IN THE DAYS *of* POOR RICHARD

John Wolcott Adams

IN THE DAYS
OF POOR RICHARD

By
IRVING BACHELLER
Author of
**The Light in The Clearing
A Man for the Ages, Etc.**

ILLUSTRATED BY
JOHN WOLCOTT ADAMS

INDIANAPOLIS
THE BOBBS-MERRILL COMPANY
PUBLISHERS

Printed in the United States of America.

PRESS OF
BRAUNWORTH & CO
BOOK MANUFACTURERS
BROOKLYN, N. Y.

To My Friend

ALBERT J. BEVERIDGE

Discerning Student and Interpreter of
the Spirit of the Prophets, the Struggle
of the Heroes and the Wisdom of the
Founders of Democracy, I Dedicate
This Volume.

FOREWORD

Much of the color of the love-tale of Jack and Margaret, which is a part of the greater love-story of man and liberty, is derived from old letters, diaries, and newspaper clippings in the possession of a well-known American family.

CONTENTS

CONTENTS—*Continued*

IN THE DAYS *of*
POOR RICHARD

In the Days of Poor Richard

BOOK ONE

CHAPTER I

THE HORSE VALLEY ADVENTURE

"THE first time I saw the boy, Jack Irons, he was about nine years old. I was in Sir William Johnson's camp of magnificent Mohawk warriors at Albany. Jack was so active and successful in the games, between the red boys and the white, that the Indians called him 'Boiling Water.' His laugh and tireless spirit reminded me of a mountain brook. There was no lad, near his age, who could run so fast, or jump so far, or shoot so well with the bow or the rifle. I carried him on my back to his home, he urging me on as if I had been a battle horse and when we were come to the house, he ran about doing his chores. I helped him, and, our work accomplished, we went down to the river for a swim, and to my surprise, I found him a well taught fish. We became friends and always when I have thought of him, the words Happy Face have come to me. It was, I think, a better nickname than 'Boiling Water,' although there was much propriety in the latter. I knew that his energy given to labor would accomplish much and when I left him, I repeated the words which my father had often quoted in my hearing:

" 'Seest thou a man diligent in his calling? He shall stand before kings.' "

This glimpse of John Irons, Jr.—familiarly known as Jack Irons—is from a letter of Benjamin Franklin to his wife.

Nothing further is recorded of his boyhood until, about eight years later, what was known as the "Horse Valley Adventure" occurred. A full account of it follows with due regard for background and color:

"It was the season o' the great moon," said old Solomon Binkus, scout and interpreter, as he leaned over the camp-fire and flicked a coal out of the ashes with his forefinger and twiddled it up to his pipe bowl. In the army he was known as "old Solomon Binkus," not by reason of his age, for he was only about thirty-eight, but as a mark of deference. Those who followed him in the bush had a faith in his wisdom that was 'childlike. "I had had my feet in a pair o' sieves walkin' the white sea a fortnight," he went on. "The dry water were six foot on the level, er mebbe more, an' some o' the waves up to the tree-tops, an' nobody with me but this 'ere ol' Marier Jane* the hull trip to the Swegache country. Gol' ding my pictur'! It seemed as if the wind were a-tryin' fer to rub it off the slate. It were a pesky wind that kep' a-cuffin' me an' whistlin' in the briers on my face an' crackin' my

_____
*His rifle.

coat-tails. I were lonesome—lonesomer'n a he-bear—an' the cold grabbin' holt o' all ends o' me so as I had to stop an' argue 'bout whar my bound'ry-lines was located like I were York State. Cat's blood an' gunpowder! I had to kick an' scratch to keep my nose an' toes from gittin'—brittle."

At this point, Solomon Binkus paused to give his words a chance "to sink in." The silence which followed was broken only by the crack of burning faggots and the sound of the night wind in the tall pines above the gorge. Before Mr. Binkus resumes his narrative, which, one might know by the tilt of his head and the look of his wide open, right eye, would soon happen, the historian seizes the opportunity of finishing his introduction. He had been the best scout in the army of Sir Jeffrey Amherst. As a small boy he had been captured by the Senecas and held in the tribe a year and two months. Early in the French and Indian War, he had been caught by Algonquins and tied to a tree and tortured by hatchet throwers until rescued by a French captain. After that his opinion of Indians had been, probably, a bit colored by prejudice. Still later he had been a harpooner in a whale boat, and in his young manhood, one of those who had escaped the infamous massacre at Fort William Henry when English forces, having been captured and disarmed, were turned loose and set upon by the savages. He was a tall, brawny, broad-shouldered, homely-faced man of thirty-eight with a Roman nose and a prominent chin underscored by a short sandy throat beard. Some of the adventures had put their mark upon his weathered face, shaven generally once a week above the chin. The top of his left ear was missing. There was a long scar upon his forehead. These were like the notches on the stock of his rifle. They were a sign of the stories of adventure to be found in that wary, watchful brain of his.

Johnson enjoyed his reports on account of their humor and color and he describes him in a letter to Putnam as a man who "when he is much interested, looks as if he were taking aim with his rifle." To some it seemed that one eye of Mr. Binkus was often drawing conclusions while the other was engaged with the no less important function of discovery.

His companion was young Jack Irons—a big lad of seventeen, who lived in a fertile valley some fifty miles northwest of Fort Stanwix, in Tryon County, New York. Now, in September, 1768, they were traveling ahead of a band of Indians bent on mischief. The latter, a few days before, had come down Lake Ontario and were out in the bush somewhere between the lake and the new settlement in Horse Valley. Solomon thought that they were probably Hurons, since they, being discontented with the treaty made by the French, had again taken the war-path. This invasion, however, was a wholly unexpected bit of audacity. They had two captives—the wife and daughter of Colonel Hare, who had been spending a few weeks with Major

Duncan and his Fifty-Fifth Regiment, at Oswego. The colonel had taken these ladies of his family on a hunting trip in the bush.   They had had two guides with them, one of whom was Solomon Binkus.   The men had gone out in the early evening after moose and imprudently left the ladies in camp, where the latter had been captured.   Having returned, the scout knew that the only possible explanation for the absence of the ladies was Indians, although no peril could have been more unexpected.   He had discovered by "the sign" that it was a large band traveling eastward.   He had set out by night to get ahead of them while Hare and his other guide started for the fort.   Binkus knew every mile of the wilderness and had canoes hidden near its bigger waters.   He had crossed the lake, on which his party had been camping, and the swamp at the east end of it and was soon far ahead of the marauders.   A little after daylight, he had picked up the boy, Jack Irons, at a hunting camp on Big Deer Creek, as it was then called, and the two had set out together to warn the people in Horse Valley, where Jack lived, and to get help for a battle with the savages.

It will be seen by his words that Mr. Binkus was a man of imagination, but—again he is talking.

"I were on my way to a big Injun Pow-wow at Swegache fer Sir Bill—ayes it were in Feb'uary, the time o' the great moon o' the hard snow.   Now they be some good things 'bout Injuns but, like young brats, they take nat'ral to deviltry.   Ye may have my hide fer

sole luther if ye ketch me in an Injun village with a
load o' fire-water.   Some Injuns is smart, an' gol ding
their pictur's! they kin talk like a cat-bird.   A skunk
has a han'some coat an' acts as cute as a kitten but all
the same, which thar ain't no doubt o' it, his friendship
ain't wuth a dam.   It's a kind o' p'ison.   Injuns is like
skunks, if ye trust 'em they'll sp'ile ye.   They eat like
beasts an' think like beasts, an' live like beasts, an'
talk like angels.   Paint an' bear's grease, an' squaw-
fun, an' fur, an' wampum, an' meat, an' rum, is all they
think on.   I've et their vittles many a time an' I'm
obleeged to tell ye it's hard work.   Too much hair in
the stew!   They stick their paws in the pot an' grab
out a chunk an' chaw it an' bolt it, like a dog, an' wipe
their hands on their long hair.   They brag 'bout the
power o' their jaws, which I ain't denyin' is consid'able, havin' had an ol' buck bite off the top o' my
left ear when I were tied fast to a tree which—you hear
to me—is a good time to learn Injun language 'cause
ye pay 'tention clost.   They ain't got no heart er no
mercy.   How they kin grind up a captive, like wheat
in the millstuns, an' laugh, an' whoop at the sight o'
his blood!   Er turn him into smoke an' ashes while
they look on an' laugh—by mighty!—like he were
singin' a funny song.   They'd be men an' women only
they ain't got the works in 'em.   Suthin' missin'.   By
the hide an' horns o' the devil!   I ain't got no kind o'
patience with them mush hearts who say that Ameriky
belongs to the noble red man an' that the whites have

no right to bargain fer his land. Gol ding their pictur's!
Ye might as well say that we hain't no right in the
woods 'cause a lot o' bears an' painters got there fust,
which I ain't a-sayin' but what bears an' painters has
their rights."

Mr. Binkus paused again to put another coal on his
pipe. Then he listened a moment and looked up at
the rocks above their heads, for they were camped in
a cave at the mouth of which they had built a small
fire, in a deep gorge. Presently he went on:

"I found a heap o' Injuns at Swegache—Mohawks,
Senekys, Onandogs an' Algonks. They had been
swappin' presents an' speeches with the French. Just
a little while afore they had had a bellerin' match with
us 'bout love an' friendship. Then sudden-like they
tuk it in their heads that the French had a sharper
hatchet than the English. I were skeered, but when I
see that they was nobody drunk, I pushed right into the
big village an' asked fer the old Senecky chief Bear
Face—knowin' he were thar—an' said I had a letter
from the Big Father. They tuk me to him.

"I give him a chain o' wampum an' then read the
letter from Sir Bill. It offered the Six Nations more
land an' a fort, an' a regiment to defend 'em. Then
he give me a lot o' hedge-hog quills sewed on to buckskin an' says he:

" 'You are like a lone star in the night, my brother.
We have stretched out our necks lookin' fer ye. We
thought the Big Father had forgot us. Now we are

happy.   To-morrer our faces will turn south an' shine with bear's grease.'

"Sez I: 'You must wash no more in the same water with the French.   You must return to The Long House.   The Big Father will throw his great arm eround you.'

"I strutted up an' down, like a turkey gobbler, an' bellered out a lot o' that high-falutin' gab.   I reckon I know how to shove an idee under their hides.   Ye got to raise yer voice an' look solemn an' point at the stars. A powerful lot o' Injuns trailed back to Sir Bill, but they was a few went over to the French.   I kind o' mistrust thar's some o' them runnygades behind us. They're 'spectin' to git a lot o' plunder an' a horse apiece an' ride 'em back an' swim the river at the place o' the many islands.   We'll poke down to the trail on the edge o' the drownded lands afore sunrise an' I kind o' mistrust we'll see sign."

Jack Irons was a son of the much respected John Irons from New Hampshire who, in the fertile valley where he had settled some years before, was breeding horses for the army and sending them down to Sir William Johnson.   Hence the site of his farm had been called Horse Valley.

Mr. Binkus went to the near brook and repeatedly filled his old felt hat with water and poured it on the fire.   "Don't never keep no fire a-goin' a'ter I'm dried out," he whispered, as he stepped back into the dark cave, " 'cause ye never kin tell."

The boy was asleep on the bed of boughs. Mr. Binkus covered him with the blanket and lay down beside him and drew his coat over both.

"He'll learn that it ain't no fun to be a scout," he whispered with a yawn and in a moment was snoring.

It was black dark when he roused his companion. Solomon had been up for ten minutes and had got their rations of bread and dried venison out of his pack and brought a canteen of fresh water.

"The night has been dark. A piece o' charcoal would 'a' made a white mark on it," said Solomon.

"How do you know it's morning?" the boy asked as he rose, yawning.

"Don't ye hear that leetle bird up in the tree-top?" Solomon answered in a whisper. "He says it's mornin' jest as plain as a clock in a steeple an' that it's goin' to be cl'ar. If you'll shove this 'ere meat an' bread into yer stummick, we'll begin fer to make tracks."

They ate in silence and as he ate Solomon was getting his pack ready and strapping it on his back and adjusting his powder-horn.

"Ye see it's growin' light," he remarked presently in a whisper. "Keep clost to me an' go as still as ye kin an' don't speak out loud never—not if ye want to be sure to keep yer ha'r on yer head."

They started down the foot of the gorge then dim in the night shadows. Binkus stopped, now and then, to listen for two or three seconds and went on with long stealthy strides. His movements were panther-like, and the boy imitated them. He was a tall, handsome, big-framed lad with blond hair and blue eyes. They could soon see their way clearly. At the edge of the valley the scout stopped and peered out upon it. A deep mist lay on the meadows.

"I like day-dark in Injun country," he whispered. "Come on."

They hurried through sloppy footing in the wet grass that flung its dew into their garments from the shoulder down. Suddenly Mr. Binkus stopped. They could hear the sound of heavy feet splashing in the wet meadow.

"Scairt moose, runnin' this way!" the scout whispered. "I'll bet ye a pint o' powder an' a fish hook them Injuns is over east o' here."

It was his favorite wager—that of a pint of powder and a fish hook.

They came out upon high ground and reached the valley trail just as the sun was rising. The fog had lifted. Mr. Binkus stopped well away from the trail and listened for some minutes. He approached it slowly on his tiptoes, the boy following in a like manner. For a moment the scout stood at the edge of the trail in silence. Then, leaning low, he examined it closely and quickly raised his hand.

"Hoofs o' the devil!" he whispered as he beckoned to the boy. "See thar," he went on, pointing to the ground. "They've jest gone by. The grass ain't riz yit. Wait here."

He followed the trail a few rods with eyes bent upon it. Near a little run where there was soft dirt, he stopped again and looked intently at the earth and then hurried back.

"It's a big band. At least forty Injuns in it an' some captives, an' the devil an' Tom Walker. It's a mess which they ain't no mistake."

"I don't see why they want to be bothered with women," the boy remarked.

"Hostiges!" Solomon exclaimed. "Makes 'em feel safer. Grab 'em when they kin. If overtook by a stouter force they're in shape fer a dicker. The chief stands up an' sings like a bird—'bout the moon an' the stars an' the brooks an' the rivers an' the wrongs o' the red man, but it wouldn't be wuth the song o' a barn swaller less he can show ye that the wimmen are all right. If they've been treated proper, it's the same as proved. Ye let 'em out o' the bear trap which it has often happened. But you hear to me, when they go off this way it's to kill an' grab an' hustle back with the booty. They won't stop at butcherin'!"

"I'm afraid my folks are in danger," said the boy as he changed color.

"Er mebbe Peter Boneses'—'cordin' to the way they go. We got to cut eround 'em an' plow straight through the bush an' over Cobble Hill an' swim the big creek an' we'll beat 'em easy."

It was a curious, long, loose stride, the knees never quite straightened, with which the scout made his way

through the forest.   It covered ground so swiftly that
the boy had, now and then, to break into a dog-trot in
order to keep along with the old woodsman.   They
kept their pace up the steep side of Cobble Hill and
down its far slope and the valley beyond to the shore
of the Big Creek.

"I'm hot 'nough to sizzle an' smoke when I tech
water," said the scout as he waded in, holding his rifle
and powder-horn in his left hand above the creek's
surface.

They had a few strokes of swimming at mid-stream
but managed to keep their powder dry.

"Now we've got jest 'nough hoppin' to keep us from
gittin' foundered," said Solomon, as he stood on the
farther shore and adjusted his pack.   "It ain't more'n
a mile to your house."

They hurried on, reaching the rough valley road in
a few minutes.

"Now I'll take the bee trail to your place," said the
scout.   "You cut ercrost the medder to Peter Boneses'
an' fetch 'em over with all their grit an' guns an' ammunition."

Solomon found John Irons and five of his sons and
three of his daughters digging potatoes and pulling
tops in a field near the house.   The sky was clear and
the sun shining warm.   Solomon called Irons aside
and told him of the approaching Indians.

"What are we to do?" Irons asked.

"Send the women an' the babies back to the sugar

shanty," said Solomon. "We'll stay here 'cause if we run erway the Boneses'll git their ha'r lifted. I reckon we kin conquer 'em."

"How?"

"Shoot 'em full o' meat. They must 'a' traveled all night. Them Injuns is tired an' hungry. Been three days on the trail. No time to hunt! I'll hustle some wood together an' start a fire. You bring a pair o' steers right here handy. We'll rip their hides off an' git the reek o' vittles in the air soon as God'll let us."

"My wife can use a gun as well as I can and I'm afraid she won't go," said Irons.

"All right, let her hide somewhar nigh with the guns," said Solomon. "The oldest gal kin go back with the young 'uns. Don't want no skirts in sight when they git here."

Mrs. Irons hid in the shed with the loaded guns.

Ruth Irons and the children set out for the sugar bush. The steers were quickly led up and slaughtered. As a hide ripper, Solomon was a man of experience. The loins of one animal were cooking on turnspits and a big pot of beef, onions and potatoes boiling over the fire when Jack arrived with the Bones family.

"It smells good here," said Jack.

"Ayes! The air be gittin' the right scent on it," said Solomon, as he was ripping the hide off the other steer. "I reckon it'll start the sap in their mouths. You roll out the rum bar'l an' stave it in. Mis' Bones knows

how to shoot. Put her in the shed with yer mother an'
the guns, an' take her young 'uns to the sugar shanty
'cept Isr'el who's big 'nough to help."

A little later Solomon left the fire. Both his eye
and his ear had caught "sign"—a clamor among the
moose birds in the distant bush and a flock of pigeons
flying from the west.

"Don't none o' ye stir till I come back," he said, as
he turned into the trail. A few rods away he lay down
with his ear to the ground and could distinctly hear the
tramp of many feet approaching in the distance. He
went on a little farther and presently concealed himself
in the bushes close to the trail. He had not long to
wait, for soon a red scout came on ahead of the party.
He was a young Huron brave, his face painted black
and yellow. His head was encircled by a snake skin.
A fox's tail rose above his brow and dropped back on
his crown. A birch-bark horn hung over his shoulder.

Solomon stepped out of the bushes after he had
passed and said in the Huron tongue: "Welcome, my
red brother, I hear that a large band o' yer folks is
comin' and we have got a feast ready."

The young brave had been startled by the sudden
appearance of Solomon, but the friendly words had
reassured him.

"We are on a long journey," said the brave.

"And the flesh of a fat ox will help ye on yer way.
Kin ye smell it?"

"Brother, it is like the smell of the great village in

the Happy Hunting-Grounds," said the brave. "We
have traveled three sleeps from the land of the long
waters and have had only two porcupines and a small
deer to eat. We are hungry."

"And we would smoke the calumet of peace with
you," said Solomon.

They walked on together and in a moment came in
sight of the little farm-house. The brave looked at
the house and the three men who stood by the fire.

"Come with me and you shall see that we are few,"
Solomon remarked.

They entered the house and barn and walked around
them, and this, in effect, is what Solomon said to
him:

"I am the chief scout of the Great Father. My word
is like that of old Flame Tongue—your mighty chief.
You and your people are on a bad errand. No good
can come of it. You are far from your own country. A large force is now on your trail. If you rob
or kill any one you will be hung. We know your
plans. A bad white chief has brought you here. He
has a wooden leg with an iron ring around the bottom
of it. He come down lake in a big boat with you.
Night before last you stole two white women."

A look of fear and astonishment came upon the face
of the Indian.

"You are a son of the Great Spirit!" he exclaimed.

"And I would keep yer feet out o' the snare. Let
me be yer chief. You shall have a horse and fifty

beaver skins and be taken to the border and set free. I, the scout of the Great Father, have said it, and if it be not as I say, may I never see the Happy Hunting-Grounds."

The brave answered:

"My white brother has spoken well and he shall be my chief. I like not this journey. I shall bid them to the feast. They will eat and sleep like the gray wolf for they are hungry and their feet are sore."

The brave put his horn to his mouth and uttered a wild cry that rang in the distant hills. Then arose a great whooping and kintecawing back in the bush. The young Huron went out to meet the band. Returning soon, he said to Solomon that his chief, the great Splitnose, would have words with him.

Turning to John Irons, Solomon said: "He's an outlaw chief. We must treat him like a king. I'll bring 'em in. You keep the meat a-sizzlin'!"

The scout went with the brave to his chief and made a speech of welcome, after which the wily old Splitnose, in his wonderful head-dress of buckskin and eagle feathers, and his band in war-paint, followed Solomon to the feast. Silently they filed out of the bush and sat on the grass around the fire. There were no captives among them—none at least of the white skin.

Solomon did not betray his disappointment. Not a word was spoken. He and John Irons and his son began removing the spits from the fire and putting

more meat upon them and cutting the cooked roasts
into large pieces and passing it on a big earthen platter.
The Indians eagerly seized the hot meat and began to
devour it. While waiting to be served, some of the
young braves danced at the fire's edge with short, ex-
plosive, yelping, barking cries answered by dozens of
guttural protesting grunts from the older men, who sat
eating or eagerly waiting their turn to grab meat. It
was a trying moment. Would the whole band leap up
and start a dance which might end in boiling blood
and tiger fury and a massacre? But the young Huron
brave stopped them, aided no doubt by the smell of
the cooking flesh and the protest of the older men.
There would be no war-dance—at least not yet—too
much hunger in the band and the means of satisfying
it were too close and tempting. Solomon had foreseen
the peril and his cunning had prevented it.

In a letter he has thus described the incident: "It
were a band o' cutthroat robbers an' runnygades from
the Ohio country—Hurons, Algonks an' Mingos an'
all kinds o' cast off red rubbish with an old Algonk
chief o' the name o' Splitnose. They stuffed their
hides with the meat till they was stiff as a foundered
hoss. They grabbed an' chawed an' bolted it like so
many hogs an' reached out fer more, which is the differ'nce betwixt an Injun an' a white man. The white
man gen'ally knows 'nough to shove down the brakes
on a side-hill. The Injun ain't got no brakes on his
wheels. Injuns is a good deal like white brats. Let 'em

find the sugar tub when their ma is to meetin' an' they won't worry 'bout the bellyache till it comes. Them Injuns filled themselves to the gullet an' begun to lay back, all swelled up, an' roll an' grunt an' go to sleep. By an' by they was only two that was up an' pawin' eround in the stew pot fer 'nother bone, lookin' kind o' unsart'in an' jaw weary. In a minute they wiped their hands on their ha'r an' lay back fer rest. They was drunk with the meat, as drunk as a Chinee a'ter a pipe o' opium. We white men stretched out with the rest on 'em till we see they was all in the land o' nod. Then we riz an' set up a hussle. Hones' we could 'a' killed 'em with a hammer an' done it delib'rit. I started to pull the young Huron out o' the bunch. He jumped up very supple. He wasn't asleep. He had knowed better than to swaller a yard o' meat.

"Whar was the wimmen? I knowed that a part o' the band would be back in the bush with them 'ere wimmen. I'd seed suthin' in the trail over by the drownded lands that looked kind o' neevarious. It were like the end o' a wooden leg with an iron ring at the bottom an' consid'able weight on it. An Injun wouldn't have a wooden leg, least ways not one with an iron ring at the butt. My ol' thinker had been chawin' that cud all day an' o' a sudden it come to me that a white man were runnin' the hull crew. That's how I had gained ground with the red scout. I took him out in the aidge o' the bush an' sez I:

"'What's yer name?'

" 'Buckeye,' sez he.

" 'Who's the white man that's with ye?'

" 'Mike Harpe.'

" 'Are the white wimmin with him?'

" 'Yes.'

" 'How many Injuns?'

" 'Two.'

" 'What's yer signal o' victory?'

" 'The call o' the moose.'

" 'Now, Buckeye, you come with us,' I sez.

"I knowed that the white man were runnin' the hull party an' I itched to git holt o' him. Gol ding his pictur'! He'd sent the Injuns on ahead fer to do his dirty work. The Ohio country were full o' robber whelps which I kind o' mistrusted he were one on 'em who had raked up this 'ere band o' runnygades an' gone off fer plunder. We got holt o' most o' their guns very quiet, an' I put John Irons an' two o' his boys an' Peter Bones an' his boy Isr'el an' the two women with loaded guns on guard over 'em. If any on 'em woke up they was to ride the nightmare er lay still. Jack an' me an' Buckeye sneaked back up the trail fer 'bout twenty rod with our guns, an' then I told the young Injun to shoot off the moose call. Wall, sir, ye could 'a' heerd it from Albany to Wing's Falls. The answer come an' jest as I 'spected, 'twere within a quarter o' a mile. I put Jack erbout fifty feet further up the trail than I were, an' Buckeye nigh him, an' tol' 'em what to do. We skootched down in the bushes an' heerd 'em comin'! Purty soon they hove in sight—two Injuns, the two wimmin captives an' a white man—the wust-lookin' bulldog brute that I ever seen—stumpin' erlong lively on a wooden leg, with a gun an' a cane. He had a broad head an' a big lop mouth an' thick lips an' a long, red, warty nose an' small black eyes an' a growth o' beard that looked like hog's bristles. He were stout built. Stood 'bout five foot seven. Never see sech a sight in my life. I hopped out afore 'em an' Jack an' Buckeye on their heels. The Injun had my ol' hanger.

" 'Drop yer guns,' says I.

"The white man done as he were told. I spoke English an' mebbe them two Injuns didn't understan' me. We'll never know. Ol' Red Snout leaned over to pick up his gun, seein' as we'd fired ours. There was a price on his head an' he'd made up his mind to fight. Jack grabbed him. He were stout as a lion an' tore 'way from the boy an' started to pullin' a long knife out o' his boot leg. Jack didn't give him time. They had it hammer an' tongs. Red Snout were a reg'lar fightin' man. He jest stuck that 'ere stump in the ground an' braced ag'in' it an' kep' a-slashin' an' jabbin' with his club cane an' yellin' an' cussin' like a fiend o' hell. He knocked the boy down an' I reckon he'd 'a' mellered his head proper if he'd 'a' been spryer on his pins. But Jack sprung up like he were made o' Injy rubber. The bulldog devil had drawed his long knife. Jack were smart. He hopped behind a tree. Buckeye, who hadn't no gun, was jumpin' fer cover. The peg-leg cuss swore a blue streak an' flung the knife at him. It went cl'ar through his body an' he fell on his face an' me standin' thar loadin' my gun. I didn't know but he'd lick us all. But Jack had jumped on him 'fore he got holt o' the knife ag'in.

"I thought sure he'd floor the boy an' me not quite loaded, but Jack were as spry as a rat terrier. He dodged an' rushed in an' grabbed holt o' the club an' fetched the cuss a whack in the paunch with his bare fist, an' ol' Red Snout went down like a steer under the ax.

"'Look out! there's 'nother man comin',' the young womern hollered.

"She needn't 'a' tuk the trouble 'cause afore she spoke I were lookin' at him through the sight o' my ol' Marier which I'd managed to git it loaded ag'in. He were runnin' towards me. He tuk jest one more step, if I don't make no mistake.

"The ol' brute that Jack had knocked down quivered an' lay still a minit an' when he come to, we turned him eround an' started him towards Canady an' tol' him to keep a-goin'! When he were 'bout ten rods off, I put a bullet in his ol' wooden leg fer to hurry him erlong. So the wust man-killer that ever trod dirt got erway from us with only a sore belly, we never knowin' who he were. I wish I'd 'a' killed the cuss, but as 'twere, we had consid'able trouble on our hands. Right erway we heard two guns go off over by the house. I knowed that our firin' had prob'ly woke up some o' the sleepers. We pounded the ground an' got thar as quick as we could. The two wimmen wa'n't fur behind. They didn't cocalate to lose us—you hear to me. Two young braves had sprung up an' been told to lie down ag'in. But the English language ain't no help to an Injun under them surcumstances. They don't understan' it an' thar ain't no time when ignerunce is more costly. They was some others awake, but they had learnt suthin'. They was keepin' quiet, an' I sez to 'em :

" 'If ye lay still ye'll all be safe. We won't do ye a bit o' harm. You've got in bad comp'ny, but ye ain't done nothin' but steal a pair o' wimmen. If ye behave proper from now on, ye'll be sent hum.'

"We didn't have no more trouble with them. I put one o' Boneses' boys on a hoss an' hustled him up the valley fer help. The wimmen captives was bawlin'. I tol' 'em to straighten out their faces an' go with Jack an' his father down to Fort Stanwix. They were kind o' leg weary an' excited, but they hadn't been hurt yit. Another day er two would 'a' fixed 'em. Jack an' his father an' mother tuk 'em back to the pastur', an' Jack run up to the barn fer ropes an' bridles. In a little while they got some hoofs under 'em an' picked up the childern an' toddled off. I went out in the bush to find Buckeye an' he were dead as the whale that swallered Jonah."

So ends the letter of Solomon Binkus.

Jack Irons and his family and that of Peter Bones—

the boys and girls riding two on a horse—with the captives filed down the Mohawk trail. It was a considerable cavalcade of twenty-one people and twenty-four horses and colts, the latter following.

Solomon Binkus and Peter Bones and his son Israel stood on guard until the boy John Bones returned with help from the upper valley. A dozen men and boys completed the disarming of the band and that evening set out with them on the south trail.

2

It is doubtful if this history would have been written but for an accidental and highly interesting circumstance. In the first party young Jack Irons rode a colt, just broken, with the girl captive, now happily released. The boy had helped every one to get away; then there seemed to be no ridable horse for him. He walked for a distance by the stranger's mount as the latter was wild. The girl was silent for a time after the colt had settled down, now and then wiping tears from her eyes. By and by she asked:

"May I lead the colt while you ride?"

"Oh, no, I am not tired," was his answer.

"I want to do something for you."

"Why?"

"I am so grateful. I feel like the King's cat. I am trying to express my feelings. I think I know, now, why the Indian women do the drudgery."

As she looked at him her dark eyes were very serious.

"I have done little," said he. "It is Mr. Binkus who rescued you. We live in a wild country among savages and the white folks have to protect each other. We're used to it."

"I never saw or expected to see men like you," she went on. "I have read of them in books, but I never hoped to see them and talk to them. You are like Ajax and Achilles."

"Then I shall say that you are like the fair lady for whom they fought."

"I will not ride and see you walking."

"Then sit forward as far as you can and I will ride with you," he answered.

In a moment he was on the colt's back behind her. She was a comely maiden. An authority no less respectable than Major Duncan has written that she was a tall, well shaped, fun loving girl a little past sixteen and good to look upon, "with dark eyes and auburn hair, the latter long and heavy and in the sunlight richly colored"; that she had slender fingers and a beautiful skin, all showing that she had been delicately bred. He adds that he envied the boy who had ridden before and behind her half the length of Tryon County.

It was a close association and Jack found it so agreeable that he often referred to that ride as the most exciting adventure of his life.

"What is your name?" he asked.

"Margaret Hare," she answered.

"How did they catch you?"

"Oh, they came suddenly and stealthily, as they do in the story books, when we were alone in camp. My father and the guides had gone out to hunt."

"Did they treat you well?"

"The Indians let us alone, but the two white men annoyed and frightened us. The old chief kept us near him."

"The old chief knew better than to let any harm come to you until they were sure of getting away with their plunder."

"We were in the valley of death and you have led us out of it. I am sure that I do not look as if I were worth saving. I suppose that I must have turned into an old woman. Is my hair white?"

"No. You are the best-looking girl I ever saw," he declared with rustic frankness.

"I never had a compliment that pleased me so much," she answered, as her elbows tightened a little on his hands which were clinging to her coat. "I almost loved you for what you did to the old villain. I saw blood on the side of your head. I fear he hurt you?"

"He jabbed me once. It is nothing."

"How brave you were!"

"I think I am more scared now than I was then," said Jack.

"Scared! Why?"

"I am not used to girls except my sisters."

She laughed and answered:

"And I am not used to heroes. I am sure you can not be so scared as I am, but I rather enjoy it. I like to be scared—a little. This is so different."

"I like you," he declared with a laugh.

"I feared you would not like an English girl. So many North Americans hate England."

"The English have been hard on us."

"What do you mean?"

"They send us governors whom we do not like; they make laws for us which we have to obey; they impose hard taxes which are not just and they will not let us have a word to say about it."

"I think it is wrong and I'm going to stand up for you," the girl answered.

"Where do you live?" he asked.

"In London. I am an English girl, but please do not hate me for that. I want to do what is right and I shall never let any one say a word against Americans without taking their part."

"That's good," the boy answered. "I'd love to go to London."

"Well, why don't you?"

"It's a long way off."

"Do you like good-looking girls?"

"I'd rather look at them than eat."

"Well, there are many in London."

"One is enough," said Jack.

"I'd love to show them a real hero."

"Don't call me that. If you would just call me Jack Irons I'd like it better. But first you'll want to know how I behave. I am not a fighter."

"I am sure that your character is as good as your face."

"Gosh! I hope it ain't quite so dark colored," said Jack.

"I knew all about you when you took my hand and helped me on the pony—or nearly all. You are a gentleman."

"I hope so."

"Are you a Presbyterian?"

"No—Church of England."

"I was sure of that. I have seen Indians and Shakers, but I have never seen a Presbyterian."

When the sun was low and the company ahead were stopping to make a camp for the night, the boy and girl dismounted. She turned facing him and asked:

"You didn't mean it when you said that I was good-looking—did you?"

The bashful youth had imagination and, like many lads of his time, a romantic temperament and the love of poetry. There were many books in his father's home and the boy had lived his leisure in them. He thought a moment and answered:

"Yes, I think you are as beautiful as a young doe playing in the water-lilies."

"And you look as if you believed yourself," said she. "I am sure you would like me better if I were fixed up a little."

"I do not think so."

"How much better a boy's head looks with his hair cut close like yours. Our boys have long hair. They do not look so much like—men."

"Long hair is not for rough work in the bush," the boy remarked.

"You really look brave and strong. One would know that you could do things."

"I've always had to do things."

They came up to the party who had stopped to camp for the night. It was a clear warm evening. After they had hobbled the horses in a near meadow flat, Jack and his father made a lean-to for the women and children and roofed it with bark. Then they cut wood and built a fire and gathered boughs for bedding. Later, tea was made and beefsteaks and bacon grilled on spits of green birch, the dripping fat being caught on slices of toasting bread whereon the meat was presently served.

The masterful power with which the stalwart youth and his father swung the ax and their cunning craftsmanship impressed the English woman and her daughter and were soon to be the topic of many a London tea party. Mrs. Hare spoke of it as she was eating her supper.

"It may surprise you further to learn that the boy is fairly familiar with the Æneid and the Odes of Horace and the history of France and England," said John Irons.

"That is the most astonishing thing I have ever heard!" she exclaimed. "How has he done it?"

"The minister was his master until we went into the bush. Then I had to be farmer and school-teacher. There is a great thirst for learning in this New World."

"How do you find time for it?"

"Oh, we have leisure here—more than you have. In England even your wealthy young men are overworked. They dine out and play cards until three in the morning and sleep until midday. Then luncheon and the cock fight and tea and Parliament! The best of us have only three steady habits. We work and study and sleep."

"And fight savages," said the woman.

"We do that, sometimes, but it is not often necessary. If it were not for white savages, there would be no red ones. You would find America a good country to live in."

"At least I hope it will be good to sleep in this night," the woman answered, yawning. "Dreamland is now the only country I care for."

The ladies and children, being near spent by the day's travel and excitement, turned in soon after supper. The men slept on their blankets, by the fire, and

were up before daylight for a dip in the creek near by.
While they were getting breakfast, the women and
children had their turn at the creekside.

That day the released captives were in better spirits.
Soon after noon the company came to a swollen river
where the horses had some swimming to do. The
older animals and the following colts went through all
right, but the young stallion which Jack and Margaret
were riding, began to rear and plunge. The girl in her
fright jumped off his back in swift water and was
swept into the rapids and tumbled about and put in
some danger before Jack could dismount and bring
her ashore.

"You have increased my debt to you," she said, when
at last they were mounted again. "What a story this
is! It is terribly exciting."

"Getting into deeper water," said Jack. "I'm not
going to let you spoil it by drowning."

"I wonder what is coming next," said she.

"I don't know. So far it's as good as *Robinson
Crusoe.*"

"With a book you can skip and see what happens,"
she laughed. "But we shall have to read everything
in this story. I'd love to know all about you."

He told her with boyish frankness of his plans which
included learning and statesmanship and a city home.
He told also of his adventures in the forest with his
father.

Meanwhile, the elder John Irons and Mrs. Hare

were getting acquainted as they rode along. The woman had been surprised by the man's intimate knowledge of English history and had spoken of it.

"Well, you see my wife is a granddaughter of Horatio Walpole of Wolterton and my mother was in a like way related to Thomas Pitt so you see I have a right to my interest in the history of the home land," said John Irons.

"You have in your veins some of the best blood of England and so I am sure that you must be a loyal subject of the King," Mrs. Hare remarked.

"No, because I think this German King has no share in the spirit of his country," Irons answered. "Our ancient respect for human rights and fair play is not in this man."

He presented his reasons for the opinion and while the woman made no answer, she had heard for the first time the argument of the New World and was impressed by it.

Late in the day they came out on a rough road, faring down into the settled country, and that night they stopped at a small inn. At the supper table a wizened old woman was telling fortunes in a tea cup.

Miss Hare and her mother drained their cups and passed them to the old woman. The latter looked into the cup of the young lady and immediately her tongue began to rattle.

"Two ways lie before you," she piped in a shrill

voice. "One leads to happiness and many children and wealth and a long life. It is steep and rough at the beginning and then it is smooth and peaceful. Yes. It crosses the sea. The other way is smooth at the start and then it grows steep and rough and in it I see tears and blood and dark clouds and, do you see that?" she demanded with a look of excitement, as she pointed into the cup. "It is a very evil thing. I will tell you no more."

The wizened old woman rose and, with a determined look in her face, left the room.

Mrs. Hare and her daughter seemed to be much troubled by the vision of the fortune-teller.

"I hope you do not believe in that kind of rubbish," John Irons remarked.

"I believe implicitly in the gift of second sight," said Mrs. Hare. "In England women are so impatient to know their fortunes that they will not wait upon Time, and the seers are prosperous."

"I have no faith in it," said Mr. Irons. "What she said might apply to the future of any young person. Undoubtedly there are two ways ahead of your daughter and perhaps more. Each must choose his own way wisely or come to trouble. It is the ancient law."

They rode on next morning in a rough road between clearings in the forest, the boy and girl being again together on the colt's back, she in front.

"You did not have your fortune told," said Miss Margaret.

"It *has* been told," Jack answered. "I am to be married in England to a beautiful young lady. I thought that sounded well and that I had better hold on to it. I might go further and fare worse."

"Tell me the kind of girl you would fancy."

"I wouldn't dare tell you."

"Why?"

"For fear it would spoil my luck."

They rode on with light hearts under a clear sky, their spirits playing together like birds in the sunlight, touching wings and then flying apart, until it all came to a climax quite unforeseen. The story has been passed from sire to son and from mother to daughter in a certain family of central New York and there are those now living who could tell it. These two were young and beautiful and well content with each other, it is said. So it would seem that Fate could not let them alone.

"We are near our journey's end," said he, by and by.

"Oh, then, let us go very slowly," she urged.

Another step and they had passed the hidden gate between reality and enchantment. It would appear that she had spoken the magic words which had opened it. They rode, for a time, without further speech, in a land not of this world, although, in some degree, familiar to the best of its people. Only they may cross that border who have kept much of the innocence of childhood and felt the delightful fear of youth that was in those two—they only may know the great enchantment. Does it not make an undying memory and bring to the face of age, long afterward, the smile of joy and gratitude?

The next word? What should it be? Both wondered and held their tongues for fear—one can not help thinking—and really they had little need of words. The peal of a hermit thrush filled the silence with its golden, largo chime and overtones and died away and rang out again and again. That voice spoke for them far better than either could have spoken, and they were content.

"There was no voice on land or sea so fit for the hour and the ears that heard it," she wrote, long afterward, in a letter.

They must have felt it in the longing of their own hearts and, perhaps, even a touch of the pathos in the years to come. They rode on in silence, feeling now the beauty of the green woods. It had become a magic garden full of new and wonderful things. Some power had entered them and opened their eyes. The thrush's song grew fainter in the distance. The boy was first to speak.

"I think that bird must have had a long flight sometime," he said.

"Why?"

"I am sure that he has heard the music of Paradise. I wonder if you are as happy as I am."

"I was never so happy," she answered.

"What a beautiful country we are in! I have forgotten all about the danger and the hardship and the evil men. Have you ever seen any place like it?"

"No. For a time we have been riding in fairyland."

"I know why," said the boy.

"Why?"

"It is because we are riding together. It is because I see you."

"Oh, dear! I can not see *you*. Let us get off and walk," she proposed.

They dismounted.

"Did you mean that honestly?"

"Honestly," he answered.

She looked up at him and put her hand over her mouth.

"I was going to say something. It would have been most unmaidenly," she remarked.

"There's something in me that will not stay unsaid. I love you," he declared.

She held up her hand with a serious look in her eyes. Then, for a moment, the boy returned to the world of reality.

"I am sorry. Forgive me. I ought not to have said it," he stammered.

"But didn't you really mean it?" she asked with troubled eyes.

"I mean that and more, but I ought not to have said it now. It isn't fair. You have just escaped from a great danger and have got a notion that you are in debt to me and you don't know much about me anyhow."

She stood in his path looking up at him.

"Jack," she whispered. "Please say it again."

No, it was not gone. They were still in the magic garden.

"I love you and I wish this journey could go on forever," he said.

She stepped closer and he put his arm around her and kissed her lips. She ran away a few steps. Then, indeed, they were back on the familiar trail in the thirty-mile bush. A moose bird was screaming at them. She turned and said:

"I wanted you to know but I have said nothing. I couldn't. I am under a sacred promise. You are a gentleman and you will not kiss me or speak of love again until you have talked with my father. It is the custom of our country. But I want you to know that I am very happy."

"I don't know how I dared to say and do what I did, but I couldn't help it."

"*I* couldn't help it either. I just longed to know if you dared."

"The rest will be in the future—perhaps far in the future."

His voice trembled a little.

"Not far if you come to me, but I can wait—I will

wait." She took his hand as they were walking beside each other and added: *"For you."*

"I, too, will wait," he answered, "and as long as I have to."

Mrs. Hare, walking down the trail to meet them, had come near. Their journey out of the wilderness had ended, but for each a new life had begun.

The husband and father of the two ladies had reached the fort only an hour or so ahead of the mounted party and preparations were being made for an expedition to cut off the retreat of the Indians. He was known to most of his friends in America only as Colonel Benjamin Hare—a royal commissioner who had come to the colonies to inspect and report upon the defenses of His Majesty. He wore the uniform of a Colonel of the King's Guard. There is an old letter of John Irons which says that he was a splendid figure of a man, tall and well proportioned and about forty, with dark eyes, his hair and mustache just beginning to show gray.

"I shall not try here to measure my gratitude," he said to Mr. Irons. "I will see you to-morrow."

"You owe me nothing," Irons answered. "The rescue of your wife and daughter is due to the resourceful and famous scout—Solomon Binkus."

"Dear old rough-barked hickory man!" the Colonel exclaimed. "I hope to see him soon."

He went at once with his wife and daughter to

rooms in the fort.   That evening he satisfied himself
as to the character and standing of John Irons, learning that he was a patriot of large influence and considerable means.

The latter family and that of Peter Bones were well
quartered in tents with a part of the Fifty-Fifth Regiment then at Fort Stanwix.   Next morning Jack went
to breakfast with Colonel Hare and his wife and
daughter in their rooms, after which the Colonel invited the boy to take a walk with him out to the little
settlement of Mill River.   Jack, being overawed, was
rather slow in declaring himself and the Colonel presently remarked:

"You and my daughter seem to have got well acquainted."

"Yes, sir; but not as well as I could wish," Jack
answered.   "Our journey ended too soon.   I love your
daughter, sir, and I hope you will let me tell her and
ask her to be my wife sometime."

"You are both too young," said the Colonel.   "Besides you have known each other not quite three days
and I have known you not as many hours.   We are
deeply grateful to you, but it is better for you and for
her that this matter should not be hurried.   After a
year has passed, if you think you still care to see each
other, I will ask you to come to England.   I think you
are a fine, manly, brave chap, but really you will admit
that I have a right to know you better before my
daughter engages to marry you."

Jack freely admitted that the request was well founded, albeit he declared, frankly, that he would like to be got acquainted with as soon as possible.

"We must take the first ship back to England," said the Colonel. "You are both young and in a matter of this kind there should be no haste. If your affection is real, it will be none the worse for a little keeping."

Solomon Binkus and Peter and Israel and John Bones and some settlers north of Horse Valley arrived next day with the captured Indians, who, under a military guard, were sent on to the Great Father at Johnson Castle.

Colonel Hare was astonished that neither Solomon Binkus nor John Irons nor his son would accept any gift for the great service they had done him.

"I owe you more than I can ever pay," he said to the faithful Binkus. "Money would not be good enough for your reward."

Solomon stepped close to the great man and said in a low tone:

"Them young 'uns has growed kind o' love sick an' I wouldn't wonder. I don't ask only one thing. Don't make no mistake 'bout this 'ere boy. In the bush we have a way o' pickin' out men. We see how they stan' up to danger an' hard work an' goin' hungry. Jack is a reg'lar he-man. I know 'em when I see 'em, which—it's a sure fact—I've seen all kinds. He's got brains an' courage, an' a tough arm an' a good heart. He'd 'die fer a friend any day. Ye kin't do no more. So

don't make no mistake 'bout him. He ain't no hemlock
bow. I cocalate there ain't no better man-timber nowhere—no, sir, not nowhere in this world—call it
king er lord er duke er any name ye like. So, sir, if
ye feel like doin' suthin' fer me—which I didn't never
expect it, when I done what I did—I'll say be good to
the boy. You'd never have to be 'shamed o' him."

"He's a likely lad," said Colonel Hare. "And I am
rather impressed by your words, although they present
a view that is new to me. We shall be returning soon
and I dare say they will presently forget each other, but
if not, and he becomes a good man—as good a man as
his father—let us say—and she should wish to marry
him, I would gladly put her hand in his."

A letter of the handsome British officer to his friend,
Doctor Benjamin Franklin, reviews the history of this
adventure and speaks of the learning, intelligence and
agreeable personality of John Irons. Both Colonel
and Mrs. Hare liked the boy and his parents and invited
them to come to England, although the latter took the
invitation as a mere mark of courtesy.

At Fort Stanwix, John Irons sold his farm and
house and stock to Peter Bones and decided to move
his family to Albany where he could educate his children. Both he and his wife had grown weary of the
loneliness of the back country, and the peril from which
they had been delivered was a deciding factor. So it
happened that the Irons family and Solomon went to
Albany by bateaux with the Hares. It was a delight-

ful trip in good autumn weather in which Colonel
Hare has acknowledged that both he and his wife acquired a deep respect "for these sinewy, wise, upright
Americans, some of whom are as well learned, I should
say, as most men you would meet in London."

They stopped at Schenectady, landing in a brawl
between Whigs and Tories which soon developed into
a small riot over the erection of a liberty pole. Loud
and bitter words were being hurled between the two
factions. The liberty lovers, being in much larger
force, had erected the pole without violent opposition.

"Just what does this mean?" the Colonel asked John
Irons.

"It means that the whole country is in a ferment of
dissatisfaction," said Irons. "We object to being taxed
by a Parliament in which we are not represented. The
trouble should be stopped not by force but by action
that will satisfy our sense of injustice—not a very difficult thing. A military force, quartered in Boston,
has done great mischief."

"What liberty do you want?"

"Liberty to have a voice in the selection of our governors and magistrates and in the making of the laws
we are expected to obey."

"I think it is a just demand," said the Colonel.

Solomon Binkus had listened with keen interest.

"I sucked in the love o' liberty with my mother's
milk," he said. "Ye mustn't try to make me do nothin'
that goes ag'in' my common sense; if ye do, ye're goin'

to have a gosh hell o' a time with the ol' man which, you hear to me, will last as long as I do. These days there ortn't to be no sech thing 'mong white men as bein' born into captivity an' forced to obey a master, no argeyment bein' allowed. If your wife an' gal had been took erway by the Injuns, that's what would 'a' happened to 'em, which I'm sart'in they wouldn't 'a' liked it, ner you nuther, which I mean to say it respec'-ful, sir."

The Colonel wore a look of conviction.

"I see how you feel about it," he said.

"It's the way all America feels about it," said Irons. "There are not five thousand men in the colonies who would differ with that view."

Having arrived in the river city, John Irons went, with his family, to The King's Arms. That very day the Hares took ship for New York on their way to England. Jack and Solomon went to the landing with them.

"Where is my boy?" Mrs. Irons asked when Binkus returned alone.

"Gone down the river," said the latter.

"Gone down the river!" Mrs. Irons exclaimed. "Why! Isn't that he coming yonder?"

"It's only part o' him," said Solomon. "His heart has gone down the river. But it'll be comin' back. It 'minds me o' the fust time I throwed a harpoon into a sperm whale. He went off like a bullet an' sounded an' took my harpoon an' a lot o' good rope with him

an' got away with it. Fer days I couldn't think o'
nothin' but that 'ere whale. Then he b'gun to grow
smaller an' less important. Jack has lost his fust
whale."

"He looks heart-broken—poor boy!"

"But ye orto have seen her. She's got the ol' harpoon in her side an' she were spoutin' tears an' shakin'
her flukes as she moved away."

CHAPTER II

SOLOMON BINKUS in his talk with Colonel Hare had signalized the arrival of a new type of man born of new conditions. When Lord Howe and General Abercrombie got to Albany with regiments of fine, high-bred, young fellows from London, Manchester and Liverpool, out for a holiday and magnificent in their uniforms of scarlet and gold, each with his beautiful and abundant hair done up in a queue, Mr. Binkus laughed and said they looked "terrible pert." He told the virile and profane Captain Lee of Howe's staff, that the first thing to do was to "make a haystack o' their hair an' give 'em men's clothes."

"A cart-load o' hair was mowed off," to quote again from Solomon, and all their splendor shorn away for a reason apparent to them before they had gone far on their ill-fated expedition. Hair-dressing and fine millinery and drawing-room clothes were not for the bush.

An inherited sense of old wrongs was the mental background of this new type of man. Life in the bush had strengthened his arm, his will and his courage. His words fell as forcefully as his ax under provocation. He was deliberate as became one whose scalp was often in danger; trained to think of the common

44

welfare of his neighborhood and rather careless about the look of his coat and trousers.

John Irons and Solomon Binkus were differing examples of the new man. Of large stature, Irons had a reputation of being the strongest man in the New Hampshire grants. No name was better known or respected in all the western valleys. His father, a man of some means, had left him a reasonable competence.

Certain old records of Cumberland County speak of his unusual gifts, the best of which was, perhaps, modesty. He had once entertained Sir William Johnson at his house and had moved west, when the French and Indian War began, on the invitation of the governor, bringing his horses with him. For years he had been breeding and training saddle horses for the markets in New England. On moving he had turned his stock into Sir William's pasture and built a log house at the fort and served as an aid and counselor of the great man. Meanwhile his wife and children had lived in Albany. When the back country was thought safe to live in, at the urgent solicitation of Sir Jeffrey Amherst, he had gone to the northern valley with his herd, and prospered there.

Albany had one wide street which ran along the river-front. It ended at the gate of a big, common pasture some four hundred yards south of the landing which was near the center of the little city. In the north it ran into "the great road" beyond the ample grounds of Colonel Schuyler. The fort and hospital stood on the top of the big hill. Close to the shore was a fringe of elms, some of them tall and stately, their columns feathered with wild grape-vines. A wide space between the trees and the street had been turned into well-kept gardens, and their verdure was a pleasant thing to see. The town lay along the foot of a steep hill, and, midway, a huddle of buildings climbed a few rods up the slope. At the top was the English Church and below it were the Town Hall, the market and the Dutch Meeting-House. Other thoroughfares west of the main one were being laid out and settled.

John Irons was well known to Colonel Schuyler. The good man gave the newcomers a hearty welcome and was able to sell them a house ready furnished— the same having been lately vacated by an officer summoned to England. So it happened that John Irons and his family were quickly and comfortably settled in their new home and the children at work in school. He soon bought some land, partly cleared, a mile or so down the river and began to improve it.

"You've had lonesome days enough, mother," he said to his wife. "We'll live here in the village. I'll buy some good, young niggers if I can, and build a house for 'em, and go back and forth in the saddle."

The best families had negro slaves which were, in the main, like Abraham's servants, each having been

born in the house of his master. They were regarded
with affection.

It was a peaceful, happy, mutually helpful, God-
fearing community in which the affairs of each were
the concern of all. Every summer day, emigrants
were passing and stopping, on their way west, towing
bateaux for use in the upper waters of the Mohawk.
These were mostly Irish and German people seeking
cheap land, and seeing not the danger in wars to
come.

There is an old letter from John Irons to his sister
in Braintree which says that Jack, of whom he had a
great pride, was getting on famously in school. "But
he shows no favor to any of the girls, having lost his
heart to a young English maid whom he helped to
rescue from the Indians. We think it lucky that she
should be far away so that he may better keep his
resolution to be educated and his composure in the
task."

The arrival of the mail was an event in Albany those
days. Letters had come to be regarded there as common property. They were passed from hand to hand
and read in neighborhood assemblies. Often they told
of great hardship and stirring adventures in the wilderness and of events beyond the sea.

Every week the mail brought papers from the three
big cities, which were read eagerly and loaned or exchanged until their contents had traveled through every
street. Benjamin Franklin's *Pennsylvania Gazette*

came to John Irons, and having been read aloud by the fireside was given to Simon Grover in exchange for Rivington's *New York Weekly*.

Jack was in a coasting party on Gallows Hill when his father brought him a fat letter from England. He went home at once to read it. The letter was from Margaret Hare—a love-letter which proposed a rather difficult problem. It is now a bit of paper so brittle with age it has to be delicately handled. Its neatly drawn chirography is faded to a light yellow, but how alive it is with youthful ardor:

"I think of you and pray for you very often," it says. "I hope you have not forgotten me or must I look for another to help me enjoy that happy fortune of which you have heard? Please tell me truly. My father has met Doctor Franklin who told of the night he spent at your home and that he thought you were a noble and promising lad. What a pleasure it was to hear him say that! We are much alarmed by events in America. My mother and I stand up for Americans, but my father has changed his views since we came down the Mohawk together. You must remember that he is a friend of the King. I hope that you and your father will be patient and take no part in the riots and house burnings. You have English blood in your veins and old England ought to be dear to you. She really loves America very much, indeed, if not as much as I love you. Can you not endure the wrongs for her sake and mine in the hope that they will soon be

righted? Whatever happens I shall not cease to love
you, but the fear comes to me that, if you turn against
England, I shall love in vain. There are days when
the future looks dark and I hope that your answer will
break the clouds that hang over it."

So ran a part of the letter, colored somewhat by the
diplomacy of a shrewd mother, one would say who
read it carefully. The neighbors had heard of its arrival and many of them dropped in that evening, but
they went home none the wiser. After the company
had gone, Jack showed the letter to his father and
mother.

"My boy, it is a time to stand firm," said his father.

"I think so, too," the boy answered.

"Are you still in love with her?" his mother asked.

The boy blushed as he looked down into the fire and
did not answer.

"She is a pretty miss," the woman went on. "But
if you have to choose between her and liberty, what
will you say?"

"I can answer for Jack," said John Irons. "He
will say that we in America will give up father and
mother and home and life and everything we hold
dear for the love of liberty."

"Of course I could not be a Tory," Jack declared.

The boy had studiously read the books which Doctor
Franklin had sent to him—*Pilgrim's Progress, Plu-
tarch's Lives,* and a number of the works of Daniel
Defoe. He had discussed them with his father and at

the latter's suggestion had set down his impressions. His father had assured him that it was well done, but had said to Mrs. Irons that it showed "a remarkable rightness of mind and temper and unexpected aptitude in the art of expression."

It is likely that the boy wrote many letters which Miss Margaret never saw before his arguments were set down in the firm, gentle and winning tone which satisfied his spirit. Having finished his letter, at last, he read it aloud to his father and mother one evening as they sat together, by the fireside, after the rest of the family had gone to bed. Tears of pride came to the eyes of the man and woman when the long letter was finished.

"I love old England," it said, "because it is your home and because it was the home of my fathers. But I am sure it is not old England which made the laws we hate and sent soldiers to Boston. Is it not another England which the King and his ministers invented? I ask you to be true to old England which, my father has told me, stood for justice and human rights.

"But after all, what has politics to do with you and me as a pair of human beings? Our love is a thing above that. The acts of the King or my fellow countrymen can not affect my love for you, and to know that you are of the same mind holds me above despair. I would think it a great hardship if either King or colony had the power to put a tax on you—a tax which demanded my principles. Can not your father differ

with me in politics—although when you were here I
made sure that he agreed with us—and keep his faith
in me as a gentleman? I can not believe that he would
like me if I had a character so small and so easily
shifted about that I would change it to please him. I
am sure, too, that if there is anything in me you love,
it is my character. Therefore, if I were to change it
I should lose your love and his respect also. Is that
not true?"

This was part of the letter which Jack had written.

"My boy, it is a good letter and they will have to
like you the better for it," said John Irons.

Old Solomon Binkus was often at the Irons home
those days. He had gone back in the bush, since the
war ended, and, that winter, his traps were on many
streams and ponds between Albany and Lake Champlain. He came down over the hills for a night with
his friends when he reached the southern end of his
beat. It was probably because the boy had loved the
tales of the trapper and the trapper had found in the
boy something which his life had missed, that an affection began to grow up between them. Solomon was
a childless widower.

"My wife! I tell ye, sir, she had the eyes an' feet o'
the young doe an' her cheeks were like the wild, red
rose," the scout was wont to say on occasion. "I orto
have knowed better. Yes, sir, I orto. We lived way
back in the bush an' the child come 'fore we 'spected
it one night. I done what I could but suthin' went

'wrong. They tuk the high trail, both on 'em. I rigged up a sled an' drawed their poor remains into a settlement. That were a hard walk—you hear to me. No, sir, I couldn't never marry no other womern—not if she was a queen covered with dimon's—never. I 'member *her* so. Some folks it's easy to fergit an' some it ain't. That's the way o' it."

Mr. and Mrs. Irons respected the scout, pitying his lonely plight and loving his cheerful company. He never spoke of his troubles unless some thoughtless person had put him to it.

2

That winter the Irons family and Solomon Binkus went often to the meetings of the Sons of Liberty. One purpose of this organization was to induce people to manufacture their own necessities and thus avoid buying the products of Great Britain. Factories were busy making looms and spinning-wheels; skilled men and women taught the arts of spinning, weaving and tailoring. The slogan "Home Made or Nothing," traveled far and wide.

Late in February, Jack Irons and Solomon Binkus went east as delegates to a large meeting of the Sons of Liberty in Springfield. They traveled on snow-shoes and by stage, finding the bitterness of the people growing more intense as they proceeded. They found many women using thorns instead of pins and knitting one pair of stockings with the ravelings of another.

They were also flossing out their silk gowns and spinning the floss into gloves with cotton. All this was to
avoid buying goods sent over from Great Britain.

Jack tells in a letter to his mother of overtaking a
young man with a pack on his back and an ax in his
hand on his way to Harvard College. He was planning to work in a mill to pay his board and tuition.

"We hear in every house we enter the stories and
maxims of Poor Richard," the boy wrote in his letter.
"A number of them were quoted in the meeting.
Doctor Franklin is everywhere these days."

The meeting over, Jack and Solomon went on by
stage to Boston for a look at the big city.

They arrived there on the fifth of March a little
after dark. The moon was shining. A snow flurry
had whitened the streets. The air was still and cold.
They had their suppers at The Ship and Anchor.
While they were eating they heard that a company of
British soldiers who were encamped near the Presbyterian Meeting-House had beaten their drums on Sunday so that no worshiper could hear the preaching.

"And the worst of it is we are compelled to furnish
them food and quarters while they insult and annoy
us," said a minister who sat at the table.

After supper Jack and Solomon went out for a walk.
They heard violent talk among people gathered at the
street corners. They soon overtook a noisy crowd of
boys and young men carrying clubs. In front of Mur-
ray's Barracks where the Twenty-Ninth Regiment was

quartered, there was a chattering crowd of men and boys. Some of them were hooting and cursing at two sentinels. The streets were lighted by oil lamps and by candles in the windows of the houses.

In Cornhill they came upon a larger and more violent assemblage of the same kind. They made their way through it and saw beyond, a captain, a corporal and six private soldiers standing, face to face, with the crowd. Men were jeering at them; boys hurling abusive epithets. The boys, as they are apt to do, reflected, with some exaggeration, the passions of their elders. It was a crowd of rough fellows—mostly wharfmen and sailors. Solomon sensed the danger in the situation. He and Jack moved out of the jeering mob. Then suddenly a thing happened which may have saved one or both of their lives. The Captain drew his sword and flashed a dark light upon Solomon and called out:

"Hello, Binkus! What the hell do you want?"

"Who be ye?" Solomon asked.

"Preston."

"Preston! Cat's blood an' gunpowder! What's the matter?"

Preston, an old comrade of Solomon, said to him:

"Go around to headquarters and tell them we are cut off by a mob and in a bad mess. I'm a little scared. I don't want to get hurt or do any hurting."

Jack and Solomon passed through the guard and hurried on. Then there were hisses and cries of

"Tories! Rotten Tories!" As the two went on they heard missiles falling behind them and among the soldiers.

"They's goin' to be bad trouble thar," said Solomon. "Them lads ain't to blame. They're only doin' as they're commanded. It's the dam' King that orto be hetchelled."

They were hurrying on, as he spoke, and the words were scarcely out of his mouth when they heard the command to fire and a rifle volley—then loud cries of pain and shrill curses and running feet. They turned and started back. People were rushing out of their houses, some with guns in their hands. In a moment the street was full.

"The soldiers are slaying people," a man shouted. "Men of Boston, we must arm ourselves and fight."

It was a scene of wild confusion. They could get no farther on Cornhill. The crowd began to pour into side-streets. Rumors were flying about that many had been killed and wounded. An hour or so later Jack and Solomon were seized by a group of ruffians.

"Here are the damn Tories!" one of them shouted.

"Friends o' murderers!" was the cry of another. "Le's hang 'em!"

Solomon immediately knocked the man down who had called them Tories and seized another and tossed him so far in the crowd as to give it pause.

"I don't mind bein' hung," he shouted, "not if it's done proper, but no man kin call me a Tory lessen my hands are tied, without gittin' hurt. An' if my hands was tied I'd do some hollerin', now you hear to me."

A man back in the crowd let out a laugh as loud as the braying of an ass. Others followed his example. The danger was passed. Solomon shouted:

"I used to know Preston when I were a scout in Amherst's army fightin' Injuns an' Frenchmen, which they's more'n twenty notches on the stock o' my rifle an' fourteen on my pelt, an' my name is Solomon Binkus from Albany, New York, an' if you'll excuse us, we'll put fer hum as soon as we kin git erway convenient."

They started for The Ship and Anchor with a number of men and boys following and trying to talk with them.

"I'll tell ye, Jack, they's trouble ahead," said Solomon as they made their way through the crowded streets.

Many were saying that there could be no more peace with England.

In the morning they learned that three men had been killed and five others wounded by the soldiers. Squads of men and boys with loaded muskets were marching into town from the country.

Jack and Solomon attended the town meeting that day in the old South Meeting-House. It was a quiet and orderly crowd that listened to the speeches of Josiah Quincy, John Hancock and Samuel Adams, demanding calmly but firmly that the soldiers be forth-

John Wolcott Adams

with removed from the city. The famous John Hancock cut a great figure in Boston those days. It is not surprising that Jack was impressed by his grandeur for he had entered the meeting-house in a scarlet velvet cap and a blue damask gown lined with velvet and strode to the platform with a dignity even above his garments. As he faced about the boy did not fail to notice and admire the white satin waistcoat and white silk stockings and red morocco slippers. Mr. Quincy made a statement which stuck like a bur in Jack Irons' memory of that day and perhaps all the faster because he did not quite understand it. The speaker said: "The dragon's teeth have been sown."

The chairman asked if there was any citizen present who had been on the scene at or about the time of the shooting. Solomon Binkus arose and held up his hand and was asked to go to the minister's room and confer with the committee.

Mr. John Adams called at the inn that evening and announced that he was to defend Captain Preston and would require the help of Jack and Solomon as witnesses. For that reason they were detained some days in Boston and released finally on the promise to return when their services were required.

They left Boston by stage and one evening in early April, traveling afoot, they saw the familiar boneheads around the pasture lands above Albany where the farmers had crowned their fence stakes with the skeleton heads of deer, moose, sheep and cattle in which birds had the habit of building their nests. It had been thawing for days, but the night had fallen clear and cold. They had stopped at the house of a settler some miles northeast of Albany to get a sled load of Solomon's pelts which had been stretched and hung there. Weary of the brittle snow, they took to the river a mile or so above the little city, Solomon hauling his sled. Jack had put on the new skates which he had bought in Bennington where they had gone for a visit with old friends. They were out on the clear ice, far from either shore, when they heard an alarming peal of "river thunder"—a name which Binkus applied to a curious phenomenon often accompanied by great danger to those on the rotted roof of the Hudson. The hidden water had been swelling. Suddenly it had made a rip in the great ice vault a mile long with a noise like the explosion of a barrel of powder. The rip ran north and south about midstream. They were on the west sheet and felt it waver and subside till it had found a bearing on the river surface.

"We must git off o' here quick," said Binkus. "She's goin' to break up."

"Let me have the sled and as soon as I get going, you hop on," said Jack.

The boy began skating straight toward the shore, drawing the sled and its load, Solomon kicking out behind with his spiked boots until they were well under way. They heard the east sheet breaking up before they had made half the distance to safe footing. Then their own began to crack into sections as big "as a ten-acre lot," Mr. Binkus said, "an' the noise was like a battle, but Jack kept a-goin' an' me settin' light an' my mind a-pushin' like a scairt deer." Water was flooding over the ice which had broken near shore, but the skater jumped the crack before it was wider than a man's hand and took the sled with him. They reached the river's edge before the ice began heaving and there the sloped snow had been wet and frozen to rocks and bushes, so they were able to make their way through it.

"Now, we're even," said Solomon when they had hauled the sled up the river bank while he looked back at the ice now breaking and beginning to pile up, "I done you a favor an' you've done me one. It's my turn next."

This was the third in the remarkable series of adventures which came to these men.

They had a hearty welcome at the little house near The King's Arms, where they sat until midnight telling of their adventures. In the midst of it, Jack said to his father:

"I heard a speaker say in Boston that the dragon's teeth had been sown. What does that mean?"

"It means that war is coming," said John Irons. "We might as well get ready for it."

These words, coming from his father, gave him a shock of surprise. He began to think of the effect of war on his own fortunes.

3

Solomon sent his furs to market and went to work on the farm of John Irons and lived with the family. The boy returned to school. After the hay had been cut and stacked in mid-summer, they were summoned to Boston to testify in the trial of Preston. They left in September taking with them a drove of horses.

"It will be good for Jack," John Irons had said to his wife. "He'll be the better prepared for his work in Philadelphia next fall."

Two important letters had arrived that summer. One from Benjamin Franklin to John Irons, offering Jack a chance to learn the printer's trade in his Philadelphia shop and board and lodging in his home. "If the boy is disposed to make a wise improvement of his time," the great man had written, "I shall see that he has an opportunity to take a course at our Academy. I am sure he would be a help and comfort to Mrs. Franklin. She, I think, will love to mother him. Do not be afraid to send him away from home. It will help him along toward manhood. I was much impressed by his letter to Miss Margaret Hare, which her mother had the goodness to show me. He has a fine spirit and a rare gift for expressing it. She and the girl were convinced by its argument, but the Colonel himself is an obdurate Tory—he being a favorite of the King. The girl, now very charming and much admired, is, I happen to know, deeply in love with your son. I have promised her that, if she will wait for him, I will bring him over in good time and act as your vicar at the wedding. This, she and her mother are the more ready to do because of their superstition that God has clearly indicated him as the man who would bring her happiness and good fortune. I find that many European women are apt to entertain and enjoy superstition and to believe in omens—not the only drop of old pagan blood that lingers in their veins. I am sending, by this boat, some more books for Jack to read."

The other letter was from Margaret Hare to the boy, in which she had said that they were glad to learn that he and Mr. Binkus were friends of Captain Preston and inclined to help him in his trouble. "Since I read your letter I am more in love with you than ever," she had written. "My father was pleased with it. He thinks that all cause of complaint will be removed. Until it is, I do not ask you to be a Tory, but only to be patient."

Jack and Solomon were the whole day getting their horses across Van Deusen's ferry and headed eastward in the rough road. Mr. Binkus wore his hanger—an old Damascus blade inherited from his father—and carried his long musket and an abundant store of ammunition; Jack wore his two pistols, in the use of which he had become most expert.

When the horses had "got the kinks worked out," as Solomon put it, and were a trifle tired, they browsed along quietly with the man and boy riding before and behind them. By and by they struck into the twenty-mile bush beyond the valley farms. In the second day of their travel they passed an Albany trader going east with small kegs of rum on a pack of horses and toward evening came to an Indian village. They were both at the head of the herd.

"Stop," said Solomon as they saw the smoke of the fires ahead. "We got to behave proper."

He put his hands to his mouth and shouted a loud halloo, which was quickly answered. Then two old men came out to him and the talk which followed in the Mohawk dialect was thus reported by the scout to his companion:

"We wish to see the chief," said Solomon. "We have gifts for him."

"Come with us," said one of the old men as they led Solomon to the Stranger's House. The old men went from hut to hut announcing the newcomers. Victuals and pipes and tobacco were sent to the Stranger's House for them. This structure looked like a small barn and was made of rived spruce. Inside, the chief sat on a pile of unthrashed wheat. He had a head and face which reminded Jack of the old Roman emperors shown in the Historical Collections. There was re-markable dignity in his deep-lined face. His name was Thunder Tongue. The house had no windows.

Many skins hung from its one cross-beam above their heads.

Mr. Binkus presented beaver skins and a handsome belt. Then the chief sent out some women to watch the horses and to bring Jack into the village. Near by were small fields of wheat and maize. The two travelers sat down with the chief, who talked freely to Solomon Binkus.

"If white man comes to our village cold, we warm him; wet, we dry him; hungry, we feed him," he said. "When Injun man goes to Albany and asks for food, they say, 'Where's your money? Get out, you Injun dog!' The white man he comes with scaura and trades it for skins. It steals away the wisdom of the young braves. It bends my neck with trouble. It is bad."

They noted this just feeling of resentment in the old chief and expressed their sympathy. Soon the Albany trader came with his pack of rum. The chief greeted him cheerfully and asked for scaura.

"I have enough to make a hundred men happy," the trader answered.

"Bring it to me, for I have a sad heart," said Thunder Tongue.

When the Dutch trader went to his horse for the kegs, Solomon said to the chief:

"Why do you let him bring trouble to your village and steal away the wisdom of your warriors?"

"Tell me why the creek flows to the great river and I will answer you," said the chief.

He began drinking as soon as the trader came with the kegs, while the young warriors gathered about the door, each with skins on his arm.   Soon every male Indian was staggering and whooping and the squaws with the children had started into the thickets.

Solomon nudged Jack and left the hut, followed by the boy.

"Come on.   Let's git out o' here.   The squaws an' the young 'uns are sneakin'.   You hear to me—thar'll be hell to pay here soon."

So while the braves were gathered about the trader and were draining cups of fire-water, the travelers made haste to mount and get around the village and back into their trail with the herd.   They traveled some miles in the long twilight and stopped at the Stony Brook Ford, where there were good water and sufficient grazing.

"Here's whar the ol' Green Mountain Trail comes down from the north an' crosses the one we're on," said Solomon.

They dismounted and Solomon hobbled a number of horses while Jack was building a fire.   The scout, returning from the wild meadow, began to examine some tracks he had found at the trail crossing.   Suddenly he gave a whistle of surprise and knelt on the ground.

"Look 'ere, Jack," he called.

The boy ran to his side.

"Now this 'ere is suthin' cur'user than the right

hoof o' the devil," said Solomon Binkus, as he pointed with his forefinger at a print in the soft dirt.

Jack saw the print of the wooden stump with the iron ring around its base which the boy had not forgotten. Near it were a number of moccasin tracks.

"What does this mean?" he asked.

"Wall, sir, I cocalate it means that ol' Mike Harpe has been chased out o' the Ohio country an' has come down the big river an' into Lake Champlain with some o' his band an' gone to cuttin' up an' been obleeged to take to the bush. They've robbed somebody an' are puttin' fer salt water. They'll hire a boat an' go south an' then p'int fer the 'Ganies. Ol' Red Snout shoved his leg in that 'ere gravel sometime this forenoon prob'ly."

They brewed tea to wet their buttered biscuit and jerked venison.

Solomon looked as if he were sighting on a gun barrel when he said:

"Now ye see what's the matter with this 'ere Injun business. They're jest a lot o' childern scattered all over the bush an' they don't have to look fer deviltry. Deviltry is lookin' fer them an' when they git together thar's trouble."

Solomon stopped, now and then, to peer off into the bush as he talked while the dusk was falling. Suddenly he put his finger to his lips. His keen eyes had detected a movement in the shadowy trail.

"Hide an' horns o' the devil!" he exclaimed in a low

tone. "This 'ere may be suthin' neevarious. Shove ol' Marier this way an' grab yer pistols an' set still."

He crept on his hands and knees with the strap of his rifle in his teeth to the edge of the bush, where he sat for a moment looking and listening. Suddenly Solomon arose and went back in the trail, indicating with a movement of his hand that the boy was not to follow. About fifteen rods from their camp-fire he found an Indian maiden sitting on the ground with bowed head. A low moan came from her lips. Her skin was of a light copper color. There was a wreath of wild flowers in her hair.

"My purty maid, are your people near?" Solomon asked in the Mohawk tongue.

She looked up at him, her beautiful dark eyes full of tears, and sorrowfully shook her head.

"My father was a great white chief," she said. "Always a little bird tells me to love the white man. The beautiful young pale face on a red horse took my heart with him. I go, too."

"You must go back to your people," said Solomon.

Again she shook her head, and, pointing up the trail, whispered:

"They will burn the Little White Birch. No more will I go in the trail of the red man. It is like climbing a thorn tree."

He touched her brow tenderly and she seized his hand and held it against her cheek.

"I follow the beautiful pale face," she whispered.

Solomon observed that her lips were shapely and her teeth white.

"What is your name?" he asked.

"They call me the Little White Birch."

Solomon told her to sit still and that he would bring food to her.

"It's jest only a little squaw," he said to Jack when he returned to the camp-fire. "Follered us from that 'ere Injun village. I guess she were skeered o' them drunken braves. I'm goin' to take some meat an' bread an' tea to her. No, you better stay here. She's as skeery as a wild deer."

After Solomon had given her food he made her take his coat for a blanket and left her alone.

Next morning she was still there. Solomon gave her food again and when they resumed their journey they saw her following.

"She'll go to the end o' the road, I guess," said Solomon. "I'll tell ye what we'll do. We'll leave her at Mr. Wheelock's School."

Their trail bore no further signs of Harpe and his followers.

"I'll bet ye a pint o' powder an' a fish hook they was p'intin' south," said Solomon.

They reached the Indian school about noon. A kindly old Mohawk squaw who worked there was sent back in the trail to find the maiden. In a few minutes the squaw came in with her. Solomon left money with the good master and promised to send more.

When the travelers went on that afternoon the Little White Birch stood by the door looking down the road at them.

"She has a coat o' red on her skin, but the heart o' the white man," said Solomon.

In a moment Jack heard him muttering, "It's a damn wicked thing to do—which there ain't no mistake."

They had come to wagon roads improving as they approached towns and villages, in the first of which they began selling the drove. When they reached Boston, nearly a week later, they had only the two horses which they rode.

The trial had just begun. Being ardent Whigs, their testimony made an impression. Jack's letter to his father says that Mr. Adams complimented them when they left the stand.

There is an old letter of Solomon Binkus which briefly describes the journey. He speaks of the "pompy" men who examined them. "They grinned at me all the time an' the ol' big wig Jedge in the womern's dress got mad if I tried to crack a joke," he wrote in his letter. "He looked like he had paid too much fer his whistle an' thought I had sold it to him. Thought he were goin' to box my ears. John Addums is erbout as sharp as a razor. Took a likin' to Jack an' me. I tol' him he were smart 'nough to be a trapper."

The two came back in the saddle and reached Albany late in October.

CHAPTER III

THE JOURNEY TO PHILADELPHIA

THE *New York Mercury* of November 4, 1770, contains this item:

"John Irons, Jr., and Solomon Binkus, the famous scout, arrived Wednesday morning on the schooner *Ariel* from Albany. Mr. Binkus is on his way to Alexandria, Virginia, where he is to meet Major Washington and accompany him to the Great Kanawha River in the Far West."

Solomon was soon to meet an officer with whom he was to find the amplest scope for his talents. Jack was on his way to Philadelphia. They had found the ship crowded and Jack and two other boys "pigged together"—in the expressive phrase of that time—on the cabin floor, through the two nights of their journey. Jack minded not the hardness of the floor, but there was much drinking and arguing and expounding of the common law in the forward end of the cabin, which often interrupted his slumbers.

He was overawed by the length and number of the crowded streets of New York and by "the great height" of many of its buildings. The grandeur of Broadway and the fashionable folk who frequented it was the subject of a long letter which he indited to his mother from The City Tavern.

He took the boat to Amboy as Benjamin Franklin had done, but without mishap, and thence traveled by stage to Burlington. There he met Mr. John Adams of Boston, who was on his way to Philadelphia. He was a full-faced, ruddy, strong-built man of about thirty-five years, with thick, wavy dark hair that fell in well trimmed tufts on either cheek and almost concealed his ears. It was beginning to show gray. He had a prominent forehead, large blue and expressive eyes and a voice clear and resonant. He was handsomely dressed.

Mr. Adams greeted the boy warmly and told him that the testimony which he and Solomon Binkus gave had saved the life of Captain Preston. The great lawyer took much interest in the boy and accompanied him to the top of the stage, the weather being clear and warm. Mr. Adams sat facing Jack, and beside the latter was a slim man with a small sad countenance which wore a permanent look of astonishment. Jack says in a letter that his beard "was not composed of hair, but hairs as straight and numerable as those in a cat's whiskers." They were also gray like his eyes. After the stage had started this man turned to Jack and asked:

"What is your name, boy?"

"John Irons."

The man opened his eyes wider and drew in his breath between parted lips as if he had heard a most astonishing fact.

"My name is Pinhorn, sir—Eliphalet Pinhorn," he reciprocated. "I have been visiting my wife in New-ark."

Jack thought it a singular thing that a man should have been visiting his wife.

"May I ask where you are going?" the man inquired of the boy.

"To Philadelphia."

Mr. Pinhorn turned toward him with a look of increased astonishment and demanded:

"Been there before?"

"Never."

The man made a sound that was between a sigh and a groan. Then, almost sternly and in a confidential tone, as if suddenly impressed by the peril of an immortal soul, he said:

"Young man, beware! I say to you, beware!"

Each stiff gray hair on his chin seemed to erect itself into an animated exclamation point. Turning again, he whispered:

"You will soon shake its dust from your feet."

"Why?"

"A sinking place! Every one bankrupt or nearly so. Display! Nothing but display! Feasting, drinking! No thought of to-morrow! Ungodly city!"

In concluding his indictment, Mr. Pinhorn partly covered his mouth and whispered the one word: "Babylon!"

A moment of silence followed, after which he

added: "I would never build a house or risk a penny in business there."

"I am going to work in Doctor Benjamin Franklin's print shop," said Jack proudly.

Mr. Pinhorn turned with a look of consternation clearly indicating that this was the last straw. He warned in a half whisper:

"Again I say beware! That is the word—beware!"

He almost shuddered as he spoke, and leaning close to the boy's ear, added in a confidential tone:

"The King of Babylon! A sinking business! An evil man!" He looked sternly into the eyes of the boy and whispered: "Very! Oh, very!" He sat back in his seat again, while the expression of his whole figure seemed to say, "Thank God, my conscience is clear, whatever happens to you."

Jack was so taken down by all this that, for a moment, his head swam. Mr. Pinhorn added:

"Prospered, but how? That is the question. Took the money of a friend and spent it. Many could tell you. Wine! Women! Infidelity! House built on the sands!"

Mr. Adams had heard most of the gloomy talk of the slim man. Suddenly he said to the slanderer:

"My friend, did I hear you say that you have been visiting your wife?"

"You did, sir."

"Well, I do not wonder that she lives in another part of the country," said Mr. Adams. "I should think that Philadelphia would feel like moving away from you. I have heard you say that it was a sinking city. It is nothing of the kind. It is floating in spite of the fact that there are human sinkers in it like yourself. I hate the heart of lead. This is the land of hope and faith and confidence. If you do not like it here, go back to England. *We* do not put our money into holes in the wall. We lend it to our neighbors because they are worthy of being trusted. We believe in our neighbors. We put our cash into business and borrow more to increase our profits. It is true that many men in Philadelphia are in debt, but they are mostly good for what they owe. It is a thriving place. I could not help hearing you speak evil of Doctor Franklin. He is my friend. I am proud to say it and I should be no friend of his if I allowed your words to go unrebuked. Yours, sir, is a leaden soul. It is without hope or trust in the things of this life. You seem not to know that a new world is born. It is a world of three tenses. We who really live in it are chiefly interested in what a man is and is likely *to be,* not in what he *was.* Doctor Franklin would not hesitate to tell you that his youth was not all it should have been. He does not conceal his errors. There is no more honest gentleman in the wide world than Doctor Franklin."

Mr. Adams had spoken with feeling and a look of indignation in his eyes. He was a frank, fearless character. All who sat on the top of the coach had heard him and when he had finished they clapped their hands.

Jack was much relieved. He had been put in mind of what Doctor Franklin had said long ago, one evening in Albany, of his struggle against the faults and follies of his youth. For a moment Mr. Pinhorn was dumb with astonishment.

"Nevertheless, sir, I hold to my convictions," he said.

"Of course you do," Mr. Adams answered. "No man like you ever recovered from his convictions, for the reason that his convictions are stronger than he is."

Mr. Pinhorn partly covered his mouth and turned to the boy and whispered:

"It is a time of violent men. Let us hold our peace."

At the next stop where they halted for dinner Mr. Adams asked the boy to sit down with him at the table. When they were seated the great man said:

"I have to be on guard against catching fire these days. Sometimes I feel the need of a companion with a fire bucket. My headlight is hope and I have little patience with these whispering, croaking Tories and with the barons of the south and the upper Hudson. I used to hold the plow on my father's farm and I am still plowing as your father is."

Jack turned with a look of inquiry.

"We are breaking new land," Mr. Adams went on. "We are treading the ordeal path among the red-hot plowshares of politics."

"It is what I should like to do," said the boy.

"You will be needed, but we must be without fear,

remembering that almost every man who has gained real distinction in politics has met a violent death. There are the shining examples of Brutus, Cassius, Hampden and Sidney, but it is worth while."

"I believe you taught school at Worcester," said Jack.

"And I learned at least one thing doing it—that school-teaching is not for me. It would have turned me into a shrub. Too much piddling! It is hard enough to teach men that they have rights which even a king must respect."

"Let me remind you, sir," said Mr. Pinhorn, who sat at the same table, "that the King can do no wrong."

"But his ministers can do as they please," Mr. Adams rejoined, whereat the whole company broke into laughter.

Mr. Pinhorn covered his mouth with astonishment, but presently allowed himself to say: "Sir, I hold to my convictions."

"You are wrong, sir. It is your convictions that hold to you. They are like the dead limbs on a tree," Mr. Adams answered. "The motto of Great Britain would seem to be, 'Do no right and suffer no wrong.' They search our ships; they impress our seamen; they impose taxes through a Parliament in which we are not represented, and if we threaten resistance they would have us tried for treason. Nero used to say that he wished that the inhabitants of Rome had only one neck, so that he could dispose of them with a single blow. It was a rather merciful wish, after all. A neck had better be chopped off than held under the yoke of tyranny."

"Sir, England shielded, protected, us from French and Indians," Mr. Pinhorn declared with high indignation.

"It protected its commerce. We were protecting British interests and ourselves. Connecticut had five thousand under arms; Massachusetts, seven thousand; New York, New Jersey and New Hampshire, many more. Massachusetts taxed herself thirteen shillings and four pence to the pound of income. New Jersey expended a pound a head to help pay for the war. On that score England is our debtor."

The horn sounded. The travelers arose from the tables and hurried out to the coach.

"It was a good dinner," Mr. Adams said to Jack when they had climbed to their seat. "We should be eating potatoes and drinking water, instead of which we have two kinds of meat and wine and pudding and bread and tea and many jellies. Still, I am a better philosopher after dinner than before it. But if we lived simpler, we should pay fewer taxes."

As they rode along a lady passenger sang the ballad of John Barleycorn, in the chorus of which Mr. Adams joined with much spirit.

"My capacity for getting fun out of a song is like the gift of a weasel for sucking eggs," he said.

So they fared along, and when Jack was taking leave of the distinguished lawyer at The Black Horse Tavern in Philadelphia the latter invited the boy to visit him in Boston if his way should lead him there.

2

The frank, fearless, sledge-hammer talk of the lawyer made a deep impression on the boy, as a long letter written next day to his father and mother clearly shows. He went to the house of the printer, where he did not receive the warm welcome he had expected. Deborah Franklin was a fat, hard-working, illiterate, economical housewife. She had a great pride in her husband, but had fallen hopelessly behind him. She regarded with awe and slight understanding the accomplishments of his virile, restless, on-pushing intellect. She did not know how to enjoy the prosperity that had come to them. It was a neat and cleanly home, but, as of old, Deborah was doing most of the work herself. She would not have had it otherwise.

"Ben thinks we ortn't to be doin' nothin' but settin' eroun' in silk dresses an' readin' books an' gabbin' with comp'ny," she said. "Men don't know how hard 'tis to git help that cleans good an' cooks decent. Everybody feels so kind o' big an' inderpendent they won't stan' it to be found fault with."

Her daughter, Mrs. Bache, and the latter's children were there. Suddenly confronted by the problem of a strange lad coming into the house to live with them, they were a bit dismayed. But presently their motherly hearts were touched by the look of the big, gentle-faced, homesick boy. They made a room ready for him on the top floor and showed him the wonders of the big house—the library, the electrical apparatus, the rocking chair with its fan swayed by the movement of the chair, the new stove and grate which the Doctor had invented. That evening, after an excellent supper, they sat down for a visit in the library, when Jack suggested that he would like to have a part of the work to do.

"I can sweep and clean as well as any one," he said. "My mother taught me how to do that. You must call on me for any help you need."

"Now I wouldn't wonder but what we'll git erlong real happy," said Mrs. Franklin. "If you'll git up 'arly an' dust the main floor an' do the broom work an' fill the wood boxes an' fetch water, I'll see ye don't go hungry."

"I suppose you will be going to England if the Doctor is detained there," said Jack.

"No, sir," Mrs. Franklin answered. "I wouldn't go out on that ol' ocean—not if ye would give me a million pounds. It's too big an' deep an' awful! No, sir! Ben got a big bishop to write me a letter an' tell me I'd better come over an' look a'ter him. But Ben knowed all the time that I wouldn't go a step."

There were those who said that her dread of the sea had been a blessing to Ben, for Mrs. Franklin had no graces and little gift for communication. But there was no more honest, hard-working, economical house-wife in Philadelphia.

Jack went to the shop and was put to work next morning. He had to carry beer and suffer a lot of humiliating imposition from older boys in the big shop, but he bore it patiently and made friends and good progress. That winter he took dancing lessons from the famous John Trotter of New York and practised fencing with the well-known Master Brissac. He also took a course in geometry and trigonometry at the Academy and wrote an article describing his trip to Boston for *The Gazette*. The latter was warmly praised by the editor and reprinted in New York and Boston journals. He joined the company for home defense and excelled in the games, on training day, especially at the running, wrestling, boxing and target shooting. There were many shooting galleries in Philadelphia wherein Jack had shown a knack of shooting with the rifle and pistol, which had won for him the Franklin medal for marksmanship. In the back country the favorite amusement of himself and father had been shooting at a mark.

Somehow the boy managed to do a **great** deal of work and to find time for tramping in the woods along the Schuylkill and for skating and swimming with the other boys. Mrs. Franklin and Mrs. Bache grew fond of Jack and before the new year came had begun to treat him with a kind of motherly affection.

William, the Doctor's son, who was the governor

of the province of New Jersey, came to the house at
Christmas time.   He was a silent, morose, dignified,
self-seeking man, who astonished Jack with his rabid
Toryism.   He nettled the boy by treating the opinions
of the latter with smiling toleration and by calling his
own father—the great Doctor—"a misguided man."

Jack forged ahead, not only in the printer's art, but
on toward the fulness of his strength.   Under the
stimulation of city life and continuous study, his talents grew like wheat in black soil.   In the summer of
'seventy-three he began to contribute to the columns of
The Gazette.   Certain of his articles brought him compliments from the best people for their wit, penetration
and good humor.   He had entered upon a career of
great promise when the current of his life quickened
like that of a river come to a steeper grade.   It began
with a letter from Margaret Hare, dated July 14, 1773.
In it she writes:

"When you get this please sit down and count up
the years that have passed since we parted.   Then
think how our plans have gone awry.   You must also
think of me waiting here for you in the midst of a
marrying world.   All my friends have taken their
mates and passed on.   I went to Doctor Franklin
to-day and told him that I was an old lady well past
nineteen and accused him of having a heart of stone.
He said that he had not sent for you because you were
making such handsome progress in your work.   I
said: 'You do not think of the rapid progress I am

making toward old age. You forget, too, that I need a husband as badly as *The Gazette* needs a philosopher. I rebel. You have made me. an American—you and Jack. I will no longer consent to taxation without representation. Year by year I am giving up some of my youth and I am not being consulted about it.'

"Said he: 'I would demand justice of the king. I suppose he thinks that his country can not yet afford a queen. I shall tell him that he is imitating George the Third and that he had better listen to the voice of the people.'

"Now, my beloved hero, the English girl who is not married at nineteen is thought to be hopeless. There are fine lads who have asked my father for the right to court me and still I am waiting for my brave deliverer and he comes not. I can not forget the thrush's song and the enchanted woods. They hold me. If they have not held you—if for any reason your heart has changed—you will not fail to tell me, will you? Is it necessary that you should be great and wise and rich and learned before you come to me? Little by little, after many talks with the venerable Franklin, I have got the American notion that I would like to go away with you and help you to accomplish these things and enjoy the happiness which was ours, for a little time, and of which you speak in your letters. Surely there was something very great in those moments. It does not fade and has it not kept us true to their promise? But, Jack, how long am I to wait? You must tell me."

This letter went to the heart of the young man.
She had deftly set before him the gross unfairness of
delay. He felt it. Ever since the parting he had been
eager to go, but his father was not a rich man and the
family was large. His own salary had been little more
than was needed for clothing and books. That autumn
it had been doubled and the editor had assured him that
higher pay would be forthcoming. He hesitated to tell
the girl how little he earned and how small, when meas-
ured in money, his progress had seemed to be. He
was in despair when his friend Solomon Binkus arrived from Virginia. For two years the latter had
been looking after the interests of Major Washington
out in the Ohio River country. They dined together
that evening at The Crooked Billet and Solomon told
him of his adventures in the West, and frontier
stories of the notorious, one-legged robber, Micah
Harpe, and his den on the shore of the Ohio and of
the cunning of the outlaw in evading capture.

"I got his partner, Mike Fink, and Major Washing-
ton give me fifty pounds for the job," said Solomon.
"They say Harpe's son disappeared long time ago an'
I wouldn't wonder if you an' me had seen him do it."

"The white man that hung back in the bushes so
long? I'll never forget him," said Jack.

"Them wimmen couldn't 'a' been in wuss hands."

"It was a lucky day for them and for me," Jack answered. "I have here a letter from Margaret. I wish
you would read it."

Solomon read the girl's letter and said:

"If I was you I'd swim the big pond if nec'sary. This 'ere is a real simon pure, four-masted womern an' she wants you fer Captain. As the feller said when he seen a black fox, 'Come on, boys, it's time fer to wear out yer boots.' "

"I'm tied to my job."

"Then break yer halter," said Solomon.

"I haven't money enough to get married and keep a wife."

"What an ignorant cuss you be!" Solomon exclaimed. "You don't 'pear to know when ye're well off."

"What do you mean?"

"I mean that ye're wuth at least a thousan' pounds cash money."

"I would not ask my father for help and I have only forty pounds in the bank," Jack answered.

Solomon took out his wallet and removed from it a worn and soiled piece of paper and studied the memoranda it contained. Then he did some ciphering with a piece of lead. In a moment he said:

"You have got a thousan' an' fifteen pounds an' six shillin' fer to do with as ye please an' no questions asked—nary one."

"You mean you've got it."

"Which means that Jack Irons owns it hide, horns an' taller."

Tears came to the boy's eyes. He looked down for

a moment without speaking. "Thank you, Solomon," he said presently. "I can't use your money. It wouldn't be right."

Solomon shut one eye an' squinted with the other as if he were taking aim along the top of a gun barrel. Then he shook his head and drawled:

"Cat's blood an' gunpowder! That 'ere slaps me in the face an' kicks me on the shin," Solomon answered. "I've walked an' paddled eighty mile in a day an' been stabbed an' shot at an' had to run fer my life, which it ain't no fun—you hear to me. Who do ye s'pose I done it fer but you an' my kentry? There ain't nobody o' my name an' blood on this side o' the ocean—not nobody at all. An' if I kin't work fer you, Jack, I'd just erbout as soon quit. This 'ere money ain't no good to me 'cept fer body cover an' powder an' balls. I'd as leave drop it in the river. It bothers me. I don't need it. When I git hum I go an' hide it in the bush somewhars—jest to git it out o' my way. I been thinkin' all up the road from Virginny o' this 'ere gol demnable money an' what I were a-goin' to do with it an' what it could do to me. An', sez I, I'm ergoin' to ask Jack to take it an' use it fer a wall 'twixt him an' trouble, an' the idee hurried me erlong—honest! Kind o' made me happy. Course, if I had a wife an' chil- dern, 'twould be different, but I ain't got no one. An' now ye tell me ye don't want it, which it makes me feel lonesomer 'n a tarred Tory an' kind o' sorrowful— ayes, sir, it does."

Solomon's voice sank to a whisper.

"Forgive me," said Jack. "I didn't know you felt that way. But I'm glad you do. I'll take it on the understanding that as long as I live what I have shall also be yours."

"I've two hundred poun' an' six shillin' in my pocket an' a lot more hid in the bush. It's all yourn to the last round penny. I reckon it'll purty nigh bridge the slough. I want ye to be married respectable like a gentleman—slick duds, plenty o' cakes an' pies an' no slightin' the minister er the rum bar'l.

"Major Washington give me a letter to take to Ben Franklin on t'other side o' the ocean. Ye see ev'ry letter that's sent ercrost is opened an' read afore it gits to him lessen it's guarded keerful. This 'ere one, I guess, has suthin' powerful secret in it. He pays all the bills. So I'll be goin' erlong with ye on the nex' ship an' when we git thar I want to shake hands with the gal and tell her how to make ye behave."

That evening Jack went to the manager of *The Gazette* and asked for a six months' leave of absence.

"And why would ye be leaving?" asked the manager, a braw Scot.

"I expect to be married."

"In England?"

"Yes."

"I'll agree if the winsome, wee thing will give ye time to send us news letters from London. Doctor

Franklin could give ye help. He has been boiling over with praise o' you and has asked me to broach the matter. Ye'll be sailing on the next ship."

Before there was any sailing Jack and Solomon had time to go to Albany for a visit. They found the family well and prosperous, the town growing. John Irons said that land near the city was increasing rapidly in value. Solomon went away into the woods the morning of their arrival and returned in the afternoon with his money, which he gave to John Irons to be invested in land. Jack, having had a delightful stay at home, took a schooner for New York that evening with Solomon.

The night before they sailed for England his friends in the craft gave Jack a dinner at The Gray Goose Tavern. He describes the event in a long letter. To his astonishment the mayor and other well-known men were present and expressed their admiration for his talents.

The table was spread with broiled fish and roasted fowls and mutton and towering spiced hams and sweet potatoes and mince pies and cakes and jellies.

"The spirit of hospitality expresses itself here in ham—often, also, in fowls, fish and mutton, but always and chiefly in ham—cooked and decorated with the greatest care and surrounded by forms, flavors and colors calculated to please the eye and fill the human system with a deep, enduring and memorable satisfaction," he writes.

In the midst of the festivities it was announced that
Jack was to be married and as was the custom of the
time, every man at the table proposed a toast and drank
to it.   One addressed himself to the eyes of the fortunate young lady.   Then her lips, her eyebrows, her
neck, her hands, her feet, her disposition and her future husband were each in turn enthusiastically toasted
by other guests in bumpers of French wine.   He adds
that these compliments were "so moist and numerous
that they became more and more indistinct, noisy and
irrational" and that before they ended "Nearly every
one stood up singing his own favorite song.   There
is a stage of emotion which can only be expressed in
noises.   That stage had been reached.   They put me
in mind of David Culver's bird shop where many song
birds—all of a different feather—engage in a kind
of tournament, each pouring out his soul with a desperate determination to be heard.   It was all very friendly
and good natured but it was, also, very wild."

CHAPTER IV

THE CROSSING

THERE were curious events in the voyage of Jack and Solomon. The date of the letter above referred to would indicate that they sailed on or about the eleventh of October, 1773. Their ship was *The Snow* which had arrived the week before with some fifty Irish servants, indentured for their passage. These latter were, in a sense, slaves placed in bondage to sundry employers by the captain of the ship for a term of years until the sum due to the owners for their transportation had been paid—a sum far too large, it would seem.

Jack was sick for a number of days after the voyage began but Solomon, who was up and about and cheerful in the roughest weather, having spent a part of his youth at sea, took care of his young friend. Jack tells in a letter that he was often awakened in the night by vermin and every morning by the crowing of cocks. Those days a part of every ship was known as "the hen coops" where ducks, geese and chickens were confined. They came in due time through the butcher shop and the galley to the cabin table. The cook was an able, swearing man whose culinary experience had been acquired on a Nantucket whaler. Cooks who could stand up for service every day in a small ship

on an angry sea when the galley rattled like a dice box
in the hands of a nervous player, were hard to get.
Their constitutions were apt to be better than their art.
The food was of poor quality, the cooking a tax upon
jaw, palate and digestion, the service unclean. When
good weather came, by and by, and those who had not
tasted food for days began to feel the pangs of hunger
the ship was filled with a most passionate lot of pilgrims. It was then that Solomon presented the peti-
tion of the passengers to the captain.

"Cap'n, we're 'bout wore out with whale meat an'
slobgollion. We're all down by the head."

"So'm I," said the Captain. "This 'ere man had a
good recommend an' said he could cook perfect."

"A man like that kin cook the passengers with their
own heat," said Solomon. "I feel like my belly was
full o' hot rocks. If you'll let me into the galley, I'll
right ye up an' shift the way o' the wind an' the course
o' the ship. I'll swing the bow toward Heaven 'stead
o' Hell an' keep her p'inted straight an' it won't cost
ye a penny. They's too much swearin' on this 'ere ship.
Can't nobody be a Christian with his guts a-b'ilin'. His
tongue'll break loose an' make his soul look like a
waggin with a smashed wheel an' a bu'sted ex. A cook
could do more good here than a minister."

"Can you cook?"

"You try me an' I'll agree to happy ye up so ye
won't know yerself. Yer meat won't be raw ner petri-
fied an' there won't be no insecks in the biscuit."

"He'll make a row."

"I hope so. Leave him to me. I'm a leetle bit in need o' exercise, but ye needn't worry. I know how to manage him—perfect. You come with me to the galley an' tell him to git out of it. I'll do the rest."

Solomon's advice was complied with. The cook—Thomas Crowpot by name—was ordered out of the galley. The sea cook is said to be the father of profanity. His reputation has come down through the ages untarnished, it would seem, by any example of philosophical moderation. Perhaps it is because, in the old days, his calling was a hard one and only those of a singular recklessness were willing to engage in it. *The Snow's* cook was no exception. He was a big, brawny, black Yankee with a claw foot look in his eyes. Profanity whizzed through the open door like buckshot from a musket. He had been engaged for the voyage and would not give up his job to any man.

"Don't be so snappish," said Solomon. Turning to the Captain he added: "Don't ye see here's the big spring. This 'ere man could blister a bull's heel by talkin' to it. He's hidin' his candle. This ain't no job fer him. I say he orto be promoted."

With an outburst still profane but distinctly milder the cook wished to know what they meant.

Solomon squinted with his rifle eye as if he were taking careful aim at a small mark.

"Why, ye see we passengers have been swearin' stiddy fer a week," he drawled. "We're wore out.

We need a rest. You're a trained swearer. Ye do it perfect. Ye ortn't to have nothin' else to do. We want you to go for'ard an' find a comf'table place an' set down an' do all the swearin' fer the hull ship from now on. You'll git yer pay jest the same as if ye done the cookin'. It's a big job but I guess ye're ekal to it. I'll agree that they won't nobody try to grab it. Ye may have a little help afore the mast but none abaft."

This unexpected proposition calmed the cook. The prospect of full pay and nothing to do pleased him. He surrendered.

An excellent dinner was cooked and served that day. The lobscouse made of pork, fowl and sliced potatoes was a dish to remember. But the former cook got a line of food calculated to assist him in the performance of his singular duty. Happiness returned to the ship and Solomon was cheered when at length he came out of the galley. Officers and passengers rendered him more homage after that than they paid to the rich and famous Mr. Girard who was among their number. That day this notice was written on the blackboard:

"Thomas Crowpot has been engaged to do all the swearing that's necessary on this voyage. Any one who needs his services will find him on the forward deck. Small and large jobs will be attended to while you wait."

2

Often in calm weather Jack and Solomon amused themselves and the other passengers with pistol practise by tossing small objects into the air and shooting at them over the ship's side. They rarely missed even the smallest object thrown. Jack was voted the best marksman of the two when he crushed with his bullet four black walnuts out of five thrown by Mr. Girard.

In the course of the voyage they overhauled *The Star,* a four-masted ship bound from New York to Dover. For hours the two vessels were so close that the passengers engaged in a kind of battle. Those on *The Star* began it by hurling turnips at the men on the other ship who responded with a volley of apples. Solomon discerned on the deck of the stranger Captain Preston and an English officer of the name of Hawk whom he had known at Oswego and hailed them. Then said Solomon:

"It's a ship load o' Tories who've had enough of Ameriky. They's a cuss on that tub that I helped put a coat o' tar an' feathers on in the Ohio kentry. He's the one with the black pipe in his mouth. I don't know his name but they use to call him Slops—the dirtiest, low-downdest, damn Tory traitor that ever lived. Helped the Injuns out thar in the West. See that 'ere black pipe? Allus carries it in his mouth 'cept when he's eatin'. I guess he goes to sleep with it. It's one o' the features o' his face. We tarred him plenty now you hear to me."

That evening a boat was lowered and the Captain of *The Snow* crossed a hundred yards of quiet sea to dine with the Captain of *The Star* in the cabin of the latter. Next day a stiff wind came out of the west. All sail was spread, the ships began to jump and gore the waves and *The Star* ran away from the smaller ship and was soon out of sight. Weeks of rough going followed. Meanwhile Solomon stuck to his task. Every one was sick but Jack and the officers, and there was not much cooking to be done.

Because he had to take off his coat while he was working in the galley, Solomon gave the precious letter into Jack's keeping.

Near the end of the sixth week at sea they spied land.

"We cheered, for the ocean had shown us a tiger's heart," the young man wrote. "For weeks it had leaped and struck at us and tumbled us about. The crossing is more like hardship than anything that has happened to me. One woman died and was buried at sea. A man had his leg broken by being thrown violently against the bulwarks and the best of us were bumped a little.

"Some days ago a New Yorker who was suspected of cheating at cards on the complaint of several passengers was put on trial and convicted through the evidence of one who had seen him marking a pack of the ship's cards. He was condemned to be carried up to the round top and made fast there, in view of all the ship's company for three hours and to pay a fine of two bottles of brandy. He refused to pay his fine and we excommunicated the culprit refusing either to eat, drink or speak with him until he should submit. To-day he gave up and paid his fine. Man is a sociable being and the bitterest of all punishments is exclusion. He couldn't stand it."

About noon on the twenty-ninth of November they made Dover and anchored in the Downs. Deal was about three miles away and its boats came off for them. They made a circuit and sailed close in shore. Each boat that went out for passengers had its own landing. Its men threw a rope across the breakers. This was quickly put on a windlass. With the rope winding on its windlass the boat was slowly hauled through the surge, its occupants being drenched and sprinkled with salt water. They made their way to the inn of The Three Kings where two men stood watching as they approached. One of them Jack recognized as the man Slops with the black pipe in his mouth.

"That's him," said the man with the black pipe pointing at Solomon, whereupon the latter was promptly arrested.

"What have I done?" he asked.

"You'll learn directly at 'eadquarters," said the officer.

Solomon shook hands with Jack and said: "I'm glad I met ye," and turned and walked away with the two men.

Jack was tempted to follow them but feeling a hidden purpose in Solomon's conduct went into the inn.

So the friends parted, Jack being puzzled and dis-

tressed by the swift change in the color of their affairs. The letter to Doctor Franklin was in his pocket
—a lucky circumstance. He decided to go to London
and deliver the letter and seek advice regarding the
relief of Solomon. At the desk in the lobby of The
Three Kings he learned that he must take the post
chaise for Canterbury which would not be leaving
until six P. M. This gave him time to take counsel in
behalf of his friend. Turning toward the door he met
Captain Preston, who greeted him with great warmth
and wished to know where was Major Binkus.

Jack told the Captain of the arrest of his friend.

"I expected it," said Preston. "So I have waited
here for your ship. It's that mongrel chap on *The
Star* who got a tarring from Binkus and his friends.
He saw Binkus on your deck, as I did, and proclaimed
his purpose. So I am here to do what I can to help
you. I can not forget that you two men saved my
life. Are there any papers on his person which are
likely to make him trouble?"

"No," said Jack, thinking of the letter lying safely
in his own pocket.

"That's the important thing," Preston resumed.
"Binkus is a famous scout who is known to be anti-
British. Such a man coming here is supposed to be
carrying papers. Between ourselves they would arrest
him on any pretext. You leave this matter in my
hands. If he had no papers he'll be coming on in a
day or two."

"I'd like to go with you to find him," said Jack.

"Better not," Preston answered with a smile.

"Why?"

"Because I suspect you have the papers. They'll get you, too, if they learn you are his friend. Keep away from him. Sit quietly here in the inn until the post chaise starts for Canterbury. Don't let any one pick a quarrel with you and remember this is all a sacred confidence between friends."

"I thank you and my heart is in every word," said Jack as he pressed the hand of the Captain. "After all friendship is a thing above politics—even the politics of these bitter days."

3

He sat down with a sense of relief and spent the rest of the afternoon reading the London papers although he longed to go and look at the fortress of Deal Castle. He had tea at five and set out on the mail carriage, with his box and bag, an hour later. The road was rough and muddy with deep holes in it. At one point the chaise rattled and bumped over a plowed field. Before dark he saw a man hanging in a gibbet by the roadside. At ten o'clock they passed the huge gate of Canterbury and drew up at an inn called The King's Head. The landlady and two waiters attended for orders. He had some supper and went to bed. Awakened at five A. M. by the sound of a bugle he arose and dressed hurriedly and found the post chaise waiting. They went on the King's Road from Canterbury and a mile out they came to a big, white gate in the dim light of the early morning.

A young man clapped his mouth to the window and shouted:

"Sixpence, Yer Honor!"

It was a real turnpike and Jack stuck his head out of the window for a look at it. They stopped for breakfast at an inn far down the pike and went on through Sittingborn, Faversham, Rochester and the lovely valley of the River Medway of which Jack had read.

At every stop it amused him to hear the words "Chaise an' pair," flying from host to waiter and waiter to hostler and back in the wink of an eye.

Jack spent the night at The Rose in Dartford and went on next morning over Gadshill and Shootershill and Blackheath. Then the Thames and Greenwich and Deptfort from which he could see the crowds and domes and towers of the big city. A little past two o'clock he rode over London bridge and was set down at The Spread Eagle where he paid a shilling a mile for his passage and ate his dinner.

Such, those days, was the crossing and the trip up to London, as Jack describes it in his letters.

CHAPTER V

THE stir and prodigious reach of London had appalled the young man. His fancy had built and peopled it, but having found no sufficient material for its task in New York, Boston and Philadelphia, had scored a failure. It had built too small and too humbly. He was in no way prepared for the noise, the size, the magnificence, the beauty of it. In spite of that, something in his mental inheritance had soon awakened a sense of recognition and familiarity. He imagined that the sooty odor and the bells, and the clatter of wheels and horses' feet and the voices—the air was full of voices—were like the echoes of a remote past.

The thought thrilled him that somewhere in the great crowd, of which he was now a part, were the two human beings he had come so far to see. He put on his best clothes and with the letter which had been carefully treasured—under his pillow at night and pinned to his pocket lining through the day—set out in a cab for the lodgings of Doctor Franklin. Through a maze of streets where people were "thick as the brush in the forests of Tryon County" he proceeded until after a journey of some thirty minutes the cab stopped at the home of the famous American on Bloomsbury

98

Square. Doctor Franklin was in and would see him presently, so the liveried servant informed the young man after his card had been taken to the Doctor's office. He was shown into a reception room and asked to wait, where others were waiting. An hour passed and the day was growing dusk when all the callers save Jack had been disposed of. Then Franklin entered. Jack remembered the strong, well-knit frame and kindly gray eyes of the philosopher. His thick hair, hanging below his collar, was now white. He was very grand in a suit of black Manchester velvet with white silk stockings and bright silver buckles on his shoes. There was a gentle dignity in his face when he took the boy's hand and said with a smile:

"You are so big, Jack. You have built a six foot, two inch man out of that small lad I knew in Albany, and well finished, too—great thighs, heavy shoulders, a mustache, a noble brow and shall I say the eye of Mars? It's a wonder what time and meat and bread and potatoes and air can accomplish. But perhaps industry and good reading have done some work on the job."

Jack blushed and answered. "It would be hard to fix the blame."

Franklin put his hand on the young man's shoulder and said:

"She is a lovely girl, Jack. You have excellent good taste. I congratulate you. Her pulchritude has a background of good character and she is alive with

the spirit of the New World. I have given her no
chance to forget you if that had been possible. Since
I became the agent in England of yourself and sundry
American provinces, I have seen her often but never
without longing for the gift of youth. How is my
family?"

"They are well. I bring you letters."

"Come up to my office and we'll give an hour to the
news."

When they were seated before the grate fire in the
large, pleasant room above stairs whose windows
looked out upon the Square, the young man said:

"First I shall give you, sir, a letter from Major
Washington. It was entrusted to a friend of mine who
came on the same ship with me. He was arrested at
Deal but, fortunately, the letter was in my pocket."

"Arrested? Why?"

"I think, sir, the charge was that he had helped to
tar and feather a British subject."

"Feathers and tar are poor arguments," the Doctor
remarked as he broke the seal of the letter.

It was a long letter and Franklin sat for near half
an hour thoughtfully reading and rereading it. By
and by he folded and put it into his pocket, saying as
he did so: "An angry man can not even trust himself. I sent some letters to America on condition that
they should be read by a committee of good men and
treated in absolute confidence and returned to me.
Certain members of that committee had so much gun

powder in their hearts it took fire and their prudence and my reputation have been seriously damaged, I fear. The contents of those letters are now probably known to you."

"Are they the Hutchinson, Rogers and Oliver letters?"

"The same."

"I think they are known to every one in America that reads. We were indignant that these men born and raised among us should have said that a colony ought not to enjoy all the liberties of a parent state and that we should be subjected to coercive measures. They had expressed no such opinion save in these private letters. It looked like a base effort to curry favor with the English government."

"Yes, they were overworking the curry comb," said Franklin. "I had been protesting against an armed force in Boston. The government declared that our own best people were in favor of it. I, knowing better, denied the statement. To prove their claim a distinguished baronet put the letters in my hands. He gave me leave to send them to America on condition that they should not be published. Of course they proved nothing but the treachery of Hutchinson, Rogers and Oliver. Now I seem to be tarred by the same stick."

Jack delivered sundry letters from the family of the great man who read them carefully.

"It's good to hear from home," he said when he had

finished. "You've heard of the three Greenlanders, off the rocks and ice where there was not dirt enough to raise a bushel of cabbages or light enough for half the year to make a shadow, who having seen the world and its splendors said it was interesting, but that they would prefer to live at home?"

"These days America is an unhappy land," said Jack. "We are like a wildcat in captivity—a growling, quarrelsome lot."

"Well, the British use the right to govern us like a baby rattle and they find us a poor toy. This petty island, compared with America, is but a stepping stone in a brook. There's scarcely enough of it out of water to keep one's feet dry. In two generations our population will exceed that of the British Isles. But with so many lying agents over there what chance have they to learn anything about us? They will expect to hear you tell of people being tomahawked in Philadelphia —a city as well governed as any in England. They can not understand that most of us would gladly spend nineteen shillings to the pound for the right to spend the other shilling as we please."

"Can they not be made to understand us?" Jack inquired.

"The power to learn is like your hand—you must use it or it will wither and die. There are brilliant intellects here which have lost the capacity to learn. I think that profound knowledge is not for high heads."

"I wonder just what you mean."

"Oh, the moment you lose humility, you stop learning," the Doctor went on. "There are two doors to
every intellect. One lets knowledge in, the other lets
it out. We must keep both doors in use. The mind is
like a purse: if you keep paying out money, you must,
now and then, put some into your purse or it will be
empty. I once knew a man who was a liberal spender
but never did any earning. We soon found that he
had been making counterfeit money. The King's intellects have often put me in mind of him. They are
flush with knowledge but they never learn anything.
They can tell you all you may want to know but it is
counterfeit knowledge."

"How about Lord North?"

"He has nailed up the door. The African zebra is
a good student compared to him. It is a maxim of
Walpole and North that all men are equally corrupt."

"It is a hateful notion!" Jack exclaimed.

"But not without some warrant. You may be sure
that a man who has spent his life in hospitals will have
no high opinion of the health of mankind. He and his
friends are so engrossed by their cards and cock fights
and horses and hounds that they have little time for
such a trivial matter as the problems of America.
They postpone their consideration and meanwhile the
house is catching fire. By and by these boys are going
to get burned. They think us a lot of semi-savages
not to be taken seriously. Our New England farmers
are supposed to be like the peasants of Europe. The

fact is, our average farmer is a man of better intellect and character than the average member of Parliament."

"The King's intellects would seem to be out of order," said Jack.

"And too cynical. They think only of revenues. They remind me of the report of the Reverend Commissary Blair who, having projected a college in Virginia, came to England to ask King William for help. The Queen in the King's absence ordered her Attorney-General to draw a charter with a grant of two thousand pounds. The Attorney opposed it on the ground that they were in a war and needed the money for better purposes.

"'But, Your Honor, Virginia is in great need of ministers,' said the commissary. 'It has souls to be saved.'

"'Souls—damn your souls! Make tobacco,' said the Queen's lawyer.

"The counselors of royalty have no high opinion of souls or principles. Think of these taxes on exports needed by neighbors. The minds that invented them had the genius of a pickpocket."

"I see that you are not in love with England, sir," said Jack.

"My boy, you do not see straight," the Doctor answered. "I am fond of England. At heart she is sound. The King is a kind of wooden leg. He has no feeling and no connection whatever with her heart and

little with her intellect.   The people are out of sympathy with the King.   The best minds in England are
directly opposed to the King's policy; so are most of
the people, but they are helpless.   He has throttled the
voting power of the country.   Jack, I have told you
all this and shall tell you more because—well, you
know Plato said that he would rather be a blockhead
than have all knowledge and nobody to share it.   You
ought to know the truth but I have told you only for
your own information."

"I am going to write letters to *The Gazette* but I
shall not quote you, sir, without permission," said Jack.

At this point the attendant entered and announced
that Mr. Thomas Paine had called to get his manuscript.

"Bring him up," said the Doctor.

In a moment a slim, dark-eyed man of about thirty-
three in shabby, ill-fitting garments entered the room.

Doctor Franklin shook his hand and gave him a
bundle of manuscript and said:

"It is well done but I think it unsound.   I would
not publish it."

"Why?" Paine asked with a look of disappointment.

"Well, it is spitting against the wind and he who
spits against the wind spits in his own face.   It would
be a dangerous book.   Think how great a portion of
mankind are weak and ignorant men and women;
think how many are young and inexperienced and incapable of serious thought.   They need religion to

support their virtue and restrain them from vice. If men are so wicked with religion what would they be without it? Lay the manuscript away and we will have a talk about it later."

"I should like to talk with you about it," the man answered with a smile and departed, the bundle under his arm.

"Now, Jack," said Franklin, as he looked at his watch, "I can give you a quarter of an hour before I must go and dress for dinner. Please tell me about your resources. Are you able to get married?"

Jack told him of his prospects and especially of the generosity of his friend Solomon Binkus and of the plight the latter was in.

"He must be a remarkable man," said Franklin. "With Preston's help he will be coming on to London in a day or so. If necessary you and I will go down there. We shall not neglect him. Have you any dinner clothes? They will be important to you."

"I thought, sir, that I should best wait until I had arrived here."

"You thought wisely. I shall introduce you to a good cloth mechanic. Go to him at once and get one suit for dinner and perhaps two for the street. It costs money to be a gentleman here. It's a fine art. While you are in London you'll have to get the uniform and fall in line and go through the evolutions or you will be a 'North American savage.' You shall meet the Hares in my house as soon as your clothes are

ready. Ask the tailor to hurry up. They must be finished by Wednesday noon. You had better have lodgings near me. I will attend to that for you."

The Doctor sat down and wrote on a number of
cards. "These will provide for cloth, linen, leather
and hats," he said. "Let the bills be sent to me.
Then you will not be cheated. Come in to-morrow
at half after two."

2

Jack bade the Doctor good night and drove to The
Spread Eagle where, before he went to bed, he wrote
to his parents and a long letter to *The Pennsylvania
Gazette,* describing his voyage and his arrival substantially as the facts are here recorded. Next morning he
ordered every detail in his "uniforms" for morning
and evening wear and returning again to the inn found
Solomon waiting in the lobby.

"Here I be," said the scout and trapper.

"What happened to you?"

"S'arched an' shoved me into a dark hole in the
wall. Ye know, Jack, with you an' me, it allus 'pears
to be workin'."

"What?"

"Good luck. Cur'us thing the papers was on you
'stid of me—ayes, sir, 'twas. Did ye hand 'em over
safe?"

"Last night I put 'em in Franklin's hands."

"Hunkidory! I'm ready fer to go hum."

"Not yet I hope. I want you to help me see the
place."

"Wall, sir, I'll be p'intin' fer hum soon es I kin hop on a ship. Couldn't stan' it here, too much noise an' deviltry. This 'ere city is like a twenty-mile bush full o' drunk Injuns—Maumees, hostyle as the devil. I went out fer a walk an' a crowd follered me eround which I don't like it. 'Look at the North American,' they kep' a-sayin'. As soon as I touched shore the tommyhawk landed on me. But fer Cap. Preston I'd be in that 'ere dark hole now. He see the Jedge an' the Jedge called fer Slops an' Slops had slopped over. He were layin' under a tree dead drunk. The Jedge let me go an' Preston come on with me. Now 'twere funny he turned up jest as he done; funny I got app'inted cook o' *The Snow* so as I had to give that 'ere paper to you. I tell ye it's workin'—allus workin'."

"Doctor Franklin wants to see you," said Jack. "Put on your Sunday clothes an' we'll go over to his house. I think I can lead you there. If we get lost we'll jump into a cab."

When they set out Solomon was dressed in fine shoes and brown wool stockings and drab trousers, a butternut jacket and blue coat, and a big, black three-cornered hat. His slouching gait and large body and weathered face and the variety of colors in his costume began at once to attract the attention of the crowd. A half-drunk harridan surveyed him, from top to toe, and made a profound bow as he passed. A number of small boys scurried along with them, curiously staring into the face of Solomon.

"Ain't this like comin' into a savage tribe that ain't seen no civilized human bein' fer years?"

"Wot is it?" a voice shouted.

" 'E's a blarsted bush w'acker from North Hamerica, 'e is," another answered.

Jack stopped a cab and they got into it.

"Show us some of the great buildings and land us in an hour at 10 Bloomsbury Square, East," he said.

With a sense of relief they were whisked away in the stream of traffic.

They passed the King's palace and the great town houses of the Duke of Bedford and Lord Balcarras, each of which was pointed out by the driver. Suddenly every vehicle near them stopped, while their male occupants sat with bared heads. Jack observed a curious procession on the sidewalk passing between two lines of halted people.

"Hit's their Majesties!" the driver whispered under his breath.

The King—a stout, red-nosed, blue-jowled man, with big, gray, staring eyes—was in a sedan chair surmounted by a crown. He was dressed in light cloth with silver buttons. Queen Charlotte, also in a chair, was dressed in lemon colored silk ornamented with brocaded flowers. The two were smiling and bowing as they passed. In a moment the procession entered a great gate. Then there was a crack of whips and the traffic resumed its hurried pace.

"Hit's their Majesties, sir, goin' to a drawin'-room

at Lord Rawdon's, sir," the driver explained as he drove on.

"Did you see the unnatural look in his gray eyes?" said Jack, turning to Solomon.

"Ayes! Kind o' skeered like! 'Twere a han'some yoke o' men totin' him—well broke, too, I guess. Pulled even an' nobody yellin' gee er haw er whoa hush."

"You know it isn't proper for kings and queens to, walk in public," Jack answered.

Again Solomon had on his shooting face. With his left eye closed, he took deliberate aim with the other at the subject before them and thus discharged his impressions.

"Uh huh! I suppose 'twouldn't do fer 'em to be like other folks so they have to have some extry pairs o' legs to kind o' put on when they go ou'doors. I wonder if they ain't obleeged to have an extry set o' brains fer public use."

"They have quantities of 'em all made and furnished to order and stored in the court," said Jack. "His own mind is only for use in the private rooms."

"I should think 'twould git out o' order," Solomon remarked.

"It does. They say he's been as crazy as a loon."

Soon the two observers became interested in a band of sooty-faced chimney sweeps decorated with ribbands and gilt paper. They were making musical sounds with their brushes and scrapers and soliciting gifts from the passing crowd and, now and then, scrambling for tossed coins.

In the Ave Mary Lane they saw a procession of milk men and maids carrying wreaths of flowers on wheel-barrows, the first of which held a large white pyramid which seemed to be a symbol of their calling. They were also begging.

"It's a lickpenny place," said Jack.

"Somebody's got to do some 'arnin' to pay fer all the foolin' eround," Solomon answered. "If I was to stay here I'd git myself ragged up like these 'ere savages and jine the tribe er else I'd lose the use o' my legs an' spend all my money bein' toted. I ain't used to settin' down when I move, you hear to me."

"I'll take you to Doctor Franklin's tailor," Jack proposed.

"Major Washington tol' me whar to go. I got the name an' the street all writ down plain in my wallet but I got t' go hum."

They had stopped at the door of the famous American. Jack and Solomon went in and sat down with a dozen others to await their turn.

When they had been conducted to the presence of the great man he took Solomon's hand and said:

"Mr. Binkus, I am glad to bid you welcome."

He looked down at the sinewy, big-boned, right hand of the scout, still holding it.

"Will you step over to the window a moment and give me a look at your hands?" he asked.

They went to the window and the Doctor put on his spectacles and examined them closely.

"I have never seen such an able, Samsonian fist," he went on. "I think the look of those hands would let you into Paradise. What a record of human service is writ upon them! Hands like that have laid the foundations of America. They have been generous hands. They tell me all I need to know of your spirit, your lungs, your heart and your stomach."

"They're purty heavy—that's why I gen'ally carry 'em in my pockets when I ain't busy," said Solomon.

"Over here a pair of hands like that are thought to be a disgrace. They are like the bloody hands of Macbeth. Certain people would look at them and say: 'My God, man, you are guilty of hard work. You have produced food for the hungry and fuel for the cold. You are not an idler. You have refused to waste your time with Vice and Folly. Avaunt and quit my sight.' In America every one works—even the horse, the ass and the ox. Only the hog is a gentleman. There are many mischievous opinions in Europe but the worst is that useful labor is dishonorable. Do you like London?"

Solomon put his face in shape for a long shot. Jack has written that he seemed to be looking for hostile "Injuns" some distance away and to be waiting for another stir in the bushes. Suddenly he pulled his trigger.

"London an' I is kind o' skeered o' one 'nother.

It 'minds me o' the fust time I run into ol' Thorny
Tree. They was a young brave with him an' both on
'em had guns. They knowed me an' I knowed them.
Looked as if there'd have to be some killin' done. We
both made the sign o' friendship an' kep' edgin' erway
f'm one 'nother careless like but keepin' close watch.
Sudden as scat they run like hell in one direction an' I
in t'other. I guess I look bad to London an' London
looks bad to me, but I'll have to do all the runnin' this
time."

The Doctor laughed. "It has never seen a man just
like you before," he observed. "I saw Sir Jeffrey Amherst this morning and told him you were in London.
He is fond of you and paid you many compliments and
made me promise to bring you to his home."

"I'd like to smoke a pipe with ol' Jeff," Solomon
answered. "They ain't no nonsense 'bout him. I
learnt him how to talk Injun an' read rapids an' build
a fire with tinder an' elbow grease. He knows me
plenty. He staked his life on me a dozen times in the
Injun war."

"How is Major Washington?" the Doctor asked.

"Stout as a pot o' ginger," Solomon answered. "I
rassled with him one evenin' down in Virginny an' I'll
never tackle him ag'in, you hear to me. His right
flipper is as big as mine an' when it takes holt ye'd
think it were goin' to strip the shuck off yer soul."

"He's in every way a big man," said the Doctor.
"On the whole, he's about our biggest man. An officer

who came out of the ambuscade at Fort Duquesne with thirty living men out of three companies and four shot holes in his coat must have an engagement with Destiny. Evidently his work was not finished. You have traveled about some. What is the feeling over there toward England?"

"They're like a b'ilin' pot everywhere. England has got to step careful now."

"Tell Sir Jeffrey that, if you see him, just that. Don't mince matters. Jack, I'll send my man with you and Mr. Binkus to show you the new lodgings. We found them this morning."

CHAPTER VI

THE LOVERS

THE fashionable tailor was done with Jack's equipment. Franklin had seen and approved the admirably shaped and fitted garments. The young man and his friend Solomon had moved to their new lodgings on Bloomsbury Square. The scout had acquired a suit for street wear and was now able to walk abroad without exciting the multitudes. The Doctor was planning what he called "a snug little party." So he announced when Jack and Solomon came, adding:

"But first you are to meet Margaret and her mother here at half after four."

Jack made careful preparation for that event. Fortunately it was a clear, bright day after foggy weather. Solomon had refused to go with Jack for fear of being in the way.

"I want to see her an' her folks but I reckon ye'll have yer hands full to-day," he remarked. "Ye don't need no scout on that kind o' reconnoiterin'. You go on ahead an' git through with yer smackin an' bym-by I'll straggle in."

Precisely at four thirty-five Jack presented himself at the lodgings of his distinguished friend. He has said in a letter, when his dramatic adventures were all behind him, that this was the most thrilling moment he had known. "The butler had told me that the ladies were there," he wrote. "Upon my word it put me out of breath climbing that little flight of stairs. But it was in fact the end of a long journey. It is curious that my feeling then should remind me, as it does, of moments when I have been close up to the enemy, within his lines, and lying hard against the ground in some thicket while British soldiers were tramping so near I could feel the ground shake. In the room I saw Lady Hare and Doctor Franklin standing side by side. What a smile he wore as he looked at me! I have never known a human being who had such a cheering light in his countenance. I have seen it brighten the darkest days of the war aided by the light of his words. His faith and good cheer were immovable. I felt the latter when he said:

"'See the look of alarm in his face. Now for a pretty drama!'

"Mrs. Hare gave me her hand and I kissed it and said that I had expected to see Margaret and hoped that she was not ill. There was a thistledown touch on my cheek from behind and turning I saw the laughing face I sought looking up at me. I tell you, my mother, there never was such a pair of eyes. Their long, dark lashes and the glow between them I remember chiefly. The latter was the friendly light of her spirit. To me it was like a candle in the window to guide my feet. 'Come,' it seemed to say. 'Here is a welcome for you.' I saw the pink in her cheeks, the crimson in her lips, the white of her neck, the glow of her abundant hair, the shapeliness of brow and nose and chin in that first glance. I saw the beating of her heart even. I remember there was a tiny mole on her temple under the edge of that beautiful, golden crown of hers. It did not escape my eye. I tell you she was fair as the first violets in Meadowvale on a dewy morning. Of course she was at her best. It was the last moment in years of waiting in which her imagination had furnished me with endowments too romantic. I have seen great moments, as you know, but this is the one I could least afford to give up. I had long been wondering what I should do when it came. Now it was come and there was no taking thought of what we should do. That would seem to have been settled out of court. I kissed her lips and she kissed mine and for a few moments I think we could have stood in a half bushel measure. Then the Doctor laughed and gave her Ladyship a smack on the cheek.

" 'I don't know about you, my Lady, but it fills me with the glow of youth to see such going on,' he remarked. 'I'm only twenty-one and nobody knows it— nobody suspects it even. These wrinkles and gray hair are only a mask that covers the heart of a boy.'

" 'I confess that such a scene does push me back into my girlhood,' said Lady Hare. 'Alas! I feel the old thrill.'

"Franklin came and stood before us with his hands upon our shoulders, his face shining with happiness.

" 'Margaret, a woman needs something to hold on to in this slippery world,' said he. 'Here is a man that stands as firm as an oak tree.'

"He kissed us as did Lady Hare, also, and then we all sat down together and laughed. I would not forget, if I could, that we had to wipe our eyes. No, my life has not been all blood and iron.

"Would you not call it a wonder that we had kept the sacred fire which had been kindled in our hearts, so long before, and our faith in each other? It is because we were both of a steadfast breed of folk—the English—trained to cling to the things that are worth while. Once they think they are right how hard it is to turn them aside! Let us never forget that some of the best of our traits have come from England.

"Suddenly Solomon arrived. Of course where Solomon is one would expect solecisms. They were not wanting. I had not tried to prepare him for the ordeal. Solomon is bound to be himself wherever he is, and why not? There is no better man living.

" 'You're as purty as a golden robin,' he said to Margaret, shaking her hand in his big one.

"He was not so much put out as I thought he would be. I never saw a gentler man with women. As hard as iron in a fight there has always been a curious vein of chivalry in the old scout. He stood and joked with the girl, in his odd fashion, and set us all laughing. Margaret and her mother enjoyed his talk and spoke of it, often, after that.

" 'Wal, Mis Hare,' he said to Her Ladyship, 'if ye graft this 'ere sprout on yer fam'ly tree I'll bet ye a pint o' powder an' a fish hook ye won't never be sorry fer it.'

"It did not seem to occur to him that there were those to whom a pint of powder and a fish hook would be no great temptation.

2

"I dressed and went to dine with the Hares that evening. They lived in a large house on a fashionable 'road' as certain of the streets were called. It was a typical upper class, English home. There were many fine old things in it but no bright colors, nothing to dazzle or astonish you like the wooden Indian in war paint and feathers and the stuffed bear and high colored rugs in the parlor of Mr. Gosport in Philadelphia. Every piece of furniture was like the quiet, still footed servants who came and went making the smallest possible demand upon your attention.

"I was shown into the library where Sir Benjamin sat alone reading a newspaper. He greeted me politely.

" 'The news is disquieting,' he said presently. 'What have you to tell us of the situation in America?'

" 'It is critical,' I answered. 'It can be mended, however, if the government will act promptly.'

" 'What should it do?'

" 'Make concessions, sir, stop shipping tea for a time. Don't try to force an export with a duty on it.

I think the government should not shake the mailed fist at us.'

" 'But think of the violence and the destruction of property!'

" 'All that will abate and disappear if the cause is removed. We who keep our affection for England have done our best to hold the passions of the people in check but we get no help from this side of the ocean.'

"Sir Benjamin sat thoughtfully feeling his silvered mustache. He had grown stouter and fuller-faced since we had parted in Albany when he had looked like a prosperous, well-bred merchant in military dress and had been limbered and soiled by knocking about in the bush. Now he wore a white wig and ruffles and looked as dignified as a Tory magistrate.

"In the moment of silence I mustered up my courage and spoke out.

" 'Sir Benjamin,' I said. 'I have come to claim your daughter under the promise you gave me at Fort Stanwix. I have not ceased to love her and if she continues to love me I am sure that our wishes will have your favor and blessing.'

" 'I have not forgotten the promise,' he said. 'But America has changed. It is likely to be a hotbed of rebellion—perhaps even the scene of a bloody war. I must consider my daughter's happiness.'

" 'Conditions in America, sir, are not so bad as you take them to be,' I assured him.

" 'I hope you are right,' he answered. 'I am told that the whole matter rests with your Doctor Franklin. If we are to go on from bad to worse he will be responsible.'

" 'If it rests with him I can assure you, sir, that our troubles will end,' I said, looking only at the surface of the matter and speaking confidently out of the bottomless pit of my inexperience as the young are like to do.

" 'I believe you are right,' he declared and went on with a smile. 'Now, my young friend, the girl has a notion that she loves you. I am aware of that—so are you, I happen to know. Through Doctor Franklin's influence we have allowed her to receive your letters and to answer them. I have no doubt of your sincerity, or hers, but I did not foresee what has come to pass. She is our only child and you can scarcely blame me if I balk at a marriage which promises to turn her away from us and fill our family with dissension.'

" 'May we not respect each other and disagree in politics?' I asked.

" 'In politics, yes, but not in war. I begin to see danger of war and that is full of the bitterness of death. If Doctor Franklin will do what he can to reestablish loyalty and order in the colonies my fear will be removed and I shall welcome you to my family.'

"I began to show a glint of intelligence and said: 'If the ministers will cooperate it will not be difficult.'

" 'The ministers will do anything it is in their power to do.'

"Then the timely entrance of Margaret and her mother.

" 'I suppose that I shall shock my father but I can not help it,' said the girl as she kissed me.

"You may be sure that I had my part in that game. She stood beside me, her arm around my waist and mine around her shoulders.

" 'Father, can you blame me for loving this big, splendid hero who saved us from the Indians and the bandits? It is unlike you to be such a hardened wretch. But for him you would have neither wife nor daughter.'

"She put it on thick but I held my peace as I have done many a time in the presence of a woman's cunning. Anyhow she is apt to believe herself and in a matter of the heart can find her way through difficulties which would appal a man.

" 'Keep yourself in bounds, my daughter,' her father answered. 'I know his merits and should like to see you married and hope to, but I must ask you to be patient until you can go to a loyal colony with your husband.'

"It was a pleasant dinner through which they kept me telling of my adventures in the bush. Save the immediate family only Mrs. Biggars, a sister of Lady Hare, and a young nephew of Sir Benjamin were at the table."

Jack has said in another of his letters that Mrs.

Biggars was a sweet, stout lady whose manner of address reminded him of an affectionate house cat. "That means, as you will know, that I liked her," he added.

"The ladies sat together at one end of the table. The baronet pumped me for knowledge of the hunting and fishing in the northern part of Tryon County where Solomon and I had spent a week, having left our boat in Lake Champlain and journeyed off in the mountains.

" 'Champlain was a man of imagination,' said my host. 'He tells of trying to land on a log lying against the lake shore and of discovering, suddenly, that it was an immense fish.'

" 'Since I learned that I was to meet you I have been reading a book entitled *The Animals of North America*,' said Mrs. Biggars. 'I have learned that bears often climb after and above the hunter and double themselves up and fall toward him, knocking him out of the tree. Have you seen it done?'

" 'I think it was never done outside a book,' I answered. 'I never saw a bear that was not running away from me. They hate the look of a man.'

"Mrs. Biggars was filled with astonishment and went on: 'The author tells of an animal on the borders of Canada that resembles a horse. It has cloven hoofs, a shaggy mane, a horn right out of its forehead and a tail like that of a pig. When hunted it spews hot water upon the dogs. I wonder if you could have seen such an animal?'

" 'No, that's another nightmare,' I answered. 'People go hunting for nightmares in America. They enjoy them and often think they have found them when they have not. It all comes of trying to talk with Indians and of guessing at the things they say.'

"Sir Benjamin remarked that when a man wrote about nature he seemed to regard himself as a first deputy of God.

" 'And undertakes to lend him a hand in the work of creation,' I suggested. 'Even your great Doctor Johnson has stated that swallows spend the winter at the bottom of the streams, forgetting that they might find it a rather slippery place to hang on to and a winter a long time to hold their breaths. Even Goldsmith has been divinely reckless in his treatment of *Animated Nature.*'

" 'I am surprised, sir, at your familiarity with English authors,' he declared. 'When we think of America we are apt to think of savages and poverty and ignorance and log huts.'

" 'You forget, sir, that we have about all the best books and the leisure to read them,' I answered.

" 'You undoubtedly have the best game,' said he. 'Tell us about the shooting and fishing.'

"I told of the deer, the moose and the caribou, all of which I had killed, and of our fishing on the long river of the north with a lure made of the feathers of a woodpecker, and of covering the bottom of our canoe with beautiful speckled fish. All this warmed the heart of Sir Benjamin who questioned me as to every detail in my experience on trail and river. He was a born sportsman and my stories had put a smile on his face so that I felt sure he had a better feeling for me when we arose from the table.

"Then I had an hour alone with Margaret in a corner of the great hall. We reviewed the years that had passed since our adventure and there was one detail in her history of which I must tell you. She had had many suitors, and among them one Lionel Clarke —a son of the distinguished General. Her father had urged her to accept the young man, but she had stood firmly for me.

" 'You see, this heart of mine is a stubborn thing,' she said as she looked into my eyes.

"Then it was that we gave to each other the long pledge, often on the lips of lovers since Eros strung his bow, but never more deeply felt.

" 'I am sure the sky will clear soon,' she said to me at last.

"Indeed as I bade them good night, I saw encouraging signs of that. Sir Benjamin had taken a liking to me. He pressed my hand as we drank a glass of Madeira together and said:

" 'My boy, I drink to the happiness of England, the colonies and you.' "

" ' "Time and I" and the will of God,' I whispered, as I left their door."

CHAPTER VII

THE DAWN

THE young man was elated by the look and sentiments which had gone with the parting cup at Sir Benjamin's. But Franklin, whom he saw the next day, liked not the attitude of the Baronet.

"He is one of the King's men on the Big chess board," said the old philosopher. "All that he said to you has the sound of strategy. I have reason to believe that they are trying to tow us into port and Margaret is only one of many ropes. Hare's attitude is not that of an honest man."

"Is it not true that every one who touches the King gets some of that tar on him?" Jack queried.

"It would seem so and yet we must be fair to him. We are not to think that the King is the only black pot on the fire. He is probably the best of kings but I can not think of one king who would be respectable in Boston or Philadelphia. Their expenses have been great, their taxes robbery, so they have had to study the magic arts of seeming to be just and righteous. They have been a lot of conjurers trained to create illusions."

"I suppose that Britain is no worse than other kingdoms," said the young man.

"On the whole she is the best of them. Under the

126

surface here I find the love of liberty and all good
things. Chatham, Burke and Fox are their voices. We
are not to wonder that Lord North puts a price on
every man. His is the soul of a past in which most
men have had their price. It was the old way of removing difficulties in the management of a state. It
succeeded. A new day is at hand. Its forerunners
are here. He has not seen the signs in the sky or heard
the cocks crowing. He is still asleep. I know many
men in England whom he could not buy."

Only three days before the philosopher had had a
talk with North at the urgent request of Howe, who,
to his credit, was eager for reconciliation. The King's
friend and minister was contemptuous.

"I am quite indifferent to war," he had cynically declared at last. "The confiscations it would produce
will provide for many of our friends."

It was an astonishing bit of frankness.

"I take this opportunity of assuring Your Lordship
that for all the property you seize or destroy in America, you will pay to the last farthing," said Franklin.

This treatment was like that he had received from
other members of the government since the unfortunate publication of the Hutchinson, Rogers and
Oliver letters. They seemed to entertain the notion
that he had forfeited the respect due a gentleman.

A few days after Franklin had given air to his suspicion that the government party would try to tow him
into port three stout British ships had broken their

cables on him. An invitation not likely to be received
by one who had really forfeited the respect of gentlemen was in his hands. The shrewd philosopher did
not think twice about it. He knew that here was the
first step in a change of tactics. He could not properly
decline to accept it and so he went to dine and spend
the night with a most distinguished company at the
country seat of Lord Howe.

On his return he told his young friend of the portal
and lodge in a great triumphal arch marking the entrance to the estate of His Lordship; of the mile long
road to the big house straight as a gun barrel and
smooth as a carpet; of the immense single oaks; of the
artificial stream circling the front of the house and the
beautiful bridge leading to its entrance; of the double
flight of steps under the grand portico; of the great
hall with its ceiling forty feet high, supported by fluted
Corinthian columns of red-veined alabaster; of the
rare old tapestries on a golden background in the sa-
loon; of the immense corridors connecting the wings
of the structure. The dinner and its guests and its
setting were calculated to impress the son of the Boston
soap boiler who represented the important colonies in
America.

Some of the best people were there—Lord and Lady
Cathcart, Lord and Lady Hyde, Lord and Lady Dart-
mouth. Sir William Erskine, Sir Henry Clinton, Sir
James Baird, Sir Benjamin Hare and their ladies
were also present. Doctor Franklin said that the

punch was calculated to promote cheerfulness and high sentiment. As was the custom at like functions, the ladies sat together at one end of the table, Franklin being seated at the right of Lady Howe, who was most gracious and entertaining. The first toast was to the venerable philosopher.

"My Ladies, Lords and gentlemen," said the host, "we must look to our conduct in the presence of one who talked with Sir William Wyndham and was a visitor in the house of Sir Hans Sloane before we were born; whose tireless intellect has been a confidant of Nature, a playmate of the Lightning and an inventor of ingenious and useful things; whose wisdom has given to Philadelphia a public library, a work house, good paving, excellent schools, a protection against fire as efficient as any in the world and the best newspaper in the colonies. Good health and long life to him and may his love of the old sod increase with his years."

The toast was drunk with expressions of approval, and Franklin only arose and bowed and briefly spoke his acknowledgments in a single sentence, and then added:

"Lord Howe can assure you that public men receive more praise and more blame than they really merit. I have heard much said for and against Benjamin Franklin, but there could be no better testimony in his favor than the good opinion of Lord Howe, for which I can never cease to be grateful. For years I have been weighing the evidence, and my verdict is that Franklin has meant well."

He said to Jack that he felt the need of being "as discreet as a tombstone."

A member of that party has told in his memoirs how he kept the ladies laughing with his merry jests.

"I see by *The Observer* they are going to open cod and whale fisheries in the great lakes of the Northwest," Lady Howe said to him.

He answered very gently: "Your Ladyship, has it never occurred to you that it would be a sublime spectacle to stand at the foot of the great falls of Niagara and see the whales leaping over them?"

"What do you regard as your most important discovery?" one of the ladies inquired.

"Well, first, I naturally think of the hospitality of this house and the beauty and charm of the Lady Howe and her friends," Franklin answered with characteristic diplomacy. "Then there is this wine," he added, lifting his glass. "Its importance is as great as its age and this is old enough to command even my veneration. It reminds me of another discovery of mine: the value of the human elbow. I was telling the King's physician of that this morning and it seemed to amuse him. But for the human elbow every person would need a neck longer than that of a goose to do his eating and drinking."

"I had never thought of that," Lady Howe laughingly answered. "It surely does have some effect on one's manners."

"And his personal appearance and the cost of his neckwear," said Franklin. "Here is another discovery."

He took a leathern case from his pocket and removed from it a sealed glass tube half full of a colorless liquid.

"Kindly hold that in your hand and see what happens," he said to Lady Howe. "It contains plain water."

In half a moment the water began to boil.

"It shows how easily water boils in a vacuum," said Franklin as the ladies were amusing themselves with this odd toy. "It enables us to understand why a little heat produces great agitation in certain intellects," he added.

"Doctor, we are neglecting politics," said Lord Hyde. "You lay much stress upon thrift. Do you not agree with me that a man who has not the judgment to practise thrift and acquire property has not the judgment to vote?"

"Property is all right, but let's make it stay in its own stall," said Franklin. "It should never be a qualification of the voter, because it would lead us up to this dilemma: if I have a jackass I can vote. If the jackass dies I can not vote. Therefore, my vote would represent the jackass and not me."

The dinner over, Lady Howe conducted Doctor Franklin to the library, where she asked him to sit down. There were no other persons in the room. She sat near him and began to speak of the misfortunes of the colony of Massachusetts Bay.

"Your Ladyship, we are all alike," he answered. "I have never seen a man who could not bear the misfortunes of another like a Christian. The trouble is our ministers find it too easy to bear them."

"I wish you would speak with Lord Howe frankly of these troubles. He is just by. Will you give me leave to send for him?"

"By all means, madame, if you think best."

Lord Howe joined them in a moment. He was most polite.

"I am sensible of the fact that you have been mistreated by the ministry," he said. "I have not approved of their conduct. I am unconnected with those men save through personal friendships. My zeal for the public welfare is my only excuse for asking you to open your mind."

Lady Howe arose and offered to withdraw.

"Your Ladyship, why not honor us with your presence?" Franklin asked. "For my part I can see no reason for making a secret of a business of this nature. As to His Lordship's mention of my mistreatment, that done my country is so much greater I dismiss all thought of the other. From the King's speech I judge that no accommodation can be expected."

"The plan is now to send a commission to the colonies, as you have urged," said His Lordship.

Then said Lady Howe: "I wish, my brother Franklin, that you were to be sent thither. I should like that much better than General Howe's going to command the army there."

A rather tense moment followed. Franklin broke its silence by saying in a gentle tone:

"I think, madame, they should provide the General with more honorable employment. I beg that your Ladyship will not misjudge me. I am not capable of taking an office from this government while it is acting with so much hostility toward my country."

"The ministers have the opinion that you can compose the situation if you will," Lord Howe declared. "Many of us have unbounded faith in your ability. I would not think of trying to influence your judgment by a selfish motive, but certainly you may, with reason, expect any reward which it is in the power of the government to bestow."

Then came an answer which should live in history, as one of the great credits of human nature, and all men, especially those of English blood, should feel a certain pride in it. The answer was:

"Your Lordship, I am not looking for rewards, but only for justice."

"Let us try to agree as to what is the justice of the matter," Howe answered. "Will you not draft a plan on which you would be willing to cooperate?"

"That I will be glad to do."

Persisting in his misjudgment, Howe suggested:

"As you have friends here and constituents in America to keep well with, perhaps it would better not be in your handwriting. Send it to Lady Howe and she will copy it and return the original."

Then said the sturdy old Yankee: "I desire, my friends, that there shall be no secrecy about it."

Lord and Lady Howe showed signs of great disappointment as he bade them good night and begged to be sent to his room.

"I am growing old, and have to ask for like indulgence from every hostess," he pleaded.

Howe was not willing to leave a stone unturned. He could not dismiss the notion from his mind that the purchase could be effected if the bid were raised. He drew the Doctor aside and said:

"We do not expect your assistance without proper consideration. I shall insist upon generous and ample appointments for the men you take with you and especially for you as well as a firm promise of *subsequent rewards.*"

What crown had he in mind for the white and venerable brow of the man who stood before him? Beneath that brow was a new type of statesman, born of the hardships and perils and high faith of a new world, and then and there as these two faced each other—the soul of the past and the soul of the future—a moment was come than which there had been no

greater in human history.   In America, France and
England the cocks had been crowing and now the first
light of the dawn of a new day fell upon the figure of
the man who in honor and understanding towered
above his fellows.   Now, for a moment, on the character of this man the unfathomable plan of God for
future ages would seem to have been resting.

In his sixty-eight years he had discovered, among
other things, the vanity of wealth and splendor.   It
was no more to him than the idle wind.   These are
his exact words as he stood with a gentle smile on his
face: "If you wish to use me, give me the propositions
and dismiss all thought of rewards from your mind.
They would destroy the influence you propose to use."

Howe, a good man as men went those days, had got
beyond his depth.   His philosophy comprehended no
such mystery.   What manner of man was this son of a
soap boiler who had smiled and shaken his white head
and spoken like a kindly father to the folly of a child
when these offers of wealth and honor and power had
been made to him?   Did he not understand that it was
really the King who had spoken?

The old gentleman climbed the great staircase and
went to his chamber, while Lord Howe was, no doubt,
communicating the result of his interview to his other
guests.   There were those among them who freely pre-
dicted that war was inevitable.

In the morning at eight o'clock Franklin rode into
town with Lord Howe. They discussed the motion of

the Prime Minister under the terms of which the colonies were to pay money into the British Treasury until Parliament should decide they had paid enough.

"It is impossible," said Franklin. "No chance is offered us to judge the propriety of the measure or our ability to pay. These grants are demanded under a claimed right to tax us at pleasure and compel payments by armed force. Your Lordship, it is like the proposition of a highwayman who presents a pistol at the window of your coach and demands enough to satisfy his greed—no specific sum being named—or there is the pistol."

"You are a most remarkable man, but you do not understand the government," said His Lordship. "You will not let yourself see the other side of the proposition. You are highly esteemed in America and if you could but see the justice of our claim you would be as highly esteemed here and honored and rewarded far beyond any expectation you are likely to have."

"If any one supposes that I could prevail upon my countrymen to take black for white or wrong for right, he does not know them or me," said Franklin. "My people are incapable of being so imposed upon and I am incapable of attempting it."

Next evening came the good Doctor Barclay, a friend of Franklin, and a noted philanthropist. They played chess together, and after the game, while they were draining glasses of Madeira, the philanthropist said:

"Here's to peace and good will between England and her colonies. The prosperity of both depends upon it."

They drank the toast and then Barclay proposed:

"Let us use our efforts to that end. Power is a great thing to have and the noblest gift a government can bestow is within your reach."

"Barclay, this is what I would call spitting in the soup," said Franklin. "It's excellent soup, too. I am sure the ministry would rather give me a seat in a cart to Tyburn than any other place whatever. I would despise myself if I needed an inducement to serve a great cause."

The philanthropist entered upon a wearisome argument, which lasted for nearly an hour.

"Barclay, your opinions on this problem remind me of the iron money of Lycurgus," observed Franklin.

The philanthropist desired to know why.

"Because of their bulk. A cart load of them is not worth a shilling."

In all parts of Britain those days one heard much ridicule of the New England home and conscience. Now the ministry and its friends had begun to butt their heads against the immovable wall of character which had grown out of them and of which Lord Chatham had said:

"It has made certain of our able men look like school boys."

2

There was at that time a man of great power whose voice spoke for the soul of England. He had studied the spirit of the New World and probed to its foundations. He will help us to understand the new diplomacy which had filled the ministers with astonishment.

The same week Jack was invited to breakfast with Mr. Edmund Burke and Doctor Franklin. He was awed by the brilliancy of the massive, trumpet-tongued orator and statesman.

He writes: "Burke has a most ungainly figure. His gait is awkward, his gestures clumsy, his eyes are covered with large spectacles. He is careless of his dress. His pockets bulged with papers. He spoke rapidly and with a strong Irish brogue. Power is the thing his face and form express. His knowledge is astounding. It is easy to talk with Franklin, but *I* could not talk with him. He humbled and embarrassed me. His words shone as they fell from his lips. I can give you but a feeble notion of them. This was his idea, but I remember only a few of his glowing words:

" 'I fancy that man, like most other inventions, was, at first, a disappointment. There seems to have been some doubt, for a time, as to whether the contrivance could be made to work. In fact, there is good ground for believing that it wouldn't work.

" 'It was a failure. The tendency to indolence and folly had to be overcome. Sundry improvements were necessary. An imagination and the love of adventure were added to the great machine. They were the things needed. Not all the friction of hardship and peril could stop it then. From that time, as they say in business, man was a paying institution.

" 'The lure of adventure led to the discovery of law and truth. The best child of adventure is revelation. Man is so fashioned that if he can see a glimmer of the truth he seeks, he will make for it no matter what may be in his way. The promise of an exciting time solves the problem of help. America was born of sublime faith and a great adventure—the greatest in history—that of the three caravels. High faith is the great need of the world. Columbus had it, and I think, sir, that the Pilgrims had it and that the same quality of faith is in you. In these dark years you are like the lanterns of Pharus to your people.

" 'When prodigious things are to be done, how carefully men are prepared and chosen for their doing!'

"He said many things, but these words addressed to my venerable friend impressed me deeply. It occurs to me that Burke has been chosen to speak for the soul of Britain.

"When we think of the choosing of God, who but the sturdy yeomen of our mother land could have withstood the inhospitalities of the New World and established its spirit!

"Now their Son, Benjamin Franklin, full grown in the new school of liberty, has been chosen of God to define the inalienable rights of freemen. I think the stage is being set for the second great adventure in our history.   Let us have no fear of it.   Our land is sown with the new faith.   It can not fail."

This conviction was the result of some rather full days in the British capital.

CHAPTER VIII

AN APPOINTMENT AND A CHALLENGE

SOLOMON BINKUS had left the city with Preston to visit Sir Jeffrey Amherst in his country seat, near London. Sir Benjamin had taken Jack to dine with him at two of his clubs and after dining they had gone to see the great actor Robert Bensley as Malvolio and the Comedian Dodd as Sir Andrew Aguecheek. The Britisher had been most polite, but had seemed studiously to avoid mention of the subject nearest the heart of the young man. After that the latter was invited to a revel and a cock fight, but declined the honor and went to spend an evening with his friend, the philosopher. For days Franklin had been shut in with gout. Jack had found him in his room with one of his feet wrapped in bandages and resting on a chair.

"I am glad you came, my son," said the good Doctor. "I am in need of better company than this foot. Solitude is like water—good for a dip, but you can not live in it. Margaret has been here trying to give me comfort, although she needs it more for herself."

"Margaret!" the boy exclaimed. "Why does she need comfort?"

"Oh, largely on your account, my son! Her father

141

is obdurate and the cause is clear to me. This court-
ship of yours is taking an international aspect."

He gave his young friend a full account of the night
at Lord Howe's and the interviews which had followed it.

"All London knows how I stand now. They will
not try again to bribe me. The displeasure of Sir Benjamin will react upon you."

"What shall I do if he continues to be obdurate?"

"Shove my table this way and I'll show you a problem in prudential algebra," said the philosopher. "It's
a way I have of setting down all the factors and
striking out those that are equal and arriving at the
visible result."

With his pen and a sheet of paper he set down the
factors in the problem and his estimate of their rela-
tive value as follows:

The Problem.

A father =	Margaret, her mother and Jack =	.3 + 1
A patrimony = 10	Happiness for Jack and Margaret =	100 + 90
Margaret's old friends =	Margaret's new friends =	
A father's love =	A husband's love =	10 + 9
A father's tyranny ⌐ -	Your respect for human rights =	5 + 6
		106

"Now there is the problem, and while we may differ
on the estimates, I think that most sane Americans
would agree that the balance is overwhelmingly in

favor of throwing off the yoke of tyranny, and asserting your rights, established by agreement as well as by nature. In a like manner I work out all my important problems, so that every factor is visible and subject to change.

"I only fear that I may not be able to provide for her in a suitable manner," said Jack.

"Oh, you are well off," said the philosopher. "You have some capital and recognized talent and occupation for it. When I reached Philadelphia I had an empty stomach and also a Dutch dollar, a few pennies, two soiled shirts and a pair of dirty stockings in my pockets. Many years passed and I had a family before I was as well off as you are."

Dinner was brought in and Jack ate with the Doctor and when the table was cleared they played with magic squares—an invention of the philosopher with which he was wont to divert himself and friends of an evening. When Jack was about to go, the Doctor asked:

"Will you hand me that little red book? I wish to put down a credit mark for my conscience. This old foot of mine has been rather impudent to-day. There have been moments when I could have expressed my opinion of it with joyous violence. But I did not. I let it carry on like a tinker in a public house, and never said a word."

He showed the boy an interesting table containing the days of the week, at the head of seven columns, and opposite cross-columns below were the virtues he aimed to acquire—patience, temperance, frugality and the like. The book contained a table for every week in the year. It had been his practise, at the end of each day, to enter a black mark opposite the virtues in which he had failed.

It was a curious and impressive document—a frank, candid record in black and white of the history of a human soul. To Jack it had a sacred aspect like the story of the trials of Job.

"I begin to understand how you have built up this wonderful structure we call Franklin," he said.

"Oh, it is but a poor and shaky thing at best, likely to tumble in a high wind—but some work has gone into it," said the old gentleman. "You see these white pages are rather spotted, but when I look over the history of my spirit, as I do now and then, I observe that the pages are slowly getting cleaner. There is not so much ink on them as there used to be. You see I was once a free thinker. I had no gods to bother me, and my friends were of the same stripe. In time I discovered that they were a lot of scamps and that I was little better. I found myself in the wrong road and immediately faced about. Then I began keeping these tables. They have been a help to me."

This reminded Jack of the evil words of the melancholy Mr. Pinhorn which had been so promptly rebuked by his friend John Adams on the ride to Philadelphia. The young man made a copy of one of the tables and was saying good night to his venerable friend when the latter remarked:

"I shall go to Sir John Pringle's in the morning for advice. He is a noted physician. My man will be having a day off. Could you go with me at ten?"

"Gladly," said Jack.

"Then I shall pick you up at your lodgings. You will see your rival at Pringle's. He is at home on leave and has been going to Sir John's office every Tuesday morning at ten-thirty with his father, General Clarke, a gruff, gouty old hero of the French and Indian wars and an aggressive Tory. He is forever tossing and goring the Whigs. It may be the only chance you will have to see that rival of yours. He is a handsome lad."

Doctor Franklin, with his crutch beside him in the cab, called for his young friend at the hour appointed.

"I go to his office when I have need of his advice," said the Doctor. "If ever he came to me, the wretch would charge me two guineas. We have much argument over the processes of life in the human body, of which I have gained some little knowledge. Often he flatters me by seeking my counsel in difficult cases."

The office of the Doctor Baronet was on the first floor of a large building in Gough Square, Fleet Street. A number of gentlemen sat in comfortable chairs in a large waiting room.

"Sir John will see you in a moment, sir," an attendant said to Doctor Franklin as they entered. The moment was a very long one.

"In London there are many people who disagree with the clock," Franklin laughed. "In this office, even the moments have the gout. They limp along with slow feet."

It was a gloomy room. The chairs, lounges and tables had a venerable look like that of the men who came there with warped legs and old mahogany faces. The red rugs and hangings suggested "the effect of old port on the human countenance, being of a hue like unto that of many cheeks and noses in the waiting company," as the young man wrote. The door to the private room of the great physician creaked on its hinges with a kind of groan when he came out accompanied by a limping patient.

"Wait here for a minute—a gout minute," said Franklin to his young friend. "When Pringle dismisses me, I will present you."

Jack sat and waited while the room filled with ruddy, crotchety gentlemen supported by canes or crutches—elderly, old and of middle age. Among those of the latter class was a giant of a man, erect and dignified, accompanied by a big blond youngster in a lieutenant's uniform. He sat down and began to talk with another patient of the troubles in America.

"I see the damned Yankees have thrown another cargo of tea overboard," said he in a tone of anger.

"This time it was in Cape Cod. We must give those Yahoos a lesson."

Jack surmised now that here was the aggressive Tory General of whom the Doctor had spoken and that the young man was his son.

"I fear that it would be a costly business sending men to fight across three thousand miles of sea," said the other.

"Bosh! There is not one Yankee in a hundred that has the courage of a rabbit. With a thousand British grenadiers, I would undertake to go from one end of America to another and amputate the heads of the males, partly by force and partly by coaxing."

A laugh followed these insulting words. Jack Irons rose quickly and approached the man who had uttered them. The young American was angry, but he managed to say with good composure:

"I am an American, sir, and I demand a retraction of those words or a chance to match my courage against yours."

A murmur of surprise greeted his challenge.

The Britisher turned quickly with color mounting to his brow and surveyed the sturdy form of the young man.

"I take back nothing that I say," he declared.

"Then, in behalf of my slandered countrymen, I demand the right to fight you or any Britisher who has the courage to take up your quarrel."

Jack Irons had spoken calmly like one who had weighed his words.

The young Lieutenant who had entered the room with the fiery, middle-aged Britisher, rose and faced the American and said:

"I will take up his quarrel, sir. Here is my card."

"And here is mine," said Jack. "When will you be at home?"

"At noon to-morrow."

"Some friend of mine will call upon you," Jack assured the other.

A look of surprise came to the face of the Lieutenant as he surveyed the card in his hand. Jack was prepared for the name he read which was that of Lionel Clarke.

Franklin wrote some weeks later in a letter to John Irons of Albany: "When I came out of the physician's office I saw nothing in Jack's face and manner to suggest the serious proceeding he had entered upon. If I had, or if some one had dropped a hint to me, I should have done what I could to prevent this unfortunate affair. He chatted with Sir John a moment and we went out as if nothing unusual had happened. On the way to my house we talked of the good weather we were having, of the late news from America and of my summons to appear before the Privy Council. He betrayed no sign of the folly which was on foot. I saw him only once after he helped me into the house and left me to go to his lodgings. But often I find myself

thinking of his handsome face and heroic figure and
gentle voice and hand. He was like a loving son
to me."

2

That evening Solomon arrived with Preston.

Solomon gave a whistle of relief as he entered their
lodgings on Bloomsbury Square and dropped into a
chair.

"Wal, sir! We been flyin' eround as brisk as a
bee," he remarked. "I feel as if I had spraint one leg
and spavined t'other. The sun was over the fore yard
when we got back, and since then, we went to see the
wild animals, a hip'pottermas, an' lions, an' tigers, an'
snakes, an' a bird with a neck as long as a hoe handle,
an' a head like a tommyhawk. I wouldn't wonder if
he could peck some, an' they say he can fetch a kick
that would knock a hoss down. Gosh! I kind o' felt
fer my gun! Gol darn his pictur'! Think o' bein'
kicked by a bird an' havin' to be picked up an' carried
off to be mended. We took a long, crooked trail hum
an' walked all the way. It's kind o' hard footin'.'"

Solomon spoke with the animation of a boy. At last
he had found something in London which had pleased
and excited him.

"Did you have a good time at Sir Jeffrey's?" the
young man asked.

"Better'n a barn raisin'! Say, hones', I never seen
nothin' like it—'twere so blandiferous! At fust I were
a leetle bit like a man tied to a tree—felt so helpless

an' unsart'in. Didn't know what were goin' to happen. Then ol' Jeff come an' ontied me, as ye might say, an' I 'gun to feel right. 'Course Preston tol' me not to be skeered—that the doin's would be friendly, an' they was. Gol darn my pictur'! I'll bet a pint o' powder an' a fish hook thar ain't no nicer womern in this world than ol' Jeff's wife—not one. I give her my jack-knife. She ast me fer it. 'Twere a good knife, but I were glad to give it to her. Gosh! I dunno what she wants to do with it. Mebbe she likes to whittle. They's some does. I kind o' like it myself. I warned her to be keerful not to cut herself 'cause 'twere sharper'n the tooth o' a weasel. The vittles was tasty —no common ven'son er moose meat, but the best roast beef, an' mutton, an' ham an' jest 'nough Santa Cruz rum to keep the timber floatin'! They snickered when I tol' 'em I'd take my tea bar' foot. I set 'mongst a lot o' young folks, mostly gals, full o' laugh an' ginger, an' as purty to look at as a flock o' red birds, an' I sot thar tellin' stories 'bout the Injun wars, an' bear, an' moose, an' painters till the moon were down an' a clock hollered one. Then I let each o' them gals snip off a grab o' my hair. I dunno what they wanted to do with it, but they 'pear to be as fond o' takin' hair as Injuns. Mebbe 'twas fer good luck. I wouldn't wonder if my head looks like it was shingled. Ayes! I had an almighty good time.

"These 'ere British is good folks as fur as I've been able to look 'em over. It's the gov'ment that's down on us an' the gov'ment ain't the people—you hear to me. They's lots o' good, friendly folks here, but I'm ready to go hum. They's a ship leaves Dover Thursday 'fore sunrise an' my name is put down."

Jack told them in detail of the unfortunate event of the morning.

Solomon whistled while his face began to get ready for a shot.

"Neevarious!" he exclaimed. "Here's suthin' that'll have to be 'tended to 'fore I take the water."

"Clarke is full of hartshorn and vinegar," said Preston. "He was like that in America. He could make more trouble in ten minutes than a regiment could mend in a year. He is what you would call 'a mean cuss.' But for him and Lord Cornwallis, I should be back in the service. They blame me for the present posture of affairs in America."

"Jack, I'm glad that young pup ain't me," said Solomon. "Thar never was a man better cocalated to please a friend er hurt an enemy. If he was to say pistols I guess that ol' sling o' yours would bu'st out laughin' an' I ain't no idee he could stan' a minnit in front o' your hanger."

"It's bad business, and especially for you," said Preston. "Dueling is not so much in favor here as in France. Of course there are duels, but the best people in England are set against the practise. You would be sure to get the worst of it. The old General is a favorite of the King. He is booked for knighthood. If you were to kill his son in the present state of feeling here, your neck would be in danger. If you were to injure him you would have to make a lucky escape, or go to prison. It is not a pleasant outlook for one who is engaged to an English girl. He has a great advantage over you."

"True, but it gives me a better chance to vindicate the courage of an American. I shall fight. I would rather die than lie down to such an insult. There has been too much of that kind of talk here. It can not go on in my hearing without being trumped. If I were capable of taking such an insult, I could never again face the girl I love. There must be an apology as public as the insult or a fight. I don't want to kill any man, but I must show them that their cap doesn't fit me."

Jack and Solomon sat up late. The young man had tried to see Margaret that evening, but the door boy at Sir Benjamin's had informed him that the family was not at home. He rightly suspected that the boy had done this under orders from the Baronet. He wrote a long letter to the girl apprising her of late developments in the relations of the ministry and Doctor Franklin, regarding which the latter desired no secrecy, and of his own unhappy situation.

"If I could bear such an insult in silence," he added, "I should be unworthy of the fairest and dearest girl on earth. With such an estimate of you, I must keep myself in good countenance. Whatever happens, be

sure that I am loving you with all my heart, and longing for the time when I can make you my wife."

This letter he put into his pocket with the purpose
of asking Preston to deliver it if circumstances should
drive him out of England or into prison.

Captain Preston went with Solomon Binkus next
day to the address on the card of Lieutenant Clarke.
It was the house of the General, who was waiting with
his son in the reception room. They walked together
to the Almack Club. The General was self-contained.
It would seem that his bad opinion of Yankees was
not quite so comprehensive as it had been. The whole
proceeding went forward ·with the utmost politeness.

"General, Mr. Binkus and John Irons, Jr., are my
friends," said Captain Preston.

"Indeed!" the General answered.

"Yes, and they are friends of England. They saved
my neck in America. I have assured young Irons that
your words, if they were correctly reported to me, were
spoken in haste, and that they do not express your
real opinion."

"And what, sir, were the words reported to you?"
the General asked.

Preston repeated them.

"That is my opinion."

"It is mine also," young Clarke declared.

Solomon's face changed quickly. He took deliberate
aim at the enemy and drawled:

"Can't be yer opinion is wuth more than the lives o' these young fellers that's goin' to fight."

"Gentlemen, you will save time by dropping all thought of apologies," said the General.

"Then it only remains for you to choose your weapons and agree with us as to time and place," said Preston.

"I choose pistols," said the young Britisher. "The time and place may suit your convenience, so it be soon and not too far away."

"Let us say the cow wallow on Shooter's Hill, near the oaks, at sunrise to-morrow," Preston proposed.

"I agree," the Lieutenant answered.

"Whatever comes of it, let us have secrecy and all possible protection from each side to the other when the affair is ended," said Preston.

"I agree to that also," was the answer of young Clarke.

When they were leaving, Solomon said to Preston: "That 'ere Gin'ral is as big as Goliar."

CHAPTER IX

THE ENCOUNTER

SOLOMON, Jack and their friend left London that afternoon in the saddle and took lodgings at The Rose and Garter, less than a mile from the scene appointed for the encounter. That morning the Americans had sent a friend of Preston by post chaise to Deal, with Solomon's luggage. Preston had also engaged the celebrated surgeon, Doctor Brooks, to spend the night with them so that he would be sure to be on hand in the morning. The doctor had officiated at no less than a dozen duels and enjoyed these affairs so keenly that he was glad to give his help without a fee. The party had gone out in the saddle because Preston had said that the horses might be useful.

So, having discussed the perils of the immediate future, they had done all it was in their power to do to prepare for them. Late that evening the General and his son and four other gentlemen arrived at The Rose and Garter. Certain of them had spent the afternoon in the neighborhood shooting birds and rabbits.

Solomon got Jack to bed early and sat for a time in their room tinkering with the pistols. When the locks were working "right," as he put it, he polished their grips and barrels.

"Now I reckon they'll speak out when ye pull the

trigger," he said to Jack. "An' yer eyesight 'll skate erlong easy on the top o' them bar'ls."

"It's a miserable kind of business," said the young man, who was lying in bed and looking at his friend. "We Americans have a rather hard time of it, I say. Life is a fight from beginning to end. We have had to fight with the wilderness for our land and with the Indians and the French for our lives, and now the British come along and tell us what we must and mustn't do and burn up our houses."

"An' spit on us an' talk as if we was a lot o' boar pigs," said Solomon. "But ol' Jeff tol' me 'twere the King an' his crowd that was makin' all the trouble."

"Well, the King and his army can make us trouble enough," Jack answered. "It's as necessary for an American to know how to fight as to know how to walk."

"Now ye stop worryin' an' go to sleep 'er I'll take ye crost my knee," said Solomon. "They ain't goin' to be no great damage done, not if ye do as I tell ye. I've been an' looked the ground over an' if we have to leg it, I know which way to go."

Solomon had heard from Preston that evening that the Lieutenant was the best pistol shot in his regiment, but he kept the gossip to himself, knowing it would not improve the aim of his young friend. But Solomon was made uneasy by this report.

"My boy kin throw a bullet straight as a plumb line an' quick as lightnin'," he had said to Preston. "It's as nat'ral fer him as drawin' his breath. That 'ere chap may git bored 'fore he has time to pull. I ain't much skeered."

Jack was nervous, although not from fear. His estimate of the value of human life had been increased by his affection for Margaret. When Solomon had gone to bed and the lights were blown, the young man felt every side of his predicament to see if there were any peaceable way out of it. For hours he labored with this hopeless task, until he fell into a troubled sleep, in which he saw great battalions marching toward each other. On one side, the figures of himself and Solomon were repeated thousands of times, and on the other was a host of Lionel Clarkes.

The words came to his ear: "My son, we're goin' to fight the first battle o' the war."

Jack awoke suddenly and opened his eyes. The candle was lighted. Solomon was leaning over him. He was drawing on his trousers.

"Come, my son," said the scout in a gentle voice. "They ain't a cloud an' the moon has got a smile on her face. Come, my young David. Here's the breeches an' the purty stockin's an' shoes, an' the lily white shirt. Slip 'em on an' we'll kneel down an' have a word o' prayer. This 'ere ain't no common fight. It's a battle with tyranny. It's like the fight o' David an' Goliar. Here's yer ol' sling waitin' fer ye!"

Solomon felt the pistols and stroked their grips with a loving hand.

Side by side they knelt by the bed together for a moment of silent prayer.

Others were stirring in the inn. They could hear footsteps and low voices in a room near them. Jack put on his suit of brown velvet and his white silk stockings and best linen, which he had brought in a small bag. Jack was looking at the pistols, when there came a rap at the door. Preston entered with Doctor Brooks.

"We are to go out quietly ahead of the others," said the Captain. "They will follow in five minutes."

Solomon had put on the old hanger which had come to England with him in his box. He put the pistols in his pocket and they left the inn by a rear door. A groom was waiting there with the horses saddled and bridled. They mounted them and rode to the field of honor. When they dismounted on the ground chosen, the day was dawning, but the great oaks were still waist deep in gloom. It was cold.

Preston called his friends to his side and said:

"You will fight at twenty paces. I shall count three and when I drop my handkerchief you are both to fire."

Solomon turned to Jack and said:

"If ye fire quick mebbe ye'll take the crook out o' his finger 'fore it has time to pull."

The other party was coming. There were six men in it. The General and his son and one other were in military dress. The General was chatting with a friend. The pistols were loaded by Solomon and General Clarke, while each watched the other. The Lieutenant's friends and seconds stood close together laughing at some jest.

"That's funny, I'll say, what—what!" said one of the gentlemen.

Jack turned to look at him, for there had been a curious inflection in his "what, what!" He was a stout, highly colored man with large, staring gray eyes. The young American wondered where he had seen him before.

Preston paced the ground and laid down strips of white ribband marking the distance which was to separate the principals. He summoned the young men and said: "Gentlemen, is there no way in which your honor can be satisfied without fighting?"

They shook their heads.

"Your stations have been chosen by lot. Irons, yours is there. Take your ground, gentlemen."

The young men walked to their places and at this point the graphic Major Solomon Binkus, whose keen eyes observed every detail of the scene, is able to assume the position of narrator, the words which follow being from a letter he wrote to John Irons of Albany.

"Our young David stood up thar as straight an' han'some as a young spruce on a still day—not a quiver in ary twig. The Clarke boy was a leetle pale an' when he raised his pistol I could see a twitch in his lips. He looked kind o' stiff. I see they was one thing 'bout shootin' he hadn't learnt. It don't do to tighten up. I were skeered—I don't deny it—'cause a gun don't allus have to be p'inted careful to kill a man.

"We all stood watchin' every move. I could hear a bird singin' twenty rod,—'twere that still. Preston stood a leetle out o' line 'bout half-way betwixt 'em. Up come his hand with the han'kerchief in it. Then Jack raised his pistol and took a peek down the line he wanted. The han'kerchief was in the air. Don't seem so it had fell an inch when the pistols went pop! pop! Jack's hollered fust. Clarke's pistol fell. His arm dropped an' swung limp as a rope's end. His hand turned red an' blood began to spurt above it. I see Jack's bullet had jumped into his right wrist an' tore it wide open. The Lieutenant staggered, bleedin' like a stuck whale. He'd 'a' gone to the ground but his friends grabbed him. I run to Jack.

"'Be ye hit?' I says.

"'I think his bullet teched me a little on the top o' the left shoulder,' says he.

"I see his coat were tore an' we took it off an' the jacket, an' I ripped the shirt some an' see that the bullet had kind o' scuffed its foot on him goin' by, an' left a track in the skin. It didn't mount to nothin'. The Doctor washed it off an' put a plaster on.

"'Looks as if he'd drawed a line on yer heart an' yer bullet had lifted his aim,' I says. 'Ye shoot quick, Jack, an' mebbe that's what saved ye.'

"It looked kind o' neevarious like that 'ere English-man had intended they was goin' to be one Yankee less. Jack put on his jacket an' his coat an' we stepped over to see how they was gettin' erlong with the other feller. The two doctors was tryin' fer to fix his arm and he were groanin' severe. Jack leaned over and looked down at him.

" 'I'm sorry,' he says. 'Is there anything I can do?'

" 'No, sir. You've done enuff,' growled the old General.

"One o' his party stepped up to Jack. He were dressed like a high-up officer in the army. They was a cur'ous look in his eyes—kind o' skeered like. Seemed so I'd seen him afore somewheres.

" 'I fancy ye're a good shot, sir—a good shot, sir—what—what?' he says to Jack, an' the words come as fast as a bird's twitter.

" 'I've had a lot o' practise,' says our boy.

" 'Kin ye kill that bird—what—what?' says he, p'intin' at a hawk that were a-cuttin' circles in the air.

" 'If he comes clus' 'nough,' says Jack.

"I passed him the loaded pistol. In 'bout two seconds he lifted it and bang she went, an' down come the hawk.

"Them fellers all looked at one 'nother.

" 'Gin'ral, shake hands with this 'ere boy,' says the man with the skeered eyes. 'If he is a Yankey he's a decent lad—what—what?'

"The Gin'ral shook hands with Jack an', says he: 'Young man, I have no doubt o' yer curidge or yer decency.'

"A grand pair o' hosses an' a closed coach druv up an' the ol' what-whatter an' two other men got into it an' hustled off 'cross the field towards the pike which it looked as if they was in a hurry. 'Fore he were out o' sight a military amb'lance druv up. Preston come over to us an' says he:

" 'We better be goin'.'

" 'Do ye know who he were?' asks Jack.

" 'If ye know ye better fergit it,' says Preston.

" 'How could I? He were the King o' England,' says Jack. 'I knowed him by the look o' his eyes.'

" 'Sart'in sure,' says I. 'He's the man that wus bein' toted in a chair.'

" 'Hush! I tell ye to fergit it,' says Preston.

" 'I can fergit all but the fact that he behaved like a gentleman,' says Jack.

" 'I 'spose he were usin' his private brain,' says I."

This, with some slight changes in spelling, paragraphing and punctuation, is the account which Solomon Binkus gave of the most exciting adventure these two friends had met with.

Preston came to Jack and whispered: "The outcome is a great surprise to the other side. Young Clarke is a dead shot. An injured officer of the English army may cause unexpected embarrassment. But you have time enough and no haste. You can take the post chaise and reach the ship well ahead of her sailing."

"I am of a mind not to go with you," Jack said to Solomon. "When I go, I shall take Margaret with me."

So it happened that Jack returned to London while Solomon waited for the post chaise to Deal.

CHAPTER X

THE LADY OF THE HIDDEN FACE

NEXT morning at ten, the door boy at his lodgings informed Jack that a lady was waiting to see him in the parlor. The lady was deeply veiled. She did not speak, but arose as he entered the room and handed him a note. She was tall and erect with a fine carriage. Her silence was impressive, her costume admirable.

The note in a script unfamiliar to the young man was as follows:

"You will find Margaret waiting in a coach at eleven to-day at the corner of Harley Street and Twickenham Road."

The veiled lady walked to the door and turned and stood looking at him.

Her attitude said clearly: "Well, what is your answer?"

"I will be there at eleven," said the young man.

The veiled lady nodded, as if to indicate that her mission was ended, and withdrew.

Jack was thrilled by the information but wondered why it was so wrapped in mystery. Not ten minutes had passed after the departure of the veiled lady when a messenger came with a note from Sir Benjamin Hare. In a cordial tone, it invited Jack to breakfast at the Almack Club at twelve-thirty. The young man returned his acceptance by the same messenger, and in his best morning suit went to meet Margaret. A cab conveyed him to the corner named. There was the coach with shades drawn low, waiting. A footman stood near it. The door was opened and he saw Margaret looking out at him and shaking her hand.

"You see what a sly thing I am!" she said when, the greetings over, he sat by her side and the coach was moving. "A London girl knows how to get her way. She is terribly wise, Jack."

"But, tell me, who was the veiled lady?"

"A go-between. She makes her living that way. She is wise, discreet and reliable. There is employment for many such in this wicked city. I feel disgraced, Jack. I hope you will not think that I am accustomed to dark and secret ways. This has worried and distressed me, but I had to see you."

"And I was longing for a look at you," he said.

"I was sure you would not know how to pull these ropes of intrigue. I have heard all about them. I couldn't help that, you know, and be a young lady who is quite alive."

"Our time is short and I have much to say," said Jack. "I am to breakfast with your father at the Almack Club at twelve-thirty."

She clapped her hands and said, with a laughing face, "I knew he would ask you!"

"Margaret, I want to take you to America with the

approval of your father, if possible, and without it, if necessary."

"I think you will get his approval," said the girl with enthusiasm. "He has heard all about the duel. He says every one he met, of the court party, last evening, was speaking of it. They agree that the old General needed that lesson. Jack, how proud I am of you!"

She pressed his hand in both of hers.

"I couldn't help knowing how to shoot," he answered. "And I would not be worthy to touch this fair hand of yours if I had failed to resent an insult."

"Although he is a friend of the General, my father was pleased," she went on. "He calls you a good sport. 'A young man of high spirit who is not to be played with,' that is what he said. Now, Jack, if you do not stick too hard on principles—if you can yield only a little, I am sure he will let us be married."

"I am eager to hear what he may say now," said Jack. "Whatever it may be, let us stick together and go to America and be happy. It would be a dark world without you. May I see you to-morrow?"

"At the same hour and place," she answered.

They talked of the home they would have in Philadelphia and planned its garden, Jack having told of the site he had bought with great trees and a river view. They spent an hour which lent its abundant happiness to many a long year and when they parted, soon after twelve o'clock, Jack hurried away to keep his appointment.

2

Sir Benjamin received the young man with a warm greeting and friendly words. Their breakfast was served in a small room where they were alone together, and when they were seated the Baronet observed:

"I have heard of the duel. It has set some of the best tongues in England wagging in praise of 'the Yankee boy.' One would scarcely have expected that."

"No, I was prepared to run for my life—not that I planned to do any great damage," said Jack.

"You can shoot straight—that is evident. They call your delivery of that bullet swift, accurate and merciful. Your behavior has pleased some very eminent people. The blustering talk of the General excites no sympathy here. In London, strangers are not likely to be treated as you were."

"If I did not believe that I should be leaving it," said Jack. "I should not like to take up dueling for an amusement, as some men have done in France."

"You are a well built man inside and out," Sir Benjamin answered. "You might have a great future in England. I speak advisedly."

Their talk had taken a turn quite unexpected. It flattered the young man. He blushed and answered:

"Sir Benjamin, I have no great faith in my talents."

"On terms which I would call easy, you could have fame, honor and riches, I would say."

"At present I want only your daughter. As to the rest, I shall make myself content with what may naturally come to me."

"And let me name the terms on which I should be glad to welcome you to my family."

"What are the terms?"

"Loyalty to your King and a will to understand and assist his plans."

"I could not follow him unless he will change his plans."

The Baronet put down his fork and looked up at the young man. "Do you really mean what you say?" he demanded. "Is it so difficult for you to do your duty as a British subject?"

"Sir Benjamin, always I have been taught that it is the duty of a British subject to resist oppression. The plans of the King are oppressive. I can not fall in with them. I love Margaret as I love my life, but I must keep myself worthy of her. If I could think so well of my conduct, it is because I have principles that are inviolable."

"At least I hope you would promise me not to take up arms against the King."

"Please don't ask me to do that. It would grieve me to fight against England. I hope it may never be, but I would rather fight than submit to tyranny."

The Baronet made no reply to this declaration so firmly made. A new look came into his face. Indignation and resentment were there, but he did not forget the duty of a host. He began to speak of other things. The breakfast went on to its end in an atmosphere of cool politeness.

When they were out upon the street together, Sir Benjamin turned to him and said:

"Now that we are on neutral ground, I want to say that you Americans are a stiff-necked lot of people. You are not like any other breed of men. I am done with you. My way can not be yours. Let us part as friends and gentlemen ought to part. I say good-by with a sense of regret. I shall never forget your service to my wife and daughter."

"Think not of that," said the young man. "What I did for them I would do for any one who needed my help."

"I have to ask you to give up all hope of marrying my daughter."

"That I can not do," said Jack. "Over that hope I have no control. I might as well promise not to breathe."

"But I must ask you to give me your word as a gentleman that you will hold no further communication with her."

"Sir Benjamin, I shall be frank with you. It is an unfair request. I can not agree to it."

"What do you say?" the Englishman asked in a tone of astonishment, and his query was emphasized with a firm tap of his cane on the pavement.

"I hate to displease you, sir, but if I made such a promise, I would be sure to break it."

"Then, sir, I shall see to it that you have no opportunity to oppose my will."

In spite of his fine restraint, the eyes of the Baronet glowed with anger, as he quickly turned from the young man and hurried away.

"Here is more tyranny," the American thought as he went in the opposite direction. "But I do not believe he can keep us apart."

"I walked on and on," he wrote to a friend. "Never had I felt such a sense of loss and loneliness and dejection. I almost resented the inflexible tyranny of my own spirit which had turned him against me. I accused myself of a kind of selfishness in the matter. Had it been right in me to take a course which endangered the happiness of another, to say nothing of my own? But I couldn't have done otherwise, not if I had known that a mountain were to fall upon me. I am like all of those who follow the star in the west. We do as we must. I had not seen Franklin since my duel, and largely because I had been ashamed to face him. Now I felt the need of his wisdom and so I turned my steps toward his door."

3

"I am like the land of Goshen amid the plagues of Egypt," said Franklin, when the young man was admitted to his office. "My gout is gone and I am in good spirits in spite of your adventure."

"And I suppose you will scold me for the adventure."

"You will scold yourself when the consequences

have arrived. They will be sure to give you a spanking. The deed is done, and well done. On the whole I think it has been good for the cause, but bad for you."

"Why?"

"You may have to run out of England to save your neck and the face of the King. He was there, I believe?"

"Yes, sir."

"The injured lad is in a bad way. The wound caught an infection. Intense fever and swelling have set in. I helped Sir John Pringle to amputate the arm this afternoon, but even that may not save the patient. Here is a storm to warn the wandering linnet to his shade. A ship goes to-morrow evening. Get ready to take it. In that case your marriage will have to be delayed. Rash men are often compelled to live on hope and die fasting."

"With Sir Benjamin, the duel has been a help instead of a hindrance," said the young man. "My stubborn soul has been the great obstacle."

Then he told of his interview with Sir Benjamin Hare.

Franklin put his hand on Jack's shoulder and said with a smile:

"My son, I love you. I could wish you to be no different. Cheer up. Time will lay the dust, and perhaps sooner than you think."

"I hope to see Margaret to-morrow morning."

"Ah, then, 'what Grecian arts of soft persuasion!'"
Franklin quoted. "I hope that she, too, will follow
the great star in the west!"

"I hope so, but I greatly fear that our meeting will
be prevented."

"Did you get my note of to-day at your lodgings?"
Franklin asked.

"No," said Jack. "I left there soon after ten."

"Lord Chatham has kindly offered to secure admission for you and me to the House of Lords. He is
making an important motion. Come, let us go and
see the hereditary legislators."

Lord Stanhope met them at the door of the House
of Lords. There was a great bustle among the officers when His Lordship announced their names and
his desire to have them admitted. The officers hurried
in after members and there was some delay, in the
course of which the Americans were turned from the
division reserved for eldest sons and brothers of peers.
Not less than ten minutes were consumed in the process
of seating Franklin and his friend.

Soon Lord Chatham arose and moved that His
Majesty's forces be withdrawn from Boston. With a
singular charm of personality and address, the great
dissenter made his speech. Jack wrote in his diary
that evening: "The most captivating figure that ever
I saw is a well-bred Englishman trained in the art of
public speaking." The words were no doubt inspired
by the impressive speech of Chatham, which is now an

imperishable part of the history of England. These words from it the young man remembered:

"If the ministers thus persevere in misleading and misadvising the King, I will not say that they can alienate the affection of his subjects from his crown, but I will affirm that they will make his crown not worth his wearing; I will not say that the King is betrayed, but I will say that the kingdom is undone."

Lord Sandwich in a petulant speech declared that the motion ought not to be received. He could never believe it the production of a British peer. Turning toward Franklin, he flung out:

"I fancy that I have in my eye the person who drew it up—one of the bitterest and most mischievous enemies this country has ever known."

"Franklin sat immovable and without the slightest change in his countenance," Jack wrote in a letter to *The Pennsylvania Gazette*.

Chatham declared that the motion was his own, and added:

"If I were the first minister of this country, charged with the settling of its momentous business, I should not be ashamed to call to my assistance a man so perfectly acquainted with all American affairs, as the gentleman so injuriously referred to—one whom all Europe holds in high estimation for his knowledge and wisdom, which are an honor, not only to England, but to human nature."

"Franklin told me that this was harder for him to

bear than the abuse, but he kept his countenance **as** blank as a sheet of white paper," Jack wrote. "There was much vehement declamation against the measure and it was rejected.

"When we had left the chamber, Franklin said to me:

" 'That motion was made by the first statesman of the age, who took the helm of state when the latter was in the depths of despondency and led it to glorious victory through a war with two of the mightiest kingdoms in Europe. Only a few of those men had the slightest understanding of its merits. Yet they would not even consider it in a second reading. They are satisfied with their ignorance. They have nothing to learn. Hereditary legislators! There would be more propriety in hereditary professors of mathematics! Heredity is a great success with only one kind of creature.'

" 'What creature?' I asked.

" 'The ass,' he answered, with as serious a countenance as I have seen him wear.

"No further word was spoken as we rode back to his home," the young man wrote. "We knew the die had been cast. We had seen it fall carelessly out of the hand of Ignorance, obeying intellects swelled with hereditary passion and conceit. I now had something to say to my countrymen."

CHAPTER XI

THAT evening Jack received a brief note from Preston. It said:

"I learn that young Clarke is very ill. I think you would better get out of England for fear of what may come. A trial would be apt to cause embarrassment in high places. Can I give you assistance?"

Jack returned this note by the same messenger:

"Thanks, good friend, I shall go as soon as my business is finished, which I hope may be to-morrow."

Just before the young man went to bed a brief note arrived from Margaret. It read:

"DEAREST JACK. My father has learned of our meeting yesterday and of how it came about. He is angry. He forbids another meeting. I shall not submit to his tyranny. We must assert our rights like good Americans. I have a plan. You will learn of it when we meet to-morrow at eleven. Do not send an answer. Lovingly, MARGARET."

He slept little, and in the morning awaited with keen impatience the hour of his appointment.

On his way to the place he heard a newsboy shouting the words "duel" and "Yankee," followed by the suggestive statement: "Bloody murder in high life."

Evidently Lionel Clarke had died of his wound. He saw people standing in groups and reading the paper. He began to share the nervousness of Preston and the wise, far-seeing Franklin. He jumped into a cab and was at the corner some minutes ahead of time. Precisely at eleven he saw the coach draw near. He hurried to its side. The footman dismounted and opened the door. Inside he saw, not Margaret, but the lady of the hidden face.

"You are to get in, sir, and make a little journey with the madame," said the footman.

Jack got into the coach. Its door closed, the horses started with a jump and he was on his way whither he knew not. Nor did he know the reason for the rapid pace at which the horses had begun to travel.

"If you do not mind, sir, we will not lift the shades," said the veiled lady, as the coach started. "We shall see Margaret soon, I hope."

She had a colorless, cold voice and what was then known in London as the "patrician manner." Her tone and silence seemed to say: "Please remember this is all a matter of business and not a highly agreeable business to me."

"Where is Margaret?" he asked.

"A long way from here. We shall meet her at The Ship and Anchor in Gravesend. She will be making the journey by another road."

She had answered in a voice as cold as the day and in the manner of one who had said quite enough.

"Where is Gravesend?"

"On the Thames near the sea," she answered briskly, as if in pity of his ignorance.

He saw the plan now—an admirable plan. They were to meet near the port of sailing and be married and go aboard the ship and away. It was the plan of Margaret and much better than any he could have made, for he knew little of London and its ports.

"Should I not take my baggage with me?"

"There is not time for that," the veiled lady answered. "We must make haste. I have some clothes for you in a bag."

She pointed to a leathern case under the front seat.

He sat thinking of the cleverness of Margaret as they left the edge of the city and hurried away on the east turnpike. A mist was coming up from the sea. The air ahead had the color of a wool stack. They stopped at an inn to feed and water the horses and went on in a dense fog, which covered the hedge rows on either side and lay thick on the earth so that the horses seemed to be wading in it. Their pace slowed to a walk. From that time on, the road was like a long ford over which they proceeded with caution, the driver now and then winding a horn.

Each sat quietly in a corner of the seat with a wall of cold fog between them. The young man liked it better than the wall of mystery through which he had been able to see the silent, veiled form beside him.

"Do you have much weather like this?" he ventured to inquire by and by.

This answer came out of the bank of fog: "Yes,"

as if she would have him understand that she was not being paid for conversation.

From that time forward they rode in a silence broken only by the creaking of the coach and the sound of the horses' hoofs. Darkness had fallen when they reached the little city of Gravesend. The Ship and Anchor stood by the water's edge.

"You will please wait here," said the stern lady in a milder voice than she had used before, as the coach drew up at the inn door, "I shall see if she has come."

His strange companion entered the inn and returned presently, saying: "She has not yet arrived. Delayed by the fog. We will have our dinner, if you please."

Jack had not broken his fast since nine and felt keenly the need of refreshment, but he answered:

"I think that I would better wait for Margaret."

"No, she will have dined at Tillbury," said the masterful lady. "It will save time. Please come and have dinner, sir."

He followed her into the inn. The landlady, a stout, obsequious woman, led them to a small dining-room above stairs lighted by many candles where an open fire was burning cheerfully.

A handsomely dressed man waited by them for orders and retired with the landlady when they were given.

From this point the scene at the inn is described in the diary of the American.

"She drew off her hat and veil and a young woman

about twenty-eight years of age and of astonishing beauty stood before me."

" 'There, now, I am out of business,' she remarked in a pleasant voice as she sat down at the table which had been spread before the fireplace. 'I will do my best to be a companion to you until Margaret arrives.'

"She looked into my eyes and smiled. Her sheath of ice had fallen from her.

" 'You will please forgive my impertinence,' said she. 'I earn my living by it. In a world of sentiment and passion I must be as cold and bloodless as a stone, but in fact, I am very—very human.'

"The waiter came with a tray containing soup, glasses and a bottle of sherry. We sat down at the table and our waiter filled two glasses with the sherry.

" 'Thank you, but self-denial is another duty of mine,' she remarked when I offered her a glass of the wine. 'I live in a tipsy world and drink—water. I live in a merry world and keep a stern face. It is a vile world and yet I am unpolluted.'

"I drank my glass of wine and had begun to eat my soup when a strange feeling came over me. My plate seemed to be sinking through the table. The wall and fireplace were receding into dim distance. I knew then that I had tasted the cup of Circe. My hands fell through my lap and suddenly the day ended. It was like sawing off a board. The end had fallen. There is nothing more to be said of it because my brain had ceased to receive and record impressions. I was as totally out of business as a man in his grave. When I came to, I was in a berth on the ship *King William* bound for New York. As soon as I knew anything, I knew that I had been tricked. My clothes had been removed and were lying on a chair near me. My watch and money were undisturbed. I had a severe pain in my head. I dressed and went up on deck. The Captain was there.

" 'You must have had a night of it in Gravesend,' he said. "You were like a dead man when they brought you aboard."

" 'Where am I going?' I asked.

" 'To New York,' he answered with a laugh. 'You must have had a time!'

"How much is the fare?"

" 'Young man, that need not concern you,' said the Captain. 'Your fare has been paid in full. I saw them put a letter in your pocket. Have you read it?' "

Jack found the letter and read:

"DEAR SIR—When you see this you will be well out of danger and, it is hoped, none the worse for your dissipation. This from one who admires your skill and courage and who advises you to keep out of England for at least a year.

"A WELL WISHER."

He looked back over the stern of the ship. The shore had fallen out of sight. The sky was clear. The sun shining. The wind was blowing from the east.

He stood for a long time looking toward the land he had left.

"Oh, ye wings of the wind! take my love to her and give her news of me and bid her to be steadfast in her faith and hope," he whispered.

He leaned against the bulwark and tried to think.

"Sir Benjamin has seen to it," he said to himself. "I shall have no opportunity to meet her again."

He reviewed the events of the day and their under-current of intrigue. The King himself might have been concerned in that and Preston also. It had been on the whole a rather decent performance, he mused, and perhaps it had kept him out of worse trouble than he was now in. But what had happened to Margaret? He reread her note.

"My father has learned of our meeting and of how it came about," he quoted.

"More bribery," he thought. "The intrigante natu-rally sold her services to the highest bidder."

He recalled the violent haste with which the coach had rolled away from the place of meeting. Had that been due to a fear that Margaret would defeat their plans?

All these speculations and regrets were soon put away. But for a long time one cause of worry was barking at his heels. It slept beside him and often touched and awoke him at night. He had been respon-sible for the death of a human being. What an un-lucky hour he had had at Sir John Pringle's! Yet he found a degree of comfort in the hope that those proud men might now have a better thought of the Yankees.

CHAPTER XII

AFTER Jack had been whirled out of London, Franklin called at his lodgings and learned that he had not been seen for a day. The wise philosopher entertained no doubt that the young man had taken ship agreeably with the advice given him. A report had been running through the clubs of London that Lionel Clarke had succumbed. In fact he had had a bad turn but had rallied. Jack must have heard the false report and taken ship suddenly.

Doctor Franklin went that day to the meeting of the Privy Council, whither he had been sternly summoned for examination in the matter of the letters of Hutchinson *et al*. For an hour he had stood unmoved while Alexander Wedderburn, the wittiest barrister in the kingdom, poured upon him a torrent of abuse. Even the judges, against all traditions of decorum in the high courts of·Britain, laughed at the cleverness of the assault. That was the speech of which Charles James Fox declared that it was the most expensive bit of oratory which had been heard in England since it had cost the kingdom its colonies.

It was alleged that in some manner Franklin had stolen the letters and violated their sacred privacy. It is known now that an English nobleman had put them in his hands to read and that he was in no way responsible for their publication.   The truth, if it could have been told, would have bent the proud heads of Wedderburn and the judges to whom he appealed, in confusion.   But Franklin held his peace, as a man of honor was bound to do.   He stood erect and dignified with a face like one carved in wood.

The counsel for the colonies made a weak defense. The triumph was complete.   The venerable man was convicted of conduct inconsistent with the character of a gentleman and deprived of his office as Postmaster General of the Colonies.

But he had two friends in court.   They were the Lady Hare and her daughter.   They followed him out of the chamber.   In the great hallway, Margaret, her eyes wet with tears, embraced and kissed the philosopher.

"I want you to know that I am your friend and that I love America," she said.

"My daughter, it has been a hard hour, but I am sixty-eight years old and have learned many things," he answered.   "Time is the only avenger I need.   It will lay the dust."

The girl embraced and kissed him again and said in a voice shaking with emotion:

"I wish my father and all Englishmen to know that I am your friend and that I have a love that can not be turned aside or destroyed and that I will have my right as a human being."

"Come let us go and talk together—we three," he proposed.

They took a cab and drove away.

"You will think all this a singular proceeding," Lady Hare remarked. "I must tell you that rebellion has started in our home. Its peace is quite destroyed. Margaret has declared her right to the use of her own mind."

"Well, if she is to use any mind it will have to be that one," Franklin answered. "I do not see why women should not be entitled to use their minds as well as their hands and feet."

"I was kept at home yesterday by force," said Margaret. "Every door locked and guarded! It was brutal tyranny."

"The poor child has my sympathy but what can I do?" Lady Hare inquired.

"Being an American, you can expect but one answer from me," said the philosopher. "To us tyranny in home or state is intolerable. They tried it on me when I was a boy and I ran away."

"That is what I shall do if necessary," said Margaret.

"Oh, my child! How would you live?" her mother asked.

"I will answer that question for her, if you will let me," said Franklin. "If she needs it, she shall have an allowance out of my purse."

"Thank you, but that would raise a scandal," said the woman.

"Oh, Your Ladyship, I am old enough to be her grandfather."

"I wish to go with Jack, if you know where he is," Margaret declared, looking up into the face of the philosopher.

"I think he is pushing toward America," Franklin answered. "Being alarmed at the condition of his adversary, I advised him to slip away. A ship went yesterday. Probably he's on it. He had no chance to see me or to pick up his baggage."

"I shall follow him soon," the girl declared.

"If you will only contain yourself, you will get along with your father very well," said Lady Hare. "I know him better than you. He has promised to take you to America in December. You must wait and be patient. After all, your father has a large claim upon you."

"I think you will do well to wait, my child," said the philosopher. "Jack will keep and you are both young. Fathers are like other children. They make mistakes —they even do wrong now and then. They have to be forgiven and allowed a chance to repent and improve their conduct. Your father is a good man. Try to win him to your cause."

"And die a maiden," said the girl with a sigh.

"Impossible!" Franklin exclaimed.

"I shall marry Jack or never marry. I would rather be his wife than the Queen of England."

"This is surely the age of romance," said the smiling philosopher as the ladies alighted at their door. "I wish I were young again."

BOOK TWO

CHAPTER XIII

THE FERMENT

On his voyage to New York, Jack wrote long letters to Margaret and to Doctor Franklin, which were deposited in the Post-Office on his arrival, the tenth of March. He observed a great change in the spirit of the people. They were no longer content with words. The ferment was showing itself in acts of open and violent disorder. The statue of George III, near the Battery, was treated to a volley of decayed eggs, in the evening of his arrival. This hot blood was due to the effort to prevent free speech in the colonies and the proposal to send political prisoners to England for trial.

Jack took the first boat to Albany and found Solomon working on the Irons farm. In his diary he tells of the delightful days of rest he enjoyed with his family. Solomon had told them of the great adventure but Jack would have little to say of it, having no pride in that achievement.

Soon the scout left on a mission for the Committee of Safety to distant settlements in the great north bush.

"I'll be spendin' the hull moon in the wilderness,"

he said to Jack. "Goin' to Virginny when I get back, an' I'll look fer ye on the way down."

Jack set out for Philadelphia the day after Solomon left. He stopped at Kinderhook on his way down the river and addressed its people on conditions in England. A young Tory interrupted his remarks. At the barbecue, which followed, this young man was seized and punished by a number of stalwart girls who removed his collar and jacket by force and covered his head and neck with molasses and the fuzz of cat tails. Jack interceded for the Tory and stopped the proceeding.

"My friends, we must control our anger," he said. "Let us not try to subdue tyranny by using it ourselves."

Everywhere he found the people in such a temper that Tories had to hold their peace or suffer punishment. At the office he learned that his most important letters had failed to pass the hidden censorship of mail in England. He began, at once, to write a series of articles which hastened the crisis. The first of them was a talk with Franklin, which told how his mail had been tampered with; that no letter had come to his hand through the Post-Office which had not been opened with apparent indifference as to the evidence of its violation. The Doctor's words regarding free speech in America and the proposal to try the bolder critics for treason were read and discussed in every

household from the sea to the mountains and from
Maine to Florida.

"Grievances can not be redressed unless they are
known and they can not be known save through complaints and petitions," the philosopher had said.   "If
these are taken as affronts and the messengers punished, the vent of grief is stopped up—a dangerous
thing in any state.   It is sure to produce an explosion.

"An evil magistrate with the power to punish for
words would be armed with a terrible weapon.

"Augustus Cæsar, with the avowed purpose of pre-
serving Romans from defamation, made libel subject
to the penalties of treason.   Thenceforward every
man's life hung by a thread easily severed by some
lying informer.

"Soon it was resolved by all good judges of law that
whoever should insinuate the least doubt of Nero's
preeminence in the noble art of fiddling should be
deemed a traitor.   Grief became treason and one lady
was put to death for bewailing the fate of her mur-
dered son.   In time, silence became treason, and even
a look was considered an overt act."

These words of the wise philosopher strengthened
the spirit of the land for its great ordeal.

Jack described the prejudice of the Lords who, content with their ignorance, spurned every effort to inform them of the conditions in America.

"And this little tail is wagging the great dog of

England, most of whose people believe in the justice of our complaints," he wrote.

The young man's work had set the bells ringing and they were the bells of revolt. The arrival of General Gage at Boston in May, to be civil governor and commander-in-chief for the continent, and the blockade of the port twenty days later, compelling its population who had been fed by the sea to starve or subsist on the bounty of others, drove the most conservative citizens into the open. Parties went out Tory hunting. Every suspected man was compelled to declare himself and if incorrigible, was sent away. Town meetings were held even under the eyes of the King's soldiers and no tribunal was allowed to sit in any court-house. At Salem, a meeting was held behind locked doors with the Governor and his Secretary shouting a proclamation through its keyhole, declaring it to be dissolved. The meeting proceeded to its end, and when the citizens filed out, they had invited the thirteen colonies to a General Congress in Philadelphia.

It was Solomon Binkus who conveyed the invitation to Pennsylvania and Virginia. He had gone on a second mission to Springfield and Boston and had been in the meeting at Salem with General Ward. Another man carried that historic call to the colonies farther south. In five weeks, delegates were chosen, and early in August, they were traveling on many different roads toward the Quaker City. Crowds gathered in every town and village they passed. Solomon, who rode with the Virginia delegation, told Jack that he hadn't heard so much noise since the Injun war.

"They was poundin' the bells, an shootin' cannons everywhere," he declared. "Men, women and children crowded 'round us an' split their lungs yellin'. They's a streak o' sore throats all the way from Alexandry to here."

Solomon and his young friend met John Adams on the street. The distinguished Massachusetts lawyer said to Jack when the greetings were over:

"Young man, your pen has been not writing, but making history."

"Does it mean war?" Jack queried.

Mr. Adams wiped his brow with his handkerchief and said: "People in our circumstances have seldom grown old or died in their beds."

"We ought to be getting ready," said Jack.

"And we are doing little but eat and drink and shout and bluster," Mr. Adams answered. "We are being entertained here with meats and curds and custards and jellies and tarts and floating islands and Madeira wine. It is for you to induce the people of Philadelphia to begin to save. We need to learn Franklin's philosophy of thrift."

Colonel Washington was a member of the Virginia delegation. Jack wrote that he was in uniform, blue coat and red waistcoat and breeches; that he was a big man standing very erect and about six feet, two inches in height; that his eyes were blue, his complexion light and rather florid, his face slightly pockmarked, his brown hair tinged with gray; that he had the largest hands, save those of Solomon Binkus, that he had ever seen. His letter contains these informing words:

"I never quite realized the full meaning of the word 'dignity' until I saw this man and heard his deep rich voice. There was a kind of magnificence in his manner and person when he said:

" 'I will raise one thousand men toward the relief of Boston and subsist them at my own expense.'

"That was all he said and it was the most eloquent speech made in the convention. It won the hearts of the New Englanders. Thereafter, he was the central figure in that Congress of trusted men. It is also evident that he will be the central figure on this side of the ocean when the storm breaks. Next day, he announced that he was, as yet, opposed to any definite move toward independence. So the delegates contented themselves with a declaration of rights opposing importations and especially slaves."

When the Congress adjourned October twenty-sixth to meet again on the tenth of May, there was little hope of peace among those who had had a part in its proceedings.

Jack, who knew the conditions in England, knew also that war would come soon, and freely expressed his views.

2

Letters had come from Margaret giving him the welcome news that Lionel Clarke had recovered and announcing that her own little revolution had achieved success. She and her father would be taking ship for Boston in December. Jack had urged that she try to induce him to start at once, fearing that December would be too late, and so it fell out. When the news of the Congress reached London, the King made new plans. He began to prepare for war. Sir Benjamin Hare, who was to be the first deputy of General Gage, was assigned to a brigade and immediately put his regiments in training for service overseas. He had spent six months in America and was supposed, in England, to have learned the art of bush fighting. Such was the easy optimism of the cheerful young Minister of War, and his confrères, in the House of Lords. After the arrival of the *King William* at Gravesend on the eighth of December, no English women went down to the sea in ships for a long time. Thereafter the water roads were thought to be only for fighting men. Jack's hope was that armed resistance would convince the British of their folly.

"A change of front in the Parliament would quickly end the war," he was wont to say. Not that he quite believed it. But young men in love are apt to say things which they do not quite believe. In February, 1775, he gave up his work on *The Gazette* to aid in the problem of defense. Solomon, then in Albany, had

written that he was going the twentieth of that
month on a mission to the Six Nations of The Long
House.

It was unusual for the northern tribes to hold a
council in winter—especially during the moon of the
hard snow, but the growing bitterness of the white
men had alarmed them. They had learned that another and greater war was at hand and they were restless for fear of it. The quarrel was of no concern to
the red man, but he foresaw the deadly peril of choosing the wrong side. So the wise men of the tribes
were coming into council.

"If we fight England, we got to have the Injuns on
our side er else Tryon County won't be no healthy
place fer white folks," Solomon wrote. "I wished you
could go 'long with me an' show 'em the kind o' shootin' we'll do ag'in' the English an' tell 'em they could
count the leaves in the bush easier than the men in the
home o' the south wind, an' all good shooters. Put on
a big, two-story bearskin cap with a red ribband tied
around it an' bring plenty o' gewgaws. I don't care
what they be so long as they shine an' rattle. I cocalate you an' me could do good work."

Immediately the young man packed his box and set
out by stage on his way to the North. Near West
Point, he left the sleigh, which had stopped for repairs,
and put on his skates and with the wind mostly at his
back, made Albany early that evening on the river
roof. He found the family and Solomon eating sup-

per, with the table drawn close to the fireside, it being
a cold night.

"I think that St. Nicholas was never more welcome
in any home or the creator of more happiness than I
was that night," he wrote in a letter to Margaret, sent
through his friend Doctor Franklin. "What a glow
was in the faces of my mother and father and Solomon
Binkus—the man who was so liked in London! What
cries of joy came from the children! They clung to
me and my little brother, Josiah, sat on my knee while
I ate my sausage and flapjacks and maple molasses. I
shall never forget that supper hour for, belike, I was
hungry enough to eat an ox. You would never see a
homecoming like that in England, I fancy. Here the
family ties are very strong. We have no opera, no
theater, no balls and only now and then a simple party
of neighborhood folk. We work hard and are weary
at night. So our pleasures are few and mostly those
shared in the family circles. A little thing, such as a
homecoming, or a new book, brings a joy that we remember as long as we live. I hope that you will not
be appalled by the simplicity of my father's home and
neighborhood. There is something very sweet and
beautiful in it, which, I am sure, you would not fail
to discover.

"Philadelphia and Boston are more like the cities
you know. They are getting ambitious and are beginning to ape the manners of England but, even there,
you would find most people like my own. The at-

tempts at grandeur are often ludicrous. In Philadelphia, I have seen men sitting at public banquets without coat or collar and drinking out of bottles."

Next day, Jack and Solomon set out with packs and snow-shoes for The Long House, which was the great highway of the Indians. It cut the province from the Hudson to Lake Erie. In summer it was roofed by the leaves of the forest. The chief villages of the Six Tribes were on or near it. This trail was probably the ancient route of the cloven hoof on its way to the prairies—the thoroughfare of the elk and the buffalo. How wisely it was chosen, time has shown, for now it is covered with iron rails, the surveyors having tried in vain to find a better one.

Late in the second day out, they came suddenly on a young moose. Jack presented his piece and brought the animal down. They skinned him and cut out the loins and a part of each hind quarter. When Solomon wrapped the meat in a part of the hide and slung it over his shoulder, night was falling.

"Cat's blood an' gunpowder! The ol' night has a sly foot," said Solomon. "We won't see no Crow Hill tavern. We got t' make a snow house."

On the south side of a steep hill near them was a deep, hard frozen drift. Solomon cut the crust with his hatchet and began moving big blocks of snow. Soon he had made a cavern in the great white pile, a fathom deep and high, and as long as a full grown man. They put in a floor of balsam boughs and

spread their blankets on it.   Then they cut a small
dead pine and built a fire a few feet in front of their
house and fried some bacon and a steak and made
snow water and a pot of tea.   The steak and bacon
were eaten on slices of bread without knife or fork.
Their repast over, Solomon made a rack and began
jerking the meat with a slow fire of green hardwood
smoldering some three feet below it.   The "jerk"
under way, they reclined on their blankets in the snow
house secure from the touch of a cold wind that swept
down the hillside, looking out at the dying firelight
while Solomon told of his adventures in the Ohio
country.

Jack was a bit afflicted with "snow-shoe evil," being
unaccustomed to that kind of travel, and he never forgot the sense of relief and comfort which he found in
the snow house, or the droll talk of Solomon.

"You're havin' more trouble to git married than a
Mingo brave," Solomon said to Jack. " 'Mongst them,
when a boy an' gal want to git married, both fam'lies
have to go an' take a sweat together.   They heat a lot
o' rocks an' roll 'em into a pen made o' sticks put in
crotches an' covered over with skins an' blankets.   The
hot rocks turn it into a kind o' oven.   They all crawl
in thar an' begin to sweat an' hoot an' holler.   You
kin hear 'em a mile off.   It's a reg'lar hootin' match.
I'd call it a kind o' camp meetin'.   When they holler
it means that the devil is lettin' go.   They're bein'
purified.   It kind o' seasons 'em so they kin stan' the

heat o' a family quarrel. When Injuns have had the
grease sweat out of 'em, they know suthin' has happened. The women'll talk fer years 'bout the weddin'
sweat."

Now and then, as he talked, Solomon arose to put
more wood on the fire and keep "the jerk sizzling."
Just before he lay down for the night, he took some
hard wood coals and stored them in a griddle full of
hot ashes so as to save tinder in the morning.

They were awakened in the night by the ravening
of a pack of wolves at the carcass of the slain moose,
which lay within twenty rods of the snow camp. They
were growling and snapping as they tore the meat
from the bones. Solomon rose and drew on his boots.

"Cat's blood an' gunpowder! I thought the smell
o' the jerk would bring 'em," Solomon whispered.
"Say, they's quite a passel o' wolves thar—you hear
to me. No, I ain't skeered o' them thar whelps, but it's
ag'in' my principles to go to sleep if they's nuthin' but
air 'twixt me an' them. They might be jest fools
'nough to think I were good eatin'; which I ain't. I
guess it's 'bout time to take keer o' this 'ere jerk an'
start up a fire. I won't give them loafers nothin' but
hell, if they come 'round here—not a crumb."

Solomon went to work with his ax in the moon-
light, while Jack kindled up the fire.

"We don't need to tear off our buttons hurryin',"
said the former, as he flung down a dead spruce by the
fireside and began chopping it into sticks. "They

won't be lookin' for more fodder till they've picked the bones o' that 'ere moose. Don't make it a big fire er you'll melt our roof. We jest need a little belt o' blaze eround our front. Our rear is safe. Chain lightnin' couldn't slide down this 'ere hill without puttin' on the brakes."

Soon they had a good stack of wood inside the fire line and in the pile were some straight young birches. Solomon made stakes of these and drove them deep in the snow close up to the entrance of their refuge, making a stockade with an opening in the middle large enough for a man to pass through. Then they sat down on their blankets, going out often to put wood on the fire. While sitting quietly with their rifles in hand, they observed that the growling and yelping had ceased.

"They've got that 'ere moose in their packs," Solomon whispered. "Now keep yer eye peeled. They'll be snoopin' eround here to git our share. You see."

In half a moment, Jack's rifle spoke, followed by the loud yelp of a wolf well away from the firelight.

"Uh, huh! You warmed the wax in his ear, that's sart'in;" said Solomon as Jack was reloading. "Did ye hear him say 'Don't'?"

The scout's rifle spoke and another wolf yelped.

"Yer welcome," Solomon shouted. "I slammed that 'er hunk o' lead into the pack leader—a whale of a wolf. The ol' Cap'n stepped right up clus. Seen 'im plain—gray, long legged ol' whelp. He were walkin' towards the fire when he stubbed his toe. It's all over now. They'll snook erway. The army has lost its Gin'ral."

They saw nothing more of the wolf pack and after an hour or so of watching, they put more wood on the fire, filled the opening in their stockade and lay down to rest. Solomon called it a night of "one-eyed sleep" when they got up at daylight and rekindled the fire and washed their hands and faces in the snow. The two dead wolves lay within fifty feet of the fire and Solomon cut off the tail of the larger one for a souvenir.

They had more steak and bread, moistened with tea, for breakfast and set out again with a good store of jerked meat in their packs. So they proceeded on their journey, as sundry faded clippings inform us, spending their nights thereafter at rude inns or in the cabins of settlers until they had passed the village of the Mohawks, where they found only a few old Indians and their squaws and many dogs and young children. The chief and his sachems and warriors and their wives had gone on to the great council fire in the land of Kiodote, the Thorny Tree.

They spent a night in the little cabin tavern of Bill Scott on the upper waters of the Mohawk. Mrs. Scott, a comely woman of twenty-six, had been a sister of Solomon's wife. She and the scout had a pleasant visit about old times in Cherry Valley where they had spent a part of their childhood, and she was most

thoughtful and generous in providing for their comfort. The Scotts had lost two children and another,
a baby, was lying asleep in the cradle. Scott was a
hard working, sullen sort of a man who made his living chiefly by selling rum to the Indians. Solomon
used to say that he had been "hooked by the love o'
money an' et up by land hunger."

"You'll have to git away from The Long House,"
Solomon said to Scott. "One reason I come here was
to tell ye."

"What makes ye think so?" Scott asked.

"The Injuns'll hug ye when they're drunk but they'll
hate ye when they're sober," Solomon answered.
"They lay all their trouble to fire-water an' they're
right. If the cat jumps the wrong way an' they go on
the war-path, ye got to look out."

"I ain't no way skeered," was Scott's answer. He
had a hoarse, damp voice that suggested the sound of
rum gurgling out of a jug. His red face indicated
that he was himself too fond of the look and taste of
fire-water.

"Ye got to git erway from here I tell ye," Solomon
insisted.

Scott stroked his sandy beard and answered: "I
guess I know my business 'bout as well as you do."

"Le's go back to Cherry Valley, Bill," the woman
urged.

"Oh, keep yer trap shet," Scott said to her.

"He's as selfish as a he-bear," said Solomon as he

and Jack were leaving soon after daylight. "Don't think o' nuthin' but gittin' rich. Keeps swappin' fire-water fer land an' no idee o' the danger."

They left the woman in tears.

"It's awful lonesome here. I'll never see ye ag'in," she declared as she stood wiping her eyes with her apron.

"Here now—you behave!" Solomon exclaimed. "I'll toddle up to your door some time next summer."

"Mirandy is a likely womern—I tell ye," Solomon whispered as they went away. "He is a mean devil! Ain't the kind of a man fer her—nary bit. A rum bottle is the only comp'ny he keers fer."

They often spoke of the pathetic loneliness of this good-looking, kindly, mismated woman. Jack and Solomon reached the council on the fifth day of their travel. There, a level plain in the forest was covered with Indians and the snow trodden smooth. Around it were their tents and huts and houses. There were males and females, many of the latter in rich silks and scarlet cloths bordered with gold fringe. Some wore brooches and rings in their noses. Among them were handsome faces and erect and noble forms.

In the center of the plain stood a great stack of wood and green boughs of spruce and balsam built up in layers for the evening council fire.

Old Kiodote knew Solomon and remembered Jack, whom he had seen in the great council at Albany in 1761.

"He says your name was 'Boiling Water,' " Solomon said to Jack after a moment's talk with the chief.

"He has a good memory," the young man answered.

The two white men were invited to take part in the games. All the warriors had heard of Solomon's skill with a rifle. "Son of the Thunder," they called him in the League of the Iroquois. The red men gathered in great numbers to see him shoot. Again, as of old, they were thrilled by his feats with the rifle, but when Jack began his quick and deadly firing, crushing butternuts thrown into the air, with rifle and pistol, a kind of awe possessed the crowd. Many came and touched him and stared into his face and called him "The Brother of Death."

3

Solomon's speech that evening before the council fire impressed the Indians. He had given much thought to its composition and Jack had helped him in the invention of vivid phrases loved by the red men. He addressed them in the dialect of the Senecas, that being the one with which he was most familiar. He spoke of the thunder cloud of war coming up in the east and the cause of it and begged them to fight with their white neighbors, under the leadership of The Great Spirit for the justice which He loved. Solomon had brought them many gifts in token of the friendship of himself and his people.

Old Theandenaga, of the Mohawks, answered him in a speech distinguished by its noble expressions of good will and by an eloquent, but not ill-tempered, account of the wrongs of the red men. He laid particular stress on the corrupting of the young braves with fire-water.

"Let all bad feeling be buried in a deep pool," Solomon answered. "There are bad white men and there are bad Indians but they are not many. The good men are like the leaves of the forest—you can not count them—but the bad man is like the scent pedlar.* Though he is but one, he can make much trouble."

Every judgment of the league in council had to be unanimous. They voted in sections, whereupon each section sent its representative into the higher council and no verdict was announced until its members were of one mind. The deliberations were proceeding toward a favorable judgment as Solomon thought, when Guy Johnson arrived from Johnson Castle with a train of pack bearers. A wild night of drunken revelry followed his arrival. Jack and Solomon were lodging at a log inn, kept by a Dutch trader, half a mile or so from the scene of the council. A little past midnight, the trader came up into the loft where they were sleeping on a heap of straw and awakened Solomon.

"Come down the ladder," said the Dutchman. "A young squaw has come out from the council. She will speak to you."

Solomon slipped on his trousers, coat and boots, and

---

* The skunk.

went below. The squaw was sitting on the floor against the wall. A blanket was drawn over the back of her head. Her handsome face had a familiar look.

"Put out the light," she whispered in English.

The candle was quickly snuffed and then:

"I am the Little White Birch," she said. "You and my beautiful young brave were good to me. You took me to the school and he kissed my cheek and spoke words like the song of the little brown bird of the forest. I have come here to warn you. Turn away from the great camp of the red man. Make your feet go fast. The young warriors are drunk. They will come here to slay you. I say go like the rabbit when he is scared. Before daylight, put half a sleep between you and them."

Solomon called Jack and in the darkness they quickly got ready to go. The Dutchman could give them only a loaf of bread, some salt and a slab of bacon. The squaw stood on the door-step watching while they were getting ready. Snow was falling.

"They are near," she whispered when the men came out. "I have heard them."

She held Jack's hand to her lips and said:

"Let me feel your face. I can not see it. I shall see it not again this side of the Happy Hunting-Grounds."

For a second she touched the face of the young man and he kissed her forehead.

"This way," she whispered. "Now go like the snow in the wind, my beautiful pale face."

"Can we help you?" Jack queried. "Will you go with us back to the white man's school?"

"No, I am old woman now. I have taken the yoke of the red man. In the Happy Hunting-Grounds maybe the Great Spirit will give me a pale face. Then I will go with my father and his people and my beautiful young brave will take me to his house and not be ashamed. Go now. Good-by."

"Little White Birch, I give you this," said Jack, as he put in her hand the tail of the great gray wolf, beautifully adorned with silver braid and blue ribbands.

It was snowing hard. Jack and Solomon started toward a belt of timber east of the log inn. Before they reached it, their clothes were white with snow—a fact which probably saved their lives. They were shot at from the edge of the bush. Solomon shouted to Jack to come on and wisely ran straight toward the spot from which the rifle flashes had proceeded. In the edge of the woods, Jack shot an Indian with his pistol. The red man was loading. So they got through what appeared to be a cordon around the house and cut into the bush.

"They won't foller us," said Solomon, as the two stopped presently to put on their snow-shoes.

"What makes you think so?"

"They don't keer to see us lessen they're hid. We

are the Son o' the Thunder an' the Brother o' Death.
It would hurt to see us. The second our eyes drop
on an Injun, he's got a hole in his guts an' they know
it. They'd ruther go an' set down with a jug o' rum."

"It was a low and devilish trick to bring fire-water
into that camp," said Jack.

"Guy Johnson is mean enough to steal acorns from
a blind hog," Solomon answered.

Suddenly they heard a loud whooping in the distance and looking back into the valley they saw a great
flare of light.

"They've put the torch to the tavern and will have a
dance," said Solomon. "We got out jest in time."

"I am afraid for the Little White Birch," said Jack.

"They'll let her alone. She is one of the wives of ol'
Theandenaga. She will lead the Dutchman an' his
family to the house o' the great chief. She won't let
'em be hurt if she kin help it. She knowed they was
a'ter us."

"Why do they want to kill us?" Jack queried.

"'Cause they're goin' to fight with the British an'
we shoot so damn well they want to git us out o' the
way an' do it sly an' without gittin' hurt. But fer the
squaw, we'd be hoppin' eround in that 'ere loft like
a pair o' rats. They'd 'a' sneaked the Dutchman an'
his folks outdoors with tommyhawks over their heads
and scattered grease an' gunpowder an' boughs on the
floor, an' set 'er goin' an' me an' you asleep above the
ladder. I reckon we'd had to do some climbin' an'

they's no tellin' where we'd 'a' landed, which there ain't do doubt 'bout that."

Solomon seemed to know his way by an instinct like that of a dog. They were in the deep woods traveling by snow light without a trail. Jack felt sure they were going wrong, but he said nothing. By and by there was a glow in the sky ahead. The snow had ceased falling and the heavens were clear.

"Ye see we're goin' right," said Solomon. "The sun'll be up in half an hour, but afore we swing to the trail we better git a bite. Gulf Brook is down yender in the valley an' I'd kind o' like to taste of it."

They proceeded down a long, wooded slope and came presently to the brook whose white floored aisle was walled with evergreen thickets heavy with snow. Beneath its crystal vault they could hear the song of the water. It was a grateful sound for they were warm and thirsty. Near the point where they deposited their packs was a big beaver dam.

Solomon took his ax and teapot and started up stream.

"Want to git cl'ar 'bove," said he.

"Why?" Jack inquired.

"This 'ere is a beaver nest," said Solomon.

He returned in a moment with his pot full of beautiful clear water of which they drank deeply.

"Ye see the beavers make a dam an' raise the water," Solomon explained. "When it gits a good ice roof so thick the sun won't burn a hole in it afore spring, they

tap the dam an' let the water out.   Then they've got
a purty house to live in with a floor o' clean water an'
a glass roof an' plenty o' green popple sticks stored
in the corners to feed on.   They have stiddy weather
down thar—no cold winds 'er deep snow to bother
'em.   When the roof rots an' breaks in the sunlight
an' slides off they patch up the dam with mud an'
sticks an' they've got a swimmin' hole to play in."

They built a fire and spread their blankets on a bed
of boughs and had some hot tea and jerked meat and
slices of bread soaked in bacon fat.

"Ye see them Injuns is doomed," said Solomon.
"Some on 'em has got good sense, but rum kind o'
kills all argeyment.   Rum is now the great chief o'
the red man.   Rum an' Johnson 'll win 'em over.   Sir
William was their Great White Father.   They trusted
him.   Guy an' John have got his name behind 'em.
The right an' wrong o' the matter ain't able to git under the Injun's hide.   They'll go with the British an'
burn, an' rob, an' kill.   The settlers 'll give hot blood
to their childern.   The Injun 'll be forever a brother
to the snake.   We an' our childern an' gran'childern 'll
curse him an' meller his head.   The League o' the Iroquois 'll be scattered like dust in the wind, an' we'll
wonder where it has gone.   But 'fore then, they's goin'
to be great trouble.   The white settlers has got to give
up their land an' move, 'er turn Tory, 'er be tommy-
hawked."

With a sense of failure, they slowly made their way back to Albany, riding the last half of it on the sled of a settler who was going to the river city with a grist and a load of furs.

CHAPTER XIV

ADVENTURES IN THE SERVICE OF THE COMMANDER-IN-CHIEF

Soon after they reached home Jack received a letter from Doctor Franklin who had given up his fruitless work in London and returned to Philadelphia.

It said: "My work in England has been fruitless and I am done with it. I bring you much love from the fair lady of your choice. That, my young friend, is a better possession than houses and lands, for even the flames of war can not destroy it. I have not seen, in all this life of mine, a dearer creature or a nobler passion. And I will tell you why it is dear to me, as well as to you. She is like the good people of England whose heart is with the colonies, but whose will is being baffled and oppressed. Let us hope it may not be for long. My good wishes for you involve the whole race whose blood is in my veins. That race has ever been like the patient ox, treading out the corn, whose leading trait is endurance.

"There is little light in the present outlook. You and Binkus will do well to come here. This, for a time, will be the center of our activities and you may be needed any moment."

Jack and Solomon went to Philadelphia soon after

news of the battle of Lexington had reached Albany in the last days of April. They were among the cheering crowds that welcomed the delegates to the Second Congress.

Colonel Washington, the only delegate in uniform, was the most impressive figure in the Congress. He had come up with a coach and six horses from Virginia. The Colonel used to say that even with six horses, one had a slow and rough journey in the mud and sand. His dignity and noble stature, the fame he had won in the Indian wars and his wisdom and modesty in council, had silenced opposition and opened his way. He was a man highly favored of Heaven. The people of Philadelphia felt the power of his personality. They seemed to regard him with affectionate awe. All eyes were on him when he walked around. Not even the magnificent Hancock or the eloquent Patrick Henry attracted so much attention. Yet he would stop in the street to speak to a child or to say a pleasant word to an old acquaintance as he did to Solomon.

That day in June when the beloved Virginian was chosen to be Commander-in-Chief of the American forces, Jack and Solomon dined with Franklin at his home. John Adams of Boston and John Brown, the great merchant of Providence, were his other guests. The distinguished men were discussing the choice of Colonel Washington.

"I think that Ward is a greater soldier," said Brown. "Washington has done no fighting since '58. Our battles will be in the open. He is a bush fighter."

"True, but he is a fighter and, like Achilles, a born master of men," Franklin answered. "His fiery energy saved Braddock's army from being utterly wiped out. His gift for deliberation won the confidence of Congress. He has wisdom and personality. He can express them in calm debate or terrific action. Above all, he has a sense of the oneness of America. Massachusetts and Georgia are as dear to him as Virginia."

"He is a Christian gentleman of proved courage and great sagacity," said Adams. "His one defeat proved him to be the master of himself. It was a noble defeat."

Doctor Franklin, who never failed to show some token of respect for every guest at his table, turned to Solomon and said:

"Major Binkus, you have been with him a good deal. What do you think of Colonel Washington?"

"I think he's a hull four hoss team an' the dog under the waggin," said Solomon.

John Adams often quoted these words of the scout and they became a saying in New England.

"To ask you a question is like priming a pump," said Franklin, as he turned to Solomon with a laugh. "Washington is about four times the average man, with something to spare and that something is the dog under the wagon. It would seem that the Lord God has bred and prepared and sent him among us to be chosen. We saw and knew and voted. There was no room for doubt in my mind."

"And while I am a friend of Ward, I am after all convinced that Washington is the man," said Brown. "Nothing so became him as when he called upon all gentlemen present to remember that he thought himself unequal to the task."

Washington set out in June with Colonel Lee and a company of Light Horse for Boston where some sixteen thousand men had assembled with their rifles and muskets to be organized into an army for the defense of Massachusetts.

2

A little later Jack and Solomon followed with eight horses and two wagons loaded with barrels of gunpowder made under the direction of Benjamin Franklin and paid for with his money. A British fleet being in American waters, the overland route was chosen as the safer one. It was a slow and toilsome journey with here and there a touch of stern adventure. Crossing the pine barrens of New Jersey, they were held up by a band of Tory refugees and deprived of all the money in their pockets. Always Solomon got a squint in one eye and a solemn look in the other when that matter was referred to.

" 'Twere all due to the freight," he said to a friend. "Ye see their guns was p'intin' our way and behind us were a ton o' gunpowder. She's awful particular comp'ny. Makes her nervous to have anybody nigh her that's bein' shot at. Ye got to be peaceful an' p'lite. Don't let no argements come up. If some feller wants yer money an' has got a gun it'll be cheaper to let him have it. I tell ye she's an uppity, hot-tempered ol' critter—got to be treated jest so er she'll stomp her foot an' say, 'Scat,' an' then—"

Solomon smiled and gave his right hand a little upward fling and said no more, having lifted the burden off his mind.

On the post road, beyond Horse Neck in Connecticut, they had a more serious adventure. They had been traveling with a crude map of each main road, showing the location of houses in the settled country where, at night, they could find shelter and hospitality. Owing to the peculiar character of their freight, the Committee in Philadelphia had requested them to avoid inns and had caused these maps to be sent to them at post-offices on the road indicating the homes of trusted patriots from twenty to thirty miles apart. About six o'clock in the evening of July twentieth, they reached the home of Israel Lockwood, three miles above Horse Neck. They had ridden through a storm which had shaken and smitten the earth with its thunder-bolts some of which had fallen near them. Mr. Lockwood directed them to leave their wagons on a large empty barn floor and asked them in to supper.

"If you'll bring suthin' out to us, I guess we better stay by her," said Solomon. "She might be nervous."

"Do you have to stay with this stuff all the while?" Lockwood asked.

"Night an' day," said Solomon. "Don't do to let 'er git lonesome. To-day when the lightnin' were slappin' the ground on both sides o' me, I wanted to hop down an' run off in the bush a mile er so fer to see the kentry, but I jest had to set an' hope that she would hold her temper an' not go to slappin' back."

"She," as Solomon called the two loads, was a most exacting mistress. They never left her alone for a moment. While one was putting away the horses the other was on guard. They slept near her at night.

Israel Lockwood sat down for a visit with them when he brought their food. While they were eating, another terrific thunder-storm arrived. In the midst of it a bolt struck the barn and rent its roof open and set the top of the mow afire. Solomon jumped to the rear wheel of one of the wagons while Jack seized the tongue. In a second it was rolling down the barn bridge and away. The barn had filled with smoke and cinders but these dauntless men rolled out the second wagon.

Rain was falling. Solomon observed a wisp of smoke coming out from under the roof of this wagon. He jumped in and found a live cinder which had burned through the cover and fallen on one of the barrels. It was eating into the wood. Solomon tossed it out in the rain and smothered "the live spot." He examined the barrels and the wagon floor and was satisfied. In speaking of that incident next day he said to Jack:

"If I hadn't 'a' had purty good control o' my legs, I guess they'd 'a' run erway with me. I had to put the whip on 'em to git 'em to step in under that wagon roof—you hear to me."

While Solomon was engaged with this trying duty, Lockwood had led the horses out of the stable below and rescued the harness. A heavy shower was falling. The flames had burst through the roof and in spite of the rain, the structure was soon destroyed.

"The wind was favorable and we all stood watching the fire, safe but helpless to do anything for our host," Jack wrote in a letter. "Fortunately there was another house near and I took the horses to its barn for the night. We slept in a woodshed close to the wagons. We slipped out of trouble by being on hand when it started. If we had gone into the house for supper, I'm inclined to think that the British would not have been driven out of Boston.

"We passed many companies of marching riflemen. In front of one of these, the fife and drum corps playing behind him, was a young Tory, who had insulted the company, and was, therefore, made to carry a gray goose in his arms with this maxim of Poor Richard on his back: 'Not every goose has feathers on him.'

"On the twentieth we reported to General Washington in Cambridge. This was the first time I saw him in the uniform of a general. He wore a blue coat with buff facings and buff underdress, a small sword, rich epaulets, a black cockade in his three-cornered hat, and a blue sash under his coat. His hair was done up in a queue. He was in boots and spurs. He received us politely, directing a young officer to go with us to the powder house. There we saw a large number of barrels.

"'All full of sand,' the officer whispered. 'We keep 'em here to fool the enemy.'

"Not far from the powder house I overheard this little dialogue between a captain and a private.

"'Bill, go get a pail o' water,' said the captain.

"'I shan't do it. 'Tain't my turn,' the private answered."

The men and officers were under many kinds of shelter in the big camp. There were tents and marquees and rude structures built of boards and roughly hewn timber, and of stone and turf and brick and brush. Some had doors and windows wrought out of withes knit together in the fashion of a basket. There were handsome young men whose thighs had never felt the touch of steel; elderly men in faded, moth-eaten uniforms and wigs.

In their possession were rifles and muskets of varying size, age and caliber. Some of them had helped to make the thunders of Naseby and Marston Moor. There were old sabers which had touched the ground when the hosts of Cromwell had knelt in prayer.

Certain of the men were swapping clothes. No uniforms had been provided for this singular assemblage of patriots all eager for service. Sergeants wore a strip of red on the right shoulder; corporals a strip of green. Field officers mounted a red cockade; captains flaunted a like signal in yellow. Generals wore a pink ribband and aides a green one.

This great body of men which had come to besiege Boston was able to shoot and dig. That is about all they knew of the art of war. Training had begun in earnest. The sergeants were working with squads; Generals Lee and Ward and Green and Putnam and Sullivan with companies and regiments from daylight to dark.

Jack was particularly interested in Putnam—a short, rugged, fat, white-haired farmer from Connecticut of bluff manners and nasal twang and of great animation for one of his years—he was then fifty-seven. He was often seen flying about the camp on a horse. The young man had read of the heroic exploits of this veteran of the Indian wars.

Their mission finished, that evening Jack and Solomon called at General Washington's headquarters.

"General, Doctor Franklin told us to turn over the hosses and wagons to you," said Solomon. "He didn't tell us what to do with ourselves 'cause 'twasn't nec'-sary an' he knew it. We want to enlist."

"For what term?"

"Till the British are licked."

"You are the kind of men I need," said Washing-

John Wolcott Adams

ton. "I shall put you on scout duty. Mr. Irons will go into my regiment of sharp shooters with the rank of captain. You have told me of his training in Philadelphia."

3

So the two friends were enlisted and began service in the army of Washington.

A letter from Jack to his mother dated July 25, 1775, is full of the camp color:

"General Charles Lee is in command of my regiment," he writes. "He is a rough, slovenly old dog of a man who seems to bark at us on the training ground. He has two or three hunting dogs that live with him in his tent and also a rare gift of profanity which is with him everywhere—save at headquarters.

"To-day I saw these notices posted in camp:

" 'Punctual attendance on divine service is required of all not on actual duty.'

" 'No burning of the pope allowed.'

" 'Fifteen stripes for denying duty.'

" 'Ten for getting drunk.'

" 'Thirty-nine for stealing and desertion.'

"Rogues are put in terror, lazy men are energized. The quarters are kept clean, the food is well cooked and in plentiful supply, but the British over in town are said to be getting hungry."

Early in August a London letter was forwarded to Jack from Philadelphia. He was filled with new hope as he read these lines:

"Dearest Jack: I am sailing for Boston on one of the next troop ships to join my father. So when the war ends—God grant it may be soon!—you will not have far to go to find me. Perhaps by Christmas time we may be together. Let us both pray for that. Meanwhile, I shall be happier for being nearer you and for doing what I can to heal the wounds made by this wretched war. I am going to be a nurse in a hospital. You see the truth is that since I met you, I like all men better, and I shall love to be trying to relieve their sufferings . . ."

It was a long letter but above is as much of it as can claim admission to these pages.

"Who but she could write such a letter?" Jack asked himself, and then he held it to his lips a moment. It thrilled him to think that even then she was probably in Boston. In the tent where he and Solomon lived when they were both in camp, he found the scout. The night before Solomon had slept out. Now he had built a small fire in front of the tent and lain down on a blanket, having delivered his report at headquarters.

"Margaret is in Boston," said Jack as soon as he entered, and then standing in the firelight read the letter to his friend.

"Thar is a real, genewine, likely gal," said the scout.

"I wish there were some way of getting to her," the young man remarked.

"Might as well think o' goin' to hell an' back ag'in," said Solomon. "Since Bunker Hill the British are like a lot o' hornets. I run on to one of 'em to-day. He fired at me an' didn't hit a thing but the air an' run like a scared rabbit. Could 'a' killed him easy but I kind o' enjoyed seein' him run. He were like chain lightnin' on a greased pole—you hear to me."

"If the General will let me, I'm going to try spy duty and see if I can get into town and out again," he proposed.

"You keep out o' that business," said Solomon. "They's too many that know ye over in town. The two Clarkes an' their friends an' Colonel Hare an' his friends, an' Cap. Preston, an' a hull passle. They know all 'bout ye. If you got snapped, they'd stan' ye ag'in' a wall an' put ye out o' the way quick. It would be pie for the Clarkes, an' the ol' man Hare wouldn't spill no tears over it. Cap. Preston couldn't save ye that's sart'in. No, sir, I won't 'low it. They's plenty o' old cusses fer such work."

For a time Jack abandoned the idea, but later, when Solomon failed to return from a scouting tour and a report reached camp that he was captured, the young man began to think of that rather romantic plan again. He had grown a full beard; his skin was tanned; his clothes were worn and torn and faded. His father, who had visited the camp bringing a supply of clothes for his son, had failed, at first, to recognize him.

December had arrived. The General was having his first great trial in keeping an army about him. Terms of enlistment were expiring. Cold weather had come.

The camp was uncomfortable. Regiments of the home-sick lads of New England were leaving or preparing to leave. Jack and a number of young ministers in the service organized a campaign of persuasion and many were prevailed upon to reenlist. But hundreds of boys were hurrying homeward on the frozen roads. The southern riflemen, who were a long journey from their homes, had not the like temptation to break away. Bitter rivalry arose between the boys of the north and the south. The latter, especially the Virginia lads, were in handsome uniforms. They looked down upon the awkward, homespun ranks in the regiments of Massachusetts, Rhode Island and Connecticut. Then came the famous snowball battle between the boys of Virginia and New England. In the midst of it, Washington arrived and, leaping from his white horse, was quickly in the thick of the fight. He seized a couple of Virginia lads and gave them a shaking.

"No more of this," he commanded.

It was all over in a moment. The men were running toward their quarters.

"There is a wholesome regard here for the Commander-in-Chief," Jack wrote to his mother. "I look not upon his heroic figure without a thought of the great burden which rests upon it and a thrill of emotion. There are many who fear him. Most severely he will punish the man who neglects his duty, but how gentle and indulgent he can be, especially to a new recruit, until the latter has learned the game of war! He is like a good father to these thousands of boys and young men. No soldier can be flogged when he is near. If he sees a fellow tied to the halberds, he will ask about his offense and order him to be taken down. In camp his black servant, Bill, is always with him. Out of camp he has an escort of light horse. Morning and evening he holds divine service in his tent. When a man does a brave act, the Chief summons him to headquarters and gives him a token of his appreciation. I hope to be called one of these days."

Soon after this letter was written, the young man was sent for. He and his company had captured a number of men in a skirmish.

"Captain, you have done well," said the General. "I want to make a scout of you. In our present circumstances it's about the most important, dangerous and difficult work there is to be done here, especially the work which Solomon Binkus undertook to do. There is no other in whom I should have so much confidence."

"You do me great honor," said Jack. "I shall make a poor showing compared with that of my friend Major Binkus, but I have some knowledge of his methods and will do my best."

"You will do well to imitate them with caution," said the General. "He was a most intrepid and astute observer. In the bush they would not have captured him. The clearings toward the sea make the work arduous and full of danger. It is only for men of your

strength and courage. Major Bartlett knows the part
of the line which Colonel Binkus traversed. He will
be going out that way to-morrow. I should like
you, sir, to go with him. After one trip I shall be
greatly pleased if you are capable of doing the work
alone."

Orders were delivered and Jack reported to Bartlett,
an agreeable, middle-aged farmer-soldier, who had
been on scout duty since July. They left camp together next morning an hour before reveille. They had
an uneventful day, mostly in wooded flats and ridges,
and from the latter looking across with a spy-glass into
Bruteland, as they called the country held by the British, and seeing only, now and then, an enemy picket or
distant camps. About midday they sat down in a
thicket together for a bite to eat and a whispered conference.

"Binkus, as you know, had his own way of scouting," said the Major. "He was an Indian fighter. He
liked to get inside the enemy lines and lie close an'
watch 'em an' mebbe hear what they were talking
about. Now an' then he would surprise a British sentinel and disarm him an' bring him into camp."

Jack wondered that his friend had never spoken of
the capture of prisoners.

"He was a modest man," said the young scout.

"He didn't want the British to know where Solomon
Binkus was at work, and I guess he was wise," said
the Major. "I advise you against taking the chances

that he took. It isn't necessary. You would be caught much sooner than he was."

That day Bartlett took Jack over Solomon's trail and gave him the lay of the land and much good advice. A young man of Jack's spirit, however, is apt to have a degree of enterprise and self-confidence not easily controlled by advice. He had been traveling alone for three days when he felt the need of more exciting action. That night he crossed the Charles River on the ice in a snow-storm and captured a sentinel and brought him back to camp.

About this time he wrote another letter to the family, in which he said:

"The boys are coming back from home and reenlisting. They have not been paid—no one has been paid—but they are coming back. More of them are coming than went away.

"They all tell one story. The women and the old men made a row about their being at home in time of war. On Sunday the minister called them shirks. Everybody looked askance at them. A committee of girls went from house to house reenlisting the boys. So here they are, and Washington has an army, such as it is."

4

Soon after that the daring spirit of the youth led him into a great adventure. It was on the night of January fifth that Jack penetrated the British lines in a snow-storm and got close to an outpost in a strip of forest. There a camp-fire was burning. He came close. His garments had been whitened by the storm. The air was thick with snow, his feet were muffled in a foot of it. He sat by a stump scarcely twenty feet from the fire, seeing those in its light, but quite invisible. There he could distinctly hear the talk of the Britishers. It related to a proposed evacuation of the city by Howe.

"I'm weary of starving to death in this God-forsaken place," said one of them. "You can't keep an army without meat or vegetables. I've eaten fish till I'm getting scales on me."

"Colonel Riffington says that the army will leave here within a fortnight," another observed.

It was important information which had come to the ear of the young scout. The talk was that of well bred Englishmen who were probably officers.

"We ought not to speak of those matters aloud," one of them remarked. "Some damned Yankee may be listening like the one we captured."

"He was Amherst's old scout," said another. "He swore a blue streak when we shoved him into jail. They don't like to be treated like rebels. They want to be prisoners of war."

"I don't know why they shouldn't," another answered. "If this isn't a war, I never saw one. There are twenty thousand men under arms across the river and they've got us nailed in here tighter than a drum.

They used to say in London that the rebellion was
a teapot tempest and that a thousand grenadiers could
march to the Alleghanies in a week and subdue the
country on the way. You are aware of how far we
have marched from the sea. It's just about to where
we are now. We've gone about five miles in eight
months. How many hundreds of years will pass
before we reach the Alleghanies? But old Gage will
tell you that it isn't a war."

'A' young man came along with his rifle on his
shoulder.

"Hello, Bill!" said one of the men. "Going out on
post?"

"I am, God help me," the youth answered. "It's
what I'd call a hell of a night."

The sentinel passed close by Jack on his way to his
post. The latter crept away and followed, gradually
closing in upon his quarry. When they were well
away from the fire, Jack came close and called, "Bill."

The sentinel stopped and faced about.

"You've forgotten something," said Jack, in a genial
tone.

"What is it?"

"Your caution," Jack answered, with his pistol
against the breast of his enemy. "I shall have to kill
you if you call or fail to obey me. Give me the rifle
and go on ahead. When I say gee go to the right, haw
to the left."

So the capture was made, and on the way out Jack picked up the sentinel who stood waiting to be relieved and took both men into camp.

From documents on the person of one of these young Britishers, it appeared that General Clarke was in command of a brigade behind the lines which Jack had been watching and robbing.

When Jack delivered his report the Chief called him a brave lad and said:

"It is valuable information you have brought to me. Do not speak of it. Let me warn you, Captain, that from now on they will try to trap you. Perhaps, even, you may look for daring enterprises on that part of their line."

The General was right. The young scout ran into a most daring and successful British enterprise on the twentieth of January. The snow had been swept away in a warm rain and the ground had frozen bare, or it would not have been possible. Jack had got to a strip of woods in a lonely bit of country near the British lines and was climbing a tall tree to take observations when he saw a movement on the ground beneath him. He stopped and quickly discovered that the tree was surrounded by British soldiers. One of them, who stood with a raised rifle, called to him:

"Irons, I will trouble you to drop your pistols and come down at once."

Jack saw that he had run into an ambush. He dropped his pistols and came down. He had disregarded the warning of the General. He should have been looking out for an ambush. A squad of five men stood about him with rifles in hand. Among them was Lionel Clarke, his right sleeve empty.

"We've got you at last—you damned rebel!" said Clarke.

"I suppose you need some one to swear at," Jack answered.

"And to shoot at," Clarke suggested.

"I thought that you would not care for another match with me," the young scout remarked as they began to move away.

"Hereafter you will be treated like a rebel and not like a gentleman," Clarke answered.

"What do you mean?"

"I mean that you will be standing, blindfolded against a wall."

"That kind of a threat doesn't scare me," Jack answered. "We have too many of your men in our hands."

CHAPTER XV

IN BOSTON JAIL

Jack was marched under a guard into the streets of Boston. Church bells were ringing. It was Sunday morning. Young Clarke came with the guard beyond the city limits. They had seemed to be very careless in the control of their prisoner. They gave him every chance to make a break for liberty. Jack was not fooled.

"I see that you want to get rid of me," said Jack to the young officer. "You'd like to have me run a race with your bullets. That is base ingratitude. I was careful of you when we met and you do not seem to know it."

"I know how well you can shoot," Clarke answered. "But you do not know how well I can shoot."

"And when I learn, I want to have a fair chance for my life."

Beyond the city limits young Clarke, who was then a captain, left them, and Jack proceeded with the others.

The streets were quiet—indeed almost deserted. There were no children playing on the common. A crowd was coming out of one of the churches. In the midst of it the prisoner saw Preston and Lady Hare. They were so near that he could have touched them

with his hand as he passed. They did not see him.
He noted the name of the church and its minister. In
a few minutes he was delivered at the jail—a noisome,
ill-smelling, badly ventilated place. The jailer was a
tall, slim, sallow man with a thin gray beard. His face
and form were familiar. He heard Jack's name with
a look of great astonishment. Then the young man
recognized him. He was Mr. Eliphalet Pinhorn, who
had so distinguished himself on the stage trip to Philadelphia some years before.

"It is a long time since we met," said Jack.

Mr. Pinhorn's face seemed to lengthen. His mouth
and eyes opened wide in a silent demand for information.

Jack reminded him of the day and circumstances.

For a moment Mr. Pinhorn held his hand against
his forehead and was dumb with astonishment. Then
he said:

"I knew! I foresaw! But it is not too late."

"Too late for what?"

"To turn, to be redeemed, loved, forgiven. Think
it over, sir. Think it over."

Jack's name and age and residence were registered.
Then Pinhorn took his arm and walked with him
down the corridor toward an open door. About half-
way to the door he stopped and put his hand on Jack's
shoulder and said with a look of great seriousness:

"A sinking cause! Death! Destruction! Misery!
The ship is going down. Leave it."

"You are misinformed. There is no leak in our ship," said Jack.

Mr. Pinhorn shut his eyes and shook his head mournfully. Then, with a wave of his hand, he pronounced the doom of the western world in one whispered word:

"Ashes!"

For a moment his face and form were alive with exclamatory suggestion. Then he shook his head and said:

"Doomed! Poor soul! Go out in the yard with your fellow rebels. They are taking the air."

The yard was an opening walled in by the main structure and its two wings and a wooden fence some fifteen feet high. There was a ragged, dirty rabble of "rebel" prisoners, among whom was Solomon Binkus, all out for an airing. The old scout had lost flesh and color. He held Jack's hand and stood for a moment without speaking.

"I never was so glad and so sorry in my life," said Solomon. "It's a hell-mogrified place to be in. Smells like a blasted whale an' is as cold as the north side of a grave stun on a Janooary night, an' starvation fare, an' they's a man here that's come down with the small-pox. How'd ye git ketched?"

Jack briefly told of his capture.

"I got sick one day an' couldn't hide 'cause I were makin' tracks in the snow so I had to give in," said Solomon. "Margaret has been here, but they won't

let 'er come no more 'count o' the smallpox. Sends
me suthin' tasty ev'ry day er two. I tol' er all 'bout
ye. I guess the smallpox couldn't keep 'er 'way if she
knowed you was here. But she won't be 'lowed to
know it. This 'ere Clarke boy has p'isoned the jail.
Nobody 'll come here 'cept them that's dragged. He's
got it all fixed fer ye. I wouldn't wonder if he'd be
glad to see ye rotted up with smallpox."

"What kind of a man is Pinhorn?"

"A whey-faced hypercrit an' a Tory. Licks the feet
o' the British when they come here."

Jack and Solomon lay for weeks in this dirty,
noisome jail, where their treatment was well calculated
to change opinions not deeply rooted in firm soil. They
did not fear the smallpox, as both were immune. But
their confinement was, as doubtless it was intended to
be, memorably punitive. They were "rebels"—law-
breakers, human rubbish whose offenses bordered upon
treason. The smallpox patient was soon taken away,
but other conditions were not improved. They slept
on straw infested with vermin. Their cover and food
were insufficient and "not fit fer a dog," in the words
of Solomon. Some of the boys gave in and were set
free on parole, and there was one, at least, who went
to work in the ranks of the British.

There is a passage in a letter of Jack Irons regarding conditions in the jail which should be quoted here:

"One boy has lung fever and every night I hear him
sobbing. His sorrow travels like fire among the

weaker men. I have heard a number of cold, half-starved, homesick lads crying like women in the middle of the night. It makes me feel like letting go myself. There is one man who swears like a trooper when it begins. I suppose that I shall be as hysterical as the rest of them in time. I don't believe General Howe knows what is going on here. The jail is run by American Tories, who are wreaking their hatred on us."

Jack sent a line to the rector of the Church of England, where he had seen Preston and Lady Howe, inviting him to call, but saw him not, and no word came from him. Letters were entrusted to Mr. Pinhorn for Preston, Margaret and General Sir Benjamin Hare with handsome payment for their delivery, but they waited in vain for an answer.

"They's suthin' wrong 'bout this 'ere business," said Solomon. "You'll find that ol' Pinhorn has got a pair o' split hoofs under his luther."

One day Jack was sent for by Mr. Pinhorn and conducted to his office.

"Honor! Good luck! Relief!" was the threefold exclamation with which the young man was greeted.

"What do you mean?" Jack inquired.

"General Howe! You! Message to Mr. Washington! To-night!"

"Do you mean General Washington?"

"No. Mister! Title not recognized here!"

"I shall take no message to 'Mr.' Washington," Jack answered. "If I did, I am sure that he would not receive it."

Mr. Pinhorn's face expressed a high degree of astonishment.

"Pride! Error! Persistent error!" he exclaimed. "Never mind! Details can be fixed. You are to go to-night. Return to-morrow!"

The prospect of getting away from his misery even for a day or two was alluring.

"Let me have the details in writing and I will let you know at once," he answered.

The plan was soon delivered. Jack was to pass the lines on the northeast front in the vicinity of Breed's Hill with a British sergeant, under a white flag, and proceed to Washington's headquarters.

"Looks kind o' neevarious," said Solomon when they were out in the jail yard together. "Looks like ye might be grabbed in the jaws o' a trap. Nobody's name is signed to this 'ere paper. There's nothin' behind the hull thing but ol' Pinhorn an'—who? I'm skeered o' Mr. Who? Pinhorn an' Who an' a Dark Night! There's a pardnership! Kind o' well mated! They want ye to put yer life in their hands. What fer? Wal, ye know it 'pears to me they'd be apt to be car'less with it. It's jest possible that there's some feller who'll be happier if you was rubbed off the slate. War is goin' on an' you belong to that breed o' pups they call rebels. A dead rebel don't cause no hard feelin's in the British army. Now, Jack, you stay where ye be. 'Tain't a fust rate place, but it's better'n a hole in the ground. Suthin' is goin' to happen—you mark my words, boy. I kind o' think Margaret is gittin' anxious to talk with me an' kin't be kept erway no longer. Mebbe the British army is goin' to move. Ye know fer two days an' nights we been hearin' cannon fire."

"Solomon, I'm not going out to be shot in the back," said the young man. "If I am to be executed, it must be done with witnesses in proper form. I shall refuse to go. If Margaret should come, and it is possible, I want you to sit down with her in front of my cell so that I can see her, but do not tell her that I am here. It would increase her trouble and do no good. Besides, I could not permit myself to touch her hand even, but I would love to look into her face."

So it happened that the proposal which had come to Jack through Mr. Pinhorn was firmly declined, whereupon the astonishment of that official was expressed in a sorrowful gesture and the exclamation: "Doomed! Stubborn youth!"

2

Solomon Binkus was indeed a shrewd man. In the faded packet of letters is one which recites the history of the confinement of the two scouts in the Boston jail. It tells of the coming of Margaret that very evening with an order from the Adjutant General directing

Mr. Pinhorn to allow her to talk with the "rebel prisoner Solomon Binkus."

The official conducted her to the iron grated door
in front of Solomon's cell.

"I will talk with him in the corridor, if you please,"
she said, as she gave the jailer a guinea, whereupon
he became most obliging. The cell door was opened
and chairs were brought for them to sit upon. Cannons were roaring again and the sound was nearer
than it had been before.

"Have you heard from Jack?" she asked when they
were seated in front of the cell of the latter.

"Yes, ma'am. He is well, but like a man shot with
rock salt."

"What do you mean?"

"Sufferin'," Solomon answered. "Kind o' riddled
with thoughts o' you an' I wouldn't wonder."

"Did you get a letter?" she asked.

"No. A young officer who was ketched an' brought
here t'other day has told me all 'bout him."

"Is the officer here?"

"Yes, ma'am," Solomon answered.

"I want to see him—I want to talk with him. I
must meet the man who has come from the presence
of my Jack."

Solomon was visibly embarrassed. He was in trouble for a moment and then he answered: "I'm 'fraid
'twouldn't do no good."

"Why?"

" 'Cause he's deef an' dumb."

"But do you not understand?   It would be a comfort to look at him."

"He's in this cell, but I wouldn't know how to call
him," Solomon assured her.

She went to Jack's door and peered at him through
the grating. He was lying on his straw bed. The
light which came from candles set in brackets on the
stone wall of the corridor was dim.

"Poor, poor fellow!" she exclaimed. "I suppose he
is thinking of his sweetheart or of some one very dear
to him. His eyes are covered with his handkerchief.
So you have lately seen the boy I love! How I wish
you could tell me about him!"

The voice of the young lady had had a curious effect upon that nerve-racked, homesick company of soldier lads in prison. Doubtless it had reminded some
of dear and familiar voices which they had lost hope
of hearing again.

One began to groan and sob, then another and another.

"Ain't that like the bawlin' o' the damned?" Solomon asked. "Some on 'em is sick; some is wore out.
They're all half starved!"

"It is dreadful!" said she, as she covered her eyes
with her handkerchief. "I can not help thinking that
any day *he* may have to come here. I shall go to
see General Howe to-night."

"To-morrer I'll git this 'ere boy to write out all he

knows 'bout Jack, but if ye see it, ye'll have to come 'ere an' let me put it straight into yer hands," Solomon assured her.

"I'll be here at ten o'clock," she said, and went away.

Pinhorn stepped into the corridor as Solomon called to Jack:

"Things be goin' to improve, ol' man. Hang on to yer hosses. The English people is to have a talk with General Howe to-night an' suthin' 'll be said, now you hear to me. That damn German King ain't a-goin' to have his way much longer here in Boston jail."

Early next morning shells began to fall in the city. Suddenly the firing ceased. At nine o'clock all prisoners in the jail were sent for, to be exchanged. Preston came with the order from General Howe and news of a truce.

"This means yer army is lightin' out," Solomon said to him.

"The city will be evacuated," was Preston's answer.

"Could I send a message to Gin'ral Hare's house?"

"The General and his brigade and family sailed for another port at eight. If you wish, I'll take your message."

Solomon delivered to Preston a letter written by Jack to Margaret. It told of his capture and imprisonment.

"Better than I, you will know if there is good ground for these dark suspicions which have come to us," he wrote. "As well as I, you will know what a trial I underwent last evening. That I had the strength to hold my peace, I am glad, knowing that you are the happier to-day because of it."

The third of March had come. The sun was shining. The wind was in the south. They were not strong enough to walk, so Preston had brought horses for them to ride. There were long patches of snow on the Dorchester Heights. A little beyond they met the brigade of Putnam. It was moving toward the city and had stopped for its noon mess. The odor of fresh beef and onions was in the air.

"Cat's blood an' gunpowder!" said Solomon. "Tie me to a tree."

"What for?" Preston asked.

"I'll kill myself eatin'," the scout declared. "I'm so gol durn hungry I kin't be trusted."

"I guess we'll have to put the brakes on each other," Jack remarked.

"An' it'll be steep goin'," said Solomon.

Washington rode up to the camp with a squad of cavalry while they were eating. He had a kind word for every liberated man. To Jack he said:

"I am glad to address you as Colonel Irons. You have suffered much, but it will be a comfort for you to know that the information you brought enabled me to hasten the departure of the British."

Turning to Solomon, he added:

"Colonel Binkus, I am indebted to you for faithful, effective and valiant service. You shall have a medal."

"Gin'ral Washington, we're a-goin' to lick 'em," said Solomon. "We're a-goin' to break their necks."

"Colonel, you are very confident," the General answered with a smile.

"You'll see," Solomon continued. "God A'mighty is sick o' tyrants. They're doomed."

"Let us hope so," said the Commander-in-Chief. "But let us not forget the words of Poor Richard: 'God helps those who help themselves.'"

CHAPTER XVI

THE Selectmen of Boston, seeing the city threatened with destruction, had made terms with Washington for the British army. It was to be allowed peaceably to abandon the city and withdraw in its fleet of one hundred and fifty vessels. The American army was now well organized and in high spirit. Washington waited on Dorchester Heights for the evacuation of Boston to be completed. Meanwhile, a large force was sent to New York to assist in the defense of that city. Jack and Solomon went with it. On account of their physical condition, horses were provided for them, and on their arrival each was to have a leave of two weeks, "for repairs," as Solomon put it. They went up to Albany for a rest and a visit and returned eager for the work which awaited them.

They spent a spring and summer of heavy toil in building defenses and training recruits. The country was aflame with excitement. Rhode Island and Connecticut declared for independence. The fire ran across their borders and down the seaboard. Other colonies were making or discussing like declarations. John Adams, on his way to Congress, told of the defeat of the Northern army in Canada and how it was heading southward "eaten with vermin, diseased, scattered, dispirited, unclad, unfed, disgraced." Colonies were ignoring the old order of things, electing their own assemblies and enacting their own laws. The Tory provincial assemblies were unable to get men enough together to make a pretense of doing business.

In June, by a narrow margin, the Congress declared for independence, on the motion of Richard Henry Lee of Virginia. A declaration was drafted and soon adopted by all the Provincial Congresses. It was engrossed on parchment and signed by the delegates of the thirteen states on the second of August. Jack went to that memorable scene as an aid to John Adams, who was then the head of the War Board.

He writes in a letter to his friends in Albany:

"They were a solemn looking lot of men with the exception of Doctor Franklin and Thomas Jefferson of Virginia. The latter wore a long-tailed buff coat with round gold buttons. He is a tall, big-boned man. I have never seen longer arms than he has. His wrists and hands are large and powerful.

"When they began to sign the parchment he smiled and said:

" 'Gentlemen, Benjamin Franklin should have written this document. The committee, however, knew well that he would be sure to put a joke in it.'

" 'Let me remind you that behind it all is the greatest joke in history,' said the philosopher.

" 'What is that?' Mr. Jefferson asked.

" 'The British House of Lords,' said Franklin.

"A smile broke through the cloud of solemnity on those many faces, and was followed by a little ripple of laughter.

"'The committee wishes you all to know that it is indebted to Doctor Franklin for wise revision of the instrument,' said Mr. Jefferson.

"When the last man had signed, Mr. Jefferson rose and said:

"'Gentlemen, we have taken a long and impor step. On this new ground we must hang together the end.'

"'We must all hang together or assuredly we all hang separately,' said Franklin with that gentl fatherly smile of his.

"Again the signers laughed.

"Last night I heard Patrick Henry speak. thrilled us with his eloquence. He is a spare but rugged man, whose hands have been used to toil like my own. They tell me that he was a small merchant, farmer and bar-keeper down in Virginia before he became a lawyer and that he educated himself largely by the reading of history. He has a rapid, magnificent diction, slightly flavored with the accent of the Scot."

2

In August, Howe had moved a part of his army from Halifax to Staten Island and offensive operations were daily expected in Washington's army. Jack hurried to his regiment, then in camp with others on the heights back of Brooklyn. The troops there were

not ready for a strong attack. General Greene, who
was in command of the division, had suddenly fallen
ill. Jack crossed the river the night of his arrival with
a message to General Washington. The latter returned with the young Colonel to survey the situation.
They found Solomon at headquarters. He had discovered British scouts in the wooded country near Graves-
   He and Jack were detailed to keep watch of that
of the island and its shores with horses posted at
enient points so that, if necessary, they could make
reports.

Next day, far beyond the outposts in the bush, they
their horses in the little stable near Remsen's cabin
the south road and went on afoot through the bush.
used to tell his friends that the singular alertness
skill of Solomon had never been so apparent as in
the adventures of that day.

"Go careful," Solomon warned as they parted.
"Keep a-goin' south an' don't worry 'bout me."

"I thought that I knew how to be careful, but Solomon took the conceit out of me," Jack was wont to
say. "I was walking along in the bush late that day
when I thought I saw a move far ahead. I stopped
and suddenly discovered that Solomon was standing
beside me.

"I was so startled that I almost let a yelp out of
me.

"He beckoned to me and I followed him. He began
to walk about as fast as I had ever seen him go. He

had been looking for me. Soon he slowed his gait and said in a low voice:

" 'Ain't ye a leetle bit car'less? An Injun wouldn't have no trouble smashin' yer head with a tommyhawk. In this 'ere business ye got to have a swivel in yer neck an' keep 'er twistin'. Ye got to know what's goin' on afore an' behind ye an' on both sides. We must p'int fer camp. This mornin' the British begun to land an army at Gravesend. Out on the road they's waggin loads o' old folks an' women, an' babies on their way to Brooklyn. We got to skitter 'long. Some o' their skirmishers have been workin' back two ways an' may have us cut off.' "

Suddenly Solomon stopped and lifted his hand and listened. Then he dropped and put his ear to the ground. He beckoned to Jack, who crept near him.

"Somebody's nigh us afore an' behind," he whispered. "We better hide till dark comes. You crawl into that ol' holler log. I'll nose myself under a brush pile."

They were in a burnt slash where the soft timber had been cut some time before. The land was covered with a thick, spotty growth of poplar and wild cherry and brush heaps and logs half-rotted. The piece of timber to which Solomon had referred was the base log of a giant hemlock abandoned, no doubt, because, when cut, it was found to be a shell. It was open only at the butt end. Its opening was covered by an immense cobweb. Jack brushed it away and crept back-

ward into the shell.   He observed that many black
hairs were caught upon the rough sides of this singular
chamber.   Through the winter it must have been the
den of a black bear.   As soon as he had settled down,
with his face some two feet from the sunlit air of the
outer world, Jack observed that the industrious spider
had begun again to throw his silvery veil over the great
hole in the log's end.   He watched the process.   First
the outer lines of the structure were woven across the
edges of the opening and made fast at points around
its imperfect circle.   Then the weaver dropped to opposite points, unreeling his slender rope behind him and
making it taut and fast.   He was no slow and clumsy
workman.   He knew his task and rushed about, rapidly strengthening his structure with parallel lines,
having a common center, until his silken floor was in
place again and ready for the death dance of flies and
bees and wasps.   Soon a bumble bee was kicking and
quivering like a stricken ox on its surface.   The spider
rushed upon him and buried his knives in the back and
sides of his prey.   The young man's observation of
this interesting process was interrupted by the sound
of voices and the tread of feet.   They were British
voices.

"They came this way.   I saw them when they
turned," a voice was saying.   "If I had been a little
closer, I could have potted both men with one bullet."

"Why didn't you take a shot anyhow?" another
asked.

"I was creeping up, trying to get closer. They have had to hide or run upon the heels of our people."

A number of men were now sitting on the very log in which Jack was hidden. The young scout saw the legs of a man standing opposite the open end of the log. Then these memorable words were spoken:

"This log is good cover for a man to hide in, but nobody is hid in it. There's a big spider's web over the opening."

There was more talk, in which it came out that nine thousand men were crossing to Gravesend.

"Come on, boys, I'm going back," said one of the party. Whereupon they went away.

Dusk was falling. Jack waited for a move from Solomon. In a few minutes he heard a stir in the brush. Then he could dimly see the face of his friend beyond the spider's web.

"Come on, my son," the latter whispered.

With a feeling of real regret, Jack rent the veil of the spider and came out of his hiding-place. He brushed the silken threads from his hair and brow as he whispered:

"That old spider saved me—good luck to him!"

"We'll keep clus together," Solomon whispered. "We got to push right on an' work 'round 'em. If any one gits in our way, he'll have to change worlds sudden, that's all. We mus' git to them hosses 'fore midnight."

Darkness had fallen, but the moon was rising when

they set out. Solomon led the way, with that long, loose stride of his. Their moccasined feet were about as noiseless as a cat's. On and on they went until Solomon stopped suddenly and stood listening and peering into the dark bush beyond. Jack could hear and see nothing. Solomon turned and took a new direction without a word and moving with the stealth of a hunted Indian. Jack followed closely. Soon they were sinking to their knees in a mossy tamarack swamp, but a few minutes of hard travel brought them to the shore of a pond.

"Wait here till I git the canoe," Solomon whispered.

The latter crept into a thicket and soon Jack could hear him cautiously shoving his canoe into the water. A little later the young man sat in the middle of the shell of birch bark while Solomon knelt in its stern with his paddle. Silently he pushed through the lilied margin of the pond into clear water. The moon was hidden behind the woods. The still surface of the pond was now a glossy, dark plane between two starry deeps—one above, the other beneath. In the shadow of the forest, near the far shore, Solomon stopped and lifted his voice in the long, weird cry of the great bush owl. This he repeated three times, when there came an answer out of the woods.

"That's a warnin' fer ol' Joe Thrasher," Solomon whispered. "He'll go out an' wake up the folks on his road an' start 'em movin'."

They landed and Solomon hid his canoe in a thicket.

"Now we kin skitter right long, but I tell ye we got purty clus to 'em back thar."

"How did you know it?"

"Got a whiff o' smoke. They was strung out from the pond landin' over 'crost the trail. They didn't cover the swamp. Must 'a' had a fire for tea early in the evenin'. Wherever they's an Englishman, thar's got to be tea."

Before midnight they reached Remsen's barn and about two o'clock entered the camp on lathering horses. As they dismounted, looking back from the heights of Brooklyn toward the southeast, they could see a great light from many fires, the flames of which were leaping into the sky.

"Guess the farmers have set their wheat stacks afire," said Solomon. "They're all scairt an' started fer town."

General Washington was with his forces some miles north of the other shore of the river. A messenger was sent for him. Next day the Commander-in-Chief found his Long Island brigades in a condition of disorder and panic. Squads and companies, eager for a fight, were prowling through the bush in the south like hunters after game. A number of the new Connecticut boys had deserted. Some of them had been captured and brought back. In speaking of the matter, Washington said:

"We must be tolerant. These lads are timid. They have been dragged from the tender scenes of domestic life. They are unused to the restraints of war. We must not be too severe."

Jack heard the Commander-in-Chief when he spoke these words.

"The man has a great heart in him, as every great man must," he wrote to his father. "I am beginning to love him. I can see that these thousands in the army are going to be bound to him by an affection like that of a son for a father. With men like Washington and Franklin to lead us, how can we fail?"

The next night Sir Henry Clinton got around the Americans and turned their left flank. Smallwood's command and that of Colonel Jack Irons were almost destroyed, twenty-two hundred having been killed or taken. Jack had his left arm shot through and escaped only by the swift and effective use of his pistols and hanger, and by good luck, his horse having been "only slightly cut in the withers." The American line gave way. Its unseasoned troops fled into Brooklyn. There was the end of the island. They could go no farther without swimming. With a British fleet in the harbor under Admiral Lord Howe, the situation was desperate. Sir Henry had only to follow and pen them in and unlimber his guns. The surrender of more than half of Washington's army would have to follow. At headquarters, the most discerning minds saw that only a miracle could prevent it.

The miracle arrived. Next day a fog thicker than the darkness of a clouded night enveloped the island

and lay upon the face of the waters. Calmly, quickly Washington got ready to move his troops. That night, under the friendly cover of the fog, they were quietly taken across the East River, with a regiment of Marblehead sea dogs, under Colonel Glover, manning the boats. Fortunately, the British army had halted, waiting for clear weather.

3

For nearly two weeks Jack was nursing his wound in Washington's army hospital, which consisted of a cabin, a tent, a number of cow stables and an old shed on the heights of Harlem. Jack had lain in a stable. Toward the end of his confinement, John Adams came to see him.

"Were you badly hurt?" the great man asked.

"Scratched a little, but I'll be back in the service to-morrow," Jack replied.

"You do not look like yourself quite. I think that I will ask the Commander-in-Chief to let you go with me to Philadelphia. I have some business there and later Franklin and I are going to Staten Island to confer with Admiral Lord Howe. We are a pair of snappish old dogs and need a young man like you to look after us. You would only have to keep out of our quarrels, attend to our luggage and make some notes in the conference."

So it happened that Jack went to Philadelphia with Mr. Adams, and, after two days at the house of Doctor Franklin, set out with the two great men for the conference on Staten Island. He went in high hope that he was to witness the last scene of the war.

In Amboy he sent a letter to his father, which said:

"Mr. Adams is a blunt, outspoken man. If things do not go to his liking, he is quick to tell you. Doctor Franklin is humorous and polite, but firm as a God-placed mountain. You may put your shoulder against the mountain and push and think it is moving, but it isn't. He is established. He has found his proper bearings and is done with moving. These two great men differ in little matters. They had a curious quarrel the other evening. We had reached New Brunswick on our way north. The taverns were crowded. I ran from one to another trying to find entertainment for my distinguished friends. At last I found a small chamber with one bed in it and a single window. The bed nearly filled the room. No better accommodation was to be had. I had left them sitting on a bench in a little grove near the large hotel, with the luggage near them. When I returned they were having a hot argument over the origin of northeast storms, the Doctor asserting that he had learned by experiment that they began in the southwest and proceeded in a north-easterly direction. I had to wait ten minutes for a chance to speak to them. Mr. Adams was hot faced, the Doctor calm and smiling. I imparted the news.

" 'God of Israel!' Mr. Adams exclaimed. "Is it not enough that I have to agree with you? Must I also sleep with you?'

" 'Sir, I hope that you must not, but if you must, I beg that you will sleep more gently than you talk,' said Franklin.

"I went with them to their quarters carrying the luggage. On the way Mr. Adams complained that he had picked up a flea somewhere.

" 'The flea, sir, is a small animal, but a big fact,' said Franklin. 'You alarm me. Two large men and a flea will be apt to crowd our quarters.'

"In the room they argued with a depth of feeling which astonished me, as to whether the one window should be open or closed. Mr. Adams had closed it.

" 'Please do not close the window,' said Franklin. 'We shall suffocate.'

" 'Sir, I am an invalid and afraid of the night air,' said Adams rather testily.

" 'The air of this room will be much worse for you than that out-of-doors,' Franklin retorted. He was then between the covers. 'I beg of you to open the window and get into bed and if I do not prove my case to your satisfaction, I will consent to its being closed.'

"I lay down on a straw filled mattress outside their door. I heard Mr. Adams open the window and get into bed. Then Doctor Franklin began to expound his theory of colds. He declared that cold air never gave any one a cold; that respiration destroyed a gallon of air a minute and that all the air in the room would be consumed in an hour. He went on and on and long before he had finished his argument, Mr. Adams was snoring, convinced rather by the length than the cogency of the reasoning. Soon the two great men, whose fame may be said to fill the earth, were asleep in the same bed in that little box of a room and snoring in a way that suggested loud contention. I had to laugh as I listened. Mr. Adams would seem to have been defeated, for, by and by, I heard him muttering as he walked the floor."

Howe's barge met the party at Amboy and conveyed them to the landing near his headquarters. It was, however, a fruitless journey. Howe wished to negotiate on the old ground now abandoned forever. The people of America had spoken for independence—a new, irrevocable fact not to be put aside by ambassadors. The colonies were lost. The concessions which the wise Franklin had so urgently recommended to the government of England, Howe seemed now inclined to offer, but they could not be entertained.

"Then my government can only maintain its dignity by fighting," said Howe.

"That is a mistaken notion," Franklin answered. "It will be much more dignified for your government to acknowledge its error than to persist in it."

"We shall fight," Howe declared.

"And you will have more fighting to do than you anticipate," said Franklin. "Nature is our friend and ally. The Lord has prepared our defenses. They are the sea, the mountains, the forest and the character of our people. Consider what you have accomplished. At an expense of eight million pounds, you have killed about eight hundred Yankees. They have cost you ten thousand pounds a head. Meanwhile, at least a hundred thousand children have been born in America. There are the factors in your problem. How much time and money will be required for the job of killing all of us?"

The British Admiral ignored the query.

"My powers are limited," said he, "but I am authorized to grant pardons and in every way to exercise the King's paternal solicitude."

"Such an offer shows that your proud nation has no flattering opinion of us," Franklin answered. "We, who are the injured parties, have not the baseness to entertain it. You will forgive me for reminding you that the King's paternal solicitude has been rather trying. It has burned our defenseless towns in mid-winter; it has incited the savages to massacre our farmers in the back country; it has driven us to a declaration of independence. Britain and America are now distinct states. Peace can be considered only on that basis. You wish to prevent our trade from passing into foreign channels. Let me remind you, also, that the profit of no trade can ever be equal to the expense of holding it with fleets and armies."

"On such a basis I am not empowered to treat with you," Howe answered. "We shall immediately move against your army."

The conference ended. The ambassadors and their secretary shook hands with the British Admiral.

"Mr. Irons, I have heard much of you," said the latter as he held Jack's hand. "You are deeply attached to a young lady whom I admire and whose father is my friend. I offer you a chance to leave this troubled land and go to London and marry and lead a peaceable, Christian life. You may keep your principles, if you wish, as I have no use for them. You will find sympathizers in England."

"Lord Howe, your kindness touches me," the young man answered. "What you propose is a great temptation. It is like Calypso's offer of immortal happiness to Ulysses. I love England. I love peace, and more than either, I love the young lady, but I couldn't go and keep my principles."

"Why not, sir?"

"Because we are all of a mind with our Mr. Patrick Henry. We put Liberty above happiness and even above life. So I must stay and help fight her battles, and when I say it I am grinding my own heart under my heel. Don't think harshly of me. I can not help it. The feeling is bred in my bones."

His Lordship smiled politely and bowed as the three men withdrew.

Franklin took the hand of the young man and pressed it silently as they were leaving the small house in which Howe had established himself.

Jack, who had been taking notes of the fruitless talk

of these great men, was sorely disappointed.   He could see no prospect now of peace.

"My hopes are burned to the ground," he said to Doctor Franklin.

"It is a time of sacrifice," the good man answered. "You have the invincible spirit that looks into the future and gives all it has.   You are America."

"I have been thinking too much of myself," Jack answered.   "Now I am ready to lay down my life in this great cause of ours."

"Boy, I like you," said Mr. Adams.   "I have arranged to have you safely conveyed to New York. There an orderly will meet and conduct you to our headquarters."

"Thank you, sir," Jack replied.   Turning to Doctor Franklin, he added:

"One remark of yours to Lord Howe impressed me. You said that Nature was our friend and ally.   It put me in mind of the fog that helped us out of Brooklyn and of a little adventure of mine."

Then he told the story of the spider's web.

"I repeat that all Nature is with us," said Franklin. "It was a sense of injustice in human nature that sent us across the great barrier of the sea into conditions where only the strong could survive.   Here we have raised up a sturdy people with three thousand miles of water between them and tyranny. Armies can not cross it and succeed long in a hostile land.   They are too far

from home. The expense of transporting and main-
taining them will bleed our enemies until they are
spent. The British King is powerful, but now he has
picked a quarrel with Almighty God, and it will go
hard with him."

CHAPTER XVII

WITH THE ARMY AND IN THE BUSH

In January, 1777, Colonel Irons writes to his father from Morristown, New Jersey, as follows:

"An army is a despotic machine. For that reason chiefly our men do not like military service. It is hard to induce them to enlist for long terms. They are released by expiration long before they have been trained and seasoned for good service. So Washington has found it difficult to fill his line with men of respectable fighting quality.

"Our great Commander lost his patience on the eve of our leaving New York. Our troops, posted at Kip's Bay on the East River to defend the landing, fled in a panic without firing a gun at the approach of Howe's army. I happened to be in a company of Light Horse with General Washington, who had gone up to survey the ground. Before his eyes two brigades of New England troops ran away, leaving us exposed to capture.

"The great Virginian was hot with indignation. He threw his hat to the ground and exclaimed:

"'Are these the kind of men with whom I am to defend America?'

"Next day our troops behaved better and succeeded

in repulsing the enemy. This put new spirit in them. Putnam got his forces out of New York and well up the shore of the North River. For weeks we lay behind our trenches on Harlem Heights, building up the fighting spirit of our men and training them for hard service. The stables, cabins and sheds of Harlem were full of our sick. Smallpox had got among them. Cold weather was coming on and few were clothed to stand it. The proclamation of Admiral Lord Howe and his brother, the General, offering pardon and protection to all who remained loyal to the crown, caused some to desert us, and many timid settlers in the outlying country, with women and children to care for, were on the fence ready to jump either way. Hundreds were driven by fear toward the British.

"In danger of being shut in, we crossed King's Bridge and retreated to White Plains. How we toiled with our baggage on that journey, many of us being yoked like oxen to the wagons! Every day troops, whose terms of enlistment had expired, were leaving us. It seemed as if our whole flying camp would soon be gone. But there were many like Solomon and me who were willing to give up everything for the cause and follow our beloved Commander into hell, if necessary. There were some four thousand of us who streaked up the Hudson with him to King's Ferry, at the foot of the Highlands, to get out of the way of the British ships. There we crossed into Jersey and dodged about, capturing a thousand men at Trenton and three hundred at Princeton, defeating the British regiments who pursued us and killing many officers and men and cutting off their army from its supplies. We have seized a goodly number of cannon and valuable stores and reclaimed New Jersey and stiffened the necks of our people. It has been, I think, a turning point in the war. Our men have fought like Homeric heroes and endured great hardships in the bitter cold with worn-out shoes and inadequate clothing. A number have been frozen to death. I loaned my last extra pair of shoes to a poor fellow whose feet had been badly cut and frozen. When I tell you that coming into Morristown I saw many bloody footprints in the snow behind the army, you will understand. We are a ragamuffin band, but we have taught the British to respect us. Send all the shoes and clothing you can scare up.

"I have seen incidents which have increased my love of Washington. When we were marching through a village in good weather there was a great crowd in the street. In the midst of it was a little girl crying out because she could not see Washington. He stopped and called for her. They brought the child and he lifted her to the saddle in front of him and carried her a little way on his big white horse.

"At the first divine service here in Morristown he observed an elderly woman, a rough clad farmer's wife, standing back in the edge of the crowd. He arose and beckoned to her to come and take his seat. She did so, and he stood through the service, save when he was kneeling. Of course, many offered him their seats, but he refused to take one.

"We have been deeply impressed and inspirited by the address of a young man of the name of Alexander Hamilton. He is scarcely twenty years of age, they tell me, but he has wit and eloquence and a maturity of understanding which astonished me. He is slender, a bit under middle stature and has a handsome face and courtly manners. He will be one of the tallest candles of our faith, or I am no prophet.

"Solomon has been a tower of strength in this campaign. I wish you could have seen him lead the charge against Mercer's men and bring in the British general, whom he had wounded. He and I are scouting around the camp every day. Our men are billeted up and down the highways and living in small huts around headquarters."

Washington had begun to show his great and singular gifts. One of them, through which he secured rest and safety for his shattered forces, shone out there in Morristown. There were only about three thousand effective men in his army. To conceal their number, he had sent them to many houses on the roads leading into the village. The British in New York numbered at least nine thousand well seasoned troops, and with good reason he feared an attack. The force at Morristown was in great danger. One day a New York merchant was brought into camp by the famous scout Solomon Binkus. The merchant had been mistreated by the British. He had sold his business and crossed the river by night and come through the lines on the wagon of a farmer friend who was bringing supplies to the American army. He gave much information as to plans and positions of the British, which was known to be correct. He wished to enlist in the American army and do what he could to help it. He was put to work in the ranks. A few days later the farmer with whom he had arrived came again and, after selling his wagon load, found the ex-merchant and conferred with him in private. That evening, when the farmer had got a mile or so from camp, he was stopped and searched by Colonel Irons. A letter was found in the farmer's pocket which clearly indicated that the ex-merchant was a spy and the farmer a Tory. Irons went at once to General Washington with his report, urging that the spy be taken up and put in confinement.

The General sat thoughtfully looking into the fire, but made no answer.

"He is here to count our men and report our weakness," said the Colonel.

"The poor fellow has not found it an easy thing to do," the General answered. "I shall see that he gets help."

They went together to the house where the Adjutant General had his home and office. To this officer Washington said:

"General, you have seen a report from one Weatherly, a New York merchant, who came with information from that city. Will you kindly do him the honor of asking him to dine with you here alone to-morrow evening? Question him as to the situation in New York in a friendly manner and impart to him such items of misinformation as you may care to give, but mainly look to this. Begin immediately to get signed returns from the brigadiers showing that we have an effective force here of twelve thousand men. These reports must be lying on your desk while you are conferring with Weatherly. Treat the man with good food and marked politeness and appreciation of the service he is likely to render us. Soon after you have eaten, I shall send an orderly here. He will deliver a message. You will ask the man to make himself at home while you are gone for half an hour or so. You will see that the window shades are drawn and the door closed and that no one disturbs the man while he is copying those returns, which he will be sure to do. Colonel Irons, I depend upon you to see to it that he has an opportunity to escape safely with his budget. I warn you not to let him fail. It is most important."

The next morning, Weatherly was ordered to report to Major Binkus for training in scout duty, and the morning after that he was taken out through the lines, mounted, with Colonel Irons and carefully lost in the pine bush. He was seen no more in the American camp. The spy delivered his report to the British and

the little remnant of an army at Morristown was safe
for the winter. Cornwallis and Howe put such confidence in this report that when Luce, another spy, came
into their camp with a count of Washington's forces,
which was substantially correct, they doubted the good
faith of the man and threw him into prison.

So the great Virginian had turned a British spy
into one of his most effective helpers.

Meanwhile good news had encouraged enlistment
for long terms. Four regiments of horse were put in
training, ten frigates were built and sent to sea and
more were under construction. The whole fighting
force of America was being reorganized. Moreover,
in this first year the Yankee privateers had so wounded
a leg of the British lion that he was roaring with rage.
Three hundred and fifty of his ships, well laden from
the West Indies, had been seized. Their cargoes were
valued at a million pounds. The fighting spirit of
America was encouraged also by events in France,
where Franklin and Silas Deane were now at work.
France had become an ally. A loan of six hundred
thousand dollars had been secured in the French capital
and expert officers from that country had begun to
arrive to join the army of Washington.

CHAPTER XVIII

IN THE spring news came of a great force of British which was being organized in Canada for a descent upon New York through Lake Champlain. Frontier settlers in Tryon County were being massacred by Indians.

Generals Herkimer and Schuyler had written to Washington, asking for the services of the famous scout, Solomon Binkus, in that region.

"He knows the Indian as no other man knows him and can speak his language and he also knows the bush," Schuyler had written. "If there is any place on earth where his help is needed just now, it is here."

"Got to leave ye, my son," Solomon said to Jack one evening soon after that.

"How so?" the young man asked.

"Goin' hum to fight Injuns. The Great Father has ordered it. I'll like it better. Gittin' lazy here. Summer's comin' an' I'm a born bush man. I'm kind o' oneasy—like a deer in a dooryard. I ain't had to run fer my life since we got here. My hoofs are complainin'. I ain't shot a gun in a month."

A look of sorrow spread over the face of Solomon.

"I'm tired of this place," said Jack. "The British are scared of us and we're scared of the British.

There's nothing going on. I'd love to go back to the big bush with you."

"I'll tell the Great Father that you're a born bush man. Mebbe he'll let ye go. They'll need us both. Rum, Injuns an' the devil have j'ined hands. The Long House will be the center o' hell an' its line fences 'll take in the hull big bush."

That day Jack's name was included in the order.

"I am sorry that it is not yet possible to pay you or any of the men who have served me so faithfully," said Washington. "If you need money I shall be glad to lend you a sum to help you through this journey."

"I ain't fightin' fer pay," Solomon answered. "I'll hoe an' dig, an' cook, an' guide fer money. But I won't fight no more fer money—partly 'cause I don't need it—partly 'cause I'm fightin' fer myself. I got a little left in my britches pocket, but if I hadn't, my ol' Marier wouldn't let me go hungry."

2

In April the two friends set out afoot for the lower end of the Highlands. On the river they hired a Dutch farmer to take them on to Albany in his sloop. After two delightful days at home, General Schuyler suggested that they could do a great service by traversing the wilderness to the valley of the great river of the north, as far as possible toward Swegachie, and reporting their observations to Crown Point or Fort Edward, if there seemed to be occasion for it, and if not, they were to proceed to General Herkimer's camp at Oris-

kany and give him what help they could in protecting
the settlers in the west.

"You would need to take all your wit and courage
with you," the General warned them. "The Indians
are in bad temper. They have taken to roasting their
prisoners at the stake and eating their flesh. This is a
hazardous undertaking. Therefore, I give you a suggestion and not an order."

"I'll go 'lone," said Solomon. "If I get et up it
needn't break nobody's heart. Let Jack go to one o'
the forts."

"No, I'd rather go into the bush with you," said
Jack. "We're both needed there. If necessary we
could separate and carry our warning in two directions. We'll take a couple of the new double-barreled
rifles and four pistols. If we had to, I think we could
fight a hole through any trouble we are likely to
have."

So it was decided that they should go together on
this scouting trip into the north bush. Solomon had
long before that invented what he called "a lightnin'
thrower" for close fighting with Indians, to be used
if one were hard pressed and outnumbered and likely
to have his scalp taken. This odd contrivance he had
never had occasion to use. It was a thin, round shell
of cast iron with a tube, a flint and plunger. The shell
was of about the size of a large apple. It was to be
filled with missiles and gunpowder. The plunger, with
its spring, was set vertically above the tube. In throw-

ing this contrivance one released its spring by the pressure of his thumb. The hammer fell and the spark it made ignited a fuse leading down to the powder. Its owner had to throw it from behind a tree or have a share in the peril it was sure to create.

While Jack was at home with his people Solomon spent a week in the foundry and forge and, before they set out on their journey, had three of these unique weapons, all loaded and packed in water-proof wrappings.

About the middle of May they proceeded in a light bark canoe to Fort Edward and carried it across country to Lake George and made their way with paddles to Ticonderoga. There they learned that scouts were operating only on and near Lake Champlain. The interior of Tryon County was said to be dangerous ground. Mohawks, Cagnawagas, Senecas, Algonquins and Hurons were thick in the bush and all on the warpath. They were torturing and eating every white man that fell in their hands, save those with a Tory mark on them.

"We're skeered o' the bush," said an elderly bearded soldier, who was sitting on a log. "A man who goes into the wildwood needs to be a good friend o' God."

"But Schuyler thinks a force of British may land somewhere along the big river and come down through the bush, building a road as they advance," said Jack.

"A thousand men could make a tol'able waggin road to Fort Edward in a month," Solomon declared.

"That's mebbe the reason the Injuns are out in the bush eatin' Yankees. They're tryin' fer to skeer us an' keep us erway. By the hide an' horns o' the devil! We got to know what's a-goin' on out thar. You fellers are a-settin' eround these 'ere forts as if ye had nothin' to do but chaw beef steak an' wipe yer rifles an' pick yer teeth. Why don't ye go out thar in the bush and do a little skeerin' yerselves? Ye're like a lot o' ol' women settin' by the fire an' tellin' ghos' stories."

"We got 'nuff to do considerin' the pay we git," said a sergeant.

"Hell an' Tophet! What do ye want o' pay?" Solomon answered. "Ain't ye willin' to fight fer yer own liberty without bein' paid fer it? Ye been kicked an' robbed an' spit on, an' dragged eround by the heels, an' ye don't want to fight 'less somebody pays ye. What a dam' corn fiddle o' a man ye mus' be!"

Solomon was putting fresh provisions in his pack as he talked.

"All the Injuns o' Kinady an' the great grass lands may be snookin' down through the bush. We're bound fer t' know what's a-goin' on out thar. We're liable to be skeered, but also an' likewise we'll do some skeerin' 'fore we give up—you hear to me."

Jack and Solomon set out in the bush that afternoon and before night fell were up on the mountain slants north of the Glassy Water, as Lake George was often called those days. But for Solomon's caution an evil fate had perhaps come to them before their first sleep on the journey. The new leaves were just out, but not quite full. The little maples and beeches flung their sprays of vivid green foliage above the darker shades of the witch hopple into the soft-lighted air of the great house of the wood and filled it with a pleasant odor. A mile or so back, Solomon had left the trail and cautioned Jack to keep close and step softly. Soon the old scout stopped and listened and put his ear to the ground. He rose and beckoned to Jack and the two turned aside and made their way stealthily up the slant of a ledge. In the edge of a little thicket on a mossy rock shelf they sat down. Solomon looked serious. There were deep furrows in the skin above his brow.

When he was excited in the bush he had the habit of swallowing and the process made a small, creaky sound in his throat. This Jack observed then and at other times. Solomon was peering down through the bushes toward the west, now and then moving his head a little. Jack looked in the same direction and presently saw a move in the bushes below, but nothing more. After a few minutes Solomon turned and whispered:

"Four Injun braves jist went by. Mebbe they're scoutin' fer a big band—mebbe not. If so, the crowd is up the trail. If they're comin' by, it'll be 'fore dark. We'll stop in this 'ere tavern. They's a cave on t'other side o' the ledge as big as a small house."

They watched until the sun had set. Then Solomon

led Jack to the cave, in which their packs were deposited.

From the cave's entrance they looked upon the undulating green roof of the forest dipping down into a deep valley, cut by the smooth surface of a broad river with mirrored shores, and lifting to the summit of a distant mountain range. Its blue peaks rose into the glow of the sunset.

"Yonder is the great stairway of Heaven!" Jack exclaimed.

"I've put up in this 'ere ol' tavern many a night," said Solomon. "Do ye see its sign?"

He pointed to a great dead pine that stood a little below it, towering with stark, outreaching limbs more than a hundred and fifty feet into the air.

"I call it The Dead Pine Tavern," Solomon remarked.

"On the road to Paradise," said Jack as he gazed down the valley, his hands shading his eyes.

"Wisht we could have a nice hot supper, but 'twon't do to build no fire. Nothin' but cold vittles! I'll go down with the pot to a spring an' git some water. You dig fer our supper in that pack o' mine an' spread it out here. I'm hungry."

They ate their bread and dried meat moistened with spring water, picked some balsam boughs and covered a corner of the mossy floor with them. When the rock chamber was filled with their fragrance, Jack said:

"If my dream comes true and Margaret and I are

married, I shall bring her here. I want her to see The Dead Pine Tavern and its outlook."

"Ayes, sir, when ye're married safe," Solomon answered. "We'll come up here fust summer an' fish, an' hunt, an' I'll run the tavern an' do the cookin' an' sweep the floor an' make the beds!"

"I'm a little discouraged," said Jack. "This war may last for years."

"Keep up on high ground er ye'll git mired down," Solomon answered. "Ain't nuther on ye very old yit, an' fust ye know these troubles 'll be over an' done."

Jack awoke at daylight and found that he was alone. Solomon returned in half an hour or so.

"Been scoutin' up the trail," he said. "Didn't see a thing but an ol' gnaw bucket. We'll jest eat a bite an' p'int off to the nor'west an' keep watch o' this 'ere trail. They's Injuns over thar on the slants. We got to know how they look an' 'bout how many head they is."

They went on, keeping well away from the trail.

"We'll have to watch it with our ears," said Solomon in a whisper.

His ear was often on the ground that morning and twice he left Jack to "snook" out to the trail and look for tracks. Solomon could imitate the call of the swamp robin, and when they were separated in the bush, he gave it so that his friend could locate him. At midday they sat down in deep shade by the side of a brook and ate their luncheon.

"This 'ere is Peppermint Brook," said Solomon. "It's 'nother one o' my taverns."

"Our food isn't going to last long at the rate we are eating it," Jack remarked. "If we can't shoot a gun what are we going to do when it's all gone?"

"Don't worry," Solomon answered. "Ye're in my kentry now an' there's a better tavern up in the high trail."

They fared along, favored by good weather, and spent that night on the shore of a little pond not more than fifty paces off the old blazed thoroughfare. Next day, about "half-way from dawn to dark," as Solomon was wont, now and then, to speak of the noon hour, they came suddenly upon fresh "sign." It was where the big north trail from the upper waters of the Mohawk joined the one near which they had been traveling. When they were approaching the point Solomon had left Jack in a thicket and cautiously crept out to the "juncshin." There was half an hour of silence before the old scout came back in sight and beckoned to Jack. His face had never looked more serious. The young man approached him. Solomon swallowed—a part of the effort to restrain his emotions.

"Want to show ye suthin'," he whispered.

The two went cautiously toward the trail. When they reached it the old scout led the way to soft ground near a brook. Then he pointed down at the mud. There were many footprints, newly made, and among them the print of that wooden peg with an iron ring around its bottom, which they had seen twice before, and which was associated with the blackest memories they knew. For some time Solomon studied the surface of the trail in silence.

"More'n twenty Injuns, two captives, a pair o' hosses, a cow an' the devil," he whispered to Jack. "Been a raid down to the Mohawk Valley. The cow an' the hosses are loaded with plunder. I've noticed that when the Injuns go out to rob an' kill folks ye find, 'mong their tracks, the print o' that 'ere iron ring. I seen it twice in the Ohio kentry. Here is the heart o' the devil an' his fire-water. Red Snout has got to be started on a new trail. His ol' peg leg is goin' down to the gate o' hell to-night."

Solomon's face had darkened with anger. There were deep furrows across his brow.

Standing before Jack about three feet away, he drew out his ram rod and tossed it to the young man, who caught it a little above the middle. Jack knew the meaning of this. They were to put their hands upon the ram rod, one above the other. The last hand it would hold was to do the killing. It was Solomon's.

"Thank God!" he whispered, as his face brightened.

He seemed to be taking careful aim with his right eye.

"It's my job," said he. "I wouldn't 'a' let ye do it if ye'd drawed the chanst. It's my job—proper. They ain't an hour ahead. Mebbe—it's jest possible—he

may go to sleep to-night 'fore I do, an' I wouldn't be
supprised.   They'll build their fire at the Caverns on
Rock Crick an' roast a captive.   We'll cross the bush
an' come up on t' other side an' see what's goin' on."

They crossed a high ridge, with Solomon tossing
his feet in that long, loose stride of his, and went down
the slope into a broad valley.   The sun sank low and
the immeasurable green roofed house of the wild was
dim and dusk when the old scout halted.   Ahead in the
distance they had heard voices and the neighing of a
horse.

"My son," said Solomon as he pointed with his finger, "do you see the brow o' the hill yonder whar the
black thickets be?"

Jack nodded.

"If ye hear to me ye'll stay this side.   This 'ere
business is kind o' neevarious.   I'm a-goin' clus up.
If I come back ye'll hear the call o' the bush owl.   If
I don't come 'fore mornin' you p'int fer hum an' the
good God go with ye."

"I shall go as far as you go," Jack answered.

Solomon spoke sternly.   The genial tone of good
comradeship had left him.

"Ye kin go, but ye ain't obleeged," said he.   "Bear
in mind, boy.   To-night I'm the Cap'n.   Do as I tell ye
—*exact.*"

He took the lightning hurlers out of the packs and
unwrapped them and tried the springs above the ham-
mers.   Earlier in the day he had looked to the priming.

Solomon gave one to Jack and put the other two in his pockets. Each examined his pistols and adjusted them in his belt. They started for the low lying ridge above the little valley of Rock Creek. It was now quite dark and looking down through the thickets of hemlock they could see the firelight of the Indians and hear the wash of the creek water. Suddenly a wild whooping among the red men, savage as the howl of wolves on the trail of a wounded bison, ran beyond them, far out into the forest, and sent its echoes traveling from hilltop to mountain side. Then came a sound which no man may hear without getting, as Solomon was wont to say, "a scar on his soul which he will carry beyond the last cape." It was the death cry of a captive. Solomon had heard it before. He knew what it meant. The fire was taking hold and the smoke had begun to smother him. Those cries were like the stabbing of a. knife and the recollection of them like blood-stains.

They hurried down the slant, brushing through the thicket, the sound of their approach being covered by the appalling cries of the victim and the demon-like tumult of the drunken braves. The two scouts were racked with soul pain as they went on so that they could scarcely hold their peace and keep their feet from running. A new sense of the capacity for evil in the heart of man entered the mind of Jack. They had come close to the frightful scene, when suddenly a deep silence fell upon it. Thank God, the victim had gone beyond the reach of pain. Something had hap-

pened in his passing—perhaps the savages had thought
it a sign from Heaven. For a moment their clamor
had ceased. The two scouts could plainly see the poor
man behind a red veil of flame. Suddenly the white
leader of the raiders approached the pyre, limping on
his wooden stump, with a stick in his hand, and
prodded the face of the victim. It was his last act.
Solomon was taking aim. His rifle spoke. Red Snout
tumbled forward into the fire. Then what a scurry
among the Indians! They vanished and so suddenly
that Jack wondered where they had gone. Solomon
stood reloading the rifle barrel he had just emptied.
Then he said:

"Come on an' do as I do."

Solomon ran until they had come near. Then he
jumped from tree to tree, stopping at each long enough
to survey the ground beyond it. This was what he
called "swapping cover." From behind a tree near
the fire he shouted in the Indian tongue:

"Red men, you have made the Great Spirit angry.
He has sent the Son of the Thunder to slay you with
his lightning."

No truer words had ever left the lips of man. His
hand rose and swung back of his shoulder and shot
forward. The round missile sailed through the firelight and beyond it and sank into black shadows in the
great cavern at Rocky Creek—a famous camping-place
in the old time. Then a flash of white light and a roar
that shook the hills! A blast of gravel and dust and

debris shot upward and pelted down upon the earth. Bits of rock and wood and an Indian's arm and foot fell in the firelight. A number of dusky figures scurried out of the mouth of the cavern and ran for their lives shouting prayers to Manitou as they disappeared in the darkness. Solomon pulled the embers from around the feet of the victim.

"Now, by the good God A'mighty, 'pears to me we got the skeer shifted so the red man'll be the rabbit fer a while an' I wouldn't wonder," said Solomon, as he stood looking down at the scene. "He ain't a-goin' to like the look o' a pale face—not overly much. Them Injuns that got erway 'll never stop runnin' till they've reached the middle o' next week."

He seized the foot of Red Snout and pulled his head out of the fire.

"You ol' hellion!" Solomon exclaimed. "You dog o' the devil! Tumbled into hell whar ye b'long at last, didn't ye? Jack, you take that luther bucket an' bring some water out o' the creek an' put out this fire. The ring on this 'ere ol' wooden leg is wuth a hundred pounds."

Solomon took the hatchet from his belt and hacked off the end of Red Snout's wooden leg and put it in his coat pocket, saying:

"From now on a white man can walk in the bush without gittin' his bones picked. Injuns is goin' to be skeered o' us—a few an' I wouldn't be supprised."

When Jack came back with the water, Solomon

poured it on the embers and looked at the swollen form which still seemed to be straining at the green withes of moose wood.

"Nothin' kin be done fer him," said the old scout. "He's gone erway. I tell ye, Jack, it g'in my soul a sweat to hear him dyin'."

A moment of silence full of the sorrow of the two men followed. Solomon broke it by saying:

"That 'ere black pill o' mine went right down into the stummick o' the hill an' give it quite a puke—you hear to me."

They went to the cavern's mouth and looked in.

"They's an awful mess in thar. I don't keer to see it," said Solomon.

Near them they discovered a warrior who had crawled out of that death chamber in the rocks. He had been stunned and wounded about the shoulders. They helped him to his feet and led him away. He was trembling with fear. Solomon found a pine torch, still burning, near where the fire had been. By its light they dressed his wounds—the old scout having with him always a small surgeon's outfit.

"Whar is t' other captive?" he asked in the Indian tongue.

"About a mile down the trail. It's a woman and a boy," said the warrior.

"Take us whar they be," Solomon commanded.

The three started slowly down the trail, the warrior leading them.

"Son of the Thunder, throw no more lightning and I will kiss your mighty hand and do as you tell me," said the Indian, as they set out.

It was now dark. Jack saw, through the opening in the forest roof above the trail, Orion and the Pleiades looking down at them, as beautiful as ever, and now he could hear the brook singing merrily.

"I could have chided the stars and the brook while the Indian and I were waiting for Solomon to bring the packs," he wrote in his diary.

CHAPTER XIX

THE VOICE OF A WOMAN SOBBING

OVER the ridge and more than a mile away was a wet, wild meadow. They found the cow and horses feeding on its edge near the trail. The moon, clouded since dark, had come out in the clear mid-heavens and thrown its light into the high windows of the forest above the ancient thoroughfare of the Indian. The red guide of the two scouts gave a call which was quickly answered. A few rods farther on, they saw a pair of old Indians sitting in blankets near a thicket of black timber. They could hear the voice of a woman sobbing near where they stood.

"Womern, don't be skeered o' us—we're friends—we're goin' to take ye hum," said Solomon.

The woman came out of the thicket with a little lad of four asleep in her arms.

"Where do ye live?" Solomon asked.

"Far south on the shore o' the Mohawk," she answered in a voice trembling with emotion.

"What's yer name?"

"I'm Bill Scott's wife," she answered.

"Cat's blood and gunpowder!" Solomon exclaimed. "I'm Sol Binkus."

She knelt before the old scout and kissed his knees

283

and could not speak for the fulness of her heart. Solomon bent over and took the sleeping lad from her arms and held him against his breast.

"Don't feel bad. We're a-goin' to take keer o' you," said Solomon. "Ayes, sir, we be! They ain't nobody goin' to harm ye—nobody at all."

There was a note of tenderness in the voice of the man as he felt the chin of the little lad with his big thumb and finger.

"Do ye know what they done with Bill?" the woman asked soon in a pleading voice.

The scout swallowed as his brain began to work on the problem in hand.

"Bill broke loose an' got erway. He's gone," Solomon answered in a sad voice.

"Did they torture him?"

"What they done I couldn't jes' tell ye. But they kin't do no more to him. He's gone."

She seemed to sense his meaning and lay crouched upon the ground with her sorrow until Solomon lifted her to her feet and said:

"Look here, little womern, this don't do no good. I'm goin' to spread my blanket under the pines an' I want ye to lay down with yer boy an' git some sleep. We got a long trip to-morrer.

" 'Tain't so bad as it might be—ye're kind o' lucky a'ter all is said an' done," he remarked as he covered the woman and the child.

The wounded warrior and the old men were not to

be found. They had sneaked away into the bush. Jack and Solomon looked about and the latter called but got no answer.

"They're skeered cl'ar down to the toe nails," said Solomon. "They couldn't stan' it here. A lightnin' thrower is a few too many. They'd ruther be nigh a rattlesnake."

The scouts had no sleep that night. They sat down by the trail side leaning against a log and lighted their pipes.

"You 'member Bill Scott?" Solomon whispered.

"Yes. We spent a night in his house."

"He were a mean cuss. Sold rum to the Injuns. I allus tol' him it were wrong but—my God A'mighty! —I never 'spected that the fire in the water were a goin' to burn him up sometime. No, sir—I never dreamed he were a-goin' to be punished so—never."

They lay back against the log with their one blanket spread and spent the night in a kind of half sleep. Every little sound was "like a kick in the ribs," as Solomon put it, and drove them "into the look and listen business." The woman was often crying out or the cow and horses getting up to feed.

"My son, go to sleep," said Solomon. "I tell ye there ain't no danger now—not a bit. I don't know much but I know Injuns—plenty."

In spite of his knowledge even Solomon himself could not sleep. A little before daylight they arose and began to stir about.

"I was badly burnt by that fire," Jack whispered.

"Inside!" Solomon answered. "So was I. My soul were a-sweatin' all night."

The morning was chilly. They gathered birch bark and dry pine and soon had a fire going. Solomon stole over to the thicket where the woman and child were lying and returned in a moment.

"They're sound asleep," he said in a low tone. "We'll let 'em alone."

He began to make tea and got out the last of their bread and dried meat and bacon. He was frying the latter when he said:

"That 'ere is a mighty likely womern."

He turned the bacon with his fork and added:

"Turrible purty when she were young. Allus hated the rum business."

Jack went out on the wild meadow and brought in the cow and milked her, filling a basin and a quart bottle.

Solomon went to the thicket and called:

"Mis' Scott!"

The woman answered.

"Here's a tow'l an' a leetle jug o' soap, Mis' Scott. Ye kin take the boy to the crick an' git washed an' then come to the fire an' eat yer breakfust."

The boy was a handsome, blond lad with blue eyes and a serious manner. His confidence in the protection of his mother was sublime.

"What's yer name?" Solomon asked, looking up at the lad whom he had lifted high in the air.

"Whig Scott," the boy answered timidly with tears in his eyes.

"What! Be ye skeered o' me?"

These words came from the little lad as he began to cry. "No, sir. I ain't skeered. I'm a brave man."

"Courage is the first virtue in which the young are schooled on the frontier," Jack wrote in a letter to his friends at home in which he told of the history of that day. "The words and manner of the boy reminded me of my own childhood.

"Solomon held Whig in his lap and fed him and soon won his confidence. The backs of the horses and the cow were so badly galled they could not be ridden, but we were able to lash the packs over a blanket on one of the horses. We drove the beasts ahead of us. The Indians had timbered the swales here and there so that we were able to pass them with little trouble. Over the worst places I had the boy on my back while Solomon carried 'Mis' Scott' in his arms as if she were a baby. He was very gentle with her. To him, as you know, a woman has been a sacred creature since his wife died. He seemed to regard the boy as a wonderful kind of plaything. At the camping-places he spent every moment of his leisure tossing him in the air or rolling on the ground with him.

"One day when the woman sat by the fire crying, the little lad touched her brow with his hand and said:

" 'Don't be skeered, mother. I'm brave. I'll take care o' you.'

"Solomon came to where I was breaking some dry sticks for the fire and said laughingly, as he wiped a tear from his cheek with the back of his great right hand:

" 'Did ye ever see sech a gol' durn cunnin' leetle cricket in yer born days—ever?'

"Always thereafter he referred to the boy as the Little Cricket.

"That would have been a sad journey but for my interest in these reactions on this great son of Pan, with whom I traveled. I think that he has found a thing he has long needed, and I wonder what will come of it.

"When he had discovered, by tracks in the trail, that the Indians who had run away from us were gone South, he had no further fear of being molested.

" 'They've gone on to tell what happened on the first o' the high slants an' to warn their folks that the Son o' the Thunder is comin' with lightnin' in his hands. Injuns is like rabbits when the Great Spirit begins to rip 'em up. They kin't stan' it.' "

That afternoon Solomon, with a hook and line and grubs, gathered from rotted stumps, caught many trout in a brook crossing the trail and fried them with slices of salt pork. In the evening they had the best supper

John Wolcott Adams

of their journey in what he called "The Catamount Tavern." It was an old bark lean-to facing an immense boulder on the shore of a pond. There, one night some years before, he had killed a catamount. It was in the foot-hills remote from the trail. In a side of the rock was a small bear den or cavern with an overhanging roof which protected it from the weather. On a shelf in the cavern was a round block of pine about two feet in diameter and a foot and a half long. This block was his preserve jar. A number of two-inch augur holes had been bored in its top and filled with jerked venison and dried berries. They had been packed with a cotton wick fastened to a small bar of wood at the bottom of each hole. Then hot deer's fat had been poured in with the meat and berries until the holes were filled within an inch or so of the top. When the fat had hardened a thin layer of melted beeswax sealed up the contents of each hole. Over all wooden plugs had been driven fast.

"They's good vittles in that 'ere block," said Solomon. "'Nough, I guess, to keep a man a week. All he has to do is knock out the plug an' pull the wick an' be happy."

"Going to do any pulling for supper?" Jack queried.

"Nary bit," said Solomon. "Too much food in the woods now. We got to be savin'. Mebbe you er I er both on us 'll be comin' through here in the winter time skeered o' Injuns an' short o' fodder. Then we'll open the pine jar."

They had fish and tea and milk and that evening as he sat on his blanket before the fire with the little lad in his lap he sang an old rig-a-dig tune and told stories and answered many a query.

Jack wrote in one of his letters that as they fared along, down toward the sown lands of the upper Mohawk, Solomon began to develop talents of which none of his friends had entertained the least suspicion.

"He has had a hard life full of fight and peril like most of us who were born in this New World," the young man wrote. "He reminds me of some of the Old Testament heroes, and is not this land we have traversed like the plains of Mamre? What a gentle creature he might have been if he had had a chance! How long, I wonder, must we be slayers of men? As long, I take it, as there are savages against whom we must defend ourselves."

The next morning they met a company of one of the regiments of General Herkimer who had gone in pursuit of Red Snout and his followers. Learning what had happened to that evil band and its leader the soldiers faced about and escorted Solomon and his party to Oriskany.

CHAPTER XX

THE FIRST FOURTH OF JULY

Mrs. Scott and her child lived in the family of General Herkimer for a month or so. Settlers remote from towns and villages had abandoned their farms. The Indians had gone into the great north bush perhaps to meet the British army which was said to be coming down from Canada in appalling numbers. Hostilities in the neighborhood of The Long House had ceased. The great Indian highway and its villages were deserted save by young children and a few ancient red men and squaws, too old for travel. Late in June, Jack and Solomon were ordered to report to General Schuyler at Albany.

"We're gettin' shoveled eroun' plenty," Solomon declared. "We'll take the womern an' the boy with us an' paddle down the Mohawk to Albany. They kind o' fell from Heaven into our hands an' we got to look a'ter 'em faithful. Fust ye know ol' Herk 'll be movin' er swallered hull by the British an' the Injuns, like Jonah was by the whale, then what 'ud become o' her an' the Leetle Cricket? We got to look a'ter 'em."

"I think my mother will be glad to give them a home," said Jack. "She really needs some help in the house these days."

291

2

The Scotts' buildings had been burned by the Indians and their boats destroyed save one large canoe
which had happened to be on the south shore of the
river out of their reach. In this Jack and Solomon
and "Mis' Scott" and the Little Cricket set out with
loaded packs in the moon of the new leaf, to use a
phrase of the Mohawks, for the city of the Great River.
They had a carry at the Wolf Riff and some shorter
ones but in the main it was a smooth and delightful
journey, between wooded shores, down the long winding lane of the Mohawk. Without fear of the Indians
they were able to shoot deer and wild fowl and build
a fire on almost any part of the shore. Mrs. Scott
insisted on her right to do the cooking. Jack kept a
diary of the trip, some pages of which the historian
has read. From them we learn:

"Mrs. Scott has bravely run the gauntlet of her
sorrows. Now there is a new look in her face. She
is a black eyed, dark haired, energetic, comely woman
of forty with cheeks as red as a ripe strawberry. Solomon calls her 'middle sized' but she seems to be large
enough to fill his eye. He shows her great deference
and chooses his words with particular care when he
speaks to her. Of late he has taken to singing. She
and the boy seem to have stirred the depths in him
and curious things are coming up to the surface—
songs and stories and droll remarks and playful tricks
and an unusual amount of laughter. I suppose that it

is the spirit of youth in him, stunned by his great sorrow. Now touched by miraculous hands he is coming back to his old self. There can be no doubt of this: the man is ten years younger than when I first knew him even. The Little Cricket has laid hold of his heart. Whig sits between the feet of Solomon in the stern during the day and insists upon sleeping with him at night.

"One morning my old friend was laughing as we stood on the river bank washing ourselves.

" 'What are you laughing at?' I asked.

" 'That gol durn leetle skeezucks!' he answered. 'He were kickin' all night like a mule fightin' a bumble bee. 'Twere a cold night an' I held him ag'in' me to keep the leetle cuss warm.'

" 'Hadn't you better let him sleep with his mother?' I asked.

" 'Wall, if it takes two to do his sleepin' mebbe I better be the one that suffers. Ain't she a likely womern?'

"Of course I agreed, for it was evident that she was likely, sometime, to make him an excellent wife and the thought of that made me happy."

They had fared along down by the rude forts and villages traveling stealthily at night in tree shadows through "the Tory zone," as the vicinity of Fort Johnson was then called, camping, now and then, in deserted farm-houses or putting up at village inns. They arrived at Albany in the morning of July fourth. Setting out from their last camp an hour before daylight they had heard the booming of cannon at sunrise. Solomon stopped his paddle and listened.

"By the hide an' horns o' the devil!" he exclaimed. "I wonder if the British have got down to Albany."

They were alarmed until they hailed a man on the river road and learned that Albany was having a celebration.

"What be they celebratin'?" Solomon asked.

"The Declaration o' Independence," the citizen answered.

"It's a good idee," said Solomon. "When we git thar this 'ere ol' rifle o' mine 'll do some talkin' if it has a chanst."

Church bells were ringing as they neared the city. Its inhabitants were assembled on the river-front. The Declaration was read and then General Schuyler made a brief address about the peril coming down from the north. He said that a large force under General Burgoyne was on Lake Champlain and that the British were then holding a council with the Six Nations on the shore of the lake above Crown Point.

"At present we are unprepared to meet this great force but I suppose that help will come and that we shall not be dismayed. The modest man who leads the British army from the north declares in his proclamation that he is 'John Burgoyne, Esq., Lieutenant General of His Majesty's forces in America, Colonel of the Queen's Regiment of Light Dragoons, Governor of Fort William in North Britain, one of the Commons

in Parliament and Commander of an Army and Fleet
Employed on an Expedition from Canada!' My
friends, such is the pride that goeth before a fall. We
are an humble, hard-working people. No man among
us can boast of a name so lavishly adorned. Our
names need only the simple but glorious adornments of
firmness, courage and devotion. With those, I verily
believe, we shall have an Ally greater than any this
world can offer. Let us all kneel where we stand while
the Reverend Mr. Munro leads us in prayer to Almighty God for His help and guidance."

It was an impressive hour and that day the same
kind of talk was heard in many places. The church
led the people. Pulpiteers of inspired vision of which,
those days, there were many, spoke with the tongues
of men and of angels. A sublime faith in "The Great
Ally" began to travel up and down the land.

CHAPTER XXI

THE AMBUSH

MRS. SCOTT and her little son were made welcome in the home of John Irons. Jack and Solomon were immediately sent up the river and through the bush to help the force at Ti. In the middle and late days of July, they reported to runners the southward progress of the British. They were ahead of Herkimer's regiment of New York militia on August third when they discovered the ambush—a misfortune for which they were in no way responsible. Herkimer and his force had gone on without them to relieve Fort Schuyler. The two scouts had ridden post to join him. They were afoot half a mile or so ahead of the commander when Jack heard the call of the swamp robin. He hurried toward his friend. Solomon was in a thicket of tamaracks.

"We got to git back quick," said the latter. "I see sign o' an ambush."

They hurried to their command and warned the General. He halted and faced his men about and began a retreat. Jack and Solomon hurried out ahead of them some twenty rods apart. In five minutes Jack heard Solomon's call again. Thoroughly alarmed, he ran in the direction of the sound. In a moment he met Solomon. The face of the latter had that stern look which came only in a crisis. Deep furrows ran across his brow. His hands were shut tight. There was an expression of anger in his eyes. He swallowed as Jack came near.

"It's an ambush sure as hell's ahead," he whispered.

As they were hurrying toward the regiment, he added:

"We got to fight an' ag'in' big odds—British an' Injuns. Don't never let yerself be took alive, my son, lessen ye want to die as Scott did. But, mebbe, we kin bu'st the circle."

In half a moment they met Herkimer.

"Git ready to fight," said Solomon. "We're surrounded."

The men were spread out in a half-circle and some hurried orders given, but before they could take a step forward the trap was sprung. "The Red Devils of Brant" were rushing at them through the timber with yells that seemed to shake the tree-tops. The regiment fired and began to advance. Some forty Indians had fallen as they fired. General Herkimer and others were wounded by a volley from the savages.

"Come on, men. Foller me an' use yer bayonets," Solomon shouted. "We'll cut our way out."

The Indians ahead had no time to load. Scores of them were run through. Others fled for their lives. But a red host was swarming up from behind and firing into the regiment. Many fell. Many made the mistake of turning to fight back and were overwhelmed

and killed or captured. A goodly number had cut their
way through with Jack and Solomon and kept going,
swapping cover as they went. Most of them were
wounded in some degree. Jack's right shoulder had
been torn by a bullet. Solomon's left hand was broken
and bleeding. The savages were almost on their heels,
not two hundred yards behind. The old scout rallied
his followers in a thicket at the top of a knoll with an
open grass meadow between them and their enemies.
There they reloaded their rifles and stood waiting.

"Don't fire—not none o' ye—till I give the word.
Jack, you take my rifle. I'm goin' to throw this 'ere
bunch o' lightnin'."

Solomon stepped out of the thicket and showed himself when the savages entered the meadow. Then he
limped up the trail as if he were badly hurt, in the
fashion of a hen partridge when one has come near
her brood. In a moment he had dodged behind cover
and crept back into the thicket.

There were about two hundred warriors who came
running across the flat toward that point where Solomon had disappeared. They yelled like demons and
overran the little meadow with astonishing speed.

"Now hold yer fire—hold yer fire till I give ye the
word, er we'll all be et up. Keep yer fingers off the
triggers now."

He sprang into the open. Astonished, the foremost
runners halted while others crowded upon them. The

"bunch of lightning" began its curved flight as Solomon leaped behind a tree and shouted, "Fire!"

" 'Tain't too much to say that the cover flew off o'
hell right thar at the edge o' the Bloody Medder that
minnit—you hear to me," he used to tell his friends.
"The air were full o' bu'sted Injun an' a barrel o' blood
an' grease went down into the ground. A dozen er so
that wasn't hurt run back ercrost the medder like the
devil were chasin' 'em all with a red-hot iron. I
reckon it'll allus be called the Bloody Medder."

In this retreat Jack had lost so much blood that he
had to be carried on a litter. Before night fell they
met General Benedict Arnold and a considerable force.
After a little rest the tireless Solomon went back into
the bush with Arnold and two regiments to find the
wounded Herkimer, if possible, and others who might
be in need of relief. They met a band of refugees
coming in with the body of the General. They reported that the far bush was echoing with the shrieks
of tortured captives.

"Beats all what an amount o' sufferin' it takes to
start a new nation," Solomon used to say.

Next day Arnold fought his way to the fort, and
many of St. Leger's Rangers and their savage allies
were slain or captured or broken into little bands and
sent flying for their lives into the northern bush. So
the siege of Fort Schuyler was raised.

"I never see no better fightin' man than Arnold,"

Solomon used to say. "I seen him fight in the middle bush an' on the Stillwater. Under fire he was a reg'-lar wolverine. Allus up ag'in' the hottest side o' hell an' sayin':

"'Come on, boys. We kin't expec' to live forever.'

"But Arnold were a sore head. Allus kickin' over the traces an' complainin' that he never got proper credit."

CHAPTER XXII

THE BINKUSSING OF COLONEL BURLEY

SOLOMON had been hit in the thigh by a rifle bullet on his way to the fort. He and Jack and other wounded men were conveyed in boats and litters to the hospital at Albany where Jack remained until the leaves were gone. Solomon recovered more quickly and was with Lincoln's militia under Colonel Brown when they joined Johnson's Rangers at Ticonderoga and cut off the supplies of the British army. Later having got around the lines of the enemy with this intelligence he had a part in the fighting on Bemus Heights and the Stillwater and saw the defeated British army under Burgoyne marching eastward in disgrace to be conveyed back to England.

Jack had recovered and was at home when Solomon arrived in Albany with the news.

"Wal, my son, I cocalate they's goin' to be a weddin' in our fam'ly afore long," said the latter.

"What makes you think so?" Jack inquired.

"'Cause John Burgoyne, High Cockylorum and Cockydoodledo, an' all his army has been licked an' kicked an' started fer hum an' made to promise that they won't be sassy no more. I tell ye the war is goin' to end. They'll see that it won't pay to keep it up."

"But you do not know that Howe has taken Philadelphia," said Jack. "His army entered it on the twenty-sixth of September. Washington is in a bad fix. You and I have been ordered to report to him at White Marsh as soon as possible."

"That ol' King 'ud keep us fightin' fer years if he had his way," said Solomon. "He don't have to bleed an' groan an' die in the swamps like them English boys have been doin'. It's too bad but we got to keep killin' 'em, an' when the bad news reaches the good folks over thar mebbe the King'll git spoke to proper. We got to keep a-goin'. Fer the fust time in my life I'm glad to git erway from the big bush. The Injuns have found us a purty tough bit o' fodder but they's no tellin', out thar in the wilderness, when a man is goin' to be roasted and chawed up."

Solomon spent a part of the evening at play with the Little Cricket and the other children and when the young ones had gone to bed, went out for a walk with "Mis' Scott" on the river-front.

Mrs. Irons had said of the latter that she was a most amiable and useful person.

"The Little Cricket has won our hearts," she added. "We love him as we love our own."

When Jack and Solomon were setting out in a hired sloop for the Highlands next morning there were tears in the dark eyes of "Mis' Scott."

"Ain't she a likely womern?" Solomon asked again when with sails spread they had begun to cut the water.

Near King's Ferry in the Highlands on the Hudson

they spent a night in the camp of the army under Putnam. There they heard the first note of discontent
with the work of their beloved Washington. It came
from the lips of one Colonel Burley of a Connecticut
regiment. The Commander-in-Chief had lost Newport, New York and Philadelphia and been defeated
on Long Island and in two pitched battles on ground
of his own choosing at Brandywine and Germantown.

The two scouts were angry.

It had been a cold, wet afternoon and they, with
others, were drying themselves around a big, open fire
of logs in front of the camp post-office.

Solomon was quick to answer the complaint of
Burley.

"He's allus been fightin' a bigger force o' well
trained, well paid men that had plenty to eat an' drink
an' wear. An' he's fit 'em with jest a shoe string o' an
army. When it come to him, it didn't know nothin'
but how to shoot an' dig a hole in the ground. The
men wouldn't enlist fer more'n six months an' as soon
as they'd learnt suthin', they put fer hum. An' with
that kind o' an army, he druv the British out o' Boston.
With a leetle bunch o' five thousand unpaid, barefoot,
ragged backed devils, he druv the British out o' Jersey an' they had twelve thousan' men in that neighborhood. He's had to dodge eround an' has kep' his army
from bein' et up, hide, horns an' taller, by the power
o' his brain. He's managed to take keer o' himself
down thar in Jersey an' Pennsylvaney with the Brit-

ish on all sides o' him, while the best fighters he had come up here to help Gates. I don't see how he could 'a' done it—damned if I do—without the help o' God."

"Gates is a real general," Burley answered. "Washington don't amount to a hill o' beans."

Solomon turned quickly and advanced upon Burley.

"I didn't 'spect to find an enemy o' my kentry in this 'ere camp," he said in a quiet tone. "Ye got to take that back, mister, an' do it prompt, er ye're goin' to be all mussed up."

"Ye could see the ha'r begin to brustle under his coat," Solomon was wont to say of Burley, in speaking of that moment. "He stepped up clus an' growled an' showed his teeth an' then he begun to git rooined."

Burley had kept a public house for sailors at New Haven and had had the reputation of being a bad man in a quarrel. Of just what happened there is a full account in a little army journal of that time called *The Camp Gazette*. Burley aimed a blow at Solomon with his fist. Then as Solomon used to put it, "the water bu'st through the dam." It was his way of describing the swift and decisive action which was crowded into the next minute. He seized Burley and hurled him to the ground. With one hand on the nape of his neck and the other on the seat of his trousers, Solomon lifted his enemy above his head and quoited him over the tent top.

Burley picked himself up and having lost his head

drew his hanger, and, like a mad bull, rushed at Solomon. Suddenly he found his way barred by Jack.

"Would you try to run a man through before he can draw?" the latter asked.

Solomon's old sword flashed out of its scabbard.

"Let him come on," he shouted. "I'm more to hum with a hanger than I be with good vittles."

Of all the words on record from the lips of this man, these are the most immodest, but it should be remembered that when he spoke them his blood was hot.

Jack gave way and the two came together with a clash of steel. A crowd had gathered about them and was increasing rapidly. They had been fighting for half a moment around the fire when Solomon broke the blade of his adversary. The latter drew his pistol! Before he could raise it Solomon had fired his own weapon. Burley's pistol dropped on the ground. Instantly its owner reeled and fell beside it. The battle which had lasted no more than a minute had come to its end. There had been three kinds of fighting in that lively duel.

Solomon's voice trembled when he cried out:

"Ary man who says a word ag'in' the Great Father is goin' to git mussed up."

He pushed his way through the crowd which had gathered around the wounded man.

"Let me bind his arm," he said.

But a surgeon had stood in the crowd. He was

then doing what he could for the shattered member of the hot-headed Colonel Burley. Jack was helping him. Some men arrived with a litter and the unfortunate officer was quickly on his way to the hospital.

Jack and Solomon set out for headquarters. They met Putnam and two officers hurrying toward the scene of the encounter. Solomon had fought in the bush with him. Twenty years before they had been friends and comrades. Solomon saluted and stopped the grizzled hero of many a great adventure.

"Binkus, what's the trouble here?" the latter asked, as the crowd who had followed the two scouts gathered about them.

Solomon gave his account of what had happened. It was quickly verified by many eye-witnesses.

"Ye done right," said the General. "Burley has got to take it back an' apologize. He ain't fit to be an officer. He behaved himself like a bully. Any man who talks as he done orto be cussed an' Binkussed an' sent to the guard house."

Within three days Burley had made an ample apology for his conduct and this bulletin was posted at headquarters:

"Liberty of speech has its limits. It must be controlled by the law of decency and the general purposes of our army and government. The man who respects no authority above his own intellect is a conceited ass and would be a tyrant if he had the chance. No word of disrespect for a superior officer will be tolerated in this army."

"The Binkussing of Burley"—a phrase which traveled far beyond the limits of Putnam's camp—and the notice of warning which followed was not without its effect on the propaganda of Gates and his friends.

2

Next day Jack and Solomon set out with a force of twelve hundred men for Washington's camp at White Marsh near Philadelphia. There Jack found a letter from Margaret. It had been sent first to Benjamin Franklin in Paris through the latter's friend Mr. David Hartley, a distinguished Englishman who was now and then sounding the Doctor on the subject of peace.

"I am sure that you will be glad to know that my love for you is not growing feeble on account of its age," she wrote. "The thought has come to me that I am England and that you are America. It will be a wonderful and beautiful thing if through all this bitterness and bloodshed we can keep our love for each other. My dear, I would have you know that in spite of this alien King and his followers, I hold to my love for you and am waiting with that patience which God has put in the soul of your race and mine, for the end of our troubles. If you could come to France I would try to meet you in Doctor Franklin's home at Passy. So I have the hope in me that you may be sent to France."

This is as much of the letter as can claim admission to our history. It gave the young man a supply of happiness sufficient to fill the many days of hardship and peril in the winter at Valley Forge. It was read to Solomon.

"Say, this 'ere letter kind o' teches my feelin's—does sart'in," said Solomon. "I'm goin' to see what kin be done."

Unknown to Jack, within three days Solomon had a private talk with the Commander-in-Chief at his headquarters. The latter had a high regard for the old scout. He maintained a dignified silence while Solomon made his little speech and then arose and offered his hand saying in a kindly tone:

"Colonel Binkus, I must bid you good night."

CHAPTER XXIII

THE GREATEST TRAIT OF A GREAT COMMANDER

JACK IRONS used to say that no man he had known had such an uncommon amount of common sense as George Washington. He wrote to his father:

"It would seem that he must be in communication with the all-seeing mind. If he were to make a serious blunder here our cause would fail. The enemy tries in vain to fool him. Their devices are as an open book to Washington. They have fooled me and Solomon and other officers but not him. I had got quite a conceit of myself in judging strategy but now it is all gone.

"One day I was scouting along the lines, a few miles from Philadelphia, when I came upon a little, ragged, old woman. She wished to go through the lines into the country to buy flour. The moment she spoke I recognized her. It was old Lydia Darrah who had done my washing for me the last year of my stay in Philadelphia.

" 'Why, Lydia, how do you do?' I asked.

" 'The way I have allus done, laddie buck,' she answered in her good Irish brogue. 'Workin' at the tub an' fightin' the divil—bad 'cess to him—but I kape me hilth an' lucky I am to do that—thanks to the

309

good God! How is me fine lad that I'd niver 'a' knowed but for the voice o' him?'

" 'Not as fine as when I wore the white ruffles but stout as a moose,' I answered. 'The war is a sad business.'

" 'It is that—may the good God defind us! We cross the sea to be rid o' the divil an' he follys an' grabs us be the neck.'

"We were on a lonely road. She looked about and seeing no one, put a dirty old needle case in my hands.

" 'Take that, me smart lad. It's fer good luck,' she answered.

"As I left her I was in doubt of the meaning of her generosity. Soon I opened the needle book and found in one of its pockets a piece of thin paper rolled tight. On it I found the information that Howe would be leaving the city next morning with five thousand men, and baggage wagons and thirteen cannon and eleven boats. The paper contained other details of the proposed British raid. I rode post to headquarters and luckily found the General in his tent. On the way I arrived at a definite conviction regarding the plans of Howe. I was eager to give it air, having no doubt of its soundness. The General gave me respectful attention while I laid the facts before him. Then I took my courage in my hands and asked:

" 'General, may I venture to express an opinion?'

" 'Certainly,' he answered.

" 'It is the plan of Howe to cross the Delaware in

his boats so as to make us believe that he is going to New York. He will recross the river above Bristol and suddenly descend upon our rear.'

"Washington sat, with his arms folded, looking very grave but made no answer.

"In other words, again I presented my conviction.

"Still he was silent and I a little embarrassed. In half a moment I ventured to ask:

" 'General, what is your opinion?'

"He answered in a kindly tone: 'Colonel Irons, the enemy has no business in our rear. The boats are only for our scouts and spies to look at. The British hope to fool us with them. To-morrow morning about daylight they will be coming down the Edgely Bye Road on our left.'

"He called an aid and ordered that our front be made ready for an attack in the early morning.

"I left headquarters with my conceit upon me and half convinced that our Chief was out in his judgment of that matter. No like notion will enter my mind again. Solomon and I have quarters on the Edgely Bye Road. A little after three next morning the British were reported coming down the road. A large number of them were killed and captured and the rest roughly handled.

"A smart Yankee soldier in his trial for playing cards yesterday, set up a defense which is the talk of the camp. For a little time it changed the tilt of the wrinkles on the grim visage of war. His claim was that he had no Bible and that the cards aided him in his devotions.

"The ace reminded him of the one God; the deuce of the Father and Son; the tray of the Trinity; the four spot of the four evangelists—Matthew, Luke, Mark and John; the five spot of the five wise and the five foolish virgins; the six spot of the six days of creation; the seven of the Sabbath; the eight of Noah and his family; the nine of the nine ungrateful lepers; the ten of the Ten Commandments; the knave of Judas; the queen was to him the Queen of Sheba and the king was the one great King of Heaven and the Universe.

" 'You will go to the guard house for three days so that, hereafter, a pack of cards will remind you only of a foolish soldier,' said Colonel Provost."

Snow and bitter winds descended upon the camp early in December. It was a worn, ragged, weary but devoted army of about eleven thousand men that followed Washington into Valley Forge to make a camp for the winter. Of these, two thousand and ninety-eight were unfit for duty. Most of the latter had neither boots nor shoes. They marched over roads frozen hard, with old rags and pieces of hide wrapped around their feet. There were many red tracks in the snow in the Valley of the Schuylkill that day. Hardly a man was dressed for cold weather. Hundreds were shivering and coughing with influenza.

"When I look at these men I can not help thinking

THE GREATEST TRAIT 313

how small are my troubles," Jack wrote to his mother.
"I will complain of them no more. Solomon and I
have given away all the clothes we have except those
on our backs. A fiercer enemy than the British is be-
sieging us here. He is Winter. It is the duty of the
people we are fighting for to defend us against this
enemy. We should not have to exhaust ourselves in
such a battle. Do they think that because God has
shown His favor at Brooklyn, Saratoga, and sundry
other places, He is in a way committed? Are they not
disposed to take it easy and over-work the Creator?
I can not resist the impression that they are praying
too much and paying too little. I fear they are lying
back and expecting God to send ravens to feed us and
angels to make our boots and weave our blankets and
clothing. He will not go into that kind of business.
The Lord is not a shoemaker or a weaver or a baker.
He can have no respect for a people who would
leave its army to starve and freeze to death in the back
country. If they are to do that their faith is rotten
with indolence and avarice.

"There are many here who have nothing to wear but
blankets with armholes, belted by a length of rope.
There are hundreds who have no blankets to cover
them at night. They have to take turns sitting by the
fire while others are asleep. For them a night's rest
is impossible. Let this letter be read to the people of
Albany and may they not lie down to sleep until they
have stirred themselves in our behalf, and if any man

dares to pray to God to help us until he has given of his abundance to that end and besought his neighbors to do the same, I could wish that his praying would choke him. Are we worthy to be saved—that is the question. If we expect God to furnish the flannel and the shoe leather, we are not. That is our part of the great task. Are we going to shirk it and fail?

"We are making a real army. The men who are able to work are being carefully trained by the crusty old Baron Steuben and a number of French officers."

That they did not fail was probably due to the fact that there were men in the army like this one who seemed to have some little understanding of the will of God and the duty of man. This letter and others like it, traveled far and wide and more than a million hands began to work for the army.

The Schuylkill was on one side of the camp and wooded ridges, protected by entrenchments, on the other. Trees were felled and log huts constructed, sixteen by fourteen feet in size. Twelve privates were quartered in each hut.

The Gates propaganda was again being pushed. Anonymous letters complaining that Washington was not protecting the people of Pennsylvania and New Jersey from depredations were appearing in sundry newspapers. By and by a committee of investigation arrived from Congress. They left satisfied that Washington had done well to keep his army alive, and that

he must have help or a large part of it would die of
cold and hunger.

2

It was on a severe day in March that Washington
sent for Jack Irons. The scout found the General sitting alone by the fireside in his office which was part of
a small farm-house. He was eating a cold luncheon
of baked beans and bread without butter. Jack had
just returned from Philadelphia where he had risked
his life as a spy, of which adventure no details are recorded save the one given in the brief talk which follows. The scout smiled as he took the chair offered.

"The British are eating no such frugal fare," he
remarked.

"I suppose not," the General answered.

"The night before I left Philadelphia Howe and his
staff had a banquet at The Three Mariners. There
were roasted hams and geese and turkeys and patties
and pies and jellies and many kinds of wine and high
merriment. The British army is well fed and clothed."

"We are not so provided but we must be patient,"
said Washington. "Our people mean well, they are as
yet unorganized. This matter of being citizens of an
independent nation at war is new to them. The men
who are trying to establish a government while they
are defending it against a powerful enemy have a most
complicated problem. Naturally, there are disagree-
ments and factions. Congress may, for a time, be di-
vided but the army must stand as one man. This thing

we call human liberty has become for me a sublime personality. In times when I could see no light, she has kept my heart from failing."

"She is like the goddess of old who fought in the battles of Agamemnon," said Jack. "Perhaps she is the angel of God who hath been given charge concerning us. Perhaps she is traveling up and down the land and overseas in our behalf."

Washington sat looking thoughtfully into the fire. In a moment he said:

"She is like a wise and beautiful mother assuring us that our sorrows will end, by and by, and that we must keep on."

The General arose and went to his desk and returned with sealed letters in his hand and said:

"Colonel, I have a task for you. I could give it to no man in whom I had not the utmost confidence. You have earned a respite from the hardships and perils of this army. Here is a purse and two letters. With them I wish you to make your way to France as soon as possible and turn over the letters to Franklin. The Doctor is much in need of help. Put your services at his disposal. A ship will be leaving Boston on the fourteenth. A good horse has been provided; your route is mapped. You will need to start after the noon mess. For the first time in ten days there will be fresh beef on the tables. Two hundred blankets have arrived and more are coming. After they have eaten, give the men a farewell talk and put them in good heart, if you

can. We are going to celebrate the winter's end which
can not be long delayed. When you have left the
table, Hamilton will talk to the boys in his witty and
inspiring fashion."

Soon after one o'clock on the seventh of March,
1778, Colonel Irons bade Solomon good-by and set
out on his long journey. That night he slept in a farm-
house some fifty miles from Valley Forge.

Next morning this brief note was written to his
mother:

"I am on my way to France, leaving mother and
father and sister and brother and friend, as the Lord
has commanded, to follow Him, I verily believe. Yesterday the thought came to me that this thing we call
the love of Liberty which is in the heart of every man
and woman of us, urging that we stop at no sacrifice
of blood and treasure, is as truly the angel of God as he
that stood with Peter in the prison house. Last night
I saw Liberty in my dreams—a beautiful woman she
was, of heroic stature with streaming hair and the
glowing eyes of youth and she was dressed in a long
white robe held at the waist by a golden girdle. And
I thought that she touched my brow and said:

" 'My son, I am sent for all the children of men and
not for America alone. You will find me in France
for my task is in many lands.'

"I left the brave old fighter, Solomon, with tears in
his eyes. What a man is Solomon! Yet, God knows,
he is the rank and file of Washington's army as it

stands to-day—ragged, honest, religious, heroic, half fed, unappreciated, but true as steel and willing, if required, to give up his comfort or his life! How may we account for such a man without the help of God and His angels?"

BOOK THREE

CHAPTER XXIV

IN FRANCE WITH FRANKLIN

JACK shipped in the packet *Mercury,* of seventy tons, under Captain Simeon Sampson, one of America's ablest naval commanders. She had been built for rapid sailing and when, the second day out, they saw a British frigate bearing down upon her they wore ship and easily ran away from their enemy. Their first landing was at St. Martin on the Isle de Rhé. They crossed the island on mules, being greeted with the cry:

"Voilà les braves Bostones!"

In France the word *Bostone* meant American revolutionist. At the ferry they embarked on a long gabbone for La Rochelle. There the young man enjoyed his first repose on a French *lit* built up of sundry layers of feather beds. He declares in his diary that he felt the need of a ladder to reach its snowy summit of white linen. He writes a whole page on the sense of comfort and the dreamless and refreshing sleep which he had found in that bed. The like of it he had not known since he had been a fighting man.

In the morning he set out in a heavy vehicle of two wheels, drawn by three horses. Its postillion in frizzed and powdered hair, under a cocked hat, with a long

319

queue on his back and in great boots, hooped with iron, rode a lively little *bidet*. Such was the French stage-coach of those days, its running gear having been planned with an eye to economy, since vehicles were taxed according to the number of their wheels. The diary informs one that when the traveler stopped for food at an inn, he was expected to furnish his own knife. The highways were patrolled, night and day, by armed horsemen and robberies were unknown. The vineyards were not walled or fenced. All travelers had a license to help themselves to as much fruit as they might wish to eat when it was on the vines.

They arrived at Chantenay on a cold rainy evening. They were settled in their rooms, happy that they had protection from the weather, when their landlord went from room to room informing them that they would have to move on.

"Why?" Jack ventured to inquire.

"Because a *seigneur* has arrived."

"A *seigneur!*" Jack exclaimed.

"*Oui,* Monsieur. He is a very great man."

"But suppose we refuse to go," said Jack.

"Then, Monsieur, I shall detain your horses. It is a law of *le grand monarque.*"

There was no dodging it. The coach and horses came back to the inn door. The passengers went out into the dark, rainy night to plod along in the mud, another six miles or so, that the *seigneur* and his suite could enjoy that comfort the weary travelers had been

forced to leave.   Such was the power of privilege with
which the great Louis had saddled his kingdom.

They proceeded to Ancenis, Angers and Breux.
From the latter city the road to Versailles was paved
with flat blocks of stone.   There were swarms of beggars in every village and city crying out, with hands
extended, as the coach passed them:

"*La charité, au nom de Dieu!*"

"France is in no healthy condition when this is possible," the young man wrote.

If he met a priest carrying a Bon Dieu in a silver
vase every one called out, "*Aux genoux!*" and then the
beholder had to kneel, even if the mud were ankle
deep.   So on a wet day one's knees were apt to be as
muddy as his feet.

The last stage from Versailles to Paris was called
the post royale.   There the postillion had to be dressed
like a gentleman.   It was a magnificent avenue,
crowded every afternoon by the wealth and beauty of
the kingdom, in gorgeously painted coaches, and
lighted at night by great lamps, with double reflectors,
over its center.   They came upon it in the morning on
their way to the capital.   There were few people traveling at that hour.   Suddenly ahead they saw a cloud of
dust.   The stage stopped.   On came a band of horsemen riding at a wild gallop.   They were the King's
couriers.

"Clear the way," they shouted.   "The King's hunt
is coming."

All travelers, hearing this command, made quickly for the sidings, there to draw rein and dismount. The deer came in sight, running for its life, the King close behind with all his train, the hounds in full cry. Near Jack the deer bounded over a hedge and took a new direction. His Majesty—a short, stout man with blue eyes and aquiline nose, wearing a lace cocked hat and brown velvet coatee and high boots with spurs—dismounted not twenty feet from the stage-coach, saying with great animation:

"*Vite! Donnez moi un cheval frais.*"

Instantly remounting, he bounded over the hedge, followed by his train.

2

A letter from Jack presents all this color of the journey and avers that he reached the house of Franklin in Passy about two o'clock in the afternoon of a pleasant May day. The savant greeted his young friend with an affectionate embrace.

"Sturdy son of my beloved country, you bring me joy and a new problem," he said.

"What is the problem?" Jack inquired.

"That of moving Margaret across the channel. I have a double task now. I must secure the happiness of America and of Jack Irons."

He read the despatches and then the Doctor and the young man set out in a coach for the palace of Vergennes, the Prime Minister. Colonel Irons was filled with astonishment at the tokens of veneration for the

white-haired man which he witnessed in the streets of
Paris.

"The person of the King could not have attracted
more respectful attention," he writes. "A crowd gathered about the coach when we were leaving it and
every man stood with uncovered head as we passed
on our way to the palace door. In the crowd there
was much whispered praise of *'Le grand savant.'* I
did not understand this until I met, in the office of the
Compte de Vergennes, the eloquent Senator Gabriel
Honore Riquetti de Mirabeau. What an impressive
name! Yet I think he deserves it. He has the eye of
Mars and the hair of Samson and the tongue of an
angel, I am told. In our talk, I assured him that in
Philadelphia Franklin came and went and was less observed than the town crier.

"'But your people seem to adore him,' I said.

"'As if he were a god,' Mirabeau answered. 'Yes,
it is true and it is right. Has he not, like Jove, hurled
the lightning of heaven in his right hand? Is he not
an unpunished Prometheus? Is he not breaking the
scepter of a tyrant?'

"Going back to his home where in the kindness of
his heart he had asked me to live, he endeavored, mod-
estly, to explain the evidences of high regard which
were being showered upon him.

"'It happens that my understanding and small control of a mysterious and violent force of nature has
appealed to the imagination of these people,' he said.

'I am the only man who has used thunderbolts for his playthings. Then, too, I am speaking for a new world to an old one. Just at present I am the voice of Human Liberty. I represent the hunger of the spirit of man. It is very strong here. You have not traveled so far in France without seeing thousands of beggars. They are everywhere. But you do not know that when a child comes in a poor family, the father and mother go to prison *pour mois de nourrice*. It is a pity that the poor can not keep their children at home. This old kingdom is a muttering Vesuvius, growing hotter, year by year, with discontent. You will presently hear its voices.' "

There was a dinner that evening at Franklin's house, at which the Marquis de Mirabeau, M. Turgot, the Madame de Brillon, the Abbé Raynal and the Compte and Comptesse d' Haudetot, Colonel Irons and three other American gentlemen were present. The Madame de Brillon was first to arrive. She entered with a careless, jaunty air and ran to meet Franklin and caught his hand and gave him a double kiss on each cheek and one on his forehead and called him "papa."

"At table she sat between me and Doctor Franklin," Jack writes. "She frequently locked her hand in the Doctor's and smiled sweetly as she looked into his eyes. I wonder what the poor, simple, hard-working Deborah Franklin would have thought of these familiarities. Yet here, I am told, no one thinks ill of that kind of thing. The best women of France seem to

John Wolcott Adams

treat their favorites with like tokens of regard. Now and then she spread her arms across the backs of our chairs, as if she would have us feel that her affection was wide enough for both.

"She assured me that all the women of France were in love with *le grand savant.*

"Franklin, hearing the compliment, remarked: 'It is because they pity my age and infirmities. First we pity, then embrace, as the great Mr. Pope has written.'

" 'We think it a compliment that the greatest intellect in the world is willing to allow itself to be, in a way, captured by the charms of women,' Madame Brillon declared.

" 'My beautiful friend! You are too generous,' the Doctor continued with a laugh. 'If the greatest man were really to come to Paris and lose his heart, I should know where to find it.'

"The Doctor speaks an imperfect and rather broken French, but these people seem to find it all the more interesting on that account. Probably to them it is like the English which we have heard in America from the lips of certain Frenchmen. How fortunate it is that I learned to speak the language of France in my boyhood!

"From the silver-tongued Mirabeau I got further knowledge of Franklin, with which I, his friend and fellow countryman, should have been acquainted, save that the sacrifices of the patriot are as common as mother's milk and cause little comment among us. The great orator was expected to display his talents, if there were any excuse for it, wherever he might be, so the ladies set up a demand for a toast. He spoke of Franklin, 'The Thrifty Prodigal,' saying:

" 'He saves only to give. There never was such a squanderer of his own immeasurable riches. For his great inventions and discoveries he has never received a penny. Twice he has put his personal fortune at the disposal of his country. Once when he paid the farmers for their horses and wagons to transport supplies for the army of Braddock, and again when he offered to pay for the tea which was thrown into Boston Harbor.'

"The great man turned to me and added:

" 'I have learned of these things, not from him, but from others who know the truth, and we love him in France because we are aware that he is working for Human Liberty and not for himself or for any greedy despot in the west.'

"It is all so true, yet in America nothing has been said of this.

"As the dinner proceeded the Abbé Raynal asked the Doctor if it was true that there were signs of degeneracy in the average male American.

" 'Let the facts before us be my answer," said Franklin. 'There are at this table four Frenchmen and four Americans. Let these gentlemen stand up.'

"The Frenchmen were undersized, the Abbé himself being a mere shrimp of a man. The Americans, Carmichael, Harmer, Humphries and myself, were big

men, the shortest being six feet tall.   The contrast
raised a laugh among the ladies.   Then said Franklin
in his kindest tones:

" 'My dear Abbé, I am aware that manhood is not a
matter of feet and inches.   I only assure you that
these are average Americans and that they are pretty
well filled with brain and spirit.'

"The Abbé spoke of a certain printed story on which
he had based his judgment.

"Franklin laughed and answered: 'I know that is
a fable, because I wrote it myself one day, long ago,
when we were short of news.' "

The guests having departed, Franklin asked the
young man to sit down for a talk by the fireside.   The
Doctor spoke of the women of France, saying:

" 'You will not understand them or me unless you remind yourself that we are in Europe and that it is the
eighteenth century.   Here the clocks are lagging.
Time moves slowly.   With the poor it stands still.
They know not the thing we call progress.'

" 'Those who have money seem to be very busy
having fun,' I said.

" 'There is no morning to their day,' he went on.
'Their dawn is noontime.   Our kind of people have
had longer days and have used them wisely.   So we
have pushed on ahead of this European caravan.   Our
fathers in New England made a great discovery.'

" 'What was it?' I asked.

" 'That righteousness was not a joke; that Christianity was not a solemn plaything for one day in the week, but a real, practical, working proposition for every day in the year; that the main support of the structure is industry; that its most vital commandment is this, "six days shalt thou labor"; that no amount of wealth can excuse a man from this duty. Every one worked. There was no idleness and therefore little poverty. The days were all for labor and the nights for rest. The wheels of progress were greased and moving.'

" 'And our love of learning helped to push them along,' I suggested.

" 'True. Our people have been mostly like you and me,' he went on. 'We long for knowledge of the truth. We build schools and libraries and colleges. We have pushed on out of the eighteenth century into a new time. There you were born. Now you have stepped a hundred years backward into Europe. You are astonished, and this brings me to my point. Here I am with a great task on my hands. It is to enlist the sympathy and help of France. I must take things, not as I could wish them to be, but as I find them. At this court women are all powerful. It has long been a maxim here that a diplomatist must stand well with the ladies. Even though he is venerable, he must be gallant, and I do not use the word in a shady sense. The ladies are not so bad as you would think them. They are playthings. To them, life is not as we know it, filled with realities. It is a beautiful drama of rich

costumes and painted scenes and ingenious words, all
set in the atmosphere of romance. The players only
pretend to believe each other. In the salon I am one
of these players. I have to be.'

" 'Mirabeau seemed to mean what he said,' was my
answer.

" 'Yes. He is one of those who often speak from
the heart. All these players love the note of sincerity
when they hear it. In the salon it is out of key, but
away from the ladies the men are often living and not
playing. Mirabeau, Condorcet, Turgot and others
have heard the call of Human Liberty. Often they
come to this house and speak out with a strong candor.'

" 'I suppose that this great drama of despotism in
France will end in a tragedy whose climax will con-
sume the stage and half the players,' I ventured to say.

" 'That is a theme, Jack, on which you and I must
be silent,' Franklin answered. 'We must hold our
mouths as with a bridle.'

"For a moment he sat looking sadly into the glowing coals on the grate. Franklin loved to talk, but no
one could better keep his own counsel.

" 'At heart I am no revolutionist,' he said presently. 'I believe in purifying—not in breaking down.
I would to God that I could have convinced the British
of their error. Mainly I am with the prophet who
says:

" ' "Stand in the old ways. View the ancient paths.

Consider them well and be not among those who are given to change." '

"I sat for a moment thinking of the cruelties I had witnessed, and asking myself if it had been really worth while. Franklin interrupted my thoughts.

" 'I wish we could discover a plan which would induce and compel nations to settle their differences without cutting each other's throats. When will human wisdom be sufficient to see the advantage of this?'

"He told me the thrilling details of his success in France; how he had won the kingdom for an ally and secured loans and the help of a fleet and army then on the sea.

" 'And you will not be surprised to learn that the British have been sounding me to see if we would be base enough to abandon our ally,' he laughed.

"In a moment he added:

" 'Come, it is late and you must write a letter to the heart of England before you lie down to rest.'

"Often thereafter he spoke of Margaret as 'the heart of England.' "

CHAPTER XXV

THE PAGEANT

JACK began to assist Franklin in his correspondence and in the many business details connected with his mission.

"I have never seen a man with a like capacity for work," the young officer writes. "Every day he is conferring with Vergennes or other representatives of the King, or with the ministers of Spain, Holland and Great Britain. The greatest intellect in the kingdom is naturally in great request. To-day, after many hours of negotiation with the Spanish minister, in came M. Dubourg, the most distinguished physician in Europe.

"'Mon chère maître,' he said. 'I have a most difficult case and as you know more about the human body than any man of my acquaintance I wish to confer with you.'

"Yesterday, Doctor Ingenhauz, physician to the Emperor of Austria, came to consult him regarding the vaccination of the royal family of France.

"In the evening, M. Robespierre, a slim, dark-skinned, studious young attorney from Arras, wearing gold-rimmed spectacles, came for information regarding lightning rods, he having doubts of their legality. While they were talking, M. Joseph Ignace Guillotin, another physician, arrived. He was looking

331

for advice regarding a proposed new method of capital punishment, and wished to know if, in the Doctor's opinion, a painless death could be produced by quickly severing the head from the body. Next morning, M. Jourdan, with hair and beard as red as the flank of my bay mare and a loud voice, came soon after breakfast, to sell us mules by the ship load.

"So you see that even I, living in his home and seeing him almost every hour of the day, have little chance to talk with him. Last night we met M. Voltaire—dramatist and historian—now in the evening of his days. We were at the Academy, where we had gone to hear an essay by D'Alembert. Franklin and Voltaire—a very thin old gentleman of eighty-four, with piercing black eyes—sat side by side on the platform. The audience demanded that the two great men should come forward and salute each other. They arose and advanced and shook hands.

"'A la Française,' the crowd demanded.

"So the two white-haired men embraced and kissed each other amidst loud applause.

"We are up at sunrise and at breakfast, for half an hour or so, I have him to myself. Then we take a little walk in the palace grounds of M. le Ray de Chaumont, Chief Forester of the kingdom, which adjoins us. To the Count's generosity Franklin is indebted for the house we live in. The Doctor loves to have me with him in the early morning. He says breakfasting alone is the most *triste* of all occupations.

" 'I think that the words of Demosthenes could not have been more sought than yours,' I said to him at breakfast this morning.

"He laughed as he answered: 'Demosthenes said that the first point in speaking was *action*. Probably he meant the action which preceded the address—a course of it which had impressed people with the integrity and understanding of the speaker. For years I have had what Doctor Johnson would call "a wise and noble curiosity" about nature and have had some success in gratifying it. Then, too, I have tried to order my life so that no man could say that Ben Franklin had intentionally done him a wrong. So I suppose that my words are entitled to a degree of respect—a far more limited degree than the French are good enough to accord them.'

"As we were leaving the table he said: 'Jack, I have an idea worthy of Demosthenes. My friend, David Hartley of London, who still has hope of peace by negotiation, wishes to come over and confer with me. I shall tell him that he may come if he will bring with him the Lady Hare and her daughter.'

" 'More thrilling words were never spoken by Demosthenes,' I answered. 'But how about Jones and his *Bonne Homme Richard?* He is now a terror to the British coasts. They would fear destruction.'

" 'I shall ask Jones to let them alone,' he said. 'They can come under a special flag.'

"Commodore Jones did not appear again in Paris

until October, when he came to Passy to report upon a famous battle.

"I was eager to meet this terror of the coasts. His impudent courage and sheer audacity had astonished the world. The wonder was that men were willing to join him in such dare devil enterprises.

"I had imagined that Jones would be a tall, gaunt, swarthy, raw-boned, swearing man of the sea. He was a sleek, silent, modest little man, with delicate hands and features. He wished to be alone with the Doctor, and so I did not hear their talk. I know that he needed money and that Franklin, having no funds, provided the sea fighter from his own purse.

"Commodore Jones had brought with him a cart-load of mail from captured British ships. In it were letters to me from Margaret.

" 'Now you are near me and yet there is an impass-able gulf between us,' she wrote. 'We hear that the seas are overrun with pirates and that no ship is safe. Our vessels are being fired upon and sunk. I would not mind being captured by a good Yankee captain, if it were carefully done. But cannons are so noisy and impolite! I have a lot of British pluck in me, but I fear that you would not like to marry a girl who limped because she had been shot in the war. And, just think of the possible effect on my disposition. So before we start Doctor Franklin will have to promise not to fire his cannons at us.'

"I showed the letter to Franklin and he laughed and said:

" 'They will be treated tenderly. The Commodore will convoy them across the channel. I shall assure Hartley of that in a letter which will go forward to-day.'

"Anxious days are upon us. Our money in America has become almost worthless and we are in extreme need of funds to pay and equip the army. We are daily expecting a loan from the King of three million livres. But Vergennes has made it clear to us that the government of France is itself in rather desperate straits. The loan has been approved, but the treasury is waiting upon certain taxes not yet collected. The moment the money is available the Prime Minister will inform us of the fact.

"On a fine autumn day we drove with the Prince of Condé in his great coach, ornamented with costly paintings, to spend a day at his country seat in Chantilly. The palace was surrounded by an artificial canal; the gardens beautified with ponds and streams and islands and cascades and grottos and labyrinths, the latter adorned with graceful sculptures. His stables were lined with polished woods; their windows covered with soft silk curtains. Of such a refinement of luxury I had never dreamed. Having seen at least a thousand beggars on the way, I was saddened by these rich, lavish details of a prince's self-indulgence.

"On the wish of our host, Franklin had taken with him a part of his electrical apparatus, with which he amused a large company of the friends of the great *Seigneur* in his palace grounds. Spirits were fired by a spark sent from one pond to another with no conductor but the water of a stream. The fowls for dinner were slain by electrical shocks and cooked over a fire kindled by a current from an electrical bottle. At the table the success of America was toasted in electrified bumpers with an accompaniment of guns fired by an electrical battery.

"A poet had written a *Chanson à Boire* to Franklin, which was read and merrily applauded at the dinner— one stanza of which ran as follows:

> " '*Tout, en fondant un empire,*
> *Vous le voyez boire et rire*
> *Le verre en main*
> *Chantons notre Benjamin.*'

"To illustrate the honest candor with which often he speaks, even in the presence of Frenchmen who are near the throne, I quote a few words from his brief address to the Prince and his friends:

" 'A good part of my life I have worked with my hands. If Your Grace will allow me to say so, I wish to see in France a deeper regard for the man who works with his hands—the man who supplies food. He really furnishes the standard of all value. The value of everything depends on the labor given to the making of it. If the labor in producing a bushel of wheat is the same as that consumed in the production of an ounce of silver, their value is the same.

" 'The food maker also supplies a country with its population. By 1900 he will have given to America a hundred million people and a power and prosperity beyond our reckoning. Frugality and Industry are the most fruitful of parents, especially where they are respected. When luxury and the cost of living have increased, people have become more cautious about marriage and populations have begun to dwindle.'

"The Bourbon Prince, a serious-minded man, felt the truth of all this and was at pains to come to my venerable friend and heartily express his appreciation.

" 'We know that we are in a bad way, but we know not how to get out of it,' he said.

"The Princess, who sat near us at table, asked the Doctor for information about the American woman.

" ' "She riseth while it is yet night and giveth meat to her household, and a portion to her maidens," ' he quoted. 'She is apt to be more industrious than her husband. She works all day and often a part of the night. She is weaver, knitter, spinner, tailor, cook, washerwoman, teacher, doctor, nurse. While she is awake her hands are never idle, and their most important work is that of slowly building up the manhood of America. Ours is to be largely a mother-made land.'

" '*Mon Dieu!* I should think she would be cross with so much to do,' said the Princess.

" 'Often she is a little cross,' Franklin answered.
'My friend, James Otis of Massachusetts, complained
of the fish one day at dinner when there was company
at the table. Mrs. Otis frankly expressed her opinion
of his bad manners. He was temperamental and himself a bit overworked. He made no answer, but in the
grace which followed the meal he said:

" ' "O Lord, we thank Thee that we have been able
to finish this dinner without getting slapped."

" 'But I would ask Your Highness to believe that our
men are mostly easier to get along with. They do not
often complain of the food. They are more likely to
praise it.'

"On our way back to Paris the Doctor said to me:

" 'The great error of Europe is entailment—entailed
estates, entailed pride, entailed luxury, entailed conceit. A boy who inherits honor will rarely honor himself. I like the method of China, where honor ascends,
but does not descend. It goes back to his parents who
taught him his virtues. It can do no harm to his parents, but it can easily ruin him and his children. I regard humility as one of the greatest virtues.'

2

"That evening our near neighbors, Le Compte de
Chaumont and M. LeVilleard, came to announce that
a dinner and ball in honor of Franklin would occur at
the palace of Compte de Chaumont less than a week
later.

" 'My good friends,' said the philosopher, 'I value

these honors which are so graciously offered me, but I
am old and have much work to do. I need rest more
than I need the honors.'

" 'It is one of the penalties of being a great savant
that people wish to see and know him,' said the Count.
'The most distinguished people in France will be
among those who do you honor. I think, if you can
recall a talk we had some weeks ago, you will wish
to be present.'

" 'Oh, then, you have heard from the Hornet.'

" 'I have a letter here which you may read at your
convenience.'

" 'My dear friend, be pleased to receive my apologies and my hearty thanks,' said Franklin. 'Not even
the gout could keep me away.'

"Next day I received a formal invitation to the dinner and ball. I told the Doctor that in view of the
work to be done, I would decline the invitation. He
begged me not to do it and insisted that he was count-
ing upon me to represent the valor and chivalry of the
New World; that as I had grown into the exact stature
of Washington and was so familiar with his manners
and able to imitate them in conversation, he wished
me to assume the costume of our Commander-in-
Chief. He did me the honor to say:

" 'There is no other man whom it would be safe to
trust in such an exalted rôle. I wish, as a favor to
me, you would see what can be done at the costumer's
and let me have a look at you.'

"I did as he wished. The result was an astonishing likeness. I dressed as I had seen the great man in the field. I wore a wig slightly tinged with gray, a blue coat, buff waistcoat and sash and sword and the top boots and spurs. When I strode across the room in the masterly fashion of our great Commander, the Doctor clapped his hands.

" 'You are as like him as one pea is like another!' he exclaimed. 'Nothing would so please our good friends, the French, who have an immense curiosity regarding *Le Grand Vasanton,* and it will give me an opportunity to instruct them as to our spirit.'

"He went to his desk and took from a drawer a cross of jeweled gold on a long necklace of silver—a gift from the King—and put it over my head so that the cross shone upon my breast.

" 'That is for the faith of our people,' he declared. 'The guests will assemble on the grounds of the Count late in the afternoon. You will ride among them on a white horse. A beautiful maiden in a white robe held at the waist with a golden girdle will receive you. She will be Human Liberty. You will dismount and kneel and kiss her hand. Then the Prime Minister of France will give to each a blessing and to you a sword and a purse. You will hold them up and say:

" ' "For these things I promise you the friendship of my people and their prosperity."

" 'You will kiss the sword and hang it beside your

own and pass the purse to me and then I shall have something to say.'

"So it was all done, but with thrilling details, of which no suspicion had come to me. I had not dreamed, for instance, that the King and Queen would be present and that the enthusiasm would be so great. You will be able to judge of my surprise when, riding my white horse through the cheering crowd, throwing flowers in my way, I came suddenly upon Margaret Hare in the white robe of Human Liberty. Now facing me after these years of trial, her spirit was equal to her part. She was like unto the angel I had seen in my dreams. The noble look of her face thrilled me. It was not so easy to maintain the calm dignity of Washington in that moment. I wanted to lift her in my arms and hold her there, as you may well believe, but, alas, I was Washington! I dismounted and fell upon one knee before her and kissed her hand not too fervently, I would have you know, in spite of my temptation. She stood erect, although tears were streaming down her cheeks and her dear hand trembled when it rested on my brow and she could only whisper the words:

" 'May the God of your fathers aid and keep you.'

"The undercurrent of restrained emotion in this little scene went out to that crowd, which represented the wealth, beauty and chivalry of France. I suppose that some of them thought it a bit of good acting.

These people love the drama as no others love it. I suspect that many of the friends of Franklin knew that she who was Liberty was indeed my long lost love. A deep silence fell upon them and then arose a wild shout of approval that seemed to come out of the very heart of France and to be warm with its noble ardor. Every one in this beautiful land—even the King and Queen and their kin—are thinking of Liberty and have begun to long for her blessing. That, perhaps, is why the scene had so impressed them.

"But we were to find in this little drama a climax wholly unexpected by either of us and of an importance to our country which I try in vain to estimate. When the Prime Minister handed the purse to Franklin he bade him open it. This the latter did, finding therein letters of credit for the three million livres granted, of which we were in sore need. With it was the news that a ship would be leaving Boulogne in the morning and that relays on the way had been provided for his messenger. The invention of our beloved diplomat was equal to the demand of the moment and so he announced:

" 'Washington is like his people. He turns from all the loves of this world to obey the call of duty. My young friend who has so well presented the look and manner of Washington will now show you his spirit.'

"He looked at his watch and added:

" 'Within forty minutes he will be riding post to Boulogne, there to take ship for America.'

"So here I am on the ship *L'Etoile* and almost in sight of Boston harbor, bringing help and comfort to our great Chief.

"I was presented to the King and Queen. Of him I have written—a stout, fat-faced man, highly colored, with a sloping forehead and large gray eyes. His coat shone with gold embroidery and jeweled stars. His close-fitting waistcoat of milk white satin had golden buttons and a curve which was not the only sign he bore of rich wine and good capon. The queen was a beautiful, dark-haired lady of some forty years, with a noble and gracious countenance. She was clad in no vesture of gold, but in sober black velvet. Her curls fell upon the loose ruff of lace around her neck. There were no jewels on or about her bare, white bosom. Her smile and gentle voice, when she gave me her bon-voyage and best wishes for the cause so dear to us, are jewels I shall not soon forget.

"Yes, I had a little talk with Margaret and her mother, who walked with me to Franklin's house. There, in his reception room, I took a good look at the dear girl, now more beautiful than ever, and held her to my heart a moment.

" 'I see you and then I have to go,' I said.

" 'It is the fault of my too romantic soul,' she answered mournfully. 'For two days we have been in hiding here. I wanted to surprise you.'

"And this protest came involuntarily from my lips:

" 'Here now is the happiness for which I have

longed, and yet forthwith I must leave it. What a mystery is the spirit of man!'

" 'When it is linked to the spirit of God it ceases to understand itself,' she answered. 'Oh, that I had the will for sacrifice which is in you!'

"She lifted the jeweled cross I wore to her lips and kissed it. I wish that I could tell you how beautiful she looked then. She is twenty-six years old and her womanhood is beginning.

" 'Now you may go,' she said. 'My heart goes with you, but I fear that we shall not meet again.'

" 'Why?' was my question.

" 'I am utterly discouraged.'

" 'You can not expect her to wait for you any longer. It is not fair,' said her mother.

" 'Margaret, I do not ask you to wait,' I said. 'I am not quite a human being. I seem to have no time for that. I am of the army of God. I shall not expect you to wait.'

"So it befell that the stern, strong hand of a soldier's duty drew me from her presence almost as soon as we had met. I kissed her and left her weeping, for there was need of haste. Soon I was galloping out of Passy on my way to the land I love. I try not to think of her, but how can I put out of mind the pathos of that moment? Whenever I close my eyes I see her beautiful figure sitting with bowed head in the twilight."

CHAPTER XXVI

In Boston harbor, Jack learned of the evacuation
of Philadelphia by the British and was transferred to
a Yankee ship putting out to sea on its way to that
city. There he found the romantic Arnold, crippled
by his wounds, living in the fine mansion erected by
William Penn. He had married a young daughter
of one of the rich Tory families, for his second wife,
and was in command of the city. Colonel Irons,
having delivered the letters to the Treasurer of the
United States, reported at Arnold's office. It was
near midday and the General had not arrived. The
young man sat down to wait and soon the great
soldier drove up with his splendid coach and pair.
His young wife sat beside him. He had little time
for talk. He was on his way to breakfast. Jack
presented his compliments and the good tidings
which he had brought from the Old Country. Arnold
listened as if he were hearing the price of codfish and
hams.

The young man was shocked by the coolness of the
Commandant. The former felt as if a pail of icy
water had been thrown upon him when Arnold
answered:

345

"Now that they have money I hope that they will pay their debt to me."

This kind of talk Jack had not heard before. He resented it but answered calmly: "A war and an army is a great extravagance for a young nation that has not yet learned the imperial art of gathering taxes. Many of us are going unpaid but if we get liberty it will be worth all it costs."

"That sounds well but there are some of us who are also in need of justice," Arnold answered as he turned away.

"General, you who have not been dismayed by force will never, I am sure, surrender to discouragement," said Jack.

The fiery Arnold turned suddenly and lifting his cane in a threatening manner said in a loud voice:

"Would you reprimand me—you damned upstart?"

"General, you may strike me, if you will, but I can not help saying that we young men must look to you older ones for a good example."

Very calmly and politely the young man spoke these words. He towered above the man Arnold in spirit and stature. The latter did not commit the folly of striking him but with a look of scorn ordered him to leave the office.

Jack obeyed the order and went at once to call upon his old friend, Governor Reed. He told the Governor of his falling out with the Major-General.

"Arnold is a sordid, selfish man and a source of

great danger to our cause," said the Governor. "He is vain and loves display and is living far beyond his means. To maintain his extravagance he has resorted to privateering and speculation, and none of it has been successful. He is deeply involved in debt. It is charged that he has used his military authority for private gain. He was tried by a court-martial but escaped with only a reprimand from the Commander-in-Chief. He is thick with the Tories. He is the type of man who would sell his master for thirty pieces of silver."

"This is alarming," said Jack.

"My boy an ill wind is blowing on us," the Governor went on. "We have all too many Arnolds in our midst. Our currency has depreciated until forty shillings will not buy what one would have bought before the war. The profit makers are rolling in luxury and the poor army starves. The honest and patriotic are impoverished while those who practise fraud and Toryism are getting rich."

Depressed by this report of conditions in America Jack set out for Washington's headquarters on the Hudson. Never had the posture of American affairs looked so hopeless. The Governor had sold him a young mare with a white star in her forehead and a short, white stocking on her left fore-leg, known in good time as the horse of destiny.

"She was a well turned, high spirited creature with good plumes, a noble eye and a beautiful head and neck," Jack wrote long after the day he parted with her. "I have never ridden a more distinguished animal. She was in every way worthy of the task ahead of her."

When he had crossed the King's Ferry the mare went lame. A little beyond the crossing he met a man on a big, roan gelding. Jack stopped him to get information about the roads in the north.

"That's a good-looking mare," the man remarked.

"And she is better than she looks," Jack answered. "But she has thrown a shoe and gone lame."

"I'll trade even and give you a sound horse," the man proposed.

"What is your name and where do you live?" Jack inquired.

"My name is Paulding and I live at Tarrytown in the neutral territory."

"I hope that you like horses."

"You can judge of that by the look of this one. You will observe that he is well fed and groomed."

"And your own look is that of a good master," said Jack, as he examined the teeth and legs of the gelding. "Pardon me for asking. I have grown fond of the mare. She must have a good master."

"I accepted his offer not knowing that a third party was looking on and laying a deeper plan than either of us were able to penetrate," Jack used to say of that deal.

He approached the little house in which the Commander-in-Chief was quartered with a feeling of dread, fearing the effect of late developments on his spirit.

The young man wrote to Margaret in care of Franklin this account of the day which followed his return to camp:

"Thank God! I saw on the face of our Commander the same old look of unshaken confidence. I knew that he could see his way and what a sense of comfort came of that knowledge! More than we can tell we are indebted to the calm and masterful face of Washington. It holds up the heart of the army in all discouragements. His faith is established. He is not afraid of evil tidings. This great, god-like personality of his has put me on my feet again. I was in need of it, for a different kind of man, of the name of Arnold, had nearly floored me."

" 'Sit down here and tell me all about Franklin,' he said with a smile.

"I told him what was going on in Paris and especially of the work of our great minister to the court of Louis XVI.

"He heard me with deep interest and when I had finished arose and gave me his hand saying:

" 'Colonel, again you have won my gratitude. We must keep our courage.'

"I told him of my unhappy meeting with Arnold.

" 'The man has his faults—he is very human, but he has been a good soldier,' Washington answered.

"The thought came to me that the love of liberty had lifted many of us above the human plane of sordid striving.

"Solomon came into camp that evening. He was so glad to see me that he could only wring my hand and utter exclamations.

" 'How is the gal?' he asked presently.

"I told him of our meeting in Passy and of my fear that we should not meet again.

" 'It seems as if the Lord were not yet willing to let us marry,' I said.

" 'Course not,' he answered. 'When yer boat is in the rapids it's no time fer to go ashore an' pick apples. I cocalate the Lord is usin' ye fer to show the Ol' World what's inside o' us Americans.'

"Margaret, I wonder if the Lord really wished to show you and others the passion which is in the heart of Washington and his army. On the way to my ship I was like one making bloody footprints in the snow. How many of them I have seen! And now is the time to tell you that Doctor Franklin has written a letter informing me how deeply our part in the little pageant had impressed Mr. Hartley and the court people of France and that he had secured another loan.

"Solomon is a man of faith. He never falters.

"He said to me: 'Don't worry. That gal has got a backbone. She ain't no rye straw. She's a-goin' to think it over.'

"Neither spoke for a time. We sat by an open fire in front of his tent as the night fell. Solomon was filling his pipe. He swallowed and his right eye began to take aim. I knew that some highly important theme would presently open the door of his intellect and come out.

" 'Jack, I been over to Albany,' he said. 'Had a long visit with Mirandy. They ain't no likelier womern in Ameriky. I'll bet a pint o' powder an' a fish hook on that. Ye kin look fer 'em till yer eyes run but ye'll be obleeged to give up.'

"He lighted his pipe and smoked a few whiffs and added: 'Knit seventy pair o' socks fer my regiment this fall.'

" 'Have you asked her to marry you?' I inquired.

" 'No. 'Tain't likely she'd have me,' he answered. 'She's had troubles enough. I wouldn't ask no womern to marry me till the war is fit out. I'm liable to git all shot up any day. I did think I'd ask her but I didn't. Got kind o' skeered an' skittish when we sot down together, an' come to think it all over, 'twouldn't 'a' been right.'

" 'You're wrong, Solomon,' I answered. 'You ought to have a home of your own and a wife to make you fond of it. How is the Little Cricket?'

" 'Cunnin'est little shaver that ever lived,' said he. 'I got him a teeny waggin an' drawed him down to the big medder an' back. He had a string hitched on to my waist an' he pulled an' hauled an' hollered whoa an' git ap till he were erbout as hoarse as a bull frog. When we got back he wanted to go all over me with a curry comb an' braid my mane.'

"The old scout roared with laughter as he thought of the child's play in which he had had a part. He told me of my own people and next to their good health it pleased me to learn that my father had given all his horses—save two—to Washington. That is what all our good men are doing. So you will see how it is that we are able to go on with this war against the great British empire.

"That night the idea came to me that I would seek an opportunity to return to France in the hope of finding you in Paris. I applied for a short furlough to give me a chance to go home and see the family. There I found a singular and disheartening situation. My father's modest fortune is now a part of the ruin of war. Soon after the beginning of hostilities he had loaned his money to men who had gone into the business of furnishing supplies to the army. He had loaned them dollars worth a hundred cents. They are paying their debts to him in dollars worth less than five cents. Many, and Washington among them, have suffered in a like manner. My father has little left but his land, two horses, a yoke of oxen and a pair of slaves. So I am too poor to give you a home in any degree worthy of you.

"Dear old Solomon has proposed to make me his heir, but now that he has met the likely womern I must not depend upon him. So I have tried to make you know the truth about me as well as I do. If your heart is equal to the discouragement I have heaped upon it I offer you this poor comfort. When the war is over I can borrow a thousand pounds to keep a roof over our heads and a fowl in the pot and pudding in the twifflers while I am clearing the way to success. The prospect is not inviting, I fear, but if, happily, it should appeal to you, I suggest that you join your father in New York at the first opportunity so that we may begin our life together as soon as the war ends. And now, whatever comes, I would wish you to keep these thoughts of me: I have loved you, but there are things which I have valued above my own happiness. If I can not have you I shall have always the memory of the hours we have spent together and of the great hope that was mine.

"While I was at home the people of our neighborhood set out at daylight one morning for a pigeon party. We had our breakfast on an island. Then the ladies sat down to knit and sew, while the men went fishing. In the afternoon we gathered berries and returned at dusk with filled pails and many fish. So our people go to the great storehouse of Nature and help themselves."

CHAPTER XXVII

WHICH CONTAINS THE ADVENTURES OF SOLOMON IN
THE TIMBER SACK AND ON THE "HAND-MADE
RIVER"

IN the spring of 1779, there were scarcely sixteen
thousand men in the American army, of which three
thousand were under Gates at Providence; five thousand in the Highlands under McDougall, who was
building new defenses at West Point, and on the east
shore of the Hudson under Putnam; seven thousand
were with Washington at Middlebrook where he had
spent a quiet winter; a few were in the south. The
British, discouraged in their efforts to conquer the
northern and middle colonies, sent a force of seven
thousand men to take Georgia and South Carolina.
They hoped that Washington, who could not be induced to risk his army in decisive action against superior numbers, would thus be compelled to scatter
and weaken it. But the Commander-in-Chief, knowing how seriously Nature, his great ally, was gnawing
at the vitals of the British, bided his time and kept his
tried regiments around him. Now and then, a staggering blow filled his enemies with a wholesome fear of
him. His sallies were as swift and unexpected as the
rush of a panther with the way of retreat always open.
Meanwhile a cry of affliction and alarm had arisen in

England. Its manufacturers were on the verge of bankruptcy, its people out of patience.

As soon as the ice was out of the lakes and rivers, Jack and Solomon joined an expedition under Sullivan against the Six Nations, who had been wreaking bloody vengeance on the frontiers of Pennsylvania and New York. The Senecas had been the worst offenders, having spilled the blood of every white family in their reach. Sullivan's expedition ascended the Chemung branch of the Susquehanna and routed a great force of Indians under Brant and Johnson at Newtown and crossed to the Valley of the Genessee, destroying orchards, crops and villages. The red men were slain and scattered. The fertile valley was turned into a flaming, smoking hell. Simultaneously a force went up the Alleghany and swept its shores with the besom of destruction.

Remembrance of the bold and growing iniquities of the savage was like a fire in the heart of the white man. His blood boiled with anger. He was without mercy. Like every reaping of the whirlwind this one had been far more plentiful than the seed from which it sprang. Those April days the power of the Indian was forever broken and his cup filled with bitterness. Solomon had spoken the truth when he left the Council Fire in the land of Kiodote:

"Hereafter the Injun will be a brother to the snake."

Jack and Solomon put their lives in danger by entering the last village ahead of the army and warning its people to flee. The killing had made them heart-sick, although they had ample reason for hating the red men.

In the absence of these able helpers Washington had moved to the Highlands. This led the British General, Sir Henry Clinton, to decide to block his return. So he sent a large force up the river and captured the fort at Stony Point and King's Ferry connecting the great road from the east with the middle states. The fort and ferry had to be retaken, and, early in July, Jack and Solomon were sent to look the ground over.

In the second day of their reconnoitering above Stony Point they came suddenly upon a British outpost. They were discovered and pursued but succeeded in eluding the enemy. Soon a large party began beating the bush with hounds. Jack escaped by hiding behind a waterfall. Solomon had a most remarkable adventure in making his way northward. Hearing the dogs behind him he ran to the shore of a bay, where a big drive of logs had been boomed in, and ran over them a good distance and dropped out of sight. He lay between two big sections of a great pine with his nose above water for an hour or so. A band of British came down to the shore and tried to run the logs but, being unaccustomed to that kind of work, were soon rolled under and floundering to their necks.

"I hadn't no skeer o' their findin' me," Solomon

said to Jack. " 'Cause they was a hundred acres o' floatin' timber in that 'ere bay. I heard 'em slippin' an' sloshin' eround nigh shore a few minutes an' then they give up an' went back in the bush. They were a strip o' open water 'twixt the logs an' the shore an' I clumb on to the timber twenty rod er more from whar I waded in so's to fool the dogs."

"What did you do with your rifle an' powder?" Jack inquired.

"Wal, ye see, they wuz some leetle logs beyond me that made a kind o' a holler an' I jest put ol' Mariet 'crost 'em an' wound the string o' my powder-horn on her bar'l. I lay thar a while an' purty soon I heard a feller comin' on the timber. He were clus up to me when he hit a log wrong an' it rolled him under. I clim' up an' grabbed my rifle an' thar were 'nother cuss out on the logs not more'n ten rod erway. He took a shot at me, but the bullet didn't come nigh 'nough so's I could hear it whisper he were bobbin' eround so. I lifted my gun an' says I:

" 'Boy, you come here to me.'

"But he thought he'd ruther go somewhar else an' he did—poor, ignorant devil! I went to t' other feller that was rasslin' with a log tryin' to git it under him. He'd flop the log an' then it would flop him. He'd throwed his rifle 'crost the timber. I goes over an' picks it up an' says I:

" 'Take it easy, my son. I'll help ye in a minute.'

"His answer wa'n't none too p'lite. He were a leetle

runt of a sergeant. I jest laughed at him an' went to t' other feller an' took the papers out o' his pockets. I see then a number o' British boys was makin' fer me on the wobbly top o' the river. They'd see me goin' as easy as a hoss on a turnpike an' they was tryin' fer to git the knack o' it. In a minute they begun poppin' at me. But shootin' on logs is like tryin' to walk a line on a wet deck in a hurricane. Ye got to know how to offset the wobble. They didn't skeer me. I went an' hauled that runt out o' the water an' with him under my right arm an' the two rifles under the left un I started treadin' logs headin' fer the north shore. They quit shootin' but come on a'ter me pell-mell. They got to comin' too fast an' I heard 'em goin' down through the roof o' the bay behind me an' rasslin' with the logs. That put meat on my bones! I could 'a' gone back an' made a mess o' the hull party with the toe o' my boot but I ain't overly fond o' killin'. Never have been. I took my time an' slopped erlong toward shore with the runt under my arm cussin' like a wildcat. We got ashore an' I made the leetle sergeant empty his pockets an' give me all the papers he had. I took the strip o' rawhide from round my belt an' put a noose above his knees an' 'nother on my wrist an' sot down to wait fer dark which the sun were then below the tree-tops. I looked with my spy-glass 'crost the bay an' could see the heads bobbin' up an' down an' a dozen men comin' out with poles to help the log rasslers. Fer some time they had 'nough to do an' I wouldn't be supprised. If we had the hull British army on floatin' timber the logs would lick 'em in a few minutes."

Solomon came in with his prisoner and accurate information as to the force of British in the Highlands.

On the night of the fifteenth of July, a detachment of Washington's troops under Wayne, preceded by the two scouts, descended upon Stony Point and King's Ferry and routed the enemy, capturing five hundred and fifty men and killing sixty. Within a few days the British came up the river in great force and Washington, unwilling to risk a battle, quietly withdrew and let them have the fort and ferry and their labor for their pains. It was a bitter disappointment to Sir Henry Clinton. The whole British empire clamored for decisive action and their great Commander was unable to bring it about and meanwhile the French were preparing to send a heavy force against them.

2

Solomon, being the ablest bush scout in the American army, was needed for every great enterprise in the wilderness. So when a small force was sent up the Penobscot River to dislodge a regiment of British from Nova Scotia, in the late summer of 1779, he went with it. The fleet which conveyed the Americans was in command of a rugged old sea cap-

tain from Connecticut of the name of Saltonstall who
had little knowledge of the arts of war. He neglected
the precautions which a careful commander would
have taken.

A force larger than his own should have guarded
the mouth of the river. Of this Solomon gave him
warning, but Captain Saltonstall did not share the
apprehension of the great scout. In consequence they
were pursued and overhauled far up the river by a
British fleet. Saltonstall in a panic ran his boats
ashore and blew them up with powder. Again a
force of Americans was compelled to suffer the bitter
penalty of ignorance. The soldiers and crews ran
wild in the bush a hundred miles from any settlement.
It was not possible to organize them. They fled in
all directions. Solomon had taken with him a bark
canoe. This he carried, heading eastward and followed by a large company, poorly provisioned. A
number of the ships' boats which had been lowered
and moved, before the destruction began, were carried on the advice of Solomon. Fortunately this
party was not pursued. Nearly every man in it had
his gun and ammunition. The scout had picked up
a goodly outfit of axes and shovels and put them in the
boats. He organized his retreat with sentries, rear
guard, signals and a plan of defense. The carriers
were shifted every hour. After two days of hard
travel through the deep woods they came to a lake
more than two miles long and about half as wide.

Their provisions were gone save a few biscuit and a sack of salt. There were sixty-four men in the party.

Solomon organized a drive. A great loop of weary men was flung around the end of the lake more than a mile from its shore. Then they began approaching the camp, barking like dogs as they advanced. In this manner three deer and a moose were driven to the water and slain. These relieved the pangs of hunger and insured the party, for some little time, against starvation. They were, however, a long way from help in an unknown wilderness with a prospect of deadly hardships. Solomon knew that the streams in this territory ran toward the sea and for that reason he had burdened the party with boats and tools.

The able scout explored a long stretch of the lake's outlet which flowed toward the south. It had a considerable channel but not enough water for boats or canoes even. That night he began cutting timber for a dam at the end of the lake above its outlet. Near sundown, next day, the dam was finished and the water began rising. A rain hurried the process. Two days later the big water plane had begun to spill into its outlet and flood the near meadow flats. The party got the boats in place some twenty rods below and ready to be launched. Solomon drove the plug out of his dam and the pent-up water began to pour through. The stream was soon flooded and the boats floating. Thus with a spirited water horse to carry them they began their journey to the sea. Men stood in the bow and stern of each boat with poles to push it along and keep it off the banks. Some ten miles below they swung into a large river and went on, more swiftly, with the aid of oars and paddles.

Thus Solomon became the hero of this ill-fated expedition. After that he was often referred to in the army as the River Maker, although the ingenious man was better known as the Lightning Hurler, that phrase having been coined in Jack's account of his adventures with Solomon in the great north bush. In the ranks he had been regarded with a kind of awe as a most redoubtable man of mysterious and uncanny gifts since he and Jack had arrived in the Highlands fresh from their adventure of "shifting the skeer"— as Solomon was wont to put it—whereupon, with no great delay, the rash Colonel Burley had his Binkussing. The scout was often urged to make a display of his terrible weapon but he held his tongue about it, nor would he play with the lightning or be induced to hurl it upon white men.

"That's only fer to save a man from bein' burnt alive an' et up," he used to say.

At the White Pine Mills near the sea they were taken aboard a lumber ship bound for Boston. Solomon returned with a great and growing influence among the common soldiers. He had spent a week in Newport and many of his comrades had reached the camp of Washington in advance of the scout's arrival.

When Solomon—a worn and ragged veteran—gained the foot of the Highlands, late in October, he learned to his joy that Stony Point and King's Ferry had been abandoned by the British. He found Jack at Stony Point and told him the story of his wasted months. Then Jack gave his friend the news of the war.

D'Estaing with a French fleet had arrived early in the month. This had led to the evacuation of Newport and Stony Point to strengthen the British position in New York. But South Carolina had been conquered by the British. It took seven hundred dollars to buy a pair of shoes with the money of that state, so that great difficulties had fallen in the way of arming and equipping a capable fighting force.

"I do not talk of it to others, but the troubles of our beloved Washington are appalling," Jack went on. "The devil loves to work with the righteous, waiting his time. He had his envoy even among the disciples of Jesus. He is among us in the person of Benedict Arnold—lover of gold. The new recruits are mostly of his stripe. He is their Captain. They demand big bounties. The faithful old guard, who have fought for the love of liberty and are still waiting for their pay, see their new comrades taking high rewards. It isn't fair. Naturally the old boys hate the newcomers. They feel like putting a coat of tar and feathers on every one of them. You and I have got to go to work and put the gold seekers out of the temple. They need to hear some of your plain talk. Our greatest peril is Arnoldism."

"You jest wait an' hear to me," said Solomon. "I got suthin' to say that'll make their ears bleed passin' through 'em.'

The evening of his arrival in camp Solomon talked at the general assembly of the troops. He was introduced with most felicitous good humor by Washington's able secretary, Mr. Alexander Hamilton. The ingenious and rare accomplishments of the scout and his heroic loyalty were rubbed with the rhetoric of an able talker until they shone.

"Boys, ye kint make no hero out o' an old scrag o' a man like me," Solomon began. "You may b'lieve what Mr. Hamilton says but I know better. I been chased by Death an' grabbed by the coat-tails frequent, but I been lucky enough to pull away. That's all. You new recruits 'a' been told how great ye be. I'm a-goin' fer to tell ye the truth. I don't like the way ye look at this job. It ain't no job o' workin' out. We're all workin' fer ourselves. It's my fight an' it's yer fight. I won't let no king put a halter on my head an', with the stale in one hand an' a whip in t' other, lead me up to the tax collector to pay fer his fun. I'd ruther fight him. Some o' you has fam'lies. Don't worry 'bout 'em. They'll be took care of. I got some confidence in the Lord myself. Couldn't 'a' lived without it. Look a' me. I'm so ragged that I got patches o' sunburn on my back an' belly. I'm what ye might call a speckled man. My feet 'a' been bled. My body looks like an ol' tree that has been clawed by a bear an' bit by woodpeckers. I've stuck my poker into the fire o' hell. I've been singed an' frost bit an' half starved an' ripped by bullets, an' all the pay I want is liberty an' it ain't due yit. I've done so little' I'm 'shamed o' myself. Money! Lord God o' Israel! If any man has come here fer to make money let him stan' up while we all pray fer his soul. These 'ere United States is your hum an' my hum an' erway down the trail afore us they's millions 'pon millions o' folks comin' an' we want 'em to be free. We're a-fightin' fer 'em an' fer ourselves. If ye don't fight ye'll git nothin' but taxes to pay the cost o' lickin' ye. It'll cost a hundred times more to be licked than it'll cost to win. Ye won't find any o' the ol' boys o' Washington squealin' erbout pay. We're lookin' fer brothers an' not pigs. Git down on yer knees with me, every one o' ye, while the Chaplain asks God A'mighty to take us all into His army."

The words of Solomon put the new men in better spirit and there was little complaining after that. They called that speech "The Binkussing of the Recruits." Solomon was the soul of the old guard.

CHAPTER XXVIII

IN WHICH ARNOLD AND HENRY THORNHILL ARRIVE
IN THE HIGHLANDS

MARGARET and her mother returned to England with David Hartley soon after Colonel Irons had left France. The British Commissioner had not been able to move the philosopher. Later, from London, he had sent a letter to Franklin seeking to induce America to desert her new ally. Franklin had answered:

"I would think the destruction of our whole country and the extirpation of our people preferable to the infamy of abandoning our allies. We may lose all but we shall act in good faith."

Here again was a new note in the history of diplomatic intercourse.

Colonel Irons' letter to Margaret Hare, with the greater part of which the reader is familiar, was forwarded by Franklin to his friend Jonathan Shipley, Bishop of St. Asaph, and by him delivered. Another letter, no less vital to the full completion of the task of these pages was found in the faded packet. It is from General Sir Benjamin Hare to his wife in London and is dated at New York, January 10, 1780. This is a part of the letter:

"I have a small house near the barracks with our

friend Colonel Ware and the best of negro slaves and every comfort. It is now a loyal city, secure from attack, and, but for the soldiers, one might think it a provincial English town. This war may last for years and as the sea is, for a time, quite safe, I have resolved to ask you and Margaret to take passage on one of the first troop ships sailing for New York, after this reaches you. Our friend Sir Roger and his regiments will be sailing in March as I am apprised by a recent letter. I am, by this post, requesting him to offer you suitable accommodations and to give you all possible assistance. The war would be over now if Washington would only fight. His caution is maddening. His army is in a desperate plight, but he will not come out and meet us in the open. He continues to lean upon the strength of the hills. But there are indications that he will be abandoned by his own army."

Those "indications" were the letters of one John Anderson, who described himself as a prominent officer in the American army. The letters were written to Sir Henry Clinton. They asked for a command in the British army and hinted at the advantage to be derived from facts, of prime importance, in the writer's possession.

Margaret and her mother sailed with Sir Roger Waite and his regiments on the tenth of March and arrived in New York on the twenty-sixth of April. *Rivington's Gazette* of the twenty-eighth of that month describes an elaborate dinner given by Major John André, Adjutant-General of the British Army, at the City Hotel to General Sir Benjamin Hare and Lady Hare and their daughter Margaret. Indeed the conditions in New York differed from those in the camp of Washington as the day differs from the night.

A Committee of Congress had just finished a visit to Washington's Highland camp. They reported that the army had received no pay in five months; that it often went "sundry successive days without meat"; that it had scarcely six days' provisions ahead; that no forage was available; that the medical department had neither sugar, tea, chocolate, wine nor spirits.

The month of May, 1780, gave Washington about the worst pinch in his career. It was the pinch of hunger. Supplies had not arrived. Famine had entered the camp and begun to threaten its life. Soldiers can get along without pay but they must have food. Mutiny broke out among the recruits.

In the midst of this trouble, Lafayette, the handsome French Marquis, then twenty-three years old, arrived on his white horse, after a winter in Paris, bringing word that a fleet and army from France were heading across the sea. This news revived the drooping spirit of the army. Soon boats began to arrive from down the river with food from the east. The crisis passed. In the north a quiet summer followed. The French fleet with six thousand men under

Rochambeau arrived at Newport, July tenth, and were immediately blockaded by the British as was a like expedition fitting out at Brest. So Washington could only hold to his plan of prudent waiting.

2

On a clear, warm day, late in July, 1780, a handsome coach drawn by four horses crossed King's Ferry and toiled up the Highland road. It carried Benedict Arnold and his wife and their baggage. Jack and Solomon passed and recognized them.

"What does that mean, I wonder?" Jack queried.

"Dun know," Solomon answered.

"I'm scared about it," said the younger scout. "I am afraid that this money seeker has the confidence of Washington. He has been a good fighting man. That goes a long way with the Chief."

Colonel Irons stopped his horse. "I am of half a mind to go back," he declared.

"Why?"

"I didn't tell the General half that Reed said to me. It was so bitter and yet I believe it was true. I ought to have told him. Perhaps I ought now to go and tell him."

"There's time 'nough," said Solomon. "Wait till we git back. Sometimes I've thought the Chief needed advice but it's allus turned out that I was the one that needed it."

The two horsemen rode on in silence. It was the middle of the afternoon of that memorable July day.

They were bound for the neutral territory between the American and British lines, infested by "cow boys" from the south and "skinners" from the north who were raiding the farms of the settlers and driving away their cattle to be sold to the opposing armies. The two scouts were sent to learn the facts and report upon them. They parted at a cross-road. It was near sundown when at a beautiful brook, bordered with spearmint and wild iris, Jack watered and fed his horse and sat down to eat his luncheon. He was thinking of Arnold and the new danger when he discovered that a man stood near him. The young scout had failed to hear his approach—a circumstance in no way remarkable since the road was little traveled and covered with moss and creeping herbage. He thought not of this, however, but only of the face and form and manner of the stranger. The face was that of a man of middle age. The young man wrote in a letter:

"It was a singularly handsome face, smooth shaven and well shaped with large, dark eyes and a skin very clean and perfect—I had almost said it was transparent. Add to all this a look of friendliness and masterful dignity and you will understand why I rose to my feet and took off my hat. His stature was above my own, his form erect. I remember nothing about his clothes save that they were dark in color and seemed to be new and admirably fitted.

" 'You are John Irons, Jr., and I am Henry

Thornhill,' said he. 'I saw you at Kinderhook where I used to live. I liked you then and, since the war began, I have known of your adventures.'

" 'I did not flatter myself that any one could know of them except my family, and my fellow scout and General Washington,' I answered.

" 'Well, I happen to have had the chance to know of them,' he went on. 'You are a true friend of the great cause. I saw you passing a little way back and I followed for I have something to say to you.'

" 'I shall be glad to hear of it,' was my answer.

" 'Washington can not be overcome by his enemies unless he is betrayed by his friends. Arnold has been put in command at West Point. He has planned the betrayal of the army.'

" 'Do you know that?' I asked.

" 'As well as I know light and darkness.'

" 'Have you told Washington?'

" 'No. As yet I have had no opportunity. I am telling him, now, through you. In his friendships he is a singularly stubborn man. The wiles of an enemy are as an open book to him but those of a friend he is not able to comprehend. He will discredit or only half believe any warning that you or I may give him. But it is for you and Solomon to warn him and be not deceived.'

" 'I shall turn about and ride back to camp,' I said.

" 'There is no need of haste,' he answered. 'Arnold does not assume command until the third of August.'

"He shaded his eyes and looked toward the west where the sun was setting and the low lying clouds were like rose colored islands in a golden sea, and added as he hurried away down the road to the south:

" 'It is a beautiful world.'

" 'Too good for fighting men,' I answered as I sat down to finish my luncheon for I was still hungry.

"While I ate, the tormenting thought came to me that I had neglected to ask for the source of his information or for his address. It was a curious oversight due to his masterly manner and that sense of the guarded tongue which an ordinary mortal is apt to feel in the presence of a great personality. I had been, in a way, self-bridled and cautious in my speech, as I have been wont to be in the presence of Washington himself. I looked down the road ahead. The stranger had rounded a bend and was now hidden by the bush. I hurried through my repast, bridled my horse and set off at a gallop expecting to overtake him, but to my astonishment he had left the road. I did not see him again, but his words were ever with me in the weeks that followed.

"I reached the Corlies farm, far down in the neutral territory, at ten o'clock and a little before dawn was with Corlies and his neighbors in a rough fight with a band of cattle thieves, in the course of which three men and a boy were seriously disabled by my pistols. We had salted a herd and concealed ourselves in the midst of it and so were able to shoot from good cover when the thieves arrived. Solomon and I spent four days in the neutral territory. When we left it a dozen cattle thieves were in need of repair and three had moved to parts unknown. Save in the southern limit, their courage had been broken.

"I had often thought of Nancy, the blaze-faced mare, that I had got from Governor Reed and traded to Mr. Paulding. I was again reminded of her by meeting a man who had just come from Tarrytown. Being near that place I rode on to Paulding's farm and spent a night in his house. I found Nancy in good flesh and spirits. She seemed to know and like the touch of my hand and, standing by her side, the notion came to me that I ought to own her. Paulding was reduced in circumstances. Having been a patriot and a money-lender, the war had impoverished him. My own horse was worn by overwork and so I proposed a trade and offered a sum to boot which he promptly accepted. I came back up the north road with the handsome, high-headed mare under my saddle. The next night I stopped with one Reuben Smith near the northern limit of the neutral territory below Stony Point. Smith had prospered by selling supplies to the patriot army. I had heard that he was a Tory and so I wished to know him. I found him a rugged, jovial, long-haired man of middle age, with a ready ringing laugh. His jokes were spoken in a low tone and followed by quick, stertorous breathing and roars and gestures of appreciation. His cheerful spirit had no doubt been a help to him in our camp.

"'I've got the habit o' laughin' at my own jokes,' said he. 'Ye see it's a lonely country here an' if I didn't give 'em a little encouragement they wouldn't come eround,' the man explained.

"He lifted a foot and swung it in the air while he bent the knee of the leg on which he was standing and opened his mouth widely and blew the air out of his lungs and clapped his hands together.

"'It also gives you exercise,' I remarked.

"'A joke is like a hoss; it has to be fed or it won't work,' he remarked, as he continued his cheerful gymnastics. I have never known a man to whom a joke was so much of an undertaking. He sobered down and added:

"'This mare is no stranger to oats an' the curry comb.'

"He looked her over carefully before he led her to the stable.

"Next morning as he stood by her noble head, Smith said to me:

"'She's a knowin' beast. She'd be smart enough to laugh at my jokes an' I wouldn't wonder.'

"He was immensely pleased with this idea of his. Then, turning serious, he asked if I would sell her.

"'You couldn't afford to own that mare,' I said.

"I had touched his vanity. In fact I did not realize how much he had made by his overcharging.

He was better able to own her than I and that he proposed to show me.

"He offered for her another horse and a sum which caused me to take account of my situation. The money would be a help to me. However, I shook my head. He increased his offer.

" 'What do you want of her?' I asked.

" 'I've always wanted to own a hoss like that,' he answered.

" 'I intended to keep the mare,' said I. 'But if you will treat her well and give her a good home I shall let you have her.'

" 'A man who likes a good joke will never drive a spavined hoss,' he answered merrily.

"So it happened that the mare Nancy fell into the hands of Reuben Smith."

CHAPTER XXIX

LOVE AND TREASON

WHEN Jack and Solomon returned to headquarters, Arnold and his wife were settled in a comfortable house overlooking the river. Colonel Irons made his report. The Commander-in-Chief complimented him and invited the young man to make a tour of the camp in his company. They mounted their horses and rode away together.

"I learn that General Arnold is to be in command here," Jack remarked soon after the ride began.

"I have not yet announced my intention," said Washington. "Who told you?"

"A man of the name of Henry Thornhill."

"I do not know him but he is curiously well informed. Arnold is an able officer. We have not many like him. He is needed here for I have to go on a long trip to eastern Connecticut to confer with Rochambeau. In the event of some unforeseen crisis Arnold would know what to do."

Then Jack spoke out: "General, I ought to have reported to you the exact words of Governor Reed. They were severe, perhaps, even, unjust. I have not repeated them to any one. But now I think you should know their full content and judge of them in your own way. The Governor insists that Arnold is

376

bad at heart—that he would sell his master for thirty pieces of silver."

Washington made no reply, for a moment, and then his words seemed to have no necessary relation to those of Jack Irons.

"General Arnold has been badly cut up in many battles," said he. "I wish him to be relieved of all trying details. You are an able and prudent man. I shall make you his chief aide with the rank of Brigadier-General. He needs rest and will concern himself little with the daily routine. In my absence, you will be the superintendent of the camp, and subject to orders I shall leave with you. Colonel Binkus will be your helper. I hope that you may be able to keep yourself on friendly terms with the General."

Jack reported to the Commander-in-Chief the warning of Thornhill, but the former made light of it.

"The air is full of evil gossip," he said. "You may hear it of me."

When they rode up to headquarters Arnold was there. To Jack's surprise the Major-General greeted him with friendly words, saying:

"I hope to know you better for I have heard much of your courage and fighting quality."

"There are good soldiers here," said Jack. "If I am one of them it is partly because I have seen you fight. You have given all of us the inspiration of a great example."

It was a sincere and deserved tribute.

On the third of August—the precise date named by
Henry Thornhill—Arnold took command of the camp
and Irons assumed his new duties. The Major-General rode with Washington every day until, on the
fourteenth of September, the latter set out with three
aides and Colonel Binkus on his trip to Connecticut.
Solomon rode with the party for two days and then returned. Thereafter Arnold left the work of his office to
Jack and gave his time to the enjoyment of the company of his wife and a leisure that suffered little inter-
ruption. For him, grim visaged war had smoothed
his wrinkled front. Like Richard he had hung up his
bruised arms. The day of Washington's departure,
Mrs. Arnold invited Jack to dinner. The young man
felt bound to accept this opportunity for more friendly
relations.

Mrs. Arnold was a handsome, vivacious, blonde
young woman of thirty. The officer speaks in a
letter of her lively talk and winning smiles and splendid figure, well fitted with a costume that reminded
him of the court ladies in France.

"What a contrast to the worn, patched uniforms
to be seen in that camp!" he added.

Soon after the dinner began, Mrs. Arnold said to
the young man, "We have heard of your romance.
Colonel and Mrs. Hare and their young daughter
spent a week in our home in Philadelphia on their
first trip to the colonies. Later Mrs. Hare wrote to
my mother of their terrible adventure in the great

north bush and spoke of Margaret's attachment for
the handsome boy who had helped to rescue them, so
I have some right to my interest in you."

"And therefor I thank you and congratulate myself," said the young man. "It is a little world after
all."

"And your story has been big enough to fill it,"
she went on. "The ladies in Philadelphia seem to
know all its details. We knew only how it began.
They have told us of the thrilling duel and how the
young lovers were separated by the war and how you
were sent out of England."

"You astonish me," said the officer. "I did not
imagine that my humble affairs would interest any
one but myself and my family. I suppose that Doctor
Franklin must have been talking about them. The
dear old soul is the only outsider who knows the
facts."

"And if he had kept them to himself he would have
been the most inhuman wretch in the world," said
Mrs. Arnold. "Women have their rights. They
need something better to talk about than Acts of
Parliament and taxes and war campaigns. I thank
God that no man can keep such a story to himself.
He has to have some one to help him enjoy it. A good
love-story is like murder. It will out."

"It has caused me a lot of misery and a lot of
happiness," said the young man.

"I long to see the end of it," the woman went on.

"I happen to know a detail in your story which may be new to you. Miss Hare is now in New York."

"In New York!"

"Oddso! In New York! We heard in Philadelphia that she and her mother had sailed with Sir Roger Waite in March. How jolly it would be if the General and I could bring you together and have a wedding at headquarters!"

"I could think of no greater happiness save that of seeing the end of the war," Jack answered.

"The war! That is a little matter. I want to see a proper end to this love-story."

She laughed and ran to the spinnet and sang *Shepherds, I Have Lost My Love.*

The General would seem to have been in bad spirits. He had spoken not half a dozen words. To him the talk of the others had been as spilled water. Jack has described him as a man of "unstable temperament."

The young man's visit was interrupted by Solomon who came to tell him that he was needed in the matter of a quarrel between some of the new recruits.

Jack and Solomon exercised unusual care in guarding the camp and organizing for defense in case of attack. It was soon after Washington's departure that Arnold went away on the road to the south. Solomon followed keeping out of his field of vision. The General returned two days later. Solomon came into Jack's hut about midnight of the day of Arnold's return with important news.

Jack was at his desk studying a map of the Highlands. The camp was at rest. The candle in Jack's hut was the only sign of life around headquarters when Solomon, having put out his horse, came to talk with his young friend. He stepped close to the desk, swallowed nervously and began his whispered report.

"Suthin' neevarious be goin' on," he began. "A British ship were lyin' nigh the mouth o' the Croton River. Arnold went aboard. An' officer got into his boat with him an' they pulled over to the west shore and went into the bush. Stayed thar till mos' night. If 'twere honest business, why did they go off in the bush alone fer a talk?"

Jack shook his head.

"Soon as I seen that I went to one o' our batteries an' tol' the Cap'n what were on my mind.

"'Damn the ol' British tub. We'll make 'er back up a little,' sez he. 'She's too clus anyhow.'

"Then he let go a shot that ripped the water front o' her bow. Say, Jack, they were some hoppin' eround on the deck o' the big British war sloop. They h'isted her sails an' she fell away down the river a mile 'er so. The sun were set when Arnold an' the officer come out o' the bush. I were in a boat with a fish rod an' could jes' see 'em with my spy-glass, the light were so dim. They stood thar lookin' fer the ship.

They couldn't see her. They went back into the bush.
It come to me what they was goin' to do. Arnold
were a-goin' to take the Britisher over to the house
o' that ol' Tory, Reub Smith. I got thar fust an' hid
in the bushes front o' the house. Sure 'nough!—
that's what were done. Arnold an' t' other feller
come erlong an' went into the house. 'Twere so dark
I couldn't see 'em but I knowed 'twere them."

"How?" the young man asked.

" 'Cause they didn't light no candle. They sot in
the dark an' they didn't talk out loud like honest men
would. I come erway. I couldn't do no more."

"I think you've done well," said Jack. "Now go
and get some rest. To-morrow may be a hard day."

2

Jack spent a bad night in the effort to be as great
as his problem. In the morning he sent Solomon and
three other able scouts to look the ground over east,
west and south of the army. One of them was to
take the road to Hartford and deliver a message to
Washington.

After the noon mess, Arnold mounted his horse and
rode away alone. The young Brigadier sent for his
trusted friend, Captain Merriwether.

"Captain, the General has set out on the east road
alone," said Jack. "He is not well. There's something wrong with his heart. I am a little worried
about him. He ought not to be traveling alone. My
horse is in front of the door. Jump on his back and

keep in sight of the General, but don't let him know what you are doing."

A little later Mrs. Arnold entered the office of the new Brigadier in a most cheerful mood.

"I have good news for you," she announced.

"What is it?"

"Soon I hope to make a happy ending of your love-story."

"God prosper you," said the young man.

She went on with great animation: "A British officer has come in a ship under a flag of truce to confer with General Arnold. I sent a letter to Margaret Hare on my own responsibility with the General's official communication. I invited her to come with the party and promised her safe conduct to our house. I expect her. For the rest we look to you."

The young man wrote: "This announcement almost took my breath. My joy was extinguished by apprehension before it could show itself. I did not speak, being for a moment confused and blinded by lightning flashes of emotion."

"It is your chance to bring the story to a pretty end," she went on. "Let us have a wedding at headquarters. On the night of the twenty-eighth, General Washington will have returned. He has agreed to dine with us that evening."

"I think that she must have observed the shadow on my face for, while she spoke, a great fear had come upon me," he testified in the Court of Inquiry.

"It seemed clear to me that, if there was a plot, the capture of Washington himself was to be a part of it and my sweetheart a helpful accessory."

"'Are you not pleased?' Mrs. Arnold asked.

"I shook off my fear and answered: 'Forgive me. It is all so unexpected and so astonishing and so very good of you! It has put my head in a whirl.'

"Gentlemen, I could see no sinister motive in this romantic enterprise of Mrs. Arnold," the testimony proceeds. "I have understood that her sympathies were British but, if so, she had been discreet enough in camp to keep them to herself. Whatever they may have been, I felt as sure then, as I do now, that she was a good woman. Her kindly interest in my little romance was just a bit of honest, human nature. It pleased me and when I think of her look of innocent, unguarded, womanly frankness, I can not believe that she had had the least part in the dark intrigue of her husband.

"I arose and kissed her hand and I remember well the words I spoke: 'Madame,' I said, 'let me not try now to express my thanks. I shall need time for friendly action and well chosen words. Do you think that Margaret will fall in with your plans?'

"She answered:

"'How can she help it? She is a woman. Have you not both been waiting these many years for the chance to marry? I think that I know a woman's heart.'

" 'You know much that I am eager to know,' I said.
'The General has not told me that he is to meet the
British. May I know all the good news?'

" 'Of course he will tell you about that,' she assured me. 'He has told me only a little. It is some
negotiation regarding an exchange of prisoners. I
am much more interested in Margaret and the
wedding. I wish you would tell me about her. I
have heard that she has become very beautiful.'

"I showed Mrs. Arnold the miniature portrait which
Margaret had given me the day of our little ride and
talk in London and then an orderly came with a
message and that gave me an excuse to put an end
to this untimely babbling for which I had no heart.
The message was from Solomon. He had got word
that the British war-ship had come back up the river
and was two miles above Stony Point with a white
flag at her masthead.

"My nerves were as taut as a fiddle string. A
cloud of mystery enveloped the camp and I was unable
to see my way. Was the whole great issue for which
so many of us had perished and fought and endured
all manner of hardships, being bartered away in the
absence of our beloved Commander? I have suffered
much but never was my spirit so dragged and torn
as when I had my trial in the thorny way of distrust.
I have had my days of conceit when I felt equal to
the work of Washington, but there was no conceit in
me then. Face to face with the looming peril, of

which warning had come to me, I felt my own weakness and the need of his masterful strength.

"I went out-of-doors.   Soon I met Merriwether
coming into camp. Arnold had returned. He had
ridden at a walk toward the headquarters of the
Second Brigade and turned about and come back
without speaking to any one. Arnold was looking
down as if absorbed in his own thoughts when Merriwether passed him in the road. He did not return
the latter's salute. It was evident that the General
had ridden away for the sole purpose of being alone.

"I went back to my hut and sat down to try to find
my way when suddenly the General appeared at my
door on his bay mare and asked me to take a little ride
with him. I mounted my horse and we rode out on
the east road together for half a mile or so.

" 'I believe that my wife had some talk with you
this morning,' he began.

" 'Yes,' I answered.

" 'A British officer has come up the river in a ship
under a white flag with a proposal regarding an exchange of prisoners. In my answer to their request
for a conference, some time ago, I enclosed a letter
from Mrs. Arnold to Miss Margaret Hare inviting
her to come to our home where she would find a hearty
welcome and her lover—now an able and most valued
officer of the staff. A note received yesterday says
that Miss Hare is one of the party. We are glad to
be able to do you this little favor.'

"I thanked him.

" 'I wish that you could go with me down the river to meet her in the morning,' he said. 'But in my absence it will, of course, be necessary for you to be on duty. Mrs. Arnold will go with me and we shall, I hope, bring the young lady safely to head-quarters.'

"He was preoccupied. His face wore a serious look. There was a melancholy note in his tone—I had observed that in other talks with him—but it was a friendly tone. It tended to put my fears at rest.

"I asked the General what he thought of the prospects of our cause.

" 'They are not promising,' he answered. 'The defeat of Gates in the south and the scattering of his army in utter rout is not an encouraging event.'

" 'I think that we shall get along better now that the Gates bubble has burst,' I answered."

This ends the testimony of "the able and most valued officer," Jack Irons, Jr.

CHAPTER XXX

"WHO IS SHE THAT LOOKETH FORTH AS THE MORN-
ING, FAIR AS THE MOON, CLEAR AS THE SUN, AND
TERRIBLE AS AN ARMY WITH BANNERS?"

THE American army had been sold by Arnold.
The noble ideal it had cherished, the blood it had
given, the bitter hardships it had suffered—torture
in the wilderness, famine in the Highlands, long
marches of half naked men in mid-winter, massacres
at Wyoming and Cherry Valley—all this had been
bartered away, like a shipload of turnips, to satisfy
the greed of one man. Again thirty pieces of silver!
Was a nation to walk the bitter way to its Calvary?
Major André, the Adjutant-General of Sir Henry
Clinton's large force in New York, was with the
traitor when he rowed from the ship to the west
shore of the Hudson and went into the bush under the
observation of Solomon with his spy-glass. Arnold
was to receive a command and large pay in the British
army. The consideration had been the delivery of
maps showing the positions of Washington's men
and the plans of his forts and other defenses, especially
those of Forts Putnam and Clinton and Battery Knox.
Much other information was put in the hands of the
British officer, including the prospective movements
of the Commander-in-Chief. He was to be taken in

388

the house of the man he had befriended.   André had
only to reach New York with his treasure and Arnold
to hold the confidence of his chief for a few days and,
before the leaves had fallen, the war would end.   The
American army and its master mind would be at the
mercy of Sir Henry Clinton.

Those September days the greatest love-story this
world had known was feeling its way in a cloud of
mystery.   The thrilling tale of Man and Liberty,
which had filled the dreams of sage and poet, had
been nearing its golden hours.   Of a surety, at last,
it would seem the lovers were to be wed.   What
time, in the flying ages, they had greeted each other
with hearts full of the hope of peace and happiness,
some tyrant king and his armies had come between
them.   Then what a carnival of lust, rapine and
bloody murder!   Man was broken on the wheel of
power and thwarted Hope sat brooding in his little
house.   History had been a long siege, like that of
Troy, to deliver a fairer Helen from the established
power of Kings.   Now, beyond three thousand miles
of sea, supported by the strength of the hills and
hearts informed and sworn to bitter duty, Man, at
last, had found his chance.   Again Liberty, in robes
white as snow and sweet as the morning, beckoned to
her lover.   Another king was come with his armies
to keep them apart.   The armies being baffled, Satan
had come also and spread his hidden snares.   Could
Satan prevail?   Was the story nearing another failure

—a tragedy dismal and complete as that of Thermopylæ?

This day we shall know. This day holds the moment which is to round out the fulness of time. It is the twenty-third of September, 1780, and the sky is clear. Now as the clock ticks its hours away, we may watch the phrases of the capable Author of the great story as they come from His pen. His most useful characters are remote and unavailable. It would seem that the villain was likely to have his way. The Author must defeat him, if possible, with some stroke of ingenuity. For this He was not unprepared.

Before the day begins it will be well to review, briefly, the hours that preceded it.

André would have reached New York that night if *The Vulture* had not changed her position on account of a shot from the battery below Stony Point. For that, credit must be given to the good scout Solomon Binkus. The ship was not in sight when the two men came out in their boat from the west shore of the river while the night was falling. Arnold had heard the shot and now that the ship had left her anchorage a fear must have come to him that his treachery was suspected.

"I may want to get away in that boat myself," he suggested to André.

"She will not return until she gets orders from you or me," the Britisher assured him.

"I wonder what has become of her," said Arnold.

"She has probably dropped down the river for some reason," André answered. "What am I to do?"

"I'll take you to the house of a man I know who lives near the river and send you to New York by horse with passports in the morning. You can reach the British lines to-morrow."

"I would like that," André exclaimed. "It would afford me a welcome survey of the terrain."

"Smith will give you a suit of clothes that will fit you well enough," said the traitor. "You and he are about of a size. It will be better for you to be in citizen's dress."

So it happened that in the darkness of the September evening Smith and André, the latter riding the blazed-face mare, set out for King's Ferry, where they were taken across the river. They rode a few miles south of the landing to the shore of Crom Pond and spent the night with a friend of Smith. In the morning the latter went on with André until they had passed Pine's Bridge on the Croton River. Then he turned back.

Now André fared along down the road alone on the back of the mare Nancy. He came to an outpost of the Highland army and presented his pass. It was examined and endorsed and he went on his way. He met transport wagons, a squad of cavalry and, later, a regiment of militia coming up from western Connecticut, but no one stopped him. In the faded hat and coat and trousers of Reuben Smith, this man, who called himself John Anderson, was not much unlike the farmer folk who were riding hither and thither in the neutral territory, on their petit errands. His face was different. It was the well kept face of an English aristocrat with handsome dark eyes and hair beginning to turn gray. Still, shadowed by the brim of the old hat, his face was not likely to attract much attention from the casual observer. The handsome mare he rode was a help in this matter. She took and held the eyes of those who passed him. He went on unchallenged. A little past the hour of the high sun he stopped to drink at a wayside spring and to give his horse some oats out of one of the saddlebags. It was then that a patriot soldier came along riding northward. He was one of Solomon's scouts. The latter stopped to let his horse drink. As his keen eyes surveyed the south-bound traveler, John Anderson felt his danger. At that moment the scout was within reach of immortal fame had he only known it. He was not so well informed as Solomon. He asked a few questions and called for the pass of the stranger. That was unquestionable. The scout resumed his journey.

André resolved not to stop again. He put the bit in the mare's mouth, mounted her and rode on with his treasure. The most difficult part of his journey was behind him. Within twelve hours he should be at Clinton's headquarters.

Suddenly he came to a fork in the road and held

up his horse, uncertain which way to go. Now the great moment was come. Shall he turn to the right or the left? On his decision rests the fate of the New World and one of the most vital issues in all history, it would seem. The left-hand road would have taken him safely to New York, it is fair to assume. He hesitates. The day is waning. It is a lonely piece of road. There is no one to tell him. The mare shows a preference for the turn to the right. Why? Because it leads to Tarrytown, her former home, and a good master. André lets her have her way. She hurries on, for she knows where there is food and drink and gentle hands. So a leg of the mighty hazard has been safely won by the mare Nancy. The officer rode on, and what now was in his way? A wonder and a mystery greater even than that of Nancy and the fork in the road. A little out of Tarrytown on the highway the horseman traveled, a group of three men were hidden in the bush—ragged, profane, abominable cattle thieves waiting for cows to come down out of the wild land to be milked. They were "skinners" in the patriot militia, some have said; some that they were farmers' sons not in the army. However that may have been, they were undoubtedly rough, hard-fisted fellows full of the lawless spirit bred by five years of desperate warfare. They were looking for Tories as well as for cattle. Tories were their richest prey, for the latter would give high rewards to be excused from the oath of allegiance.

They came out upon André and challenged him. The latter knew that he had passed the American outposts and thought that he was near the British lines. He was not familiar with the geography of the upper east shore. He knew that the so-called neutral territory was overrun by two parties—the British being called the "Lower" and the Yankees the "Upper."

"What party do you belong to?" André demanded.

"The Lower," said one of the Yankees.

It was, no doubt, a deliberate lie calculated to inspire frankness in a possible Tory. That was the moment for André to have produced his passports, which would have opened the road for him. Instead he committed a fatal error, the like of which it would be hard to find in all the records of human action.

"I am a British officer," he declared. "Please take me to your post."

They were keen-minded men who quickly surrounded him. A British officer! Why was he in the dress of a Yankee farmer? The pass could not save him now from these rough, strong handed fellows. The die was cast. They demanded the right of search. He saw his error and changed his plea.

"I am only a citizen of New York returning from family business in the country," he said.

He drew his gold watch from his pocket—that unfailing sign of the gentleman of fortune—and looked at its dial.

"You can see I am no common fellow," he added. "Let me go on about my business."

They firmly insisted on their right to search him. He began to be frightened. He offered them his watch and a purse full of gold and any amount of British goods to be allowed to go on his way.

Now here is the wonder and the mystery in this remarkable proceeding. These men were seeking plunder and here was a handsome prospect. Why did they not make the most of it and be content? The "skinners" were plunderers, but first of all and above all they were patriots. The spirit brooding over the Highlands of the Hudson and the hills of New England had entered their hearts. The man who called himself John Anderson was compelled to dismount and empty his pockets and take off his boots, in one of which was the damning evidence of Arnold's perfidy. A fortune was then within the reach of these three hard-working men of the hills, but straightway they took their prisoner and the papers, found in his boot, to the outpost commanded by Colonel Jameson.

This negotiation for the sale of the United States had met with unexpected difficulties. The "skinners" had been as hard to buy as the learned diplomat.

CHAPTER XXXI

THE LOVERS AND SOLOMON'S LAST FIGHT

MEANWHILE, Margaret and her mother had come up the river in a barge with General and Mrs. Arnold to the house of the latter. Jack had gone out on a tour of inspection. He had left headquarters after the noon meal with a curious message in his pocket and a feeling of great relief. The message had been delivered to him by the mother of a captain in one of the regiments. She said that it had been given to her by a man whom she did not know. Jack had been busy when it came and did not open it until she had gone away. It was an astonishing and most welcome message in the flowing script of a rapid penman, but clearly legible. It was without date and very brief. These were the cheering words in it:

"MY DEAR FRIEND: I have good news from down the river. The danger is passed.
"HENRY THORNHILL."

"Well, Henry Thornhill is a man who knows whereof he speaks," the young officer said to himself, as he rode away. "I should like to meet him again."

That day the phrase "Good news from down the

396

river" came repeatedly back to him. He wondered
what it meant.

Jack being out of camp, Margaret had found Solomon. Toward the day's end he had gone out on the
south road with the young lady and her mother and
Mrs. Arnold.

Jack was riding into camp from an outpost of the
army. The day was in its twilight. He had been
riding fast. He pulled up his horse as he approached
a sentry post. Three figures were standing in the
dusky road.

"Halt! Who comes there?" one of them sang out.

It was the voice of Margaret. Its challenge was
more like a phrase of music than a demand. He dismounted.

"I am one of the great army of lovers," said he.

"Advance and give the countersign," she commanded.

A moment he held her in his embrace and then he
whispered: "I love you."

"The countersign is correct, but before I let you
pass, give me one more look into your heart."

"As many as you like—but—why?"

"So I may be sure that you do not blame England
for the folly of her King."

"I swear it."

"Then I shall enlist with you against the tyrant.
He has never been my King."

Lady Hare stood with Mrs. Arnold near the lovers.

"I too demand the countersign," said the latter.

"And much goes with it," said the young man as he kissed her, and then he embraced the mother of his sweetheart and added:

"I hope that you are also to enlist with us."

"No, I am to leave my little rebel with you and return to New York."

Solomon, who had stood back in the edge of the bush, approached them and said to Lady Hare:

"I guess if the truth was known, they's more rebels in England than thar be in Ameriky."

He turned to Jack and added:

"My son, you're a reg'lar Tory privateer—grabbin' for gold. Give 'em one a piece fer me."

Margaret ran upon the old scout and kissed his bearded cheek.

"Reg'lar lightnin' hurler!" said he. "Soon as this 'ere war is over I'll take a bee line fer hum—you hear to me. This makes me sick o' fightin'."

"Will you give me a ride?" Margaret asked her lover. "I'll get on behind you."

Solomon took off the saddle and tightened the blanket girth.

"Thar, 'tain't over clean, but now ye kin both ride," said he.

Soon the two were riding, she in front, as they had ridden long before through the shady, mallowed bush in Tryon County.

"Oh, that we could hear the thrush's song again!"

"I can hear it sounding through the years," he answered. "As life goes on with me I hear many an echo from the days of my youth."

They rode a while in silence as the night fell.

"Again the night is beautiful!" she exclaimed.

"But now it is the beauty of the night and the stars," he answered.

"How they glow!"

"I think it is because the light of the future is shining on them."

"It is the light of peace and happiness. I am glad to be free."

"Soon your people shall be free," he answered her.

"My people?"

"Yes."

"Is the American army strong enough to do it?"

"No."

"The French?"

"No."

"Who then is to free us?"

"God and His ocean and His hills and forests and rivers and these children of His in America, who have been schooled to know their rights. After this King is broken there will be no other like him in England."

They dismounted at Arnold's door.

"For a time I shall have much to do, but soon I hope for great promotion and more leisure," he said.

"Tell me the good news," she urged.

"I expect to be the happiest man in the army, and the master of this house and your husband."

"And you and I shall be as one," she answered. "God speed the day when that may be true also of your people and my people."

2

He kissed her and bade her good night and returned to his many tasks. He had visited the forts and batteries. He had communicated with every outpost. His plan was complete. About midnight, when he and Solomon were lying down to rest, two horsemen came up the road at a gallop and stopped at his door. They were aides of Washington. They reported that the General was spending the night at the house of Henry Jasper, near the ferry, and would reach camp about noon next day.

"Thank God for that news," said the young man. "Solomon, I think that we can sleep better to-night."

"If you're awake two minutes from now you'll hear some snorin'," Solomon answered as he drew his boots. "I ain't had a good bar'foot sleep in a week. I don't like to have socks er luther on when I wade out into that pond. To-night, I guess, we'll smell the water lilies."

Jack was awake for an hour thinking of the great happiness which had fallen in the midst of his troubles and of Thornhill and his message. He heard the two aides going to their quarters. Then a deep

silence fell upon the camp, broken only by the rumble
of distant thunder in the mountains and the feet of
some one pacing up and down between his hut and
the house of the General. He put on his long coat
and slippers and went out-of-doors.

"Who's there?" he demanded.

"Arnold," was the answer. "Taking a little walk
before I turn in."

There was a weary, pathetic note of trouble in that
voice, long remembered by the young man, who immediately returned to his bed. He knew not that
those restless feet of Arnold were walking in the
flames of hell. Had some premonition of what had
been going on down the river come up to him? Could
he hear the feet of that horse, now galloping northward through the valleys and over the hills toward
him with evil tidings? No more for this man was
the comfort of restful sleep or the joys of home and
friendship and affection. Now the touch of his wife's
hand, the sympathetic look in her eyes and all her
babble about the coming marriage were torture to
him. He could not endure it. Worst of all, he was
in a way where there is no turning. He must go
on. He had begun to know that he was suspected.
The conduct of the scout, Solomon Binkus, had suggested that he knew what was passing. Arnold had
seen the aides of Washington as they came in. The
chief could not be far behind them. He dreaded to

stand before him. Compared to the torture now beginning for this man, the fate of Bill Scott on Rock Creek in the wilderness, had been a mercy.

Soon after sunrise came a solitary horseman, wearied by long travel, with a message from Colonel Jameson to Arnold. A man had been captured near Tarrytown with important documents on his person. He had confessed that he was Adjutant-General André of Sir Henry Clinton's army. The worst had come to pass. Now treason! disgrace! the gibbet!

Arnold was sitting at breakfast. He arose, put the message in his pocket and went out of the room. *The Vulture* lay down the river awaiting orders. The traitor walked hurriedly to the boat-landing. Solomon was there. It had been his custom when in camp to go down to the landing every morning with his spy-glass and survey the river. Only one boatman was at the dock.

"Colonel Binkus, will you help this man to take me down to the British ship?" Arnold asked. "I have an engagement with its commander and am half an hour late."

Solomon had had much curiosity about that ship. He wished to see the man who had gone into the bush and then to Smith's with Arnold.

"Sart'n," Solomon answered.

They got into a small barge with the General in the cushioned rear seat, his flag in hand.

"Make what speed you can," said the General.

The oarsmen bent to their task and the barge swept
on by the forts. A Yankee sloop overhauled and
surveyed them. If its skipper had entertained suspicions they were dissipated by the presence of Solomon Binkus in the barge.

They came up to *The Vulture* and made fast at its
landing stage where an officer waited to receive the
General. The latter ascended to the deck. In a
moment a voice called from above:

"General Arnold's boatmen may come aboard."

A British war-ship was a thing of great interest
to Solomon. Once aboard he began to look about
him at the shining guns and their gear and the tackle
and the men. He looked for Arnold, but he was not
in sight.

Among the crew then busy on the deck, Solomon
saw the Tory desperado "Slops," one time of the Ohio
River country, with his black pipe in his mouth.
Slops paused in his hauling and reeving to shake a
fist at Solomon. They were heaving the anchor.
The sails were running up. The ship had begun to
move. What was the meaning of this? Solomon
stepped to the ship's side. The stair had been hove
up and made fast. The barge was not to be seen.

"They will put you all ashore below," an officer
said to him.

Solomon knew too much about Arnold to like the
look of this. The officer went forward. Solomon
stepped to the opening in the deck rail, not yet closed,

through which he had come aboard. While he was looking down at the water, some ten feet below, a group of sailors came to fill in. His arm was roughly seized. Solomon stepped back. Before him stood the man Slops. An insulting word from the latter, a quick blow from Solomon, and Slops went through the gate out into the air and downward. The scout knew it was no time to tarry.

"A night hawk couldn't dive no quicker ner what I done," were his words to the men who picked him up. He was speaking of that half second of the twenty-fourth of September, 1780. His brief account of it was carefully put down by an officer: "I struck not twenty feet from Slops, which I seen him jes' comin' up when I took water. This 'ere ol' sloop that had overhauled us goin' down were nigh. Hadn't no more'n come up than I felt Slops' knife rip into my leg. I never had no practise in that 'ere knife work. 'Tain't fer decent folks, but my ol' Dan Skinner is allus on my belt. He'd chose the weapons an' so I fetched 'er out. Had to er die. We fit a minnit thar in the water. All the while he had that damn black pipe in his mouth. I were hacked up a leetle, but he got a big leak in *him* an' all of a sudden he wasn't thar. He'd gone. I struck out with ol' Dan Skinner 'twixt my teeth. Then I see your line and grabbed it. Whar's the British ship now?"

" 'Way below Stony P'int an' a fair wind in her sails,' the skipper answered.

"Bound fer New York," said Solomon sorrowfully. "They'd 'a' took me with 'em if I hadn't 'a' jumped. Put me over to Jasper's dock. I got to see Washington quick."

"Washington has gone up the river."

"Then take me to quarters soon as ye kin. I'll give ye ten pounds, good English gold. My God, boys! My ol' hide is leakin' bad."

He turned to the man who had been washing and binding his wounds.

"Sodder me up best ye' kin. I got to last till I see the Father."

Solomon and other men in the old army had often used the word "Father" in speaking of the Commander-in-Chief. It served, as no other could, to express their affection for him.

The wind was unfavorable and the sloop found it difficult to reach the landing near headquarters. After some delay Solomon jumped overboard and swam ashore.

What follows he could not have told. Washington was standing with his orderly in the little dooryard at headquarters as Solomon came staggering up the slope at a run and threw his body, bleeding from a dozen wounds, at the feet of his beloved Chief.

"Oh, my Father!" he cried in a broken voice and with tears streaming down his cheeks. "Arnold has sold Ameriky an' all its folks an' gone down the river."

Washington knelt beside him and felt his bloody garments.

"The Colonel is wounded," he said to his orderly. "Go for help."

The scout, weak from the loss of blood, tried to regain his feet but failed. He lay back and whispered:

"I guess the sap has all oozed out o' me but I had enough."

Washington was one of those who put him on a stretcher and carried him to the hospital.

When he was lying on his bed and his clothes were being removed, the Commander-in-Chief paid him this well deserved compliment as he held his hand:

"Colonel, when the war is won it will be only because I have had men like you to help me."

Soon Jack came to his side and then Margaret. General Washington asked the latter about Mrs. Arnold.

"My mother is doing what she can to comfort her," Margaret answered.

Solomon revived under stimulants and was able to tell them briefly of the dire struggle he had had.

"It were Slops that saved me," he whispered.

He fell into a deep and troubled sleep and when he awoke in the middle of the night he was not strong enough to lift his head. Then these faithful friends of his began to know that this big, brawny, redoubt-

able soldier was having his last fight.   He seemed to
be aware of it himself for he whispered to Jack:

"Take keer o' Mirandy an' the Little Cricket."

Late the next day he called for his Great Father.
Feebly and brokenly he had managed to say:

"Jes' want—to—feel—his hand."

Margaret had sat beside him all day helping the
nurse.

A dozen times Jack had left his work and run over
for a look at Solomon.   On one of these hurried visits
the young man had learned of the wish of his friend.
He went immediately to General Washington, who
had just returned from a tour of the forts.   The latter
saw the look of sorrow and anxiety in the face of his
officer.

"How is the Colonel?" he asked.

"I think that he is near his end," Jack answered.
"He has expressed a wish to feel your hand again."

"Let us go to him at once," said the other.   "There
has been no greater man in the army."

Together they went to the bedside of the faithful
scout.   The General took his hand.   Margaret put
her lips close to Solomon's ear and said:

"General Washington has come to see you."

Solomon opened his eyes and smiled.   Then there
was a beauty not of this world in his homely face.
And that moment, holding the hand he had loved and
served and trusted, the heroic soul of Solomon Binkus
went out upon "the lonesome trail."

Jack, who had been kneeling at his side, kissed his white cheek.

"Oh, General, I knew and loved this man!" said the young officer as he arose.

"It will be well for our people to know what men like him have endured for them," said Washington.

"I shall have to learn how to live without him," said Jack. "It will be hard."

Margaret took his arm and they went out of the door and stood a moment looking off at the glowing sky above the western hills.

"Now you have me," she whispered.

He bent and kissed her.

"No man could have a better friend and fighting mate than you," he answered.

3

" 'We spend our years as a tale that is told,' " Jack wrote from Philadelphia to his wife in Albany on the thirtieth of June, 1787: "Dear Margaret, we thought that the story was ended when Washington won. Five years have passed, as a watch in the night, and the most impressive details are just now falling out. You recall our curiosity about Henry Thornhill? When stopping at Kinderhook I learned that the only man of that name who had lived there had been lying in his grave these twenty years. He was one of the first dreamers about Liberty. What think you of that? I, for one, can not believe that the man I saw was an impostor. Was he an angel like those who

visited the prophets? · Who shall say? Naturally, I
think often of the look of him and of his sudden
disappearance in that Highland road. And, looking
back at Thornhill, this thought comes to me: Who
can tell how many angels he has met in the way of
life all unaware of the high commission of his visitor?

"On my westward trip I found that the Indians
who once dwelt in The Long House were scattered.
Only a tattered remnant remains. Near old Fort
Johnson I saw a squaw sitting in her blanket. Her
face was wrinkled with age and hardship. Her eyes
were nearly blind. She held in her withered hands
the ragged, moth eaten tail of a gray wolf. I asked
her why she kept the shabby thing.

" 'Because of the hand that gave it,' she answered
in English. 'I shall take it with me to The Happy
Hunting-Grounds. When he sees it he will know me.'

"So quickly the beautiful Little White Birch had
faded.

"At Mount Vernon, Washington was as dignified
as ever but not so grave. He almost joked when he
spoke of the sculptors and portrait painters who have
been a great bother to him since the war ended.

" 'Now no dray horse moves more readily to the
thill than I to the painter's chair,' he said.

"When I arrived the family was going in to dinner
and they waited until I could make myself ready to
join them. The jocular Light Horse Harry Lee was
there. His anecdotes delighted the great man. I had
never seen G. W. in better humor. A singularly pleas-

ant smile lighted his whole countenance. I can never forget the gentle note in his voice and his dignified bearing. It was the same whether he were addressing his guests or his family. The servants watched him closely. A look seemed to be enough to indicate his wishes. The faithful Billy was always at his side. I have never seen a sweeter atmosphere in any home. We sat an hour at the table after the family had retired from it. In speaking of his daily life he said:

"'I ride around my farms until it is time to dress for dinner, when I rarely miss seeing strange faces, come, as they say, out of respect for me. Perhaps the word curiosity would better describe the cause of it. The usual time of sitting at table brings me to candle-light when I try to answer my letters.'

"He had much to say on his favorite theme, viz.: the settling of the immense interior and bringing its trade to the Atlantic cities.

"I was coughing with a severe cold. He urged me to take some remedies which he had in the house, but I refused them.

"He went to his office while Lee and I sat down together. The latter told me of a movement in the army led by Colonel Nichola to make Washington king of America. He had seen Washington's answer to the letter of the Colonel. It was as follows:

"'Be assured, sir, no occurrence in the course of the war has given me sensations more painful than your information of there being such ideas in the army as

John Wolcott Adams

www.ingramcontent.com/pod-product-compliance
Lightning Source LLC
Chambersburg PA
CBHW020830030726
47496CB00001B/170